Kristen White

Mystic In A Minivan

Mystic Media, LLC
St. Louis, Missouri

Mystic Media, LLC
http://www.mysticinaminivan.com

ISBN: 978-0-615-31978-0

Library of Congress Control Number: 2009924101

PRINTED IN THE UNITED STATES OF AMERICA

Dedication

This book is dedicated to my mother, Becky
Your support is angel wings on Earth

In memory of Linda

Acknowledgements

Any author will admit, it takes a village to finish a book, or at least a handful of loving, loyal friends to keep you on track. Thank you to my book midwife, Anne Kosem, without her encouragement to push on through the last story line edits this book would remain unborn. Also, to my editor, Suzanne Ford for her razor sharp eyes and Mike Unterreiner for his detailed inner punctuation guide.

Thank you to my patient children and supportive family who waited out months of me glued to the computer. I am grateful to Marianne R. for opening the door to my literary creativity in her workshop. I'm also thankful to my friends: MJ, Melinda Bierman, Allison Wolff, Susan Cotter, Jamy Brase, Susan Byer and Heather Towsley who have encouraged and supported me along the way.

In deep gratitude, I thank my many teachers and mentors, namely Sonia Choquette who encouraged me to own the unfinished project and taught me to open up my intuitive channels. This process of intuitive development continued with training by Doreen Virtue. My gratitude extends to other teachers and light workers who I've only met and trained with through their books: Dr. Wayne Dyer, Emmett Fox, Carolyn Myss, Sanaya Roman, Rhonda Byrne, John Randolph Price, Catherine Ponder and Paramhansa Yogananda.

Finally, thank you to my guides and angels who channeled these words. I am deeply humbled by the experience of working with your beautiful loving energy.

Chapter 1

I am an addict.

But not in the way you might think. I have never tried drugs, like cocaine or heroin. I don't drink often, maybe a glass or two of wine a week; sometimes a month goes by before I enjoy one. The casinos or on-line poker aren't my thing. Nor do I spend my time having sex with strangers while my kids are at school. No, I'm not addicted to sex, drugs, booze or cards. My vices are much more subtle, but equally destructive.

I'm addicted to drama, gossip and complaining.

My friends and I think nothing of spending hours on end updating one another on the latest trials and tribulations of everyone we know. A lack of psychological training has given us a one-sided perspective into the poor judgment and character flaws of these foolish people, who often happen to be our friends and even spouses. The conclusion reached most often is that given the same set of circumstances, we probably would have handled it better. There really is no sacred cow when a juicy piece of gossip is available, as long as the receiver promises not to tell anyone. What we really mean is, don't tell anyone you heard it from me, but feel free to pass along the content matter.

We like to gnaw on the story awhile; much like a cow chews its cud. Who knows, perhaps it's boredom? Or maybe it runs deeper than that. Could it be that discussing the challenges others face makes us feel just a little better for a while? It's a twisted way of reconfirming, momentarily, that maybe your life is not as miserable as it sometimes seems.

But, here's the catch - when you're tuned into the "Hot and Juicy Hotline", eventually the subject matter will be about you.

My name is Jenna Sinclair. I'm the poster child for the American housewife, south of forty and north of skinny. I buy more shoes and designer handbags than pants, since my butt is still too big from the weight gained during my last pregnancy. You could say I have "size" denial. I simply refuse to acknowledge that my body is not what it used to be. Mind you, the baby is now four, and the grace period for post pregnancy pounds has expired.

My three children are under the age of ten, which means my life is organized around their elaborate carpool schedule. Everything I need to accomplish for myself must happen between the hours of 9:30 am and 2:00 pm or it has to wait for tomorrow. My daily "to-do" list on my pink Razor phone includes, but is not limited to: shopping, housecleaning, Nia or Pilates, tennis, and an extended lunch with friends. A personal favorite is the Zodiac Café at Neiman Marcus. Sprinkled into the daily mix is an occasional committee meeting for a charity or a board meeting at the Junior League. Oh, and I almost forgot, I also own a small boutique business selling artwork out of my home to my friends and designers. It's more of a hobby, really.

When I am not up to my elbows at home, I am in my car. As a mother of three small children, attending different schools and participating in a myriad of activities, I spend an inordinate amount of time shuttling my kids around my urban environment. All activities seem to be located in opposite directions, starting at the same time. It's a "Sophie's Choice" every day as to who will potentially be late. Usually it's my daughter. Last year, we were tardy forty-one times. I heard you gasp. Don't worry; I'm not applying for the Mother-of-the-Year award. I've always figured I'd give someone else a shot at maternal glory.

There is an art to the carpool, a unique blend of timing, elevated voice instructions and chaos, those outside of the club of motherhood will never fully understand or appreciate. If the clan is in the car, backpacks, books, and lunch boxes intact, leaving the driveway by

7:15 sharp, not a minute later, then it all works out perfectly. This of course implies that the routine in the morning runs smoothly, which it rarely does.

The morning routine consists of showers for the two oldest kids: Lucy, age ten and Cole, age eight, while Mia, age five, nibbles on dry cereal and watches cartoons. The next step is key. Hot breakfast, homemade lunches, finished homework, and the correct after-school gear set in the right backpack. My goal is to begin the morning routine the night before, but this is a difficult bull's eye to hit.

Here's where it gets tricky. Mia's preschool school is located 1.9 miles from the house and involves a fifteen-minute carpool line. Cole and Lucy's school is located 13.4 miles across town. It's a labyrinth, through a series of four-way stop signs, casual curbside parallel parking, and oblivious pedestrians daydreaming while strolling along on their daily dog walks. Who would have thought 13.4 miles could be so agonizing? It's like running the gauntlet in slow motion.

My youngest child, Mia, does not have to be in class until nine, but she's not decided if she is ready for this commitment, so every day we engage in a series of peace negotiations aimed at having her "in-wardrobe and on-location" by at least quarter after nine, often after I've already driven the other children to school with her pajama clad person flying shotgun from the rear bucket seat of my minivan. I know I should just take her to school in sleepwear to prove a point, but a lifetime scar from childhood humiliation is not my thing. I'm in the zone and that's the best I can do. I always take into account the unspoken "pre-school grace period rule." In other words, I tell myself that school at this age doesn't really count like it does for the big kids, so I get there when I can get there. After all, I am praying for more grace in my life; sometimes it comes, other times I simply take it.

The afternoon routine is more elaborate and requires careful planning. Lucy and Cole are in the car by 3:15 sharp and off to a slew of activities before we pick-up my youngest daughter, Mia by six pm. If we are late, she'll have to spend the night alone in the church basement where the school is located.

On Mondays, we have the Children's Choir for my daughter from 4:15 to 5:45. For my son, there's hockey practice from 5:00 to 6:30. Early arrival is of the utmost importance because the elaborate uniform of protective pads, leg warmers, and custom skates take at least twenty-two minutes to execute. On Tuesday, we have Girl Scouts at 3:15, and I am the Girl Scout leader. I have been the leader for the last five years; it's a default position. This happens to moms sometimes. We raise our hands for a small volunteer task and suddenly we own it for life. No one else has stepped forward yet. I'm no longer anticipating a reprieve. Then, there's a summer warm-up for the swim team immediately following the meeting. On Wednesday, Cole has a weekly 5:15 vision therapy appointment for thirty minutes, but it's located at a doctor's office forty-five minutes from my home, if I can perfectly time the ebb and flow of the afternoon rush hour. If not, then it takes closer to an hour to make the appointment. By the way, if you are late, you're still charged the seventy-dollar session fee anyway.

On Thursday, there is indoor soccer for my little one for 45 minutes at 4:00. Meanwhile, Lucy finishes her bi-weekly after-school running club, Girls on the Run, at 4:45. On Friday, there is a small lull in the momentum; both kids have baseball at the same time, at the same ballpark - although not on the same team, which means not on the same field.

Interspersed with this frenetic and highly orchestrated dance is a series of mandatory stops for after-school snacks at a variety of fast-food restaurants and convenience stores for "in-transit-mood-management." A hungry child is not a cooperative child.

I fondly call this daily carpool ritual "The Route."

My car is a shiny, silver minivan with electric side-doors, a sunroof, a stereo permanently tuned into Radio Disney, and a DVD player that descends from the roof. I term my minivan "The Magic School Bus," affectionately named after a favorite cartoon of the kids. Our destinations change almost daily. The seasons usher in a new sport or activity, but the basic elements of The Route are unyielding. No worries, this magic bus will take you wherever you need to go. And, there is also another type of magic going on in the "Bus." I am privy to a first-hand account of everything that happens to my kids throughout the day. I hear about their friends and foes, schoolwork success stories and failures, and the best part is the incessant chatter about things of seemingly no consequence in the "adult world." For example, the selection process of possible names

4

for a new stuffed animal, or plans to play trains and build a track around the entire living room, or who gets the first turn on the trampoline. I've come to realize, time spent on *The Route* is my path into the hearts and minds of my children, it's a journey I savor.

My home base sidekick is a spunky woman named Lolly Olive. She has short, curly, "do- it- yourself" yellow hair and a south-of-the-tracks twang. Petite in stature, but not in build, she buys her discount shoes in children's sizes for extra savings, but her t-shirts and denim shorts are more comfortable in an extra large size.

Lolly arrived in the middle of thirteen kids, a homebirth in the heartland. Her mother never bothered with a birth certificate. She believes she's somewhere between fifty-one and fifty-seven, but there's no way to know for certain. Her siblings are scattered like the puff of an expired dandelion found in the fields where she played as a child. Lolly cares for my children, a position she's held since their birth. Her job description is as varied as the selections found in the gift shop at a roadside Cracker Barrel restaurant. But, whatever the task, whether it's cleaning the overflowing cat litter box or reading to my youngest child as she drifts off to sleep, she completes it with no-nonsense diligence and a healthy dose of laughter.

Lolly is one of the people in my life I call a "rock." Everyone has "rock" people in their lives. Rocks are easy to overlook, yet they are the unwavering, constant presences upon which we tether our chaotic lives. Rock people are rarely front and center, because they don't require any emotional fireworks, also known as "personal-drama-induced-entertainment." This follows the theatrical line of reasoning employed by many females, myself included, and "Life is boring, let's make a play."

In contrast, Lolly is constant and grounded, like the sprawling oak trees in my yard. Which consequently, don't even require water. It is not until our rocks are gone that we miss them like an amputated limb, the shadow of its usefulness still lingering in the void.

I am blessed in the area of rock collections although at first glance, some of my cornerstones may look more like blowing sand. Mother is one of these whirling dervishes. She moves in and out of projects like a roadrunner, always leaving them better than when she arrived. Mother is pure energy. Always looking forward, she has achieved more than most people I know. She builds businesses and houses, stick by stick, from the ground up. Any concept my mother entertains becomes a reality before the ink of the initial outline is dry, if she even bothers to write it down. As a child, I don't remember many hugs. Life was simply too demanding for a bra-burning, female success machine. Three times married, an entrepreneur and real estate saleswoman extraordinaire, my mother made sure I had an apple red BMW and a unlimited bank account. My mother's personal life is not as successful. Much of this is due to her mouth. She shoots out critiques like armor-piercing bullets from a machine gun; no protection exists to escape the ragged, bleeding wounds her words inflict. Mother's words are harsh, laced with kind intention and the wisdom of life experience. She calls herself a "ticker tape without a censor." I tend to agree.

It is not the words however, but the actions of my mother that give her "bedrock" status. Mother is known to the rest of the world as Jacqueline "Jackie" Blackwell, a name which accurately captures her black and white opinions of the world. The experience of her mothering is layered deep in my being. Her DNA donation to me is the energy to fire up a flash of creativity into a tangible work of art and a belief that all things are possible. "Why the hell not," as she so aptly puts it. With no regard to frequency, mother has extended her checkbook; sometimes it's money for the kids' camp or school tuition, other times it's seed money to start a business of my own. But the maternal investment does not come without strings; the "I-owe-you" always arrives at a later date.

Other times, mother's support comes in the form of "boots in the dirt", like when we drove from Arizona to Florida in a moving truck we personally loaded, stopping along the way for me to interview for an entry level TV news reporter job in Austin, Texas. If I had gotten the job, she would have left me with the truck and my two dogs, and gone ahead. But, my confidence wasn't with me that day. Perhaps she should have kept her comments to herself about my "tight," newly-altered, magenta Tahari suit with its double row of shiny, brass buttons as she pulled the moving truck in front of KKTV-TV to drop me off for my big break.

Mother sometimes shares with me stories about the struggles in her life. The mistakes and challenges are so similar; it feels as if we are actors playing roles from the same script on different stages at different times. Mother is a mirror reflecting the potential of my choices, both negative and positive.

I have another maternal figure in my realm, a spiritual mother. Her gentle wisdom and reassuring insights are a welcome balm, which provide healing comfort to my chafed life. Faith Monroe is what some call a spiritual advisor or an intuitive lifestyle coach; others would consider her a psychic. Either definition is correct. Faith has salt-and-pepper hair like her outlook on life. Her clients have taught her that life offers us all similar lessons. We are the ones who add the extra spice. In essence, we enhance the flavor to make the substance more palatable, so we can digest the message. Some of us like our lives bland and constant, others prefer spicy and assaulting. Faith has taught me there is no right or wrong; it's simply a matter of degrees, like an oven set to warm or broil. The problem is, too hot, too spicy, too often, comes at a price. Faith calls it a spiritual ulcer. Too much of anything inflames us, and then it becomes difficult for our soul to digest the message, which lies underneath every life experience.

Faith is my tall glass of milk. She's the best prescription for my spiritual ulcer. Her quiet, intimate guidance cools my burning, ulcerated digestive tract. I have run to Faith "on fire" so many times, I can easily conjure the image of my hair blazing and my feet smoking as I enter the door of her office for my emergency appointment. I come seeking her "divine extinguisher", ready to coat me with fear-fighting foam before I disintegrate from the heat of my current situation, which is almost always a five-alarm blaze. Not many people know about Faith. She is my invisible tether in my otherwise visible world. Faith is a lifeline I have often grabbed onto in the darkest of moments when my burden was more than I would dare let any friend carry, lest they explode from the ridiculous force of the experience.

Finally, I have a 24/7, every day or once a month, confidant with a built in "no-bullshit-face-the–truth-o-meter". Let me tell you, this is the friend every girl needs in the gentle, but firm model. A Southern belle and Southern Baptist from Alabama, Danielle Greene was sandwiched between two beauty queens. Her mother was crowned Miss North Carolina; decades later, her younger sister wore the crown of Miss Tennessee. Danielle has warm, absorbing brown eyes that crinkle in their corners when she smiles. Her rich, chestnut hair is always styled in perfect height and proportion. She wears it in a sassy bob which brushes her shoulders. Danielle has a bible verse for almost every occasion, she knows more about hairspray and "Hallelujah" than I ever will.

We share daughters the same age, born a month apart. They were the link that brought us together while sitting side-by-side at a weekly toddler gym class. I can still clearly see our little dolls dressed in perfectly coordinated finery toddling around the petite indoor obstacle course as we chased behind them trying to keep their jaunty, matching hair bows intact. One day, I turned to Danielle and declared, "We should be friends. Let's grab lunch," and from that point forward we were.

But underneath this image of manicured perfection is a broken life glued back together again. When she was twelve, a fun-filled family outing to an amusement park ended in tragedy. Her younger sister, uncle, and cousin were all killed as their gondola broke free from its rusted tether and crashed to the pavement below. Danielle remembers vividly trying to figure out a way to brace herself during the terrifying plummet. It worked; she was the only one to make it out alive. A long scar on the outside of her leg is the only external evidence of the accident; perhaps her well-ordered life is an indication of the scars that remain within. Through her, I'm constantly present to the unspoken fact that life can change in an instant, so the pendulum swings both ways. A few years ago she moved an hour away, it sounds like a short distance, but it seems far considering my entire life exist within ten square miles.

Now that you know a little about me, how I spend my days, the places I travel and the people I see - even the twitter in my brain - I'd like to share with you the events leading up to my death...

Chapter 2

Four years earlier

"Surprise!"

A chorus of voices caught me off guard as I carried two large Gymboree shopping bags full of baby clothes into my front door.

"Oh my God!" I covered my mouth, startled. "What are you guys doing here?" I asked, still trembling slightly from the unexpected clamor.

Fourteen smiling faces beamed back at me, laughing at my shocked expression. These are female faces of friends made at my oldest child's preschool, at weekly mom's groups that visited different playgrounds, and through a wide assortment of children's activities. Clearly, they had carried off the surprise.

"I had no idea, you all scared me to death!" I laughed.

"Here, let me help you with this," Danielle said, coming forward to give me a hug. Her arms barely reached around me, with my very large, due-in-less-than-a month, pregnant belly.

"I can't believe you didn't figure this out!" she said, delighted with her secretive success.

Her warm brown eyes crinkled at the corners as she smiled at me. I could see a hint of tears threatening to spill down her face. She cries over all sentimental occasions. Sometimes even a poignant Kleenex commercial will evoke a sob or two.

"You shouldn't have. After all, this is my third baby," I scolded her lightly. *I hate being the center of attention.*

"Just relax and enjoy yourself. You've thrown baby showers for most of us," she said. "Besides, didn't you donate everything after your last child?" *Yeah, I thought I was finished. Ironically, this surprise party really started nine months ago. All mothers know babies have their own agenda, even prior to birth.*

In the short time I'd been away, the room had been transformed with pink and white balloons and assorted paper decorations. Petite clusters of sweetheart roses in shiny silver cups were on every table, their sweet fragrance filling the warm June air. It was perfect. Even the fresh flowers happened to match the blooming red and pink roses patterned boldly on my white halter maternity dress.

A pile of elegantly wrapped gifts graced a table nearby with a beautiful cake, front and center, surrounded by a garland of fresh, fragrant white Stargazer lilies. Their fuchsia centers accented the detailed pink-and-white striped sugar baby booties a top the three-tiered vanilla confection. My mother's silver coffee service gleamed on a large engraved silver tray at the end of the dining room table. My grandmother's dainty china teacups waited invitingly on a pale, green lace and linen starched cloth. Three large crystal serving bowls full of chicken salad and other delicacies from local gourmet market were also available for my unexpected guests.

I thought to myself, *how did the house get so clean?* Thankfully, my perfectionist hostess played a role in these highly orchestrated details. I felt a wash of guilt, remembering the mess I'd left earlier this morning.

My century home has two personalities, elegant and ugly. *I hope the guests decide to stay in the elegant part.* On the other side of the white, six-paneled swinging door to the dining room was my olive green kitchen circa 1950, which still desperately needed to be remodeled. This is in stark contrast to the two front rooms, the dining room and the parlor, which are charming and elegant with elaborate crown moldings, coffered ceilings, leaded glass French doors and antique furnishings.

"How are you feeling?"

"Is the baby moving a lot?"

"Any contractions?"

I was bombarded by questions, hello hugs, air kisses and happy smiles.

`"Do you think this baby will come early?" asked Elizabeth Peters, the other hostess of my party, along with Danielle. These are my two best gal pals.

She then recounted to my guests the story of the birth of my second child, Cole. He was in a hurry. Two weeks early, five contractions and four pushes, "Hello, world, I'm here!"

Elizabeth rushed to the hospital to visit. She was totally in awe; we had only finished our lunch a few hours before. I still had my lipstick and makeup on, unlike the birth of my first child, Lucy, where I labored for days. That momentous event took so long, even my hired doula asked to go home because she was exhausted.

Elizabeth, or Libby, as her close friends call her, is also the godmother of my son Cole. We each have a son the same age. We met at the Junior League a few months after I relocated here. She was also a transplant from another place. Her husband is a physician. Libby and I clicked immediately, and soon we were spending every day together, taking outings with our children. We each only had one child at the time. That was six years ago, the friendship has deepened and developed since then. Both of us have blonde hair and blue eyes; it's not uncommon for people to ask if we are sisters.

"Ding, ding, ding!" The sound of a spoon lightly tapping on a crystal glass alerted us it was time to play a game. Several pieces of pink paper were handed out and each one of the women wrote down a blurb of parenting advice.

The basket was passed up to me full of "mother's wisdom", and they all waited expectantly as I read aloud the words on each sheet of paper.

" Enjoy every moment. They grow up too fast."

"Go out on dates with your husband."

"Hug and kiss your children every day."

Everyone was smiling warmly and nodding in agreement.

"Keep your legs together until after age forty-five," one voice pierced the air with a loud cackle followed by a quick snort.

Mother! I knew immediately the source of the zinger. Mother thinks every time I have sex; I end up pregnant.

It was exactly who I suspected, my mother, Jackie Blackwell.

She was clearly entertained by her sense of humor. Mother wore a leopard print blouse, skin-tight denim pants to her shins and a cranberry red sun visor; neither her words, nor her clothes ever compliment her environment.

Never the nurturing type, when I first told her I was pregnant earlier in the year, her first response was, "Are you going to keep it?"

Even now the exchange brings a scowl to my face.

"It's not a stray puppy mother, it's a baby, and that is an offensive question," I barked back at her. "A normal grandmother would be excited and happy about the news."

Since then, at least once a week we have the same exchange. I've reached the conclusion; mother is clearly in denial about my current status in life.

"How do you have the time or resources for another baby? You need to get back out there in the world and start your TV career again." My mother's fantasy about me is forever clashing with the reality.

"That was a long time ago, Mother. Somehow I don't think those doors are still open. Have you looked at me lately? I'm close to 200 pounds bursting with my third baby."

"You should be a star," mother always proclaims. *Why can't I just be a mom?*

Her comment from the baby shower game still hung in the air. I could tell my guests were shocked. In response to her insult, the smiles faded from their faces momentarily, like melting butter losing its form. However, in the circle I now inhabit, social graces always prevail over uncertainty, at least in public.

"Let's open gifts," Libby said brightly.

"That's a great idea," Danielle chimed in.

Patterned paper, organza bows, dangling sequin booties: the boxes containing the baby gifts were a confection of merit on their own. I hated to tear the paper and expose what was inside. A completed custom scrapbook of my baby's first year, with spaces for me to add the photos; a hand-crafted bright yellow shaggy chenille diaper bag with a contrasting pink and green floral fabric lining; and a hand-painted ceramic dinner set with colorful flowers for my baby's first meals. These items were only a few of the wonderful and thoughtful gifts. I could feel my friends' loving intentions and good will oozing from each one of the packages. It was overwhelming.

After a lifetime of feeling invisible and awkward, it was delicious to experience being part of a special tribe. The initiation into motherhood creates these clans of women.

Sure, I've had my share of career success, yet it never seems to fill out the lingering loneliness of my childhood. My father was a big shot in corporate America, which meant we moved every time he had a new promotion. Almost every two years we'd zigzag the country north to east and west to south, with two extended stays in the United Kingdom and Australia. The adjustment was difficult for me: wrong clothes, wrong slang, wrong hair, wrong everything. By the time I figured it out, the boxes were being carried to the moving van again. Eventually, I stopped trying and started crying, until all of the tears dried up. Pregnancy has allowed them to flow once again.

Suddenly tears began to burn the back of my eyelids and I felt the skin on my chest start to turn red and heat up as my throat constricted. *"Not now!"* I scolded myself. I successfully fought to regain my composure. This was a time for celebration, not for tears. *"What in the world did I ever do to deserve friends such as these?"* I said to myself quietly.

I looked around the room at each of these women; beautiful, stylish, successful, smiling warmly at me and sharing their love. I paused. Time stopped for a moment, suspended in a space of non-action, a series of mere seconds, which felt like infinity. I took a mental snapshot. I downloaded the image into my heart, so I could refer back to it at a later date and feel the same joy.

Later, after the guests had all departed and we were cleaning up in my dated, olive green kitchen, I turned and gave Libby and Danielle each a big hug. "Thank you so much for today. I was completely surprised."

"You're welcome, Jenna. You've always been there for us, too. You're a tough girl to surprise," said Danielle looking at Libby in a meaningful way.

"Yeah, she kept trying to figure out what I was working on," Libby said. "Admit it, you were mad when I didn't tell you."

"Maybe a little. I thought you were trying to keep me out of the loop on something. I don't really like surprises. But this one was great. Thanks again." I smiled and looked down at the floor. *Maybe I had been a little bit of a brat. Pregnant ladies are crabby.*

"Well, we're going to go now. Steve should be back with the kids soon. I'll call you later." Libby gave me one of her signature air kisses.

I walked into the kitchen to finish cleaning up the house. I like to call my house Dora. She's a friend and an enemy, really more like a demanding high-maintenance relative. She has tons of issues. She ruins my vacation plans, spends my money, and comes unglued at the most inconvenient times. If she were a person, she'd have bad skin, warts, wrinkles, gas, constipation, sometimes diarrhea, and perhaps even a missing arm or leg. But I love her. To her credit, she has good bones, a lovely personality, and tons of untapped potential.

Dora's notable history extends back to the Civil War; a Captain of the 21st Regiment of the U.S. Cavalry built her. The original stone wall from the soldier's fort in the 1860's wraps around her front yard like an apron. The top row of stones was designed so rifles could set deep in the groove, should an attack from enemy soldiers occur. Even now, the house has the energy of a stronghold.

Dora is situated in a town that looks like Main Street, U.S.A. Charming front porches, and elaborate gardens stuffed with hostas and azaleas face each other from one block to the next. American flags fly from front doors, including ours, and children ride their bikes into the downtown area to purchase snow cones and cookies.

I know. The rule of thumb is to never fall in love with real estate; yet Dora cast a spell over us. This century-old beauty took our breath away and we had to have her. We were blinded by love. All we could see was potential.

The house has twelve foot high ceilings on both the first and second floors, eight large bedrooms, an elaborate wood paneled study, and an elegant dining room with a large bay window overlooking an acre of property graced by ten grand, sprawling oak trees. The house is located in the heart of the town's historic district like a vintage statue on top of a wedding cake.

Dora is also blessed with rotting plaster, calcified lead plumbing pipes, peeling paint, leaking radiators, a ninety-year-old tile roof, knob and tube electrical wiring, and a host of other urgent demands.

But I love her nonetheless; she's a member of my family and deserves my loyalty. Her make-over is in the works, until then I simply turn a blind eye to her glaring shortcomings and embrace her radiant potential.

Chapter 3

My husband Steve and I never lived in the same city until a month before the wedding. We have what I fondly refer to as a "modern-day-arranged-marriage". Not driven by culture, but by circumstance. We met when I was staying with friends in New York City while interviewing for a television job at NY1. He was one of their roommates. I didn't get the job, but I got a husband. In hindsight, it was the better score of the two.

We talked on the phone every night for a year and spent time together a handful of weekends and a few week-long stretches. But our careers, mine in particular, did not allow us to be located in the same city. As a news reporter for the NBC affiliate in Tampa, I was not about to quit my job to "date" someone. Jobs in television news are few and far between, although I did finally land one after the debacle in Austin. For longer than I'd care to admit, I've kept a private file folder full of rejection letters to remind me that I was, in fact, replaceable in this industry. It took years to break into the business of television news as an on-air personality. A combination of determination and degradation won the day. I was of no mind to step off the victor's platform. A long-distance boyfriend of convenience suited me fine for many years, until one day a friend of mine, fifteen years ahead of me in the business, unmarried and childless, was unceremoniously "retired" and immediately replaced by someone like me; twenty-something, cute and cheap. I've heard that at any point in our lives, we always have a variety of realities to choose from. These life path possibilities exist for us just beyond our awareness, should we decide to change our decisions about the life we want to be living. In this moment, I was given a crystal clear momentary flash of an alternative choice to where I was clearly headed. I opted to take it. My agent and my mother still don't understand.

The funny thing about a long distance boyfriend or fiancé is that you can fill in the spaces of a relationship with your own fantasies and expectations about your partner. Late at night while listening to your sweetheart's soothing voice after a long stressful day, it's easy to forget, or ignore, the "warts" on a person. We all have warts. These are the challenges and weaknesses in our personalities that are not always revealed to others until they really get to know us. Make no mistake, you really get to know someone not by what they say, but how they act and react in the daily world.

In marriage, our warts can extend beyond ourselves. After years of togetherness, I have learned that you don't just marry a person; you marry a family. You attach yourself to their beliefs, customs, traditions and communication styles; also their grudges, judgments, opinions and general long-standing angst from a variety of sources. So in addition to the wedding gifts, I now know every marriage also comes with warts and luggage. Otherwise known as family baggage.

There can be a lot. Anger and bad behavior tend to pile up when they go unaddressed. Often there is enough *stuff* inside a typical dysfunctional family to fill an entire collection of luggage, including every size bag ever offered, plus the makeup case, for first impressions, and a traveling hanging bag, for special occasions. Some families have baggage that is fresh, clean and shiny. Perfectly coordinated, allowing easy access to their issues through a series of well-organized compartments. Other families have luggage so dusty and dated the zippers are rusted and broken, making access to the stuff inside almost impossible. Eventually, in marriage, everything gets unpacked. And, like a wet towel left to mold in a plastic bag inside a hot car for an extended period of time, the *stuff* inside stinks. This is the case with my in-laws.

I could hear the phone ringing in the other room, so I scuttled to reach it as fast as my pregnant belly would allow. It'd been two weeks since the baby shower and I was counting the days until my due date.

"Hello."

"Je-- nna? Is that you? Augh. I HATE HIM!" a series of broken sobs and gasps for breath assaulted my ears from the other end of the line.

I rapidly fired out a series of questions. "Who is this? Are you alright? What's wrong?" panic rushing through my heart. *Are the kids OK? Did somebody die?* Fear gripped my throat like a vise as I waited for the bad news.

"It's Rhonda!" More sobbing followed, her voice becoming agitated as her grief turned to anger.

"Where are you? Do you need me to come to you now?" The words urgently spilled from my mouth. I still had no idea what had happened.

"That son of a bitch is cheating on me!" she barked out, more anguished sobs follow.

"Who are you talking about? Don?"

"Of course Don, who else is there?" Rhonda spat back in an ugly tone.

I struggled to get my bearings after the shock of her announcement. "Are you sure? How did you find out?" I tried to put the pieces together in my mind.

"Who is she?" The question spilled out before I could stop it. *Do I really want to get involved?*

Donald, Steve's father, met Rhonda while she was a cashier at one of his fast-food restaurants. With an ego the size of the state of Alaska, Don likes to play the role of Prince Charming. He tends to pick women who are dazzled by his assets and blinded to his attributes; women he can transform with a credit card and woo into a hotel room without a lot of questions.

Part of his behavior must be genetic. An old school Sicilian guy from the Bronx, Donald's father arrived on Ellis Island as a boy and spent his life recasting the family's fortune. The father's hard work and success established his children as doctors and lawyers. Don, a non-practicing lawyer and a middle child, inherited the machismo, but not the work ethic. His interests lie in skirts.

Rhonda is Don's second wife; for me, that would be a stepmother-in-law. It's one of the relational oddities that arise from the patchwork of broken families commonplace today. My kids call her "grandma" even though she's only nine years older than me. A daily punch card for the tanning salon guarantees her sun-tanned skin year-round. The aroma of a recently smoked cigarette is her calling card.

Over the last ten years of my marriage, she's become a friend of sorts, in that we often share similar complaints about the absurd parodies, which seem to continually plague our family's lives. The primary instigator of all of this happens to my husband's father, Donald Sinclair, the drama magnet. So it's not surprising that he is center stage once again today.

He's dark and sleek like a vintage Italian sports car with a warm brown interior, difficult to resist at first glance. Don loves travel to sunny places, his skin is always tanned, and on his medium frame he carries a small "gentleman's paunch". He wears the best of everything like a slick Manhattan lawyer, even though in reality he is simply the owner of a chain of popular burrito restaurants. Not many people I know, other than Don, wear Giorgio Armani to eat their chimichangas.

Don Sinclair draws attention to himself by discussing his business portfolio as if it were a shopping list for a gourmet market: all the things he could buy if he had the room in his cart and enough time and appetite to eat every delectable item before it perished. It goes without saying that most people only purchase one or two items at a specialty market and fantasize about the rest. Don is no exception.

Yet, people are mesmerized by the potential of Don and the illusory size of his world. He says money is never an object, unless it comes to spending it on someone other than himself. And he is always chuckling to himself about his clever ways. By the way, did I mention that the rules of the world do not apply to Don? Somewhere along the way, he qualified for a status titled "exempt". So Don tramples through life in his designer suit driving his company car, a $150K Mercedes Benz, wielding his golden passport and expecting his family entourage to pick up the pieces and repair the damage in his wake. This time is no exception.

I slowly leaned back the red chenille sofa yielding under my ample body. *"This is going to take awhile"* I propped up my feet and got ready for the latest cyclone of chaos to make landfall.

Outside, it was a breezy, cloudless day. Late June is such a pretty time of year. It was a little before noon, based on where the sun was sitting in the sky. I had to pick up my kids from camp in a few hours. I hoped this wouldn't take too long. I really needed a nap today; the squirming and kicking of my baby had been keeping me up lately.

"It's all there on his laptop, hundred's of emails between him and Amber Atkins!" The sobs had subsided, her voice gaining strength, powered by the ageless force of a scorned woman.

"Are you kidding? His assistant?" I was mystified. I'd met her only a couple of times. *Unremarkable* was all that came to mind.

My own husband is in the office twenty-five feet away from his father. *How could he not know?* That thought I kept to myself, yet she must have read my mind.

"Did Steve know anything about this?" Rhonda said in an accusing tone.

"Not that I have ever heard of!" I quickly defended him. The relationship between a stepmother and her husband's children from his first marriage is a delicate balancing act; one misstep and you fall to your death.

"These text messages are unreal. Just plain cheesy!" She blew a heavy stream of smoke into the phone and said a few curse words. Despite years of shopping at Neiman Marcus, Rhonda never seems far from the drive-thru window.

"Here, listen to this one: "How about a panty raid?""

"Or here's another, "I think you should know what people are saying behind ur back... Nice Ass!!""

"I'm sure you're disgusted." I was uncertain of what to say.

"Here, this is worse. If I ever questioned if they are having sex, here's the answer."

Ronnie read the next message, "Do U like math? If so, add a bed, subtract ur clothes, divide ur legs and we can multiply!"

Here's another, "What are u wearing?" And he used the letter "u" instead of spelling out the word 'you'."

"This one takes the cake, "If your right leg was Thanksgiving and your left leg was Christmas, could I meet you between the holidays?"

"There are hundreds all over his phone and his email account." Ronnie was screeching and reading the messages off like a roll call. I held the phone away from my ear. It was beginning to ache, not the ending I planned for my beautiful day.

"Do you think it's been going on that long, since Christmas? Maybe it was only a short fling?" I wanted to be optimistic.

"NO ONE CHEATS ON ME! IT'S OVER!" She yelled hysterically into the phone.

"I'm so sor…" She cut me off cold.

"Did I ever tell you about the time…"

By now she is in a full rant. I patiently wait for an opening in the conversation. I have always prided myself on being a good listener, but we all have our limits. Even a pause, as quick as a breath, would be enough for me to interject and get the conversation back on track with two people actually participating.

Eighteen minutes into it, there is still no sign of abatement. This freight train has left the station and it's not coming back. I fondly call this phone experience "the reading of the shit list". It's an ongoing list many people keep which spans the history of a relationship and chronicles every perceived transgression for all time. The benefit of maintaining a list is that whenever there is an argument, the list holder is fully loaded and ready for attack with an arsenal of anecdotes.

As a friend, there is nothing worse than when the list comes out, because I've already heard it all before, and it requires a huge investment of time and silence, broken only by a few grunts of agreement, so they know you haven't drifted off to sleep. In fact, I could probably read Ronnie's list myself from memory she has aired it so many times. It's my opinion that friends should be candid with one another and simply say, "You know the list!", and we would all nod our heads in emphatic agreement. Having the list "on file" is much better than having to go through it sin by sin.

"Ronnie, RHONDA!" I raise my voice to a shout, which brought her rant to an abrupt halt.

"I don't know what to say. I'm so sorry; would you like me to come over?" I'm trying to find a way to end this conversation. Suddenly I'm feeling very drained.

"No, no. I know it's time to pick up the kids. I have to go to or I'll be in the back of the carpool line. I'll call you later."

Since Ronnie is only nine years older than me, she too has kids in school and drives the daily carpool route. I stared at the phone for a while after she hung up.

What does this mean? I thought to myself.

Steve has worked for his father for years. I know he doesn't like Amber Atkins, the assistant, because he complains about her all the time. But beyond that, Ronnie is a shareholder in the business, and a divorce could be cataclysmic. Well, maybe she's wrong and this was a one-time thing. For now, I will hope for the best.

Chapter 4

Later that afternoon, I decided to call Faith from my minivan. I always have a few minutes between destinations on *the route* for a quick phone call. My pink Razor has her programmed on speed dial. Number three, right after Steve and my voicemail.

It's been more than a week since my last appointment, and this new development clearly needs exploration. I decided long ago, why stew over the many potentials of a situation when you can find out exactly what is in store through your personal psychic. Good or bad, the known is much easier than the unknown, as far as I am concerned. I guess that's my inner control freak. I simply don't like surprises.

"Thank you for calling the Soul Center, this is Faith," she answers on the first ring.

"Hi, Faith, it's Jenna. Are you with a client right now?"

" No, I just finished a reading. What's up?"

"Do you have time to fit me in? You're never going to believe what I just learned?"

"Not much surprises me, dear." We both laugh at the same time. Of course not, she's a psychic.

"How about tomorrow morning, 10?"

"Perfect, I'll look forward to it."

I can barely wait until tomorrow. Something about the anticipation of a psychic reading gives me a little buzz. It's like when a friend calls and tells you she has a big secret to share, then asks you to meet her for a tell-all and a tuxedo latte at Starbucks… in two days. The suspense is unbearable. Only with a reading, the secrets are your own, waiting patiently to be revealed to the impatient seeker; who of course would be me! Urgent, urgent, urgent, everything is always urgent. Who knows, maybe I'm addicted to psychics too.

If you've never had a reading before, here's how it works. Faith uses her radar intuition combined with the Tarot. It's a deck of cards made up of seventy-eight symbols. The Tarot is ancient; it has been described as "God's Picture Book."

Faith says it's not magic; it's only a mystical tool. She uses it in her work as a spiritual counselor. Everything depicted on the cards means something. They are loaded with colorful images and archetypes. Faith says the spirit world uses metaphorical symbols to help you learn to develop and trust your own intuition and inner guidance. It's a kind of "spirit speak", the language our spirit guides use to communicate with us. Often, I will go to Faith with a hunch about what is going on in my life, and the cards pulled during the reading will reconfirm what I already suspect. And other times, I am completely surprised by what the cards reveal. *I wonder which way it will go today?*

We were sitting across from one another in her dim reading room, and the cards were fanned out in front of us. Faith always starts out with a prayer. I placed my hands on top of her open palms and closed my eyes.

"Let us invite the energy down from the heavens and into our hearts and then release it. Next, we invite the energy up from the earth and into our hearts and then release it. And now we ask that the information, which we are about to receive, is for the highest good of all people involved. So be it and so it is. Amen."

I loved her soothing, gentle voice. I could feel a tingling sensation on the palms of my hands for a moment before I placed my hands back on my lap. I think this is the transfer of energy between us. Our vibes.

"What is it you want to know?' She picked up the deck and handed it to me so I could start shuffling.

"Well, first off, is Don really having an affair?" I finished shuffling the cards and then placed them on the table. She instructed me to cut the deck three times. Once this was completed, she collected the cards into one stack and took off the top cards one by one, laying them into a spread shaped like a cross.

"The cards say yes. They also say there are a lot more surprises to be revealed."

"Oh no, Faith, what does that mean for Steve and me? You know he works for his father. Remember, his dad owns all of the Burrito Bandit restaurants in town."

"Well, here is the Wheel of Fortune. It could be a turn for the better or a turn for the worse. But change is inevitable."

"Faith, all Steve wants is to own his own stores. Is this drama going to create that opportunity?"

"Jenna, right now it looks like everything is up in the air. But sit tight, I'm sure it will work out. There is also a warning here in the cards. Take care of yourself. A lot of people will want to lean on you for support."

"What about the baby? I'm due any minute. Will she be okay?" Faith laughed. I've asked her that question every week since learning I was pregnant. Every time, the answer was the same.

"Yes, she will be fine and there is an element of the unexpected around her birth."

"I hope she is still a girl!" I was half-joking, half-serious.

Faith laughed, "I know it's not that big of a shock, but perhaps a surprise or two."

"I'll keep you posted. Thanks for the reading. I wish it had been clearer. Everything seems so up in the air."

"Remember Jenna, we always have free will. We can make different choices at any point along the path and that will change the outcome. A lot of decisions will be made in the next few weeks and months that will determine which way this will all play out. I'll pray for you, my dear."

I hugged her goodbye. It's funny. Faith is such an important part of my life, but almost none of my friends or family know she exists.

Chapter 5

It was a warm, hot, sticky July day. The kind where the perspiration trickles down your back and it feels like a bug is crawling on you. The fact that I am nine months pregnant, and I look like an overstuffed olive ready to burst, resplendent with taunt skin covering my body from enough retained water to support the operation of a French fountain, only amplifies this unpleasant sensation. However, special occasions arrive regardless of our state of being. All I want is to sit home and watch the clock until the baby is ready to remove itself from my strained body, but today is my ten-year anniversary, and we have plans tonight.

Yes, ten years of blissful matrimony, if you can call "Utopia" a house full of kids, dogs, cats, and hermit crabs. I like to refer to my life as "happy chaos" on a good day and "hell on earth" the rest of the time. It seems like the house can never quite get to clean, we get close, but something always distracts us and we are at square one again within a day. Most of the time we pull clean clothes out of the laundry baskets; things are folded but never make it into the drawers.

Steve is a big guy who we all fondly refer to as "The Bear". His hair is as dark as mine is light, and I share his intense blue eyes, only mine are a shade lighter, with pale green accents near the iris. Even his personality is a lot like a bear, although I have never encountered one. He can be warm and snuggly, like a favorite teddy bear one moment, or he can be a loud, raging, growling beast the next.

The kids and I have invented some ways to needle him when he is in one of his rants. I say, "Kids, don't make the bear growl!" Or if we are having one of our frequent disagreements, I say, "Mom and Dad are having a bear fight!" This seems to serve two purposes. First, it quickly defuses his escalating mood swing with a cold bucket of humor; and second, it keeps the kids from being terrified by the big, loud, grouchy bear, aka Dad.

Life between us is pretty good. Being a nomad throughout my childhood, Steve is my "home". He's hard working, kind and occasionally interested in all of my social intrigues. By definition, he is a "good husband" and I am happy to be married.

Steve has packed on the pounds with each one of my pregnancies for a total of forty to spare. *Who says only women get pregnant?* We call his expanding midsection the "band of power." I personally think it makes him powerless in the sex department. Fat people don't like to have sex and my husband is no exception. But, aside from a listless libido, he makes me laugh and we like to do a lot of the same things. I also have come to learn that being in a family business has a castrating element. Don keeps Steve in line by constantly letting him know all the ways he is ineffective. Hopefully, this cycle is ending soon. Yet life is good, and we cherish our children. I can tell he is bubbling with excitement over this latest arrival.

"Honey, are you dressed yet?" Steve shouts up the stairs. "We are going to be late to meet the Peters."

"You have to come upstairs, I can't get my dress zipped," I screech.

The sound is motivating. I can hear him grudgingly taking the steps back upstairs to offer assistance.

"What can I do?" he asked.

I point to my zipper angrily. It's all part of the husband duty, doting on your two hundred pound pregnant wife. So he moves in to tuck my flesh into the confines of my strained zipper. I refuse to buy any new maternity clothes for this last couple of days, God forbid weeks, until the baby comes. I know the weight will come off right after the baby is born; at least, most of it. I'm happy to return to size 10.

"Can you believe what's going on with your father?" I asked, bewildered. "I was on the phone again with Ronnie most of the day.

She's called me every day this week with a play-by-play. Today, she said she wants a divorce. Do you think it's true?"

"Honey, you know I don't really talk to him other than business." Steve shakes his head in frustration. This is not the first time his father has been the topic of conversation in our marriage. In, fact, we talk about him most of the time. Most couples focus on the biggest problem. My husband being in business with his father is a big problem.

"Dad has his own way of doing things and consulting me for permission is not part of the protocol. In fact, I have not really seen him in the office for over a week. I think he is on vacation again."

"Well, I can't say I am surprised. There must be a lot of fires at home. But, I'm worried about what this means for you and your role at the Burrito Bandit."

"Don't worry, everything will work out." He pulls me in his arms for one of his famous bear hugs, at least as much of me as would fit in his embrace. "The business is fine. Dad may act dumb, but he's not stupid. He always covers his ass."

"Why do you trust him to cover ours?"

"He's my dad, I know him better than you do?" Steve looked down and I knew the conversation was over. *Childhood disappointment is a tough illusion to shatter.*

We drove to the restaurant in silence, each of us lost in our own thoughts. I hoped Steve was right. I had witnessed some really messy divorces lately. Another thought crossed my mind as well. W*as this a bad omen?* To learn about someone's marriage falling apart exactly on your ten-year anniversary can't be a good thing. I filed the thought away as the valet opened my door.

"Hi, sweetie!"

Libby Peters rushed up to me at the curb for a light hug and an air kiss before I could enter the restaurant. Her white blonde hair flared out like angel wings as a breeze caught it underneath. She looked exceptionally pretty tonight. I struggled inside for a moment. *Is it safe for women to have friends that look like her?* I casually glance over at my husband to see his reaction to Libby's radiance. *Nothing.* It was probably my imagination working overtime from my earlier conversation.

"Thanks again for giving me a surprise baby shower last

weekend!" I hugged her back, opting to skip the air kiss, because they always felt stupid to me.

"You didn't miss even the smallest detail!" I complimented her as we walked to our table. Libby smiled even wider, like a puffed up peacock unfurling all of its feathers.

"Have you ever thought of being an event planner?"

"Actually, the thought has crossed my mind. I get invited to so many parties." Libby looked at her husband Blake for reassurance. He offered none.

Blake was a heart surgeon. He sometimes had difficulty leaving his ego and his condescending attitude at the hospital. It didn't really matter in our friendship though; the puzzle still fit together nicely. Blake was already deep in conversation with Steve. The two men shared many of the same passions: golf, baseball and poker. They frequently left the small talk to us as they pursued their own conversational interests.

Libby and Blake have been our best couple friends for the past five years. We spend a week each summer at the beach with our families. We take turns hosting Easter egg hunts at our homes. We share an elaborate Santa costume which our husbands take turns wearing each Christmas during a kids' pajama brunch, where we get the best photos for our Christmas cards, without waiting in the long lines at the mall. Our children are the same ages, with the exception of the one I am expecting. Libby and Blake are the godparents of my son, Cole, and I am the godmother of her son, Blake, Jr. We are one big happy "family", marching through an endless calendar of shared events. Of course we would spend an anniversary together; it was more fun.

Together, Libby and I have built a circle of friends. Most of them are stay-at-home moms like us, yet a few of us have small home-based businesses on the side for a little autonomy and some financial freedom. Libby dabbles in interior designer and photography and I own an art gallery. I started it in my basement a few years back. Now, that it's grown up, the art gallery has its own retail location to call home.

Among our friends, we are the ringleaders. We plan the parties and the playgroups. We set up the court times for tennis league. I think the other girls come because we have a lot of fun together. Joy is magnetic.

Libby and I love to joke about life, especially about all of the embarrassing things that happen to us throughout the day. Like the time when she broke out in a full body rash from an antibiotic and our OB gynecologist, whose kids attend the same school as ours, insisted on giving her an anal exam. We agreed that from that point forward he was off the dinner party invitation list. Or the time I was doing a cleansing diet. The combination of herbs and roughage cause me to "toot" during a charity interview for a board position. The problem was that the "toot" had more than air in it, and I had to get out of there fast!

We have hundreds of these kinds of stories between us. A ridiculous assortment of wardrobe malfunctions, bad hair, weird body incidents and unexpected circumstances. You can call it the "history of humor." She is the first person I call if I hear, see, or experience anything of comedic potential. Laughing is good for the soul.

However, I sometimes wonder if I moved away from here, like my friend Danielle, if we would remain as close. So much of our friendship is centered on proximity and the daily diary of our circle of friends. *It's a diary of nonsense, but I love it.*

"Excuse me. Are you ready to hear today's specials?" The waiter was clearly trying to get our group moving. Twenty minutes at the table without ordering didn't look promising for a chance at a second seating and another round of gratuities on his table tonight.

"Don't worry about it, I've been here before. I'll have the grilled Chilean sea bass and orzo, with the sauce on the side," I offer with an apologetic smile. Libby and Blake miss his not-so-subtle cue, or overlook it completely.

"I'll have another glass of Pinot Grigio, and could you give us a few more minutes? I haven't had a chance to look at the menu?" Libby says dismissively. Blake did not even look up from his conversation with Steve. They were planning a guy's golf weekend in Augusta, Georgia to see the Masters'.

I felt a small growl deep in my stomach and I hoped no one heard. Last time I ate something was around lunchtime, and I was ready for some sustenance. Libby continued on about her idea to start an event planning company.

"What do you think I should call it?"

"Maybe the Art of Entertaining or Society Inc.?" I offer.

While she pauses to consider the ideas, I add, "By the way, I have decided to move the art gallery to a new storefront location."

"Really, what prompted the switch? You've only been in the current space one year."

"Parking is tough, and I think right now it's too far of a drive for some of my core customers."

"That's too bad. Your location was so convenient for me to come by for lunch and a chat."

"Well, the new gallery will be in a plaza with several popular furniture stores. They do a lot of advertising. Hopefully, I will get the benefit of their marketing dollars. Business has been a little slow."

I didn't say much more. I never like to tell anyone things are anything but fabulous. Libby misses that cue as well.

"Keep me posted." She shrugs.

"Hey, maybe I can plan your gallery grand opening!" I can see the light bulb go off as her eyes brighten up. "Let me know your budget."

I choose to let the conversation drop. *My budget is zero.* The move requires a loan from my home equity line. I privately hope and pray the new location is a fast and furious success. I need a white knight experience in my finances right now.

We pay the check and hand the valet our ticket. *I'm suddenly so tired.*

"Thanks for dinner, sweetheart." I give Steve a quick hug and a kiss as we walk to the car.

"Happy anniversary, babe." He touches my face and our eyes lock for a moment. I remember why I married him. At times like this, I see our whole beautiful life together in his gaze.

It's almost midnight and I feel my body aching all over. Visions of my comfortable bed, stacked high with pillows of all shapes and sizes, flood my mind. I think I was asleep before I hit the pillow. Later that night I awoke to more consistent aches.

It's not a simply a long day. It's labor and I'm right in the heat of it.

"Steve."

I hear him snoring next to me.

"Steve! Steve, get up!" I punch him hard in his side as another contraction ripples through my body.

"It's time!"

Too bad for my mom, Jackie. I think, secretly relieved. She desperately wanted to be at the actual birth. Both my brother and I arrived via Caesarean section in an era when that meant complete anesthesia. Mother went into the hospital to deliver a baby, fell asleep with the help of narcotics and gas, and woke up a day later to find out what happened and who arrived. Weird.

I could sympathize, so I said OK. But, I could not shake the feeling of being a spectacle for her morbid curiosity, coupled with the fact that critiques were certain to ensue.

"Honey, your vagina isn't working right. The baby seems to be stuck."

"Oh, my God, is that a hemorrhoid? It looks angry, dear."

Or maybe something like, "You're going to have a lot of work ahead of you to shed those pregnancy pounds," as she analyzes my ass and dimpled thighs hoisted in the air from the feet-forward gynecological stirrup perspective.

Whatever the dialogue, I'm not up for it. The Universe must know, because by the Grace of God, this baby is coming three weeks early, and Mother is not arriving until next week.

After three pregnancies, Steve and I know the routine. For the last week, I have had my nanny, Lolly, sleeping over at our house just in case. *Why is it that babies always want to come in the middle of the night?*

We grab our pre-packed overnight bags and head out the door. Two hours later Mia Elizabeth Sinclair is born. I barely had time to get into the hospital gown and into the labor and delivery room. After the first baby, they seem to come faster and easier each time. If I ever do it again, I know I will have to plan on a home birth or run the risk of a roadside arrival. This little rosebud is our third. I can already see the love affair blooming between her and my husband. He can't seem to put her down.

"How are you feeling?" My OB, Dr. Brad Williams asks while giving me a post birth exam.

"Fine, can I go home now?"

"You're allowed to stay up to two days. Why the rush?'

"I'm not really into hospitals and I feel fine."

"Please, just stay overnight so they can observe the baby in the nursery" the doctor gently urges me.

I agree, knowing it will be impossible to get any rest in the hospital. Plus, I already miss my other children, Cole and Lucy. The nurses are always coming in and poking, pricking or otherwise pestering the patients. It's no wonder to me that people rarely recover at the hospital; at least that's my opinion.

The next morning my cell phone rings. It's Melissa, the leasing agent from the new space I am considering for the art gallery.

"Someone else has expressed an interest in the available location for their business. They want to move forward", she informs me. "Do you still want it?"

"Yes, yes! Absolutely!" I don't even pause to think.

"Can you come down today and sign the papers?"

"I can try, but, I just had a baby last night."

"Congratulations!"

"Let me see if they have a fax machine here at the hospital so we can take care of it" I offer. "I want the space."

I'm reminded of the phrase "Time and tide wait for no man"...*or woman, or baby.* There's no way I can pass on this opportunity. Another six slow months like the last and I'll have some pretty serious business problems. *This hobby of mine is becoming a real pain in the ass.*

The baby starts to whimper and nuzzle into my chest. I offer Mia an engorged breast almost the size of her small head. She locks on and suckles contentedly. At least I have one satisfied customer.

Chapter 6

I forget how hard the first two weeks with a newborn can be. *What day is it?* I seem to have lost track. An endless blur of feedings, diaper changes and catnaps have left me totally upside down. My other children, Cole and Lucy, are somewhat curious about their new sibling, but they also want me to take them to the park and make lunch and complete another ten tasks in the next thirty minutes.

Where is Lolly?

Is clockwatching a sign of substandard mothering?

Has it only been five minutes since I last checked?

Nine-thirty will never get here.

I wish I had asked her to come at eight-thirty.

How do people do it without hired help?

This line of thinking makes time slow to a halt. *My mothering skills need an upgrade. I'll have to aim for that goal next year*, as I put on another movie to amuse my kids while I close my eyes for a minute. It's the third one today, and it's not even nine. Summer break seems to last an eternity.

The doorbell rings.

"Lolly, is that you?" I shout downstairs, too tired to get up from my glider.

The doorbell rings again twice, three times.

"Jenna, it's Libby, can I come in?" she shouts from the other side of my front door.

"Libby, what are you doing here so early?" I make my way downstairs to answer the door.

"I'm sorry I didn't call first. I didn't know what to do!" Tears spill from her eyes and start to roll down her peachy sun-kissed cheeks. She walks in the room and collapses on the first available seat.

"I think Blake is having an affair!"

"What!"

This is unbelievable. It's like a bad déjà vu! First, my mother-in-law is caught in the matrimonial Bermuda triangle and now one of my best friends. I have not even had the opportunity to tell Libby about the in-law fiasco because of the new baby. I guess it doesn't matter now.

"How did you find out?" I move over to sit beside her.

"Well, lately Blake has been going for runs late at night?"

"How late?"

"Eleven-thirty?" I raise my eyebrows.

How stupid are we women expected to be? It must be easy to overlook the truth, if you don't want to know.

"He said he was training for a marathon and couldn't sleep", she said defensively.

"Last night, at one o'clock he was still not home. I was so worried I carried the two sleeping boys to the car and drove around the neighborhood looking for him."

"Did you find him?"

At this point, she totally disintegrated. Sob after sob rolled through her body. I collected her in a big hug trying to absorb her anguish. Even without the words, I could guess what had happened.

Later, Libby filled in all of the details. She told me about a single parked car in a deserted playground parking lot a few blocks from her house. Its windows were steamed from the passionate activity of its inhabitants. The boys were asleep, so she quietly waited in her black Mercedes SUV at the edge of the lot in the shadows of the surrounding trees. *Who was inside?* Her intuition already told her what she refused to accept.

Twenty minutes passed before Blake stepped from the back seat of the red Pontiac Grand Am. He kissed the unknown blonde woman goodbye and jogged back in the direction of the house.

A thousand questions raced through her mind in a split second.

"Should I confront them?"

"What will I say?"

"Oh my God, the kids are in the car."

Libby kept her lights off and pulled out of the parking lot. She headed straight home and quickly carried the boys up to bed. Then she climbed in to bed herself.

A girl needs time to think. Right now, I'm too numb to cry; too frightened to speak.

Fortunately, she beat Blake home. He must be trying to run off the trailing end of his spent passion, she thought. Or, maybe he did not want to risk coming home and finding her awake. I waited for her to finish all of the details of her story.

"Did you see him this morning?" I asked.

"He left early for a complicated surgery. I pretended to be asleep", Libby's eyes were puffy and red from crying.

"I still have not confronted him. What should I do?"

"I have no idea?"

I could hear the baby stirring upstairs, and the movie was over. *Why can't someone invent a movie that will hold a child's interest for two or three hours?* Twenty minutes is simply not enough time to do anything.

"Oh, there you are, Lolly." A rush of relief floods over me as she walks in the door and straight upstairs to tend the baby.

"Libby, can we pick this up in a little while?" Suddenly, I can barely keep my eyes open. She's still crying softly.

"You're welcome to lie down in my guest room." I suppress a yawn.

"No, that's OK. My mom is expecting my call, and I have a few other people to call as well," she says, walking toward the door.

"Bye, sweetie. I am so sorry. Call me later." I hug Libby again, feeling tears in my own eyes as I close the door behind her.

What does this mean for our couples' friendship? I think to myself, heading upstairs to lie down. On some days, ascending these stairs feels like I am climbing out of the Grand Canyon. It's not even ten a.m. yet.

Blake you stupid bastard! You must be temporarily insane to jeopardize your entire family over some tart. She's probably a nurse. It's the last thought that crosses my mind as I drift off for a quick catnap. There's not much I can do right now.

Chapter 7

"Have you confronted him yet?" I'd called Libby on the phone for our daily check-in. The majority of our community updates occur over the telephone. "The community" being anyone we have heard of or met. The "update" portion is all of the gossip about flirtations, affairs and general social faux pas. Lately we'd been talking about her dirty laundry more than anything else.

"No, maybe it's just a one time thing."

"Honey, it's been three weeks!" I'm amazed.

"How can you act normal around a traitor like that? Are you scouring the house for more evidence? Did you find any more proof? Why the delay?" I fired off questions like lawn darts.

"Please swear you won't tell anybody. School starts next week and I don't want to be the latest hot item on everyone's chat line. You're new this year; you don't know what it is like. Besides, maybe it's just a one time thing?" Libby speculates out loud again, as if affirming it makes it the truth. I didn't tell her it doesn't work that way.

"Keep telling yourself that, but I don't believe it," I continue. "Has his behavior changed?"

"Well, he seems to be on call a lot lately."

"Have you checked his cell phone?"

"No, I don't know how." She can't see me roll my eyes over the phone. *Libby's low-tech, "I-can't-even-turn-on-the-computer" routine is annoying. Even a child knows how to send a text message these days.*

By now I have told Libby all about the affair between Steve's dad Donald Sinclair and his secretary, Amber Atkins.

It's funny, similar scenarios, but totally different reactions from the wronged wives. Ronnie is armored and out for blood. Libby is a boneless mop.

Chapter 8

"Lucy, are you excited about your first day at junior kindergarten?" I trilled, barely able to contain my own enthusiasm. Her blonde ringlets come unsprung for a moment as she vigorously nods her head.

Lucy is a beautiful child with horrible eyesight. She's had to contend with thick-coke bottle glasses since toddlerhood. I always worry about the first day at any new place for her. I don't want Lucy to feel the same painful social rejection I always had to combat as a child.

"We'll be there in a few minutes. It's only a half an hour drive from our house." I was chipper, trying to mask the first day anxiety I was feeling inside for her.

I'd already driven past five schools on the way to this one, but I barely gave them any notice. They were not what I was looking for. I had been talking this up to Lucy for months, ever since we were accepted at the prestigious Sycamore Creek Childhood Development Center. When did they stop calling it *school?* This recognition should have set off a symphony of alarm bells, but I couldn't hear a thing over the game show jackpot music that had been pounding my brain for months.

There were only two spaces available in the junior kindergarten at Sycamore Creek, and over fifty applicants. I feel like we won the lottery. Since when did anyone ever have to pay eighteen thousand dollars for a prize? Yes, that is the tuition for a year of preschool education at Sycamore Creek. Another crescendo in the music of warning notes that would have been obvious to the average woman. I am clearly tone deaf.

I'm obsessed with creating a different life for my children. I want them at the best school, booked solid with play dates and running barefoot and carefree through life. Pursuit of this ideal is a full time job, without pay; yet clearly with benefits. My former full-time beloved career-self is collecting dust on a shelf in the storage locker, which holds all of my previous selves. Who knows if I will ever dust her off again? *That's a depressing thought.* All this energy has to go somewhere. So I look at my social activities, *or obsessions*, as an investment in the future status of my family. I'm buying stock, social stock.

"We're here!" I quickly shut off the DVD screen on the ceiling of the van over protests from Lucy. Intuitively, I sense that while everyone here has the latest media technology in their cars, they pretend not to use it. Every time I pull into the driveway to the school I have to pinch myself, to prove it's not a dream.

A gallery forest, a shady stretch of trees so thick it forms a tunnel, flanks the main stone driveway, which crosses over a small bridge covering the rill gurgling through the tangle of tree roots below. This stone passageway meanders for a half a mile then gently curves to the right around a concealed bend, which reveals a quaint and inviting stone structure: The Sycamore Creek Childhood Development Center. The four-acre grounds are completely private and owned by the institution. The main entrance is flanked by a pair of graceful turrets inlaid with colorful stained glass windows depicting sheep in a pasture and a field of wildflowers. This main area, which is fondly called the "Friendship Cottage", dates back to the 1800s. It then expands and continues in both directions with two larger brick wings, which house the interactive classrooms, the experiential science lab, and the indoor/outdoor art studio. A series of natural landscapes conceal most of the modern amenities on the campus. In my opinion, it is a mystical retreat; bar none, for my child to discover the mysteries of childhood. I hope the rest of my children are accepted.

The carpool line creeps along, as we need to take alternate turns crossing the narrow bridge in both directions. I make eye contact with one of the moms across the bridge and offer a tentative smile. Why not, I'm part of the clan now. Apparently not quite yet, her eyes look through me as she drives past in her vanilla cream Lexus SUV, picking up her gold Blackberry to dial a call. *Oh well, at least I can count on a friendly face from Libby Peters.* She started sending her two boys here last year, and that's what gave me the idea to apply to the school. The parties she described sound fabulous. I can't wait to be invited.

I hope we are not going to be late. Mental note, I need to leave earlier in the future. My silver minivan looks a little lackluster once in step with the parade of fancy imported SUVs waiting for their turn to drop off the children. Funny, I've never had a complex over my car before. I'm suddenly right back in nightmare anxiety of middle school over the car: wrong color, wrong model and wrong make. *Get a grip, Jenna!* Several of the moms are hanging out of their car windows; their lacquered fingernails waving furiously, as they enthusiastically greet one another after the summer break.

"Hi, sweetie. How was Aspen this summer?" A raven-haired woman purred.

"Darling, you look so bronzed. The Greek Isles must have been fab! Let's do Starbucks and a tell-all!" Another blonde woman chirped.

"Next summer we must vacay together. It feels far too long." The entire conversation was just loud enough to let everyone know about his or her exciting travels.

I gathered that *vacay* was short for vacation. *They speak a different language here.*

After twenty minutes, we finally park and get out of the car. One woman, in the car next to me, held her hand up to her ear and mouthed an exaggerated "call-me" to her long-lost friend. Her massive diamond caught the sunlight, sending a prism of rainbow flecks across the hood of my car.

Perhaps, I do have the luck of the Irish and this IS the pot of gold at the end of the rainbow, finally a place to call home. After all, I am accepted here. At least, Lucy is. I thought to myself as I practically floated inside on my imaginary red carpet for the "meet the teacher" gathering.

Lucy was annoyed. The monogram sewn into the smocking on her pink and white gingham checked dress was making her chest itch. I kept telling her to stop pulling on her clothing. It didn't look right. I had ordered that dress handmade four months ago in preparation for her first day of school.

"Hello, everyone. Thank you so much for joining us here on this exciting day," the teacher announced.

Ms. Hamilton, Lucy's teacher, could not be a day over twenty-six. She was cheerful and spunky in the way all teachers seem to be. But that's where the similarities ended. Ms Hamilton wore her long blonde hair in a no-nonsense ponytail, but it did little to mask her streamlined attractiveness. I could swear she was wearing a blouse I had seen at Saks Fifth Avenue just last week in the new fall collection. I passed on it because the price tag was too steep.

Sycamore Creek must pay well. Whatever happened to the holy alliance of teacher and theme sweaters? You know, theme sweaters with crocheted apples and rulers stitched on the front. When I was a child, my beloved kindergarten teacher, Mrs. Walker, had a different theme sweater for every holiday, including the first day of school and the last day of school, and a few extra sweaters for the unexpected special occasions in between.

We started the meeting by introducing ourselves and saying a few words to describe our child. I wish Steve did not have to work today, he's better at these things. I could feel my palms moisten as the introductions wove their way towards me. A few parents down, I noticed a little girl dressed in what could only be a costume. A sparkly rhinestone tiara sat jauntily atop her electrified, pin-straight, dishwater brown hair. She wore a vintage women's rose color chiffon dress from the 1950's that was haphazardly pinned to stay on, and a shock of smeared red lipstick to match her glitter-encrusted Mary Jane's. I'd never seen a five-year-old dressed like that. I force myself not to stare. *No one else seems to notice. Or, they are sharing my same struggle. I don't want to be rude on the first day.*

Her mother snorts out a laugh as the turn to speak settles on her. Bootsy Simon is the name of the tattered princess and her mother is called Ruth.

"Hey, everyone. I'm Ruth, as you all probably know. Bootsy, or Boo-Boo, is my fourth child here at Sycamore Creek."

I take her in, as she is speaking, finally able to stare in that direction without being offensive. Cropped naturally curly black hair springs from her head in all directions. Ruth holds her hair back with a large white terry cloth headband that sits at the top of her forehead and the base of her hairline, forcing the hair in front to stand up straight like a solider. *I thought sweatbands were for strenuous exercise.* Yet, I don't get the impression that she is on her way to work out, unless she is auditioning for a rodeo at the insane asylum.

Ruth is wearing a brightly patterned red and orange skirt that I recognize from an exclusive boutique. A minimum investment to own one of these skirts is three hundred dollars. I've looked at them, but never pulled the trigger. The patterns are so distinctive there is no question where you bought it or how much it cost. Ruth has the riotous signature fabric combined with a pair of light blue cowboy boots and a tight yellow transparent baby tee shirt over a purple bra. Like mother like daughter, I guess.

"Hello, everyone, this is my oldest daughter Lucy Sinclair and I am Jenna. We are excited to be attending Sycamore Creek. Lucy is a creative and fun-loving child. I know she will love it here."

There, I think that introduction was inane enough to be politically correct. I still haven't gotten a read of this place yet; it's better to keep things low key at first.

"Oh by the way, Lucy's birthday is this weekend and I wanted to invite everyone from her new class. We can use it as a way to get to know one another," I cut in before the next parent starts her turn. *I never miss an opportunity to network.*

"My daughter's birthday is this week too. What day?"

"It's actually on Saturday, September 7th." I offer, turning to see who might share my precious girl's special day. To my horror, it's Ruth asking the question.

"So is mine!" Bootsy chimes in. "We were born on the same day! Wow, way cool."

Bootsy cuts across the room and plants herself next to Lucy, who politely smiles in return.

"I like your crown," Lucy's gaze was captivated by the sparkling tiara on her new friend's head.

"It's real diamonds!" Boo-boo smugly replied.

I'm tempted to believe her.

Chapter 9

"Libby, what's the deal with Ruth Simon?"

We connected later that morning to have coffee and dish about my first impression of Sycamore Creek.

"Oh yeah, her? Pretty shocking combination, the hair and the clothes," Libby said.

"Her daughter, Boop or something, is in Lucy's class," I respond.

"I don't know her very well. Our kids are not in the same class. But, what I do know is that there is tons of money there. Family money. Her husband came into it about five years ago. It's in the millions," Libby practically choked on the sum.

"Wow, I'd like to have millions just sitting around collecting dust," I lose myself in the thought.

"Now everybody wants them to sit on their charity committees, in hope of a fat donation. She's pretty connected, but I don't think she has a lot of friends. She's kind of a lone wolf type. Did you see her husband at the meet the teacher?" She looks at me with her nose scrunched up and the corner of her mouth distorted. Not a pretty expression, from a pretty girl.

"No, I can't believe she's even married."

Libby offers more dish. "Just wait till you get a load of him. It becomes even more of a mystery", she looks at me with a knowing gaze. This form of social analysis is Libby's specialty.

We laugh and talk about the teacher, the carpool line and the other moms. Now, we share the same base camp from which to pull our amusing war stories. This will be the BEST!

It didn't take long to bump into Ruth's husband, Ira Simon. He was the antithesis of his significant other, meticulously groomed from head to toe. His dark blond hair was tightly brushed back, coated with gel and then sprayed with untold gallons of hairspray for complete smoothness, not allowing even a hair to wave, much less travel astray. Peppercorn pupils were concealed behind thin frameless spectacles, the crystal clear lenses magnifying their smallness. His posture reminded me of a croissant, shoulders and hips forward making his thin belly concave. A strong angular jaw line led to a triangular chin. He didn't smile as I introduced myself during the required after school pickup in the classroom. He simply nodded in acknowledgement and looked down as he escorted Bootsy from the classroom. I felt a tingle of apprehension; this may be someone to avoid. His no-nonsense demeanor was a stark contrast to his daughter's whimsical polka dot crinoline skirt and orange rubber boots.

His wife must do all of the talking, I thought to myself as I carried Lucy's purple floral backpack to the car. It was packed full of necessary info for parents: the school directory, the semester outline, an order form for a school fundraising gift wrap sales campaign, and applications for a wide variety of parent-run committees. Time to get busy deciding where is the best place to plug in and maximize our time at Sycamore Creek.

Chapter 10

"**L**ibby, I'm on my way to Saks to pick up a few school clothes for the kids, and an outfit for the holiday party. Would you like to hook up for lunch?" *I know my budget is more along the lines of Target, but my issues about the right clothes run deep. Thank God for credit cards.*

"Sure, I don't have anything after my morning committee meeting. I can be up there in an hour, maybe ninety minutes or so."

"See you then. Let's meet at Café Tuscany. One of their harvest salads, you know, the one with the goat cheese, sounds good to me." My mouth was already watering. Nursing a baby always makes me famished.

"Yummy, me too. See you there."

I pulled into a parking place in the front slot. Lately, my parking angels had been working overtime. I always seemed to get the best spots, only steps from the door. People laugh at my tales of the parking angels; but yet they are also amazed. It works like a charm every time. I always send them ahead with a silent request. *Parking angels find me the best spot available.* Of course, I always say thank you.

The Plaza was almost empty, which was a good thing, because I had several stores on my list to visit. A new battery for my watch, a pair of running shoes, some new underwear, and possibly a dress for the Civil Arts gala next month.

Victoria's Secret was advertising a big sale, so I headed in there

45

first to check out the bras and panties. Table after table of underwear in different shapes, colors and styles were stacked high, spilling over into the drawers. Sheer sexy thongs with ruffles, cotton pink and green plaid boy shorts, nautical striped hipsters and lacy black bikinis. *When did underwear get so adventurous?* I personally like a thong style, but not a lot of patterns or bright colors. It shows through white and light colored pants and really looks tacky. Underwear should be worn and not seen, this includes panty lines and panty colors.

Steve's always saying, "What is the point of a nude colored thong? It looks like high function butt floss."

Moreover, my recently baby-filled body is hardly in shape for a thong seduction photo shoot. Perhaps something more along the lines of a photo documentary entitled "Nightmare of a Thong Wearing Amazon."

I pick up pair after pair of underwear, analyzing each one in the light to see it's truly transparent. A shiny red fabric catches my eye*; maybe I'll get this one for Steve?* I reach for the pair and hold it up to check for sheerness (too sheer makes me feel like a tart). Through the transparent veil, I see a familiar face.

Oh God! It's Don! Steve's dad! He's less than ten feet away, digging through all of the panties on the next table. I'd already passed on them. They were too naughty for my comfort. *What in the world is he doing here?*

I duck around the corner and hide behind a tall rack of fleece bathrobes, and think about what to do next. *Maybe he's buying something for Ronnie, and I should just say hello?* No, she demanded he move out of the house last week. *Oh God, this is so embarrassing!* I realize I am still clutching the glistening red panties, only now they are damp with the perspiration from my palms. Don doesn't notice me. He's obviously absorbed in some sexual reverie. A slight smile dances across his Italian skinned face, not too tan, not too white. His thick, chocolate hair is brushed back from his aquiline face. He looks younger than I remember, his expression softening his otherwise harsh features. I always think of Don as intense, demanding, but here at the panty table in Vicky Secrets he appears relaxed and aroused. *God, did I just think that?* I could see it in his eyes. They were liquid green fire, observing the wisp of white lace dangling delicately from his fingertips. *Okay, I'm definitely not saying hello. I feel like a voyeur.*

I edge toward the front of the store with my head down carrying an armload of fluffy robes like a clerk. Once I get to the front unnoticed, I drop the fuzzy wad and dash for the exit. My heart is pounding fast. It's so full of blood. I could choke on it.

Gee, Jenna, you really handled that well. Why didn't you march up to him and ask what in the hell are you doing here? My inner voice was berating me mercilessly for my cowardice. But instead of going back inside for a showdown, I slink behind a large palm in the courtyard and wait to see if he comes out with a package. Ten minutes later he is sporting not one, but two large pink paper totes. My jaw drops. *How many panties does a girl need? She must have an outfit for everyday of the week, including Sundays.* He's swinging the bags back and forth in a mindless stroll and saunters across the hall directly into the Tiffany Jewelry store. *This is a hell of a shopping spree*! I'm rooted behind the palm fronds; my other errands will have to wait. I can see from my mall jungle vantage point that he's at one of the counters in the front of the store where they display the diamonds and other precious gems. I'm less afraid now, the fear adrenaline being replaced by nauseating disgust. After about fifteen minutes, Don leaves the store carrying a small signature blue and silver bag with a white ribbon handle, in addition to his two large pink paper totes from Vicky's Secrets. I decide to abandon the tail. I've seen enough.

"Ronnie! Hi, how are you?" I dialed her number before I realized it, guilt urging action into my fingers.

"Oh, hi Jenna. I was just going to call you. It's so much worse that I thought at first," Ronnie sounded indignant and agitated.

"What do you mean?" I still hadn't decided if I was going to mention the encounter in the mall. I just wanted to check in with her out of a sense of loyalty.

"I've been gong through our financial files. Are you sitting down?"

"No."

"He bought her a car and he bought her a house. HE BOUGHT AMBER A FUCKING HOUSE!" She roared at me over the telephone.

I was numb with shock. I knew it was true. Sure, panties and diamonds, that's expected, but real estate and a BMW convertible? Hell, he could not even manage to give Steve a company credit card. *Where did the money come from?* I was under the impression that Burrito Bandit was having some financial problems. Maybe the problem comes from the ruling shareholder, the member who resides in Don's trousers.

"Ronnie, I'm so sorry," I listened to all of the gory details for a while seated silently on a mall bench. There was no need for comment. Ronnie did not come up for air, which was good because I was speechless. Then I simply had to get off the phone. My head was pounding. I forgot to mention the incident in the lingerie store. Now, it seemed like a petty crime compared to the first-degree marital felony I'd just been alerted to.

Right after I hung up the phone it rang again. "Jenna, I'm at Café Tuscany, where are you?"

"Libby, I'm so sorry. I've just had the most amazing morning since we last spoke. I'm on my way."

"See you in a minute. I'm already at a table. Oh, and guess who's here, the St. Germaine's. You know Tinsley is president of the PTO at Sycamore Creek. I'll have to introduce you to her and her sister-in-law, Frieda. Everyone calls her Freddie. It's so cute."

"Oh. Okay. See you soon.'

I took several deep breaths to compose myself as I walked down the Plaza corridor past the brightly colored shops, which usually lifts my mood considerably. Most of the time all a girl needs when she's in a funk is a little retail therapy. But, not today, no, I need a psychic tow-truck to pull me out of the emotional quick sand that has just sucked me into a suffocating hole. *Perhaps a little gloss and a squirt of fragrance will help me,* I thought as I ducked into the powder room outside of the entrance to the café.

"Hi, Libby."

"Hey, Jenna," Libby stood up to offer her signature air kisses. *I wish she would stop, we're not in France.*

"You seem a little off," Libby commented. For once she notices my strained expression.

"I am. I just witnessed Don's father buying gifts for his mistress. You know, trinkets for the tart, like see-through panties and precious gems."

48

"I know Jenna, I saw a purchase from Tiffany's on Blake's charge statement last month. I'm hoping there's a little light blue box with a white satin ribbon in my future, but if not, I know it's for her." Libby looked disappointed, but hopeful. Six months have passed and she's not mentioned a word about the affair to Blake. I've decided to stop asking.

"At this point I have little faith in cheaters. Wait until you hear what Ronnie told me." I proceeded to fill her in on all of the details of the affair between Don and his assistant Amber: the house, the car, and the naughty text messages about numerous clandestine mid-day hotel rendezvous.

"Well, I wasn't sure I was prepared to show you this, but now I feel strong enough." Libby reached into her Prada bag, pulled out a photograph, and placed it face down on the table. "I've haven't shown this to anyone yet."

"What is it?" I picked up the photo and turned it over. Settled invitingly into a grouping of fluffy pillows was a slightly chubby girl in a periwinkle blue polyester lace bra and matching panties. Behind her head was a cluster of tall white feathers that appeared to be angel wings. Her hair was frosted blonde on the ends, giving way to darker roots near her scalp. Her chin was lowered seductively with a pink tongue extended onto her glossy, pouting lips. A swath of shimmering blue eye shadow radiated from her hooded brows. Upon closer inspection, I could see a layer of cellulite on her open thighs. She looked like a corn-fed hussy on a J.C. Penney photo shoot.

"Who, or should I say what, is this?" This day was turning out to be a series of revelations, none of them pleasant. Libby, in contrast to the piglet in the photo, is a cool, elegant Pilates goddess with the style of Jackie O. *Why do men's tastes seem to swing to such extremes?*

"I've been in such denial about this whole affair business. I just wish it would end so we can go on with our lives." I could see she was upset.

"I'm sorry, Sweetie". I reached my hand across the table to comfort her. "If it's any consolation, she doesn't hold a candle to you. This chick, whoever she is, looks tacky and cheap."

"She not that cheap, Jenna, I'm beginning to think she might cost me my marriage." We silently speared our salads with new vigor, individually contemplating the new threat of sleazy, single, home-wrecking women.

Chapter 11

I decide to check in with Faith. I just love her dark little room. Every time I enter her sacred space, I see it with fresh eyes. It's smaller than my walk-in closet, yet cozy as a womb. A sea grass fan chair sits in the corner; its circular, high-back style was popular at Pier One Imports a decade ago. The card table, flanked by two chairs, is covered with an Indian-inspired purple tapestry, its intricate silver threadwork intersecting and connecting the vivid multi-patterned fabrics. A small assortment of crystals sits off to the side of the table, joined by a long bird's feather.

Two of the crystals are gifts from me. We have relatives in Hot Springs, Arkansas, and twenty-five miles outside of town is a small hamlet called Mt. Ida. It's the quartz crystal capital of the world. Little roadside shops line the state road, with plywood tables supported by cinder blocks in front, stacked full of glittering treasures from the earth. For Faith, I had picked a deep violet amethyst stone with a hole chiseled out of its center to hold a tea light candle. Amethyst represents wisdom and clear thinking. The other crystal gift was a selenite; its milky, wispy, transparency makes it look ethereal. It's supposed to support angelic connections and inspiration. It looks like something from the heavens. Both seemed like perfect choices.

Next to the crystals on the table is a lamp with a cream shade covered with a rose-colored chiffon scarf. The lamp cast a pleasant, diffused, intimate glow across the otherwise dark room. In the center of the table are her cards, the same deck she always uses.

First, I place my hands on top of hers, lying palms up on top of the table. Her skin is smooth and dry. There is an almost imperceptible current of energy crackling in the tight space between our palms. We don't grip one another. My hands rest gently on hers, a light, comfortable connection. I close my eyes and exhale slowly, deeply. After a few breaths she begins her traditional invocation.

"Take a deep breath in and get centered and balanced. Let's invite the energy from the core of the earth into our hearts and release it. Then invite the energy down from the heavens and into our hearts and release it. We ask that all of the information that we are about to receive be for the higher good of all concerned." I can feel a slight buzz throughout my body as she recites the familiar words.

"Good," She opens her eyes and exhales a deep breath. "Now, dear, what's on your mind?"

"The world has gone totally crazy, Faith." I tell her about the latest dramas with my friends and my in-laws. It's so nice to have someone to talk to who is not involved in any personal aspect of your life. Perhaps that's why some people like therapy, or even confession. It's free.

"I see you being near the tornado, but not inside it. Be careful, Jenna, or you might get sucked up in the drama yourself. Remember none of this belongs to you. Don't own it." Faith's words always hold so much clarity. I know why I can't let a week go by without seeing her.

Chapter 12

The next year was spent shuffling complaints between Libby and Ronnie. Their dramas now occupy so much real estate in my life, there's not much room for my other friends or "new construction." *An FYI, social construction requires constant new development.* Don's behavior was more outrageous than ever, now that $250 an hour divorce attorney fees were involved. One crazy night, Don ended up in jail after fighting with Ronnie over a laptop with naughty emails and company balance sheets. Domestic violence complaints require a mandatory 24-hour cooling down period.

"Steve, I'm in jail! You need to come and bail me out."

I'll never forget that call to the house. This is a classic example of the many ways Steve is always on stand-by, ready to clean up Don's disasters. Steve and I are frequently in the middle of the crossfire between Don and Ronnie, a potentially fatal position for a marriage.

Meanwhile, Libby was not sure she was ready for Blake to move out, even though it was clear to everyone but her that Blake had no intention of ending the affair. And Blake never missed an opportunity to invite Steve to join him for happy hour at the Hustler Club. Blake said it was his way to relieve the "pressure" from his prying wife. I let Steve go to the clubs, but it upset me that he always turned his cell phone off, as if calls from his wife would be a nuisance, interrupting a grinding lap dance.

Yet, as I watched Mia evolve from infant to toddler, storming around the house with no regard to her safety, I wondered why neither Libby nor Ronnie, both involved in these epic divorce dramas, were able to take even a baby step toward their own healing. It seems they are now addicted to all of the attention they are receiving from the daily play-by-play given to friends.

Chapter 13

"Jenna, it's Ruth."

"Hi, Ruth, what can I do for you?

Ever since the first day of our second year at school, Ruth Simon has had me in her sight hairs. Now that I have a year under my belt as a Sycamore Creek mom, I've gained some clout. Once she found out I owned an art gallery, she called me at least once a month for a donation of an oil painting to be used in a fund-raising auction. Ruth is a busy gal. She is on the local committee for breast cancer awareness, The Heart Association, and the City Council for the Arts, to name a few. The list is seemingly endless. I want to be socially plugged in. So, every time she asks, I say yes. Then, I look through my entire gallery to find something dynamic enough to catch people's attention and to raise at least a thousand dollars for the charity. I justify that it's good marketing, both personal and business. My business has picked up a little bit, but the charity events have not brought many clients yet.

"I was wondering if you would like to be on the committee with me for the Spring Fling Fundraiser for the Children's Hospital?"

"Wow, really?" I could feel the pearly gates opening. The *Access Granted* sign was flashing for me to enter the "inner circle."

"What do you need me to do?' I had to temper my excitement. I've learned to be enthusiastic, but not too eager.

"Just organize all of the food," Ruth clearly had experience as a nonchalant delegator.

"What does that mean?'

"I have a list of restaurants and you need to call them and see if they will donate food for the event."

I felt my heart drop a little. I'm not very good at soliciting donations; it feels like begging. Suddenly, it does not sound so glamorous. More like a tedious assignment and my to-do list is already ten pages too long. But I accept anyway. *My time cost a lot less than raiding my dwindling inventory for the sixth time this year. Maybe this time she won't need a painting.*

"Oh, by the way--do you want to donate a painting? The last one brought in a lot of bids. It made us look really good. Everybody loves your stuff."

"Sure, no problem." I privately hope this time the bids will translate into paying customers. Lord knows I need some.

The charity committees led to dinner parties. Ira is a big shot in the Local Republican fundraising machine. He's always looking for someone with a platinum wallet to invite. I'm not sure where he got that impression about us. Ira never says much during most of these social events. He's one of life's observers.

Steve once asked me what the deal was with Ira. Why he is always standing on the sidelines analyzing everyone through his monocle of judgment? I didn't have an answer. Over the past couple of months, I've often forgotten that he was in the room. But every once in a while, I would catch him looking at me and I'd smile in a friendly way. He just looked away.

Before long Ruth Simon and I were friends, not in the same way as my gossiping gal pal Libby, or my confidant Danielle. This year Danielle and I have seen less of each other, between her move, the new school and the double divorce dramas. Yet, even if a month goes by between phone calls or lunch, she is steadfast in her loyalty to our friendship. If my mother became ill, she's the first person I would call. Danny is not as tuned it to the intricacies of the local social chatter, but she's content to lend a sympathetic ear. Ruth is not someone I would hand-pick from the garden of friendship, but her presence in my life is blooming into being. *Is she a weed or a flower?*

Once during one of my weekly readings with Faith, I asked about

Ruth. Faith simply said that some people use their wardrobe to make themselves stand out. I thought about it later. Maybe the crazy clothes are a way for Ruth to get attention in the anonymous world of motherhood. Until children, I never really knew what it meant to be alone in a crowd.

Ruth was definitely wacky, but her wackiness held a strange allure for me. She didn't really seem to have many other friends, so I unofficially volunteered. The wardrobe must be frightening people away I rationalized. I did not pay attention to any other signs of social blackballing. Ruth is surrounded by acquaintances, but vacant in deep connections. I feel sympathy for her. Now that I knew the source of her motivation, it was easy to look beyond appearances. However, sometimes the outfits were still an embarrassing challenge. On particularly outrageous wardrobe days, I let Ruth walk a few steps ahead of me so that a clear connection between us was not apparent.

Ruth's favorite accessory is not from Neiman Marcus, but instead from Tennis Master. She has an extensive collection of terry cloth headbands. I have witnessed her model them all over the past year. The majority of headbands are thick white looped cotton terry cloth, but there are a few colored and striped ones in the mix. She pushes them up high on her brow, forcing her thick nest of dark curly hair to stand straight up.

One day I am going to suggest that she consider a makeover. There has to be a more successful way to differentiate yourself, without ranking a "10+" on the "weirdo-meter". Perhaps I'll invite her to join Libby and me at the pre-sale for Neiman Marcus's Last Call on Tuesday.

Chapter 14

"Jenna, Dad wants to come over and see us for dinner this weekend."

I have not seen Don since the panty raid incident at the Victoria Secret. But, out of site is not out of mind, not a day has gone by over the last few months that I have not received a slew of updates on his bad boy behavior. Ronnie is constantly calling my cell phone with 411's on Don. A year later, it's getting old.

"I found Amber's clothes in his new condo when I went to pick up the kids."

"My neighbor saw them at the airport boarding a plane for Mexico. Don said he was going to Phoenix for business."

"The credit card statements accidentally came to my house for his business charge card. Do you know how much he is spending on that slut?" *I had an idea, but I didn't want to add kindling to the inferno of vengeance.*

I now realize, Rhonda is clenching tightly to the drama of her failing marriage and refuses to release her grip. With each daily entry in her phone call blog titled <u>Sins of Don</u>, she's attempting to recruit members for her cause. I fear it will cost her sanity.

I am sympathetic and annoyed.

"Steve, I'm not sure if I can be civil to your dad. He's launched a nuclear bomb right into the heart of our family. I'm also worried about the impact on your joint business endeavors. All this money has to be coming from somewhere."

"Jenna, please, when you're nice to my dad, it make life so much easier for me."

"Why is that, Steve? I'm lucky if I speak to him a few times a year. He's never cared about my opinion before."

"Well, he's decided he wants to get back with Ronnie and he wants you to mediate."

"You have got to be kidding. I don't want to go anywhere near that one."

"Just hear what he has to say. He'll be here after six."

Don never rings the doorbell. He always bursts into our house as if it were his own.

"Jenna! Hello, gorgeous!" Don greets me with arms wide open, ready for an enthusiastic hug.

"Hello, Don." I pat him on the back perfunctorily, inside his suffocating embrace.

"How have you been?

"You look radiant. You've done a great job losing weight after the baby, what's your secret?

"Where is my gorgeous new granddaughter?"

He hit me with a rapid series of questions. He hadn't seen the baby since she was two weeks old, now she's over a year old. His sex life was dominating ninety-nine percent of his time. Yet, this sexual affair is clearly a fountain of youth for him. Don looks amazing. His dark chestnut hair was wind-brushed back from his face and his green eyes looked fresh as new grass against his arctic white pupils. *I don't think I've ever seen him look so good. Faith says people who feed on others' energy always look radiant. Like the blush a mythical vampire gets after draining its victim's blood. I believe Don is an energy vampire. I could already feel him draining me, just by his presence.*

When I'm around Don, my tendency to talk to myself is always on overdrive. Because of Steve, and their relationship tightrope, I always feel the need to operate a strong censor. So I try to keep the conversation light and simple, reserve all errant thoughts for myself, where they shout and carry on like lunatics trying to burst out of their iron-tight asylum in my mind.

"You look nice, Don. Tan and serious." A little ribbing always creeps out, no matter how hard I try to suppress it.

Don's smile rarely reaches his eyes. His eyes are too busy assessing the battleground, plotting the next strategy. Like the saying by Sun Tzu in the classic book, <u>The Art of War</u>, "Keep your friends close, and your enemies closer." *Does Don think I am a friend or a foe?*

"How old is the baby, 6 months?"

"Actually, Mia is over a year old now."

"Oh, has it been that long? Time really flies by with a newborn." Don stammered out an excuse. "Work has kept me really busy. Did Steve tell you, we're going to make a lot of money this year, tons and tons! You'll be able to own your house for cash by this time next year." His false bravado no longer holds the same seduction for me.

I call this *lottery talk*. Every time I speak to this man, he announces big money is right around the corner, but somehow it never materializes, at least it never trickles down to us.

"I'm sorry to hear you and Ronnie are facing some challenges." It was the most inane thing I could think of saying.

"What do you mean?" Don looked at me, feigning total surprise.

I froze for a minute, *what part of this is a mystery?*

"Well, Steve said you were living in a condo," I offered an explanation.

"Oh, that, it's only temporary. I'm planning to move back into my house next week. We're just having a small disagreement."

"Ok, that's good." I mumble, with no eye contact. His comments are counter-intelligence to everything I've heard over the last few months.

The denial act was more than I could bear. I knew from an earlier conversation with Ronnie that he'd been kicked out of the house, the locks were changed and lawyers were moving forward.

"I'm going to check on dinner." I walk out of the room.

While adjusting the roast, I could hear Don wrestling with Lucy and Cole in the other room. They think everything about Grandpa Don is cool: His big yellow Hummer, (one of his four cars), his loud voice, his hyperactive personality, and his constant promises to take everyone on fabulous vacations, although we have yet to go on one.

"Jenna, I've made some plans I'd like to tell you about." Don joined me in the kitchen. He was on a mission tonight.

59

"Sure, Don, what do you have in mind?

"Gabrielle and Jack are supposed to spend the holidays with me, but they don't want to go anywhere with me alone and without Ronnie. I don't think she's up for a vacation right now. She has some health concerns. But if you and Steve and the kids would go, I think it'd be a lot of fun. You know, a big giant family outing. Like we have always planned."

"Let's play it by ear, Don. If it comes together, sure, we'll probably go. Talk to Steve about it."

"Also, I was hoping you'd put in a good word with Ronnie for me. I really want to go back to my home," I thought I saw the shell crack just a little.

"Don, I don't think there is room for two hens in the coop, if you know what I mean." I looked him straight in the eyes with a meaningful stare.

"Jenna, you're such a pistol, I love that about you. There has never been anyone else. It's all in Ronnie's imagination." Don laughed and pounded me on the back like a team member, although I really wasn't referring to the same playbook. I knew he was lying, but it wasn't my place to call him out.

I wish our lives were not so intricately intertwined.

Chapter 15

"Danielle, sorry it's been awhile. This affair business is wearing me out. Both Libby and Ronnie are burning my ear off with tales from the intersection of hell and hysteria. It's been more than a year of daily entries on my "Complaint Hotline". Now Don is calling me to play mediator. It's weird and very draining. I'm dreading the holidays, again and we're planning a family trip." I finally stop ranting to take a breath.

"Jenna, you need to turn off your phone." Danielle scolded me as she surged ahead a few steps.

"I don't have it on right now," I gasp for air. Talking is ill advised during workouts. Our new boot camp instructor was kicking my double-wide booty. I'm glad Danielle encouraged me to join this exercise program, yet at this moment, I was having some doubts. The threat of vomit is an exercise deterrent.

"Danny, how did I ever let you talk me into this class?" I had my hands on my knees, bent over gulping oxygen. We both decided we needed to schedule time to be together each week to reconnect. This short course was my show of loyalty, despite the drive. The drama in my life was keeping us apart, and I hated the distance.

"You said you wanted your body back after the baby. Trust me, Landa Murphy is the best and her Creative Kick-Butt Boot Camp class is my all-time favorite." Danielle is so damn perky. Her hair even looks great during strenuous activity.

"You just can't take her too seriously. She makes up crazy shit to do, so we will have fun getting in shape."

"There is nothing fun about getting in shape!" I fought back the sudden urge to puke.

"Listen up, you pussies, I have plans for you," Landa was shouting at us like a drill sergeant, her size two body deceptively hiding the forceful voice which was now pelting us with impossible instructions. At some point, Landa had wheeled up an unnoticed wagon full of bags of unopened cat litter.

"Kitty cats let's kick butt!" she screeched. "Grab a bag and get movin'."

I picked up a ten-pound bag of Tidy Cat and slung it over my shoulder. *Danny, you'll pay for this.* I could hear her snorting laughter behind me.

"Meow, Meow, make haste ladies, not waste." Landa was possessed. She now had us jogging up and down the hill carrying our gravel-laden burdens.

"Come on Jenna, I know you have the stamina. Hang in there," Danielle was encouraging me to continue. *I've carried other people's shit around for so long, why is this workout any different?*

Chapter 16

"I will never give her a divorce even if I burn through everything I own. Which will never happen." Donald looks smugly defiant at Steve and me. "I don't care about the cost."

"I don't understand, Don, you are the one who had the affair. Why don't you want out? Amber is still part of your life. I mean, she still works for you, right?" Our conversations had taken on a new tone of candor since Don had been calling me to play mediator.

"I don't want a divorce. This is my family, and Rhonda is not going to destroy it."

I look over at Steve. He knows how I feel about this one. His dad had the affair, yet somehow it's everyone else's fault his life is crumbling like a city in the aftermath of an earthquake.

"Jenna, let it go! Please." Steve asks me quietly, in an urgent hushed tone, as his dad walks to the pool bar on the cruise ship and orders us another round of drinks. He returns with a handful of frozen margaritas in honor of our ship's docking in Mexico. We finally ended up on a *family* trip after years of empty invitations.

I ignore Steve. I can't resist. I just don't get this guy.

"Don, how much have your legal bills been so far? They have to be costing you a fortune," Steve is glaring at me now.

"You better believe it. I can outspend anyone. I'm going to win this thing!" Donald laughs out loud. This is an unbalanced game of cat and mouse; he's the lion.

How does anyone win in a divorce? The unspoken question forms in my mind, but I decide to drop it. I've watched several friends travel this path; everyone is a loser.

"Seriously, Don, I've heard you are tracking to be one of the most expensive divorces in the history of our town in the last ten years. The lawyers must love you."

Don laughs again. He's in a great mood now over the acknowledgement of his new and ever-expanding reputation as a high roller in divorce court.

"I love lawyers. That's how I get what I want in life."

Don went crazy after he realized Rhonda was not letting him move back in the house; that's when the gloves came off.

Steve gives me the "I'm warning you" stare. He always says the same thing when we argue about this stuff. "I don't want to go to war against my dad, Jenna. He will stop at nothing to win. Our family does not have the resources to survive that kind of attack." Donald seems harmless to me, more hot air than toxic gas.

"Hi guys. Are you ready to go ashore?"

Donald's two teenage kids, Gabrielle and Jack, show up on deck with Lucy, Cole and the baby in tow.

"Thanks for taking them to the game room, Gabby." I use her nickname a lot; it seems to fit this raven-haired tomboy better than the more formal Gabrielle.

"Are you coming with us?" Gabby looks at me pointedly. The unspoken message is clear, *"If you are not going, I am not going."*

Since the divorce started this summer, the two teenagers have boycotted their dad completely, with the exception of excursions or vacations which include Steve and me and our kids. This is how we ended up on Royal Caribbean Christmas cruise.

It really is the devil's caldron, all eight of us, a big dysfunctional family, floating by demand on the high seas. Without us, Jack and Gabby would not go anywhere with their Dad. Initially, Steve declined, because he does not want to be involved in any of this drama. However, his paycheck from The Burrito Bandit was a week late that month. Don said Steve picked Rhonda's side. He's a punisher, especially for disloyalty. Donald controls every aspect of the family business he operates with Steve. The Burrito Bandit has always been his strongest weapon against us. We've since learned that not being a "team player" in his personal life comes at a price. A price, Steve says, we can't afford to pay right now, with three young children to support and a mortgage to pay.

The tiny Mexican port is teeming with little shops full of jewelry, souvenirs and T-shirts. Steve and I stroll along as a mariachi band plays enthusiastically on the sidewalk, celebrating the tourists coming to pay for their dinner tonight. Tourism is a big industry in many of these poverty-stricken cruise ports. In some places, it's difficult to look beyond the squalor and enjoy a vacation.

As we were walking along, it began to dawn on me that Steve and I have not been on a vacation alone together for more than seven years. We're so preoccupied with work, the kids, and other people's problems. Life is overwhelming and we seem to be hunkered down in different corners, trying the weather the storms in our life. Lately, I've even been sleeping in the kid's rooms. I'm tired; it's easier. *I wonder: Are we having problems of our own?*

"Hey, Jenna, look at these." Steve is pointing to a square-shaped watch with mother-of- pearl face and a pink alligator band. It's lined up with a collection of similar brightly colored watches. I recognized the brand from an ad in Town and Country magazine.

"Oh, that's really pretty, sweetheart." I pick it up and hold it up to my wrist.

"Would you like it?" Steve asked.

I was surprised by the offer. I did not deserve anything.

"Really?"

"Yeah, I'd like to buy you something nice."

"Oh, Steve you're so sweet and thoughtful. Thank you. I love it!" The earlier thoughts had vanished; it must have been my imagination.

Steve carelessly threw down his platinum American Express card.

A half an hour later, our shuttle arrives to take us to the ancient Mayan ruins. The entire week long cruise consists of adventure day trips like this at the different island ports, followed by elaborate dinners at night in the elegant grand dining room. The particular ship we are sailing on has a dining room designed after the Titanic, with its dramatic two-story landing on the top of a large sweeping double staircase.

We've been assigned our own table in what I now call "the

dining room of doom." Dinnertime is a pill. Gabby and Jack give their Dad the silent treatment; while my three musketeers throw food and climb all over us, oblivious to our black-tie evening attire. It's a required five-course meal of frustration with Donald holding court at the head of the table in his white dinner jacket and black pants.

I can't wait to get home.

Chapter 17

"Faith, do you think Steve and I will get a divorce?"

"Where is that coming from?" It's not often my psychic friend looks surprised.

"Oh, I don't know. Ever since Blake moved out of the house last month, he's been going out with Steve until two and three o'clock in the morning. I know they are going to the girlie clubs. Even on weeknights," I was trying to play it cool, but it was starting to make me feel self-conscious, especially with thirty pounds of baby weight still to shed.

"You know Jenna, divorce can be energetically contagious."

"What do you mean?"

"I mean people who hang out together pick up each others' vibes and then, before long, they share the same ideas and the same actions. You may need to create a little space between yourself and everyone around you with a failing marriage. Drama breeds drama."

"You and I both know that is easier said than done." For the last 18 months, I've been getting hourly updates on the ever-growing matrimonial shit list from both Ronnie and Libby. At least Libby finally decided to take action and hire an attorney, after Blake announced he is moving out of the house and in with his mistress. But, the entire process is so draining.

"The cards say there are many hidden things yet to be revealed. I don't think your husband having an affair is one of them, but surprises can be earth-shattering in many ways."

Chapter 18

"Jenna, Blake is moving out this weekend."

"Maybe this is only temporary," I say what I think she wants to hear.

"No, I know it's final this time. I've known about the affair for a year and a half."

"I'm so sorry Libby. I know you tried everything to patch it back together again."

"Yeah, well whatever I've done apparently it was not enough. He says he can't give up the other woman. He loves us both."

It was an echo of the same story I'd heard from Ronnie all year. I tired to help out for a while, talking to both Don and Ronnie on the phone, as an unofficial referee. But it was like using a squirt bottle on a raging, out-of-control forest fire; in the end, I was the one who got burned. Now they're both a little pissed at me.

Don didn't want to give up Amber either. I don't think it's because he loves her. He told Steve, she is a *safety net*. He's just keeping her around as *"insurance"* so he doesn't end up alone in the world. The way I look at it, we're born alone, we die alone, we go to the bathroom alone, we drive to work alone, and so on. What's the big deal, everyone spends time alone. Don does not view it that way.

"Did he file for divorce?"

"No, he's calling the separation "a break", but I think what he wants is for me to file first, so he won't feel like the bad guy."

"As if he didn't break up the marriage and now abandon the family; any move after that would be anti-climatic," I said sarcastically.

"You can't imagine how hard it has been. I feel so alone." Libby hung her head down. She looked thin and gaunt. "I never thought he would leave me. We had a perfect marriage and a beautiful family. People were envious of us."

"Unfortunately not everything is as it appears to be." I wanted to be sympathetic, but we'd now been discussing the same details well over a year. It was time for Libby to start standing up again and dust herself off in preparation to take a step or two forward.

"I'm seeing that with my in-laws and their divorce." It was really ugly right now. They both had hired the most powerful, nastiest attorneys in town, who were being paid to extract blood and body parts.

"Libby, Blake seems reasonable. Maybe you can remain civil to one another and hammer out an agreement. It would be best for the kids, if you don't fight too much."

Don and Ronnie's kids are both teenagers. They are getting a lot of collateral damage from the constant war zone status of their parent's relationship. I hope Libby will be smarter. Blake seems to have calmed down a little; and now Steve has stopped going out with him. *Thank you God*! Lately, the Burrito Bandit has been front and center in the divorce and that is occupying all of Steve's focus. Don vowed to run it into the ground before he'd let Ronnie have one piece of it. This divorce has put all of Steve's ownership plans on hold indefinitely.

"At least everyone at Sycamore Creek has been so nice to me," Libby brightened at the thought of our friends at the school. "They've taken me under their wing, offered to set me up on blind dates and even brought me dinners at home."

"Yeah Libby, before long there will be someone new in your life, and you will feel so much better."

I was still trying to break into the crowd at Sycamore Creek with mixed success. People there admire the supportive friend I've been to Libby and knowing Ruth is a key that opens social doorways all over town, but not necessarily their hearts. Assistance sometimes arrives in the most unusual packages.

"How will I survive though, Jenna? I don't work. I live in a million dollar house that the boys love. I don't want to down-grade to a little cottage."

"You just have to believe that it will all work out. Something exciting could be waiting for you right around the corner." *I hope this is true.*

Chapter 19

"How much longer do I have to put up with this nonsense?" I'm trying to keep my voice down, but Steve and I have had the same argument three times this week.

"Please, hang in there with me, Jenna. I want to own some of the Burrito Bandit restaurants, at least three or four. My dad says that in a few months he'll sell me a few of my own. Then we will be free of him."

"What if he doesn't, Steve? What if it's just more of the same?" *The proverbial dangling carrot*, I thought.

"Don never delivers. It's all empty promises." I'm not convinced. Steve could see it in my face.

"He needs you, Steve, he never comes to work. Why would he let you go start a business elsewhere? Then who would run the business for him?"

"This is going to work out for us. Trust me." Steve was pleading now. Don's divorce was about to send us to lawyers of our own.

"Will you please just send out one or two resumes just in case it doesn't go our way? We have to protect our family first, Don second."

"I'll think about it. But I don't believe any opportunity will ever be as big as this one." Steve has worked with his dad so long; he has lost all perspective.

"Consider the source, Steve. Consider the source," I tried to reason.

Steve shrugs. He clearly thinks these issues with Don are my problem, not his.

"Steve, Don is totally out of control. He never comes to the office anymore. The bill for his divorce attorney is up to a million dollars. Meanwhile, every time there is an imagined transgression against Donald, somehow you are to blame and your paycheck takes a hit. We can't count on him, Honey."

Now I'm pleading with Steve. For months, I've been asking him to apply for jobs elsewhere. He refuses. Steve is convinced his best odds are with his father.

"Where do you think the money to pay for the divorce is coming from? There may not be a business to buy!" I'm so agitated. I want this man out of our lives once and for all, even if I have to verbally push him off a cliff to end our misery.

"I'm so tired of this. I'm going to call him."

"Please Jenna, whatever you do, just stay out of this." I'm already walking to the phone. *This is it!*

"Hi, Donald." He answers on the first ring.

"Hey Jenna, How are you sweetheart?" Don always answers the phone like he's hearing from his best friend for the first time in ten years. His phony enthusiasm unnerves me.

"Yes, hi, Don. The reason I am calling…" I pause for a moment. "Do you have plans for Thanksgiving?" I look at Steve. He visibly exhales and leaves the room.

"No, it's Rhonda's turn with the kids."

I take a deep breath and blurt out my invitation, "Would you like to come to our house for dinner? The kids would love to see you." Not as sincere as I would like, but an invitation all the same.

"Gee, thanks, I would love to." I could tell he was surprised by the invitation.

"What can I bring?"

"Whatever you like." I think to myself, he'll probably show up with a bottle of vintage Opus One, worth at least one hundred and fifty dollars and some Cristal champagne, set about the same price point and who knows what else. Don likes to make grand gestures when he meets new people, and insignificant gestures with everyone else.

"It's casual. I've invited three other families, Libby Peters and her two sons, Danielle and her family and a few others. I don't know if you remember meeting any of them. In fact, we are expecting anywhere between twelve to fourteen guests. Feel free to invite Ronnie and the kids. *" If you think they will come.*

"I would not count on that," Don deadpanned.

"Oh, that's too bad," And I really meant it.

Big family get-togethers are always my thing. I never had it growing up, but I always craved it. Dad was always too busy with work to make it back home to visit any family. He and my mother Jackie were constantly fighting over this topic, especially during the holidays. As an only child, it was tense and I would watch the clock or read a book until the day was over.

Now, every holiday, I make it special for Steve and the kids. We use the beautiful china and my grandmother's silver. I plan a gourmet meal. We say prayers and have many traditions that never existed for me as a child.

I wasn't really planning on seeing the kids or Ronnie. I knew what was going on. The Sinclair divorce battleground was bloody, really bloody. But, if anyone could navigate the horror of the home-wrecked holidays, I had the best shot. I knew the routine.

After dad, mother married twice more creating an obligatory parade of step- children and strangers of little permanence every holiday. So, here's the drill as I learned it. In a broken home, the holidays are a dysfunctional family theater, everyone is invited, fifty percent show up and the three-hour meal and festivities are sprinkled with small talk, smoldering animosity and big agendas. This year was no exception.

"But after dinner, we can talk about the cruise at Christmas?" Donald casually announced. *Wow, that came out of nowhere.*

"I didn't realize we were going anywhere." I tired to conceal my surprise and irritation, but I'm certain my voice betrayed me.

"Oh, didn't Steve tell you? I've reserved a space for all of us on a cruise ship out of Puerto Rico. It leaves the day after Christmas.

"Again?" I enjoyed it last year, but a second time seemed like a gamble. He goes on a cruise every year; I never imagined being part of the routine. We must have a hidden use for this year, which I'm not completely aware of.

"We travel around the western Caribbean, Grand Cayman,

Belize, and Aruba. It will be all of you and the kids. I really want you to be there."

For a second, I thought about saying what I really felt. *"Donald, I am no longer interested in being a marionette on your carnival stage. Figure it out yourself, without manipulating everyone else in my family into participating in your power struggle."*

"I expect you to come, Jenna. Otherwise there will be consequences." The hard edge to Donald's voice was unmistakable. I was shocked. He had never threatened me outright before.

He was a man used to getting what he wanted when he wanted it and how he wanted it. Usually, his wants were delivered on a silver platter, and I was once again beginning to feel like the goose held captive in the gilded cage. Surrounded by luxury, yet imprisoned nonetheless.

"Of course, Donald," I said a little too brightly, "It sounds like fun." I guess the mileage from my gracious invitation didn't get me too far.

What will I say to my mom this year? She's going to kill me if we don't come to Atlanta for Christmas.

Chapter 20

"We're here!"

The front door opened and Libby and her two boys spilled into the house. Candles warmed the entryway, the smell of pumpkin spice saturated the air and Stanley Jordan played his smooth jazz on the stereo.

"Welcome, welcome!" I rushed to greet my first guests at the door with bear hugs and air kisses.

"Here, let me take your pumpkin cheese cake. It looks delicious." I help unburden my friend Libby of her packages.

"Hi, Jenna," Libby gives me a meaningful look with a big sigh. "Thanks for inviting us. I don't know what we would have done this year. Usually we spend Thanksgiving with Blake's parents."

I return her look with an affectionate smile. "I know, sweetie. You and the boys are always welcome here." I turn to look at the two boys dressed in matching cream fisherman's sweaters, khaki pants and camel suede bucks. With their blue eyes and shaggy blond bowl haircuts, they looked like something out of a magazine ad promising family perfection. The image couldn't be farther from the truth.

"Hey guys! Give Mama J a big hug and go upstairs to find the rest of the crew. I think they are in the playroom making decorations." Long ago a group of us decided that having our children call us the formal Mrs. Peters or Mrs. Sinclair reminded us too much of our mothers and grandmothers. After all, we were more hip than that, right? So we settled on the prefix mama with our first initial as the identifier. I was Mama J, Libby was Mama L, and we had a Mama K and a Mama D, and so on and so forth. It's a system that works. We spend a lot of time together and raise our children community style, so the moms all have an understanding that it's OK for any mom in the group to supervise and redirect behavior and guide the pack of cubs through their daily activities.

"Come in the kitchen and have a glass of pinot noir. You look like you could use one." I place my hand lightly on Libby's back as a show of support as we walk into the kitchen.

I didn't want to ask if Blake was coming. When he did not arrive with the boys, I assumed he had other plans. Even though he had moved out of the house, I wanted to invite him, just in case.

Ding Dong. Ding Dong.

"Happy Turkey Day! It smells wonderful. I could eat the air!"

More guests tumbled in the front door loaded with dishes of savory food: goat cheese tarts, shitake mushroom stuffing, pumpkin pecan pie, bottles of red wine, white wine and champagne. More bear hugs and air kisses.

"We are clearly having a feast!" I laughed as I moved forward to hug my friend Danielle.

"Come in, come in!" I am so happy to have everyone at my home. The empty holidays of childhood seem like ancient history.

Wine is flowing, the turkey is roasting, women are chatting and children are racing though the house. The guys are settled in the den, cold beers in hand, watching the college football bowl games, a spread of tempting appetizers within a hands reach. The only guests left to arrive are Blake and Donald. Both of them are now at least an hour late, if they're planning to come at all.

"Jenna, I don't think Blake is going to show up here." Libby said to me quietly as we were standing at the sink shoulder to shoulder peeling the potatoes. I never had a sister, but I always wanted one. The idea of a close female companion available to listen, laugh, and share life's idiosyncrasies through childhood, dating, marriage, kids and beyond has always been a deep longing in my soul. The fact that Libby has decided to lean on me during her difficult times, and my ability to support her, has given me a taste of this sister connection. I know she is the only girl in her family, as well. Perhaps that's the connection? It's funny, until you really taste it; you never know how hungry you are for something. A sisterhood is one of these things.

"I know this has been incredibly difficult for you. I think you are doing the best you can do right now with what you have to work with." I look her directly in the eyes.

"Blake is a fool. You are a fabulous woman and his issues are about him, not you."

"I don't know if I can do it Jenna. I'm not strong like you. Lately, I can't even get out of bed." Libby's eyes begin to brim with tears, the same defeated tears she's been crying for eighteen months now. "I'm just so worried about the boys. All of my picket fence dreams are dead now."

I was about to say *Picket fences, gardens and perfect families are an illusion. They don't exist anywhere that I've seen.*

"Waooo! Waooo!" Several loud blasts pierce the air.

"Waoo! Waoo!"

All at once, the siren for the fire alarm goes off. The sound was relentless and I could not remember my emergency code.

"It must have been the bacon I accidentally burnt, which I was sautéing for the green beans." I shouted over the roar to my guests who are laughing and rolling their eyes.

"Clearly, installing a smoke detector in the kitchen was an oversight by my contractor." I try again to reach the alarm company to cancel, but the phone line is tied up with the distress call. Finally after several tries for the correct code, blessed silence. This is not the background music I had planned for my dinner party.

A few minutes later, we hear the sirens screaming down the street. I know they are headed to my house, but is it really necessary to alert the neighbors? There are pluses and minuses to having the fire station blocks from your house. An obvious minus is there is no time to tell the firemen it's a false alarm.

"Oh lord. I'll never live this one down!" I said aloud as I swing the door wide open.

"Hello, Ma'am. Where's the fire?" A large man dressed head to toe in a yellow, soot-smudged fire suit, holding a hatchet and wearing his helmet with the clear face shield in position is now standing in the middle of my celebration. Behind him several more men are jumping from their truck ready for action.

"I'm sorry to disappoint, gentlemen. This is a cooking calamity, not a real blaze."

"Do you mind if we take a look around inside, Ma'am? It's required before we can clear the scene. Just as a precaution."

"Sure, go ahead." The guys were still glued to the game. The alarm did not even faze them.

"What's the score?" One of the firemen asked as he walked through the house. Steve looked up, a little surprised that the false alarm brought a whole battalion of fireman to our feast. But then it was right back to the game.

"Clemson is ahead. But it's a tight game." Steve offered. I swear men speak their own language and they don't always use words.

"Do you want to stay for dinner?" I offered. The more the merrier.

"Sorry, ma'am, we can't accept, but thank you." It was the young guy with the axe who politely declined. He had sandy blond hair, a pair of crystal blue smiling eyes and white, perfect teeth.

Libby, Danielle and I were having a great time with the whole drama. The kids were thrilled about the personal home visit from the fire engine. *Like we planned it.* They kept pelting the guys with question like spitballs.

"How heavy is your hat?"

"Can I try it on?"

"Do you have a dog at the firehouse?"

"Do you slide down a pole?"

And my youngest, who is potty training, asked, "Do you want to watch me go potty?" Clearly, this was a person she wanted to impress.

My friends kept giggling and checking out the firemen, who happened to be the only smoking hot things on the property. No kidding, they were calendar material. I look at Libby and realize this is the first time I have really seen her laugh in a really long time. *Thank you, God, for unexpected blessings.*

"Hey guys, can you do us a favor?" I asked when they were standing in the kitchen inspecting the pan of charred bacon. They looked up from the pan, eyebrows raised.

"No offense, we do a better job at the firehouse ma'am." Our silliness was contagious.

"Yes, I will not be winning cook-of-the-year, this year!" I said sarcastically.

Then I held up a camera. "How about a few party pics to commemorate this moment of holiday history?"

Great idea! The girls scrambled to stand next to the uniformed hunks. I joined them. I definitely wanted to be included.

"Steve, Steve! Come take our picture!" I shout loud enough for my voice to reach the other room.

"I can do it." Donald Sinclair blazes in to my kitchen an hour late and not a minute sorry. He looks sleek in a black silk mock neck sweater and tan silk trousers. His dark hair is brushed back from his tan face. A pair of Elvis Costello style glasses I hadn't seen him wear before looks intellectual over his chocolate brown Italian eyes. He looks youthful and sophisticated. He looks more like Steve's brother than his father.

"Ladies, meet Donald Sinclair, Steve's father."

"What's all the excitement?" He looked around at the unfolding drama.

"Just a false alarm." I said smiling.

"That we want to turn into a photo op!" Libby offered. We both love to take pictures and make scrapbooks. This will be a fun addition. I wasn't going to let the "fire boys" leave without proof of their visit.

I handed Donald the camera.

"SMILE!"

Actually sitting down to dinner when more than fifty percent of your guests are under the age of seven is a miraculous feat to behold. Our total guest list today includes eight adults and ten children. I planned ahead and created several crafts to entertain the kids for the duration of our feast.

A Tom Turkey theme kids' table was set up in the breakfast room, away from the formal dining room. My theory was to place their table far enough away to create an adult environment in the dining room, yet close enough to hear a distress call. The table was complete with streamers, kid-created paper decorations, name cards, and crazy hats representing pilgrims and Indians. In the center of the table was a horn-shaped basket full of apples, oranges, pears and grapes all ready for little fingers to grab and eat. I also put the gravy in two squeeze bottles and made each child a molded butter pat shaped like a turkey. Moms made the plates and delivered them to our seated, squirming, giggling children at the table.

A back-up movie, Sponge Bob's Thanksgiving, was already playing in the den for little ones who had to leave the table. Over the years, I have learned that preparation is ninety percent of the battle. Let's hope it works today.

During the holidays I'm constantly reminded of why we bought this old house. One hundred and fifty Christmases and Thanksgivings were celebrated here, give or take. Family gatherings full of love, cheer, conflict and cooking, all of it, the whole caboose, was absorbed by these walls. Sometimes, when I stop and get really quiet, I can just feel the energy of the past radiating from the timber used to construct this home. It feels good. Grounded. Like home.

This year, the house is still not perfect, far from it; my kitchen is still cramped and olive-green circa 1950. Our renovation is not scheduled to begin until after the New Year. But I didn't care, I just wanted it full of people I love and care about.

On the other hand, my dining room is magnificent. *Kitchens were never a big deal a century ago. It's an idea worth reconsidering.* The best feature of the room is its tall ceilings. Center stage is an elaborate crystal chandelier dimmed to a buttery glow. A forest green silk tablecloth is covered with French paper autumn leaves. Two large hurricane glass vases sat atop the table with chubby ivory pillar candles inside surrounded by a mixture of acorns, cranberries, and green and gold glass pieces. My grandmother's silverware and my mother's crystal goblets and wineglasses twinkled in the candlelight. Keeping with tradition, I always like to bring out my best serving pieces and special china. Ivory table cards with names written by the kids and individual amber vintage glass turkey shaped soup bowls added a bit of whimsy to my table. My menu is a savory sage-rubbed turkey with cranberry and orange focaccia stuffing, cinnamon-dusted roasted butternut squash, rustic mashed rosemary and garlic red potatoes, and crunchy green beans with shallots *and bacon.* Plus a buffet of the dishes brought by everyone else.

Danielle gave me a little rub on my back, "No one does the holidays like you girl."

"Thanks for being here Danny, I've missed you lately."

"Me too, but you don't have to try so hard. There is a lot going on in your life right now. By the way, where is Jackie?"

"She's in the Caribbean with her new boyfriend."

We carried our food-laden plates into the dining room.

"Libby, I've placed you across from Donald. Who is sitting next to me?" I motioned to the chair next to me. My rectangular table can easily seat fourteen, but since we're only entertaining ten there is more room to spread out, *and for children to sneak in.*

"I believe we have met before, but I don't remember when or where." Don tapped his chin trying to put the two together. He was playing stupid-sexy.

"Yes, Don, it was at Cole's christening five years ago. I was the godmother," Libby volunteered. Thankfully, she seemed immune.

Steve and I always try to host a celebration for all of the special events in life, even if it's only a cake and some ice cream. It's a tradition often overlooked in broken homes, like the ones we came from. Steve and I are in agreement about what is important: birthdays, holidays, important events; it only takes a little extra effort to make certain they are never overlooked in our home or, worse yet, forgotten.

"Oh, yeah, I remember now." A charming smile flashed across his face directed at Libby. I glanced at her; she looked pretty in the candlelight.

I knew Don remembered. He always comments on how attractive my girlfriends are. Now that he is teetering on the edge of single, I'm certain his antennae are really up. Thankfully, no one I know would be interested in a two-time cheater.

For Don, women are like fine chocolate: expensive and difficult to refuse after just one. He was playing naïve, but he knew about the split between Blake and Libby, just as Libby knew about the split between Ronnie and Donald. Steve and I had casually mentioned the similar circumstances, with both men having an extramarital affair, a few times in passing.

After all, we talk to these individuals every day. Libby knows everything about my life, and Steve is a business partner with his father. Not much is a big secret in these intimate circles. Let's face it; they are not the first guys in the world to cheat on their wives.

"Let's all join hands and say grace."

"Thank you, Lord for the many blessing in our lives this year. We are filled with gratitude for your presence in our lives. Thank you for the opportunity to share this meal here and now with family and good friends. And may you continue to bless us and grace us in the coming year. Amen"

Excellent wine, mixed with small talk, easily led to the subject I'd been dreading since last week, *The Christmas Cruise*. How was I going to explain to Donald that there is nothing I would like to do less than float around in the Caribbean with him and his kids, again? Just so he could place a needle in Ronnie's side much like a witch doctor handles a voodoo doll? He frequently attacks her with comments about us, like, "They are my family, not yours." Technically, it's true, but the comment is in poor taste and designed to injure. *This trip is designed to reinforce this point.*

"So, Jenna, Have you decided what excursions we are going to take on our trip? Let's go scuba diving, or windsurfing." I visibly flinch. Now is not the time for me to explore this hot spot.

"Jenna, you didn't mention you were going anywhere." Libby looked at me alarmed. "When are you leaving?"

"I'm treating everyone to a cruise at Christmas around the islands." Here was the opportunity Don had been waiting for all night. Roll out the red carpet; it's time for the "Grand Gesture". Everyone at the table momentarily stopped their conversation to look at Steve and me with a little envy.

"We're just driving to my parents' house," Danielle volunteered.

"I thought we were all doing something on New Year's Eve?" Libby squeaked.

For some reason this event has preoccupied Libby's mind for the last few weeks. *Will I be alone at New Years Eve? What will I do? Will anyone kiss me? Will Blake be with HER? It's too depressing to consider.* I didn't get it. New Year's Eve has never been a big deal to me, but it is monumental to Libby.

"Why don't you come with us?" Don casually tossed the generous invitation on the table, as one would discard a paper napkin. Clearly his "Grand Gesture" was not finished with its trip down the red carpet.

WHAT? I never saw this coming.

"We'd like to come along," piped in Danielle. "But my parents would kill us," Joanne backed out. A good thing, since it was not her family that was invited.

"Why not! It will be fun," Don was eating up the attention; he had yet to take a bite of his food.

"What about the boys?" Libby hesitantly considered the idea. She looked at me for reassurance.

"Well, it would be fun to have you along." I sincerely meant it. Libby and her kids would be a welcome buffer to "Daddy-got-rocks" and his evil plans. I was so conflicted. But, perhaps this was a solution that solved more than one problem. *What's the worst that could happen? We'll get sunburned and suffer Montezuma's revenge.*

Chapter 21

There were always a lot of holiday parties and open houses to attend this time of year, sometimes two and three parties a night. I could see now that all of my hard work of the last year and a half at Sycamore Creek was really paying off, by the amount of invitations we were receiving. It felt good, really good.

"Jenna, are you and Steve coming to the Rock-n-Roll masquerade with us? Ira wants Steve to come," Ruth called me on my cell phone.

Ruth had been inviting me to so many functions lately, I was afraid I'd have to start declining. I wanted to leave room in my calendar for developing some other new contacts.

"What are you going to wear for a costume?" I could only imagine.

"I've decided to dress up as Jimmy Hendrix." *That will be interesting.*

"What about Ira? I don't think Steve will wear a costume, maybe a leather jacket."

"Ira wants his costume to be a surprise." *Everything about knowing you has been a surprise Ruth.*

"We'll see you tonight then?"

"Yes, tonight. At the Contemporary."

The Rock-n-Roll masquerade turned out to be a hot ticket. There was a line of cars around the block waiting for valet service. A crowd of partygoers dressed as various celebrities stood in line to enter the fundraising event.

"Jenna, Jenna, over here!" I recognized Ruth's voice.

The first thing I saw moving through the crowd was a giant black afro squished in the center with a multi-colored headband. *Ruth must have planned the outfit, simply because she already owned the headband.* She was wearing a green, purple and blue spiral tie-dye cotton tunic and some black leather pants with long fringe down the sides to complete the overall look. In her hands was a purple plastic guitar. It was not a pretty costume.

One glance at Ira in his costume left me speechless. Ira beat Ruth out tonight in the wardrobe contest. He was wearing a knee-length pink tunic heavily decorated with golden braids on the front panel and around the arms and repeated again at the hem. A top his head was a tall white marching band helmet. Underneath the tunic were skin-tight white leggings and little gold slippers with jingle bells on top of the toes. He had a thin black false mustache glued to his lip and his signature pupil-amplifying spectacles.

"Hello, Ira, who are you supposed to be?" I suppressed a chuckle.

"Sergeant Pepper's Lonely Hearts Club Band. You know, the Beatles," Ira said condescendingly.

I laughed, but I still didn't totally get his interpretation. Steve and I were both wearing jeans and black leather jackets. I had teased my hair a little bit and added extra black eyeliner.

The party was surprisingly fun. The band was rocking, and the open bar kept spirits high. Around eleven the dance floor was totally packed. I hadn't seen Steve for a while. He was probably talking business or music in a corner somewhere with another non-dancing spouse. Steve only dances when he's really tanked.

"Jenna! Hey, baby!!" It was Ira, drunk and swaggering towards me on the dance floor in his petal pink get-up.

"Hey Ira, want to dance?" I shouted over the music. They were our hosts. It was only polite to ask.

"Have you seen Ruth?"

"Yeah Ira, I just saw her, I think she wants to go home."

Ruth was sitting in the lobby after a fight with Ira. I offered to sit with her, but she just told me to go back inside and have fun, so I did.

"Will you come with me to find her?"

"Sure."

Ira grabbed my hand and led me into the hallway outside of the party room. I was surprised by the handholding, but a little tipsy, so I went along. We walked toward the front, when suddenly he stopped and leaned against me, pushing me into a shallow alcove. In an instant, his moist lips were pressed urgently against mine. His hand immediately reached up to grab my breast as he exhaled heavily into my mouth. A waft of booze and halitosis assaulted my senses.

At first I was too shocked to move. *What in the world is going on?*

"Jenna, don't say anything. Just grab my cock. You are so hot and sexy. I love to watch you," Ira's hot stinky breath blew the words into my ear.

He was licking the side of my face now. It was really gross.

I placed both of my hands on Ira's shoulders and pried my rose-clad attacker away from my lips.

"Don't be silly, Ira, you're drunk. Let's go find Ruth." I was trying to allow space for both of us to save face.

"No, Jenna, I have to have you. Feel how hard I am." He thrust his ramrod stiff penis, protruding from his white spandex tights, into my thigh. The sudden motion made the little gold bells on his slippers jingle.

"I believe you, Ira, and now I'm leaving." He grabbed me by the wrist as I started to walk away. I was startled by the coldness in his dead, black stare.

"Don't be such a little cunt, Jenna." His passion had suddenly converted to spite.

A film of cold sweat immediately covered my body head to toe.

"Ira, you are so out of line. I'm going to pretend this never happened." I pushed back hard as he went to grab me again, excited by the challenge of my refusal.

"You don't mean no. You're a dirty little slut. I can tell by the way you walk," he was moving toward my neck for another saliva soaked kiss.

I broke free and quickly jogged down the hall. I could hear him shouting insults in my wake. Once out of sight, I ducked into an empty room. My heart was pumping and my stomach was tied up like a sailor's knot. *What in the hell was that all about?* I sat on the cold tile floor and squeezed out a few tears of fear and frustration. This is a social SOS. *What should I do?* Ten minutes passed and I decided to go find Steve, I was ready to go home. I had made a decision.

Ira's drunk, he won't remember. I'm going to keep this to myself. I know he and Ruth are having marital problems. It must be the stress.

Chapter 22

"Have you ever heard of the Arizona Lick?'

Libby was shouting at me over the pulsating house music spun by the DJ at Carlos and Charlie's nightclub in Aruba. Our bodies kept colliding into each other, splashing liquid out of our tall hot pink drink glasses, as the crowd of dancers expanded beyond the boundaries of the dance floor.

Margaritas, Pina Coladas, Strawberry Daiquiris, Coronas, Fuzzy Navels; we had been sipping, gulping and tossing cocktail concoctions all day, ever since we set foot in this port. Steve had decided long ago to go back to the cabin. He was spent. The kids were safely tucked in bed after a day of swimming with the dolphins and a trip to the local sea turtle farm.

Don, Libby and I were the last soldiers standing. Really, we were the last soldiers dancing. In a crowded dance club, standing still is not an option. It felt like Spring Break revisited. We were having a blast! The club was on the ocean, open-air style, with floor to ceiling glassless windows spanning several of the walls. It looked a lot like a giant tiki hut with plastic chairs and sturdy wooden tables designed for dancing on. In the center of the space was a goliath bar; its counter was also crowded with bikini-clad dancers undulating to the seductive beat.

"What did you say?" I shouted back.

"Have you ever heard of the Arizona Lick?" Libby shouted in my ear. Don was a few feet a way doing a little jogging dance, it you could call it a dance. His face was sporting a flushed, excited smile. We were all a little buzzed. I didn't think he had been in a nightclub for a very long time from the look on his face. Never a club like this one.

"Come here!" Libby grabbed me by the arm, pulled me close and licked my shoulder. I was surprised, but I thought it was funny. We were letting out hair down. Her long white blonde hair was sticking to her damp face and back. It was HOT in here. Then she salted my damp skin with the saltshaker and licked it again before vigorously throwing back a shot glass of Jose Cuervo tequila. Don was mesmerized.

"Your turn!" she smiled, laughing and handing me a shot glass of tequila and the saltshaker. We were being silly. But, before I could answer, Don stuck a lime in his teeth and said. "NO! MY TURN!"

Okay, I admit it's a little weird partying with my husband's father. But I've never met this persona of Steve's dad before. I mean, I've met Businessman Don, Grandpa Don, Family Don, Patriarch Don, and Asshole Don. The list is long and varied. But Party Don, he's the new kid on the block. Honestly, this guy is a hell of a lot of fun. Unfortunately, at the time, I hadn't considered Don Juan.

Libby leaned forward and unfurled her pink tongue to slowly lick the side of Don's neck from the collar of his t-shirt to the tip of his ear. Then she salted his neck with the shaker and followed the same path again with her tongue. Next she tossed the shot glass of tequila down her throat. Topping it off, she grabbed the lime from his lips with her white teeth and bit down hard.

"OLE!" she said with a smile. Then she stumbled and fell on her butt. I looked at Don, to see if he would help her up. He was smiling like the Cheshire cat.

Lust and common sense don't reside in the same house. Perhaps they exist like owners of a vacation timeshare, sharing the same space, but never occupying it at the same time. Generally, this is not a problem unless one of the owners is out-of-control and destructive, damaging the property for everyone else. Lust is without a doubt the destructive tenant. Let's hope the damage is not beyond repair.

"What was that about last night?" I asked Libby as she sauntered up to my deck chair clad in a hot pink bikini and a flowing multicolored chiffon wrap. How many colors of bikinis does she own? So far there has been a different one every day.

"Oh yeah, that bar was over the top outrageous. I've never been anywhere like that before!"

"You were in rare form. I'm glad to see you've been having a good time. I think this trip has been good for you," I smiled at her sincerely. "It's good to see a smile on your face again."

"I can't believe tonight is New Year's Eve. I'm going to have to lay down for a nap this afternoon the recover." Libby flopped in the chair next to me, waving her hand for the deck attendant to bring her a drink. "I was so afraid I would be alone. Thanks, Jenna. This is a blast."

"You're welcome. I'm glad you're here, too."

"I could get used to this." Libby announced as she stretched out like a contented cat on the padded chaise.

I thought about her hysterically crying and vomiting last month when Blake didn't show for Thanksgiving. She was beside herself after all of the guests left.

Libby gets so emotional; it makes her physically ill. It's amazing what some sun and a change of scenery can do for your psyche. I've decided I'm not even going to mention *"the lick"* last night; it's probably nothing. Steve would die. It would really piss him off. Common sense tells me there is no way Libby would be interested in Don. He's a skirt-chaser and pathological liar, every characteristic Libby complains about in Blake, for hours on end. I can see it all on my cell phone bill, thousands of minutes, all flowing from one of two numbers.

Libby's list is aired daily, and it's the same complaints I hear from Ronnie. Why would Libby want to pick up the debris of someone else's broken relationship? *Of course she wouldn't, she is way too smart for that. I can't even imagine the two of them now complaining to me about each other.*

New Year's Eve is a main event on a cruise ship. POP! The cork exploded from the emerald green bottle of Cristal champagne. White foam bubbled over the top and spilled onto the carpet of the lounge. Cheers! Our champagne flutes chimed merrily as they connected in a toast.

"Happy New Year!"

"To new beginnings and fresh starts."

"This is really good!" Libby licked her lips and smiled. "I've never had champagne before."

"You're kidding, right. What about your wedding?" I ask in disbelief.

"Well, maybe we had a bottle of Cook's. I don't remember," Libby shrugged.

"Blake was a resident, we were on a budget."

"I've never heard of Cook's. Does that come in a box?" Don laughed at his own joke. "This is my favorite champagne, it's $200 a bottle."

"Wow!" Libby almost sprayed the liquid gold from her mouth in surprise.

"Don, Libby wasn't raised in the backwoods by a group of wolves." I tried to lightly admonish him.

"Nothing is too good for you, my dear," Don replenished her glass after she downed the rest in one smooth gulp. "Indulge yourself."

"Waiter, we're going to need another bottle," Don made a sweeping gesture.

"Libby, this is a big trip of firsts for you, I understand," Steve remarked casually. Steve usually sits on the sidelines and quietly observes. Something must have piqued his interest.

"Oh yes, I've never been on a cruise before, never flown first class, never tasted champagne. It's been amazing," Libby trilled, downing her second glass of champagne with equal gusto. *I never realized she was a 35-year-old virgin.*

"Didn't you and Blake travel together? I know we all went to the beach together a few times," Steve continued. I could tell he was skeptical of Libby's motives. *Where was he going with this?*

"Most surgeons make good money. Why would Blake be an exception?"

"Oh Steve, you know how conservative Blake is. He wants the kids college expenses completely funded before they even start grade school. We never spent money on frivolous things like champagne and luxury vacations. He wouldn't even buy me a hundred dollar piece of jewelry for my birthday. Half the price of the bottle of bubbly we just enjoyed," Libby hiccupped and giggled.

Don was not saying much, he was sitting back on the chaise sipping champagne and surveying the situation. Then it dawned on me! Pygmalion is his favorite real life drama, and now he's set his sights his next protégé. Educating a social rube on the finer things in life is one of his specialties. He's played the role a thousand times. Don loves to impress, and the naïve are easily impressed. Steve must have figured it out before me. He always knows the pitfalls when it comes to his Dad. Avoiding them is another thing altogether. Rhonda, Amber and now Libby, every single one of these women come from a modest, solid, working-class background. I never considered the connection, until now.

"Be careful of the webs you weave Jenna, you may get caught in them." Faith's warning came to mind. I felt the familiar tingle of apprehension throughout my body.

Yes, lust is about more than sex. Lust is wanting things that you don't currently possess: a certain lavish lifestyle, a wealthy husband, a new baby, or a sexy lover, a pretty, young girlfriend. After one irresistible taste, it can be hard to think about anything else. Libby Peters' world just got a little larger, reaching far beyond the navigational route of our holiday cruise. A new guest had just crashed the party, one I'd never considered.

"Libby I'd like to introduce you to Lust."

"Lust, this is my friend, Libby."

Chapter 23

"Faith, do you mind if we look at my business? Sales have been really slow, and I've been using money from my construction loan for the house remodel to keep the doors open, even though we haven't started the construction yet. Is it worth it?"

"Let me see. It appears there is someone who wants to buy the business. It looks like a young woman with dark hair."

"I know who that is. It's the gallery manager. She's always wanted to own it."

"I'm not certain if she will be able to put together the money right now. However, it looks like you might have another unexpected option."

"I hope so. It seems a shame to close it. I've owned it for six years now. When my grandmother passed away she left me an inheritance of about one hundred thousand dollars. I used it as seed money to start the art business," I looked at Faith. She was always such a patient listener.

"A few years ago sales were amazing, especially when the business was in my house. But now, hardly anyone comes into the new store. I've tried everything. I had someone come in and give it a Feng Shui analysis and I incorporated all of the suggested remedies. I've lit sage to clear away the negative energy. I've even left crystals all over the store to give it positive vibes. But nothing seems to be working. Lately, I've been burning through money ear-marked for my house. What should I do?"

"Sit tight, it appears there is a solution in the near future. But a word of caution Jenna. Dot all of your i's and cross all of your t's. Loose ends could cause you problems later on. Look, here is the card for unfinished business, and right next to it is the card of karma."

"Karma? That sounds ominous."

"Yes and no; certain events are predestined in our lives; often these are challenges that help us to grow into the person we were meant to become in this lifetime. We can't avoid these events, but there are ways to lessen their impact." She stopped and looked at the worry lines raked across my brow. *I don't think I can handle things getting any crazier.*

"Don't worry, dear, I'll be here to help you through whatever comes up. You can count on that!" She reached across the table and patted my hand in a loving, maternal way. Her reassurance comforted me, as it always does.

Chapter 24

"Ruth, I have some bad news for you."

"Yeah, what's wrong?"

"I don't think I am going to be able to donate any more paintings to your charities. I've decided to sell the business."

"Really, why?"

"It's kind of a long story. But I'll try to sum it up. Business has been a little slow, really slow, actually. I think it's partly because of the new construction going on with the furniture store next door. We look like we're closed."

"I wondered what all those trucks were doing there last month when I picked up the painting for the donation."

"We've had almost no customers for the last five months. I don't think people know we are open. Without customers, I don't have enough revenue to pay the expense of keeping it open."

"Do you think it will turn around when the furniture store reopens?"

"I hope so. But honestly, I'm not sure I can hold on. I keep borrowing money from my home equity line of credit to pay the monthly expenses of the gallery. Now, Steve wants the money back so we can pay for our massive remodeling project."

"Remodeling always costs more than you plan. We just finished our house and Ira is still having a conniption."

"My gallery manager has always wanted to buy it and I'm

seriously considering her offer."

"Do you not want to do it anymore or is it the money?"

"Probably both," I offered honestly. "Here's how I would describe it. It's like surviving the shipwreck, being on a lifeboat, seeing the land, but starving to death before the rescue crew arrives."

"That sounds bleak," Ruth was sympathetic.

"Basically, I know the new furniture store that's opening next month will probably be successful, and business will pick up again, but I've simply run out of personal resources to hold on."

"Would you consider letting me be you partner?"

"Are you serious? I never thought about it. This is the first business I've ever owned and I've never had a partner before."

"It's not so bad. Don't you remember my last business?"

"The chocolate company*?" I wasn't sure that was a real business.* I thought to myself. Ruth and a friend had teamed up to distribute locally a California-based chocolate concoction infused with herbs with names like horny goat weed, slippery elm and wet pussy willow. The haute-naughty confection was created and designed to enhance a woman's libido. It cost $75.00 a box for six "episodes." It sold well to about fifty people, gained some media attention, and then the business melted away. Ruth was left with several cases of the intriguing inventory, which became birthday presents for all of her friends and associates for the next year.

"Absolutely, how much do you want for the business?"

"Well, I was going to sell the business for $150,000. If you want to be my partner how about half: $75,000?"

"Is that all? Ira has lost that much money in the stock market in one day! It will be so much fun it won't even feel like work!" Ruth started to do a little dance around the room. I've learned she acts this way anytime she decides to start a new project.

"Don't you want to think about it awhile? Talk it over with your husband Ira? Let me at least give you my business records and let's have an attorney write up the agreement."

"Whatever, I already told you my answer. Besides this is my thing. I'm not talking to Ira about it. It's none of his business. I told you I've been talking to a divorce attorney," She looked at me adamantly. I never mentioned the night at the party. But I could see why she no longer wanted to be married to someone like him. Maybe a partnership will help her and also help me.

"I have a few ideas before we take the plunge."

"Let's talk about it at lunch next week. I have Pilates on Tuesday and Thursday but Wednesday is free. First, call your manager and tell her the deal is off," Ruth was shouting at me excitedly as she walked towards the door on her way to meet the woman she pays to organize her house.

Chapter 25

"Danielle, you are never going to believe what happened on the trip."

"Welcome back!" Danielle offered. "Did Libby and Don elope? Were they barefoot in the sand somewhere?"

"Oh, my God! How did you know?" I was shocked at her intuition. "Of course they did not elope, both of them are still married last I checked." *Thank God for this inconvenient obstacle.* "But I think there were some sparks and I'm worried about an out of control blaze."

"Jenna, I saw that coming a million miles away. Come on, we all know Libby loves the good life, isn't that why she said Blake was leaving her? She couldn't stop spending his money."

"I always thought that was just a typical nasty divorce comment. I'm still not convinced," I defended my friend Libby.

"Well please share the details," Danny inquired.

"Libby definitely got a taste of the good life on this trip. Don was in rare form. Bottles of Cristal champagne, designer handbags for both of us as souvenirs, unlimited spa treatments, the list is endless."

"Sounds like you had a good time, too."

"I did, and the kids loved all of the excursions and exotic beaches. But with Don, I am always waiting for the other shoe to drop. Like two weeks from now we will get the bill in the mail, he'll just demand another form of payment. Who knows, he may deduct the trip out of our paycheck. Trust me, Danielle, nothing is free with this guy."

"Hold on, my cell phone is ringing." I look at the caller ID: **Don Sinclair**. "Danny, it's Steve's dad, let me call you back. He never calls me. I want to see what's up. Maybe its already time for payback."

Chapter 26

"Hello."

"Hi Jenna!" *It's Mr. Happy.*

"Listen, I know it's short notice, but I have to go to Mexico next weekend for The Burrito Bandit company awards trip with Steve. Would you and Libby like to come along? I need some help with the employee pictures and organizing the event. I understand Libby is a photographer," He blurted out the unexpected invitation.

"Don, why don't you call Libby and see if she is interested? Here let me give you her phone number." *Can't a grown man organize his own social calendar?*

"I don't think I can make it. I've only been home a week and we have not even started to unpack." *Can I call you back later, perhaps in six months?*

I was looking for an excuse to decline. The cruise this year was graciously uneventful with the exception of the mismatched attraction brewing between my father-in-law and my best friend. I want to leave things on a high note with Don. Impersonal works best. Construction on my house starts next week, and I don't want Steve getting fired by his dad every other week for imagined transgressions. It's been hard enough keeping the toxic divorce out of our family's lives. But a social intrusion? It's more than I could handle. I don't want Don at all of my cocktail parties.

Besides, I know his motives and they have nothing to do with me other than *"pimp service."* History sets this precedent, the last ten years my husband has been in business with his father, they've had these incentive trips and I've never been invited. Usually, it's his mistress, Amber Atkins who always goes along and coordinates all of the activities both for him and the employees.

"Um," there was a long silence. Don does not take no for an answer.

"Don, are you still there?" I thought we had been disconnected. *It must be difficult to decide how to ask your daughter-in-law to pimp her married girlfriend to you.*

"When is the last time you and Steve took a vacation together without the kids? Every couple needs a break once in a while, right?" It was difficult to argue this reasoning.

"I don't want you guys to end up like Rhonda and me," he sounded sincere. Apparently his charm still had a little traction with me.

"I'll ask Libby. But I don't know what she will say." I'll come up with an excuse later. "Do you still want me to come if she can't make it?"

"If you'd like." *Sincerity has its limits.*

"Let me get back to you later today," I said laughing quietly to myself. *I know if Libby can't make it, you've already invited Amber.* Don never goes anywhere without back-up plan, he's too afraid of being alone.

Chapter 27

A *business partner?* The idea of joining forces with Ruth traveled around my mind for a few days until it set up residence in the naïve, hopefully optimistic section of my brain. Wasn't this the perfect solution to all of my problems? Seventy-five thousand dollars would solve a lot of problems. I could pay back the equity line the $45,000 I'd used over the past six months. Get Steve off my back. I wouldn't have to give up the business I started with seed money from my grandmother's estate. Plus now there would be new money to buy more inventories. This has to be the solution.

A visit to Faith will shine some light on the situation. Faith passes the cards to me and I start shuffling, thinking about all of my questions. With cards it's best to ask open-ended questions.

Like, "What is my financial outlook for the next six months?"

Or in my situation, "What type of business partner will Ruth be? What will our experience be like?"

I stop shuffling and then split the cards into three piles face down. She collects them all; the last cut deck is on top.

I feel the butterflies unfold their wings inside my stomach. *I hope it looks good.* One, two, three, four, five, she continues to flip cards from the top of the deck laying them on the table right side up in a pattern similar to a cross. To the left of the spread is an additional four cards lined up vertically. Out of 78 cards she only pulls ten, all that's needed to get the answers I seek.

"The card in the center is the Ace of Pentacles, this means new money is coming in, new business opportunities. I think the deal will go through," Faith smiles at me as I exhale in relief.

"That's good news, right?"

"Good and bad is all relative my dear."

"On top of the ace card is the Hierophant, this is what crosses you. It means fluctuations in life, home and business, both lucky and unlucky. It also means legal contracts, lawsuits and litigation."

"We are using a lawyer to write our purchase agreement," I offer.

"In the past, there is the card representing financial struggle and in the top position here is a card representing your fear and concerns about the future of the business. But a fear is not a reality, although it may feel like one," Faith counsels.

"The near future card," she pauses and points to a card depicting a globe, "is the world, which tells me you are going on an exciting and expansive trip."

It's all true, so far. Faith is so amazing. I am planning on asking Ruth if she wants to go to the big art buying show in New York next month.

"Faith you are always so accurate, how do you do it?"

"The last row," she points to the four cards one on top of the next, "represents the unknown, your hopes and fears, best course of action and the outcome."

"This King of Swords reversed tells me you need to beware of a man," I immediately thought of Ira.

"The next card tells me that there is a karmic or past life connection with this man and you will learn many lessons, some are quite difficult," She pauses to allow this advice to soak in. *It could also be Don; he's difficult.*

"That makes sense; I need to teach Ruth about the business. I'm sure she will have her own ideas to teach me. As far as the man, I have no idea who that could be." I shrug, dismissing the warning as she moves on.

"The last two cards show me you will get what you want, but there is a change of fortune in store. The outcome is the Wheel of Fortune reversed."

"That's great isn't it?" I am elated. My business had been down and it is turning back around. I never considered it could turn in the opposite direction. Confirmation from my most trusted advisor is what I needed.

"The Wheel of Fortune means situations are out of your control. But, the events, which follow, will create an outcome that will be impossible to miss. A new way of life is about to commence. It doesn't clarify however, what that life will look like, only that it will be different than the one you are experiencing now."

"My dreams are coming true," I feel a shiver of premonition cascade across the top of my shoulders and streamline into my gut.

"Jenna, remember we need to be careful of the webs we weave for we may get caught in them."

"Thank you Faith. *" How would I ever survive without you as my compass?* I stand up to give her a hug. I notice a slight tremble in her hands. She must be exhausted from taking care of her mother.

"Are you feeling OK?" I ask Faith.

"Don't worry about me dear, my mom is wearing me out with her illness."

"Well try to get some rest," I hug her goodbye.

It's time again for The Route. I realize Faith never tells me what to do, and she only reflects back to me the messages she receives from the Universe. I never did get a yes or no answer, about whether I should take on a partner; but it feels like a yes. I guess we all have our own free will.

Chapter 28

"Libby, I'm thinking about taking on a business partner. You'll never believe who."

"Let me guess, Ruth Simon."

"Yeah, how did you know?"

"Well you've been her pet lately on a lot of charity projects and that's generally the way it works," Libby sounded annoyed, "but has she ever had a real job?"

"I hadn't considered that," I paused for a moment. The gallery was a lot of hard work. Over the past six years I'd grown accustomed to it. There are a lot of things in a retail business that eat your time. Coding pictures for inventory, touching up frames, installing canvases and wiring the back of frames. My hand-held drill is a close personal friend. I use it often: drilling clips, connecting oils with different frames, until the customer finds the right fit. Then I wire the back with metal fasteners and tightly bound plastic coated gallery wire. My fingers are dry and calloused as a testament to that experience.

The list is endless. Small businesses are like small children: demanding, expensive and thankless, yet you love them all the same. I'm there at least thirty hours a week doing maintenance. The rest of the time, I'm there mentally trying to figure out how to change the tide and attract customers.

"She works hard at her charity stuff. I'm sure she'll be fine," I tell myself. I'm having a hard time seeing past the temptation of a much needed cash infusion.

"I'm kind of jealous, Jenna," Libby's bottom lip turned down in a pout, "I have an art background and you didn't ask me to help you."

"First off, I have asked you to help on several occasions over the past couple of years and you always have a scheduling conflict," I tried weakly to defend myself, "Second, with Blake's affair, you don't know what's going to happen and I need more security."

"I guess I see your point, but I'd be careful. You two don't seem to see eye to eye on a lot of things. She's wired differently than you are," Libby conceded. I felt she was biased.

"Don't worry, we're going to have a contract," I was glad this conversation was over. Business and friends don't usually mix well.

"Oh, by the way, do you have any interest in a trip to Mexico this weekend?" I remember the invitation from Don.

"Are you going?" Libby sounded intrigued.

"I haven't decided," her interest made me want to stay home.

Chapter 29

I almost slipped on the black ice as I ran to get into my car. It's time again to drive the daily Route. Large snowdrifts flanked both sides of the frozen road, some taller than five feet. Dirty, grey-stained ice mountains. The whole region suffered a major winter storm while we were sailing the warm sunny seas around the Islands. A light brown tan on my skin helped me feel not so cold inside, despite the twenty-degree mercury reading. It's a mental thing. I'm not a big fan of snow, or winter, or freezing rain or bulky sweaters. Jenna and January don't mix. My cell phone played the hip-hop song notifying me Steve is calling.

"Hey sweetie, what's up?"

"Jenna, guess what. My dad finally gave me the raise I've asked for since last spring. I'm getting an extra two thousand a month," Steve was bursting with enthusiasm.

"You didn't even have to ask for it?" I was skeptical. Before Thanksgiving, Don said the business was still struggling and Steve might need to take a pay cut. *I'm certain now this was a ploy to get this financial information back to Rhonda to taint their divorce. It's really starting to bother me the way he manipulates us.*

"Nope," Steve was giddy. A state I've rarely witnessed.

"Wow, that's exciting!" It was contagious. *And, what a huge relief, I was beginning to wonder if we should postpone the renovation. At least until our finances stabilize.*

"Do you still think we should put off the contractor?" I was thinking we should be conservative.

"No, let's just move ahead. I can't stand our cramped kitchen and our leaking, stinky bathroom a minute longer," Steve said confidently.

We moved in the century home thinking we would tackle the kitchen within six months. Four years later we have yet to start. Cost and circumstances always seem to get in the way.

"I really believe things are looking up." Steve sounds excited. "Dad says he wants to sell me some of the Burrito Bandit locations next month. I'm finally going to get my own business."

"I know you've wanted this for a long time, Honey. I hope it works out." I was already planning in my mind to make him a celebration dinner tonight.

"Maybe we will be able to put in a pool. The kids would love that," Steve was on a roll.

"I'll be happy with a new kitchen." I was trying not to get caught up in the excitement; nothing is for sure with Don until the ink is dry.

"If anyone deserves it, Steve, you do."

"Which locations should I pick?" Steve was excited.

"You said the company operates seventy-two restaurants. How many do you think he will be willing to part with?" *I was hoping for at least five.*

"One, two, maybe three." Steve sounded a little apologetic.

"Is that enough to live off?" I tried to hide my surprise. Steve always aims low. I don't really understand it.

"I can make it work. I just need the opportunity."

"By the way, Steve, your father invited Libby and me on your business trip to Mexico," I felt there might be a connection between the raise and the invitation.

"He did?" Steve was silent for a moment as reality clicked into place.

"Yeah, what do you think?" He finally asked, "Do you think she likes him?"

"I have no idea why she would, for a variety of obvious reasons," I rolled my eyes.

"This is pretty weird. Your friend dating my Dad…" he fell silent again, then unexpectedly started to laugh.

"If they got married it would make her Grandma Libby to our kids. If they had kids, her baby would be my sister or brother. Her five and seven year old boys, your godchildren, would become my stepbrothers. She would also be my step-mom and…" Steve was having fun with this.

"Oh my God! You have to stop!" I was laughing hard over monikers I'd never considered. Grandma Libby, it was too much.

"I have no idea if she likes him, or even why she would. Libby is not known for her brain power," I was feeling annoyed with the entire situation.

An arctic blast of air hit me in the face as the doors of the van opened for my kids in the carpool line. "But honestly, some time alone with you in Mexico sounds nice. We haven't been on a vacation away from the kids since we moved into the "money pit" house years ago." The cold weather shifted my resolve to stay home.

"Hold on for a minute Steve, I'm at Sycamore Creek, the kids are getting in the car."

"Hi guys, how was your day?" I handed each the kids a cup of hot cocoa from Starbucks' drive- thru.

"Fine." They said in a chorus as I turned on the movie in the minivan.

"Ok. I'm on the phone with daddy." Kids never give you much information fresh out of the classroom. The details of the day come out later during dinner or bath time.

"Hey, Dad. Will you be home for dinner tonight?" Cole chimed in.

Steve told me he had another late meeting. I relayed the message to the kids.

"Who's going to take me to practice?" Lucy wails. She's missed it twice this month already from these evening meetings. When Steve is tied up at work, she has to miss out on her choir practice. It's too difficult for me to bring three kids to a rehearsal located a half an hour away and to wait in the car for an hour at bedtime. Steve does it because there is a Starbucks nearby and he can read the paper.

I returned to the phone conversation, "Steve, why does he do this every week? Sleep in until noon and keep everyone at the office late? We have small kids who go to bed without a kiss goodnight from their father more often than not. It's ridiculous," in a second I was back to mad again. Knowing this man is like the eternal pendulum swinging between animosity and adoration.

"Jenna, let's just let it roll for a while and take the trip," Steve never likes to make waves. "Once I finally own my own restaurants, I will do things differently, much differently. I'm so close I can feel it." Steve sounded determined. He's held the same dream for almost a decade.

"Besides, what would Libby ever see in Dad? He's twenty years older than her and a tomcat. He's also still married and probably still doing it with his secretary Amber Atkins." I could tell he was justifying his implied consent of the relationship between our friend and his father.

"He is?" I was shocked to hear the confirmation.

"Yeah, she came back to the office the other day after lunch wearing his shirt."

"That's what I call a power lunch," I deadpanned.

"Dad always likes to work with a safety net, in life, in business, and in sex. Someone has to be giving it to him, or he's just not happy." Steve was matter of fact. "Honestly, I could care less. It seems like I'm finally on the verge of getting what I have always wanted, my own group of restaurants. Whether it's an infatuation with Libby or lunch time blow jobs from Amber, or both, I'm willing to let it run its course."

"I guess you're right," this was not a deal I was prepared to make, but I could not see any real harm at this time.

Chapter 30

"How can I help you guys?"

Ruth and I sat across the table from my friend/attorney Gloria Coin in the conference room of her modest law offices. Gloria has been a girlfriend of mine for the past five years. She offered to do the legal work for free.

"Gloria, as you know, I was going to sell the business to my gallery manager, but Ruth Simon has decided to step in and become my partner in the gallery."

"Yes, I think it sounds so exciting and I'm really looking forward to going to New York in two weeks to Art Bonanza. I love to shop," Ruth chimed in.

"There's a lot more to running a gallery than buying inventory, Ruth. Have you been advised of all of the duties you'll need to participate in?" Gloria was trying to keep us on track.

"Oh yes, I plan to be there at least three days a week," Ruth shrugged. "Ira said he did not want me to go in business with Jenna, but I'm independent. I can do what I want."

"I didn't realize Ira was against our partnership," I looked at Ruth surprised, "perhaps we should call off the deal." I immediately thought of the incident with Ira a few months back. He must still be angry with me. I'd barely seen him since that night; I made a point of avoiding him.

"Are you sure, Ruth, that you want to move forward without your husband's support and without hiring an attorney of your own to represent you in this transaction?" Gloria seemed alarmed.

"That won't be necessary. It's not that much money and, if it doesn't work out, we'll just sell the gallery and get out," she turned to look at me, "besides I don't know how long I'll even stay in this marriage. I need a business of my own." Gloria raised her eyebrows at this statement from Ruth.

"Yes we can always sell it, a lot of partnerships turn sour and I don't want to ruin our friendship over business, Ruth." I confirmed to Gloria what we had already talked about several times.

"That will never happen. I feel the same way," Ruth smiled at me. I noticed she was not wearing a headband today; it must be a special occasion.

Ruth reaches in her Chanel handbag and pulls out her matching checkbook.

"Gloria, here's a deposit to show my intent to become part of this business." Ruth starts to fill in the amount; the words "seventy five thousand dollars" filling the line in bold strokes.

"That's not necessary yet, we're a little premature. I want us to sit down several times and go over all of the details," Gloria was trying to pull us off of our speeding train.

"Gloria, just write the contract. We need to be in New York in a few weeks," Ruth instructed firmly.

"OK, whatever you want."

"Jenna, do you have any suggestions?" I shrugged.

"As you know, I've never had a partner before. You need to guide me on the legal requirements," I've already owned the business alone for seven years.

"OK Ladies, I'll meet your time table; consider it done. I'll have a basic agreement next week. But you will need to come back and iron out all of the details. We need a lot more documents like: operating agreements, buy/sell agreements, use of proceeds agreements."

"Blah, blah, blah," Ruth mimicked Gloria. She suddenly stood up and was ready to walkout. "I have to get to Pilates class. Call me later."

"Okay Ruth, I think I'm going to Mexico for a few days this weekend. We can all meet again when I get back. Just to figure out the details."

"You're quite the jet setter these days, Jenna," Ruth was teasing me.

"It seems that way, doesn't it?" *No trips for years and now one every weekend, I feel like I am the one being courted.*

Chapter 31

The warm breeze swept across the waters of the Gulf of Mexico filling the sails of our private catamaran and surging us forward at an exciting clip. Pearls of cool water danced across our skin as the boat cut effortlessly through the splashing waves. The weather the last few days in Mexico had been sheer perfection: sunny, eighty-two degrees, with an occasional gentle breeze pushing a few fluffy clouds through the azure blue sky, like a shepherd collecting his errant spring lambs. I was stretched out across the taut trampoline-like canvas deck of the chartered sailboat, my heavy-lidded blue eyes observing the sky. Lazy. Contented.

The captain of the ship had set course for a small island off Cancun called Isla Mujeres. Translated, it means "The Women's Island". I can see why the women might want to claim this little piece of heaven. Everything about this location, here and now, appealed to my soul. My senses were adrift in the luxury of nature.

Earlier in the week, Libby surprised me by quickly accepting Don's invitation to Mexico. Apparently, Blake was taking the kids for the first time after moving out and they were going to be gone for several days with their father. Libby said she was dreading the time alone and a quick vacation seemed to be the perfect distraction. Since arriving in Mexico, Libby and Don were spending some time together but it seemed more like friendship than fireworks. Steve and I were observing closely to see what was unfolding and honestly, we were relieved. After all, there is no harm in a friendship.

'Rapido! Rapido!" A command from our captain jolted me out of my indolent reverie. The boat was close to shore, and he needed our help to secure it to the beach. Don and I jumped over the side of the boat landing in the chest-high tropical waters. My bare feet sank into the soft, shifting, white sand. The crystal clear water revealed an underwater landscape of several large, grey boulders, a mountain of discarded peach conch shells, masses of white brain coral and a smattering of colorful tropical fish. Visual paradise.

We were able to secure the boat with a rope to the nearby buoy, before wading to shore with our belongings balanced on our heads. There were only two buildings on the island, a waterside café and a small luxury villa. The deck of the restaurant extended over the beach, jutting out into the ocean, allowing diners a view of the hypnotic turquoise water and the conch shell graveyard below. One had the sense the waiter would soon arrive with fishing poles in hand, allowing us to catch our own lunch. Unfortunately, this was not the case, but an ice bucket full of chilled Coronas, fresh limes, and a large plate stacked with grilled crustaceans quickly dissolved our disappointment. It was culinary perfection.

"I brought along some gear to go snorkeling. Any takers?" Don had masterminded the entire day. He chartered the boat, plotted the location and organized the meal. *Hats off to you Don, I've just had one of the best days in my life so far.* I'm beginning to see a glimpse of a person I've met once before, the same Party Don from the nightclub on the cruise: younger, more free-spirited, charming, and basically irresistible.

This is a person I'd like to get to know better. I'm certain his appeal is not lost on Libby. The boat sailed from the island to a nearby reef, popular for scuba diving and snorkeling. The plan was to leave us here at the top of the reef and to sail ahead to wait for us at the end of the reef, allowing the current to carry us back to the boat. I was a little unnerved to be left alone in the open water without a boat in clear view, but unwilling to squelch this perfect day.

The water was about thirty feet deep. I could clearly see the bottom. It was a magnificent playground for a variety of marine life. I was instantly mesmerized by a school of angelfish and began slowly kicking and drifting back to the boat with Steve, Libby, and

Donald close behind. Snorkeling is a silent adventure. The ocean water crowds out all sense of smell and sound. I share this magical other world with colorful coral, drifting sea turtles, an occasional barracuda, and so many tropical fish, I could never identify them all.

Out of the corner of my eye, I noticed a large, dark shadow just below the surface. It took a moment to register that it was Don. *Was he diving to the bottom to get one of the large shells?* No, he was holding his leg near the calf. I looked him in the eye and recognized sheer panic.

"Steve! Steve!" I burst to the surface. I was shouting over the waves as I tread water for a moment trying to catch my breath. In the course of our observations, we had all drifted apart. I could not find anyone.

"STEVE! LIBBY! ANYONE! HELP! OH MY GOD! PLEASE HELP!" I was desperate, frantic. I didn't know if I was a strong enough swimmer to save Don by myself.

I dove back under the water and swam toward Don. He was sinking toward the bottom of the ocean floor; grabbing his leg and trying to paddle with one arm back to the surface, unsuccessfully.

I reached to grab him, but he was just below my grasp. My hand sliced through the water but returned to me, empty. I'd misjudged his distance. *Oh my God! Please, someone help me!* I needed to take a breath. My lungs started burning. Searing pain. I knew he would be even deeper when I returned after a breath. I was having trouble reaching him now!

"Don! Don!" I screamed under the water. The sound was garbled and difficult to hear. It was a stupid move and it spent the last of my breath. Don didn't look at me. He was distracted by his efforts. Horrified, the unbelievable question formed in my mind.

Am I going to watch my husband's father drown? The world slowed down to a crawl. Don dead? The reality of it was even further beyond my grasp than Don himself, who was quickly plummeting to his watery fate. *Steve! Oh Steve. What will he do without his father?*

Sure, I've had my complaints about Don, but he's still family and I love him like you love a wayward child. *Rhonda? His kids? My kids?* This is a tragic nightmare. *I was powerless.* The realization swept over me like a cloak knitted with leaden threads. Right here in this moment, at the intersection of death and despair, I realized there was only one action left to take. PRAY!

GOD! Oh, please, God! I hope you are listening. Help! Jesus Christ! Archangel Michael! Everyone! Anyone! Please save Don's life! I was going down the list of saints and angels I'd learned in church as a child. The urgent plea spilled from my heart to heaven. I don't know if I actually said the words; but they were frantically loud, inside my head.

A sob burst from my lips, breaking the seal on my mouth, releasing the last of my oxygen. I inhaled a huge gulp of salt water. Coughing and sputtering, I scrambled to the surface. Now I began coughing in deep, barking spasms. The inhaled saltwater was harsh in my throat and scalded my lungs. *Where is the dammed boat?*

"Jenna, what's going on? Are you all right? Where is Steve? Don?" Libby swam to me, slapping me on my back and supporting me with her arm as we floated together with the help of our now inflated scuba vests. It's ironic, we all had the tools to save ourselves, but for some reason the vests were not previously inflated.

I'm hysterical. "Libby, its' Don! He's drowning!" I stopped to take another gasp for air. My heart was pounding so fast, I thought it would burst from my chest. "I tried, but I could not reach him." I start sobbing and coughing.

"HELP! SOMEONE HELP!" Libby starts screaming at the top of her lungs.

Suddenly, Steve and a man I've never seen before burst through the surface with an unconscious Don supported under their arms.

"Steve, Oh my God! Your Dad! You found him!" I splashed over to my husband and the unknown hero in the scuba equipment.

"I tried to save him. Dad was grabbing his leg," Steve said. He must have had a cramp."

"DAD! DAD!" Steve was pounding on Don's chest, as the other man supported him flat on the surface of the water. Steve's face was a mask of agony and fear. Steve bent over Don and blew breaths into his mouth between his own gasps for air. But, hysteria and fear were making it difficult for Steve to find enough air for both of them.

"Let's take turns," said the unknown diver, gently moving my frantic husband aside. He bent over Don and exhaled a calm, deep breath into his open mouth, visibly filling Don's lungs. One, two, three times. The mysterious diver just kept filling Don's lungs with the breath of life. The boat crew must have seen our distress, and they were now pulling up alongside. Steve scrambled to the deck of the catamaran and hurled his father on the canvas deck as if he were a forty-pound child, not a grown man. *Is he going to live? Are we too late?*

I place my head in my hands and begin to pray again. *God! Please help Don live!* I hear a hacking cough and then a gurgling sputter. Don surprises us by rolling to his side and vomiting up salt water all over the canvas decking of the sailboat. The rescue breaths must have worked.

"Who are you? How can I ever thank you?" I turned to look at the diver. He had Caribbean green eyes framed by freckled, tan skin. The combination was charming and boyish, yet his physique was strong and athletic. His wetsuit was a pale grey. It looked almost silver in the afternoon sunlight.

"I was in the area scuba diving and I saw your sinking friend. At first, I thought it was a big fish. Then I thought, perhaps someone is diving for a shell. But something about his position did not seem right," he was friendly, casual and matter of fact.

"When I got closer, I realized he was in real danger of drowning. So, I scooped him up and quickly headed for the surface. On the way up, I was met by this guy," he pointed to my husband, who was taking care of his father.

"How can I ever thank you? I don't even know your name," I was extremely curious about this angelic young man who appeared out of nowhere to save Don.

"My name is Gabriel. But my friends call me Gabe." He smiled again and I felt an aura of casual warmth radiating from his being.

"I hate to run, but it looks like everything is cool here. My diving buddies will start to wonder what happened to me. Take care!" With that, he jumped off the side of the boat and disappeared below the waves.

"Where did he go? I didn't have a chance to thank him. I'm sure Dad would want to give him a reward." Steve had heard the splash and turned to see if someone else had fallen from the boat, quickly realizing the diver had disappeared.

"Honey, I don't think he is the type who is into rewards." I looked to the clear water to see if I could find his form below the surface, but there was nothing. "I did find out his name is Gabriel."

"What hotel is he staying at? Did you get a last name?"

"No, NO! The answer to all of your questions is no. I didn't get a chance to ask," I was irritated. The experience had zapped my energy.

"Who are you guys talking about?" Libby was curious about our conversation.

"Jenna didn't get any information about the man who saved Dad's life."

"What man?" Libby asked as she was kneeling next to Don.

"You know, Libby, the scuba guy. The man with the ocean-water colored green eyes. The guy who carried Don to the surface! He was sitting on this boat talking to us. Or me at least." Sometimes this dumb blonde act of Libby's really drives me crazy.

"Jenna, I'm sorry, I have no idea who you are talking about." Libby was sincere. I could see she was telling the truth.

I looked at Steve, "Did we imagine this man?"

"Jenna, I swear I saw him. He carried Dad from the bottom of the ocean floor. I couldn't get down that far. Dad was just beyond my reach. Suddenly, this guy had him and we were swimming to the top."

"Steve, I swear I spoke to him. He told me what happened and said he needed to rejoin his friends." This entire conversation was giving me the chills. God answered my prayers in a big way today.

"Hey, can someone find me some water to rinse my mouth out?" Don was sitting up now. "This salt water tastes awful."

"Don, what in the world happened? I was afraid we had lost you." I reached over and patted him on the back after wrapping him with a fresh dry towel.

"I don't know. We were all swimming along and I remember getting a terrible cramp. Suddenly my leg was useless and I couldn't keep my head above the water. I just started to sink," Instinctively, Don reached to massage his leg.

"Do you remember who rescued you?" Steve asked, determined to solve the mystery.

"I thought it was you, Steve."

"Yeah, me and another guy. He was a scuba diver who happened to be in the area. Apparently, he saw you and came to the rescue."

"I don't remember him, but we need to get his information, so I can send him a reward or a thank you. Whatever it is you do for someone who saves your life." Don lay back on the deck and closed his eyes. The reality of his life-and-death drama was starting to settle in. We were all quiet and reflective on the sail back to the marina.

"Juan, how can I find out the names of scuba divers in the area today?" I asked the marina manager once we had docked. The journalist in me was unwilling to leave this mystery unsolved.

"Senora, it's true that most scuba charters run out of this marina," Juan offered. "But, today there was a rip-tide warning, so all afternoon trips were cancelled until tomorrow morning."

"But there was a diver over by our snorkel area," I insisted.

"That's odd. The popular scuba reef is in the opposite direction of that area, about a mile west. Most scuba divers prefer at least fifty to ninety feet of water. Your area is only thirty feet deep. It's a little on the shallow side."

"Thank you, Juan." I looked at Steve and shook my head. *I guess for some things in life there is simply no explanation.*

Libby and I left a few days early to fly home together. She told me about the night after the fateful sailing excursion and how they sat up all night talking on the beach. This in itself is not surprising, because I have never met two people more in love with the sound of their own voices. But what did surprise me was the bond that has formed between two people I never expected to connect. Libby told me about their conversation in her typical chatty gossip style and some of it broke my heart. I've kept this information to myself.

"I asked Don if he was ever in a fraternity or where he went to college?" said Libby. *She always knows what is important.* He said, "I had my son Steve at such a young age, eighteen. I've never had a chance to have a real life as a single person without the responsibility of a child. I wonder what my life would be like now if Steve had not been born."

Libby also told me matter-of-factly that Don felt he's been cheated out of the opportunity to date a lot of different women. That the women he had been married to in the past had forced him to the altar. Now, he was giving up on love and the only thing he was focused on is pursuing his dream of becoming a billionaire.

His thoughts are as shallow as the ocean reef that almost

swallowed him, I thought to myself as she prattled on about their moonlight discussion. Whatever resonated in her about this conversation escapes me. I have a sinking feeling it has something to do with his billionaire fantasies. Libby likes money. What's worse, the discussion concluded with a kiss; a deep, searing, passionate, tongue slapping kiss.

I had to stop her when she started the description of their sand dune make out session. A visual sexual image of my father-in-law with my best friend was an assault on my senses. But one thing was certain, this friendship had now taken a turn south, and it was headed into the steamy hot tropics of the volcanic region.

Chapter 32

I was tempted to call Faith from Mexico, but I waited until I got home. She would know what happened between Don and his mysterious hero.

"Faith, I think I met an angel," I told her the entire story while she nodded her head smiling.

"Jenna, angels are wonderful beings of light. History has hundreds of examples of angelic encounters. It does sound like you've had one. I'm so happy for you that you were able to experience the Grace of Divine Intervention."

Instead of being afraid, I felt a tingly warmth spread across my body. It reminded me of an electrified hug and, for a moment, I pictured Gabe's face from the boat. It made me smile. I know now; angels are real.

"So you are off to New York, Jenna?" Faith asked me about my next trip.

"Yes, next week. I hope it goes well," I was worried about Ira demanding that Ruth not get on the plane. Ruth informed me she was using her participation in my business as an act of defiance against Ira. I wanted to help Ruth, but it was becoming a little uncomfortable.

"Please prepare yourself for takeoff," The voice on the intercom system instructed us to take our seats.

I paused to catch my breath. We'd almost missed the flight this morning. Carpool was hectic. Thank God for Lolly, who watches the kids while I'm away. Ruth and I agreed to meet at the airport. At first I did not recognize her. All I saw was a blur of brown fur, akin to a wild bear rampaging through the Alaskan wilderness, rushing toward me waving its paws frantically.

"I'm here, Jenna! Wait for me!" Ruth screeched through the terminal.

I shout back, "Take it easy Ruth, I was late, too. We still have time, the plane is delayed by twenty minutes."

"Ruth, where did you get that fur coat?" I raised my eyebrows while scanning her attire.

"It was Ira's mother's. What do you think?" Ruth looked proud.

The coat was shaped like an upside down tulip. The broad, formless style from generations gone by did nothing to enhance Ruth's thin frame. In fact, she looked lost inside a giant fur-covered football. The only things sticking out were her frizzy head at the top and her pencil thin legs at the bottom, from the calves down.

"It looks very vintage, Ruth. You're making a strong fashion statement," I wanted to start the trip off on a positive note.

She smiled, satisfied with my compliment, which was really more of a comment.

We both took off our coats and stored them in the overhead compartment. Her fur animal weighed a ton. The brown fur felt dry and brittle in my hands as I helped her lift it into the bulkhead.

"Jenna, I really like your coat."

"Thanks, it's a reversible fur-lined microfiber raincoat. My mother bought it for me as a wedding present. The black sheared mink side is perfect for evenings and the raincoat side works well in snow. It's really warm, too. They're are expecting a snow storm in New York."

"I need one of those," Ruth stroked mine longingly before I placed it in the overhead next to hers.

"It's from Bloomingdale's. Every year, at this time, they have all of their coats marked down. Maybe we'll have time to stop there."

"I definitely want to do that!" Ruth said excitedly.

We settle in as the plane begins to taxi down the runway. I did not dream I would be attending the show this year. *What a lucky twist of events,* I think to myself as we leave the ground, buildings and roadways dissolving beneath us.

I look over and smile at Ruth. She looks almost pretty today, sans fur. A business trip to New York must have inspired her to tone it down. Her eyes were lined with smoky shadow and her lashes were darkened with mascara. I'd never seen her wearing makeup before.

She wore a chocolate brown suede shirt jacket with a pair of soft tan corduroy camouflage print pants and some black biker boots. Then there was the trademark pink terry cloth headband across her forehead. Without that accessory, the outfit would be almost ordinary.

"I'm so glad we had the extra points and were able to upgrade to first class," Ruth says she likes to travel in style. She bought the airline tickets and made the hotel reservations. We were planning to stay at the W Hotel, a personal favorite of mine with its sleek, understated décor.

"Thanks, Ruth, for the tickets and for becoming my partner," I impetuously grab her hand for a little squeeze. The feeling that everything might workout after all was starting to saturate my being.

I snuggle into my comfortable seat. I'd only flown first class once before. It was nice, very nice. The flight attendant served us breakfast and we ordered champagne. *Why not? We were celebrating.*

I told Ruth what to expect at Art Bonanza. I had arranged for some pre-show vendor badges so we could go early and get first pick of the paintings. This is the fifth time I have been to the show. I know the routine and the best vendors to visit.

The oil paintings are not collectables. The artists are generally unknown from China and Korea. Most canvases are purchased unsigned. The oils just look good, really good, and my customers love them. Most of my clients buy more than one. Someone once bought eighteen paintings and completed their entire house.

My business started in my home. Friends used to come over and ask where they could buy what was adorning my walls. They also wanted help with wallpaper, paint colors and furniture suggestions. So, I became an unofficial interior decorator. It seems I had an endless supply of ideas and artwork.

My mother, Jackie, owns a large art gallery in Dallas, Texas. She's constantly bringing items up to spruce up my house. One day, I was shopping for some knick knacks at an antiques mall with Danielle; when she and I noticed a booth available for rent. It gave me an idea. With a three hundred dollar deposit and two boxes of picture hangers, I stripped the walls of my house and filled up the newly rented space. Everything sold out in one weekend and I was in business.

Let me tell you, businesses take on a life and personality of their own. Pretty quickly, it crowded out a lot of other activities in my life. Fortunately, Lolly knew how to do a lot of the hard work. She worked at my house three days a week as a nanny/assistant. Since she lived 120 miles away, she spent the night Tuesday through Thursday. Almost every night we worked with the paintings and the frames. Filling orders, repairing frames, organizing the growing gallery in my rented booth and a second location in my basement. I'd already taken over the garage with my frame stock. Steve was not pleased, but he liked the extra income; it was sometimes upwards of seven thousand dollars a month. Not bad for a small business.

Business stayed vigorous over the years, until the last six months. The expenses were a lot higher when I moved into the new gallery. With Ruth's help, I believed we would quickly return to my previous success.

Ruth listened patiently to my story. She'd heard bits and pieces of it before. Now it felt important to share everything again, if we were going to be partners. I had helped her pick out several paintings for her house, some of which were featured in an article in a local magazine, which did a piece on her and Ira as up and coming young art collectors. *At least she was interested in the art world. And don't artists dress outrageously? Maybe she really is the perfect person to be involved.* This inner dialogue was evolving during a natural lull in our conversation.

"Ruth, I have an idea!" I broke the comfortable silence; flying through the clouds must have triggered my creativity.

"What is it?"

"Why don't we create a marketing campaign where we host monthly gallery events with featured artists, and a percentage of the proceeds goes to a local charity. We can use their mailing lists to invite the guests; in return, the charity gets a donation. The amount they receive will be a percentage of the sales generated during the night. We'll call it "The Art of Giving."

"Jenna, you're brilliant. Love that idea, it's what we already do," Ruth was enthusiastic.

"As soon as we get back, you need to get me all of your mailing lists. Let's try to start something in April. We are going to have a ton of new merchandise."

I could hardly wait to show her the exposition. It's hosted at The Center in Manhattan. The variety and volume of artwork available is amazing. Thousands of artists from across the world attend and exhibit at this annual event. The vendors I frequent are generally in the back of the convention hall. Since their work is not considered original by the standards of the art world; they are the bastards at this family reunion.

"I can't believe the size of this place! It's amazing!" Ruth looked like an excited little girl.

Ruth's wide-eyed gaze swept the entire span of the convention center, her jaw slack, as she digested the extent of the exhibition. Most of the vendors were still setting up tables, installing partitions, and creating their displays. We walked the distance to the back of the grand hall. I could tell Ruth's fur coat was getting heavy. She was dragging it on the floor behind her, like a brave carries his kill back to camp.

"Ruth, it looks like we are a little early here. Do you want to go to the hotel, check in, unload our heavy bags, and maybe go do something in the city for a while? I think after lunch it will be better; it's only ten a.m., no one seems to be ready."

"I love that idea!"

"Here, let me help you carry your coat," I picked up the hide and slung it over my shoulder.

"Thanks, Jenna," Ruth looked relieved. At five foot two, the coat was overwhelming for her. At over five foot nine, it was not much for me to handle, just itchy and disgusting to touch.

The W Hotel was everything I'd remembered. Sleek, sophisticated and clean; it felt a million miles away from my "mom life" of peanut butter and jelly sandwiches, dirty clothes and randomly discarded toys. We decided to share a room with two queen beds; the three hundred dollars saved on a second room would buy us six more paintings.

The décor was tone-on-tone chocolate with accents of silvery sage blue. The front desk receptionist was tickled by our excitement and gave us a high floor with a "to die for" view. A stark blue winter sky offset the grey and black skyscrapers crowding for my attention. A smattering of flurries drifted across the vista, glittering in the sunlight like shards from a pulverized martini glass.

Hello again, New York! I said to myself.

My "now-discarded-former-TV-career" self met both my husband and my agent here a lifetime ago. I knew the city well.

The cold air blasted us in the face as we exited the lobby and turned the corner onto Park Avenue. I'd forgotten about the way the buildings shield you from the weather on one side and create a wind vortex on the other. It felt like a high-powered hair dryer tricked out for cryogenics aimed at my face. I hope my nose still exists. At best, I realize I will be wearing snot icicles. I hunker down and begin to walk to the corner in hope of hailing a cab to who knows where. Survival kicks in as I fight the blistering frigid elements, Ruth needs to follow or be left behind.

"Jenna, I am so done with this coat and it's not even lunch. Let's go to Bloomingdale's!" We'd ducked into the first available cab with no destination in mind.

"That's the best idea I've heard today, Ruth. I don't think I can walk around in this weather!"

I brush my nose with my glove as it starts to thaw in the heat of the cab. *Boogers and Bloomingdale's don't mix.* The cab pulls up to the revolving doors at the front of the store. A quick dash deposits us in the heart of the handbags and cosmetics departments.

"Where are the furs?" Ruth asks the security guard who gave her an amused once over and pointed to the store directory.

Row after row of coats hung on wheeled racks lining the hallway outside the fur salon. Colorful sheared beaver jackets dyed red, blue, and even purple hung on a pipe rack, outrageously loud even in their quiet, crowded retail repose. Next was row after row of mink coats, sheared, natural, long, or short, the options were delicious.

"You can never tell until you try it on, dear." The soft, feminine voice of the sales clerk matched his thin, well-tailored appearance. He had moved in behind me as I longingly stroked the beautiful soft mocha fur of a funky jacket. I had no intention of buying a coat today. If I put one on, it would be all over. My half-hearted will power was already a puny match for my growing desire. In a few more minutes, my intuition told me will power would be throwing in the towel.

A large sign above the coats stated "Up to 75% off" in bold red letters. It was repeated again and again on each rack, as if granting us permission. That kind of discount is a powerful justification for retail misdemeanors. However, in my house, a several thousand dollar purchase, without prior permission, was more like a retail felony.

"What do you think of this one?"

Ruth was doing her little dance in a cognac colored jacket similar in style to the one I was wearing. It was reversible, with a microfiber fabric on one side and sheared dyed beaver fur in a matching color on the other side. A jaunty sash cinched the stylish jacket around her thin waist.

"You look amazing!"

"I can't believe how lightweight these coats are! I feel like I have been wearing my kid's backpack full of books, in comparison."

"I'm definitely buying this one. It's only five grand! It used to be fourteen thousand!" Ruth's casual concept of money always throws me off balance.

Funny, that's the exact same amount the contractor bid to refinish my master bathroom. My inner struggle continued. *What do I need more, a toilet that works or a fur coat?* Will power was working hard here. Then I slid my arm into the silk-lined sleeve of a gorgeous, heavily discounted sable. The luxurious marriage of fur and silk rested lightly on my shoulders, draping just below my knees. Suddenly the answer was clear... a fur coat!

I looked at the price tag with apprehension and fear. Hopefully, the one I like is closer to seventy-five percent off. Forty-seven hundred dollars was written in red ink. The die was cast. With a combination of cash and a few different credit cards, I could pull this off. My Bloomingdale's account was paid off, quietly waiting like a butler to be put into service again.

Once committed to this the course of action, it seemed harmless to try on a variety of coats. Why even stay restricted to the sales racks at this point? We are only having fun.

Ruth selects a rare chinchilla couture piece. Twenty-eight

thousand --- on sale! The whisper-soft white, grey and black pelts descended to the floor on her petite frame.

"Do you want to try?"

"No, thanks, this Russian red sable looks interesting," I look at the price, eighteen thousand dollars; it's on sale. I'm wearing my new kitchen and it feels so glamorous. Before long, the four thousand dollars we were each spending felt like a paltry amount in comparison to what we were trying on.

"I've decided I am going to buy two coats!"

"You've got to be kidding, Ruth," I was thunderstruck.

In the span of 24 hours, Ruth had traveled the expanse from her mother in-laws cast off coat to the confidence to pick up a duo of the latest fur couture. *Was this retail therapy at its finest expression, or retail revenge?*

"No, I am totally serious. These prices are great. You need to get a second coat, too," Ruth extended her future net of buyer's remorse to include me. I was tempted to jump in.

I did not want to fess up that the first one was a stretch, in a big way. I think Ruth has always believed that we are more affluent than we really are. I've never done anything to correct this assumption. The illusion seems to serve its purpose.

"I really don't need one. Besides, winter is pretty short where we live."

"You must get one. We need to treat ourselves. We'll buy them as year-end bonuses to treat ourselves for a job well done. I'll pay and the business can pay me back later, " Ruth looked determined.

"We've only been in business together for a week," I laughed. I was warming to the idea. If I can conceal it from Steve, and not hear the grief; I'm more inclined to acquiesce. We were having so much fun, in a strange way it seemed right.

"I like this sheared mink in chocolate brown with the hood. What about that elegant black mink for you, the one with the versatile collar?" Ruth was closing in on her selections.

"I do love the black, but I don't really need it," I offered weakly.

I did really like that one too. It was dressier than the one I selected. I was trying to be pragmatic and pick something casual that I could wear more frequently. As if pragmatism and fur coats can exist in the same space.

"Clerk, ring these three up." She grabbed the discarded black mink from where I had left it on the back of the salon settee.

"We also need to get monograms in the linings," Ruth announced.

I picked a pink threaded capital "J" with "Jenna" embroidered in script beneath. Ruth selected the same color and design.

"Ruth, what if the business doesn't perform. I may not be able to swing the coat," I said, already feeling guilty about buying what I knew was an excessive amount of luxury items.

"Oh, Jenna, don't worry," she shrugged nonchalantly, "I'll probably just give it to you as a gift. It's really no big deal."

I thought about the "they are worth millions" conversation I had with Libby awhile back and realized she was probably telling the truth. We were having a great time, why ruin it.

The clerk, thrilled with our spending binge, allowed us to leave our "old dogs" behind and wear our new pets for the rest of our trip. We only needed to return to Bloomie's on the way to the airport to drop them off for monogramming and shipping. Shipping is a big retail trick on expensive items; it saves hundreds of dollars in exempt sales tax. Sales tax on four fur coats totaling twenty-three thousand dollars would be close to two thousand dollars. *This savings was more money we could spend on art.* The thought helped me justify our extravagance.

At exactly one-fifteen, the cab deposits us in our new glamour back in front of The Center. We quickly place the necklace vendor badges over our heads and rush to the tables in the back. "First pick" is too important to miss.

"Hi, Jenna," Eddie Chow greets me with a warm hug as we approach his booth.

"I already pulled several of my best pieces for you."

"Thanks, you're a doll. This is my new business partner, Ruth."

"Any friend of Jenna's is a friend of mine. Nice to meet you, Ruth, let me know if you two need anything. I have your pile over here."

Eddie Chow and I had been business friends for years. Half of his family lives in the states, the rest in China. This makes it easy for him to secure the best selection right out of the studios. He's one of my top suppliers; over the years, I have purchased thousands of paintings from him.

The paintings are flat canvases stacked high in piles on top of banquet tables. They are divided by standard sizes: two by three feet, four by five feet, etc. This standardization allows for cooperation between the frame suppliers and the oil painting industries, which are situated half a globe apart.

"Ruth, the strategy I use is to flip through the piles quickly and pick what catches my eye on first impression. Then I go back through that stack and narrow down my selections." She nods at me in understanding. This amount of "shopping" definitely feels like work.

"We need to take off our coats, there's a lot to look at."

Pretty quickly we get into it. It's fun to look at all of the vibrant images: lush landscapes, pastures full of sheep, Old World portraits, crowded marketplaces in European villages, even a few abstracts and a handful of contemporary still life paintings catch my eye. We expeditiously travel from table to table in an effort to get "first pick" from as many vendors as possible. The big show opens to the public tomorrow. Then everyone has access. There are other art dealers here on the same mission. One of them, a middle aged scarlet red headed gal, dressed in a rhinestone-studded denim jacket, gives me the "evil eye" across the table. I smiled pleasantly at her and nodded. People take this stuff way too seriously.

I have noticed Ruth has a tendency to pick pastel colors. This is not so good. Over the years, I've observed that bolder primary colors -- strong combinations of red, blue, yellow and green -- attract more buyers. Here's the partnership's first obstacle. How do I manage her taste without offending her completely?

"Ruth, would you like to sort through this pile and narrow it down to what we want to buy?"

I absolutely love this piece! It's so fun." She holds up a painting of a monkey dressed in a red dress with a bowl of fruit on its head.

I laugh. *Is she joking? Or is her taste in clothing about to invade my gallery?*

Ruth doesn't laugh, she places the painting in the "buy" pile and moves to the next piece.

I guess we'll just buy what she likes; in the end it all sells. I resign myself. We can always donate it. Before long, we have amassed four hundred and thirty paintings totaling a whopping $32, 000. We'll be paying this off all year, plus I still wanted to buy some frames, and that would be at least seven to ten thousand. In all the years I've come to Art Bonanza, I've never spent more than twelve thousand dollars total.

"Do you think we should spend this much money, Ruth?' I wanted to slow us down a bit, but I didn't know how.

"We're here, aren't we? Besides, the gallery looks really depleted."

"I just want to make sure that we are committed to being in the gallery. Trust me, this will be a lot of inventory to manage."

"If I have to come every day for the rest of the month, I'll be there," Ruth gives me a determined stare.

Again, I thought about my "millions" conversation with Libby. *Could the business grow to a new level with Ruth as a partner? Maybe we needed the extra inventory?*

"Jenna, are we done with the gallery yet? I want to walk the show and look for some things for my new house."

Ruth finds and orders another ten pieces to be shipped home to her house for her personal collection. She is thrilled with the "gallery owner" discount, which is generally fifty percent off the listed retail price.

"Ira is going to kill me!" Ruth chuckles. "I just spent another twelve thousand."

By now I'm feeling some major buyer's remorse. I'm even remorseful over what she bought. Suddenly, I am exhausted.

"Ruth, let's go back to the room and rest for a while before our dinner reservations tonight and the cocktail reception at The Studio."

"Don't forget our coats, Jenna. We left them under Eddie's table," *Oh yeah, the coats.* This made our total purchases for the day over fifty thousand, I realize almost choking over the lump of fear now forming in my throat.

The bed in the hotel is one of those "heavenly beds" with the feather down puff on top, the silky six hundred thread count sheets, and a tower of fluffy down pillows. It embraces me as I stumble and collapse, nestling into the pillows. I need a little escape.

"Jenna, it's six thirty. Should we get dressed for dinner?"

Ruth's voice penetrates my dreamless state. I look over at her as she is getting dressed. I did not realize I had fallen asleep.

She then pulled on a pair of ancient once-white-now-dingy-grey cotton briefs, their saggy, shapeless form pulled up beyond her navel.

Before I could edit myself, I blurted, "Ruth, what's up with the underwear?"

She looks at me mystified, "What do you mean?"

"Oh, nothing, I just expected a color or something." I've always believed that underwear says something about our self-esteem. How we feel about our bodies and ourselves. Dingy drawers don't indicate a state of well being. I was beginning to see that Ruth was a series of contradictions.

Dinner was a blast. Ruth made a reservation for us at a French bistro in midtown with an enormous gourmet cheese counter. We ordered a cheese course, ate cheese soup, and purchased a selection of cheeses to take home. A friend of Ruth's met us for drinks before the gallery event and asked if we were "fur coat salesmen." Our new, almost matching, sheared minks must have made a statement.

The red wine, martinis, and champagne hit us pretty hard. We were giggling and drunk not far into the reception at The Studio. Liquor is a modern day truth serum.

"Jenna, you know Ira is such a neat freak?" Ruth slightly slurs her words.

"I wish Steve was. He's a stinky pig sometimes," I giggle at my candor.

"No, seriously," Ruth grabs my arm, "He spends thirty minutes a day grooming himself."

"Ruth, that's obvious, look at his hair."

"No, Jenna, his pubic hair."

"Shut up, Ruth!" I burst out laughing and she joins me. We almost collapse on the floor.

"Yes, he stands in front of the mirror with scissors and a comb." Convulsions of mirth roll through me.

"He even insisted that a magnifying mirror with an extension bar be installed on the main mirror, and he uses my blow-dryer."

"Stop, Ruth, you're killing me!" I'm slapping my leg now.

"No, I can't stop Jenna, there's more." Ruth looks at me intently. Her pupils are black pools.

"What could there possibly be?"

"He makes me lick his, you know--backside."

"No way!" The laughter abruptly dies from my body. I feel a little sick.

"You don't do it, do you?"

"Yeah, it's not that big of a deal. I'm used to it."

"Oh yeah, Ira has entire lists and elaborate charts created of how he likes things to be. He keeps them taped up inside the cabinet doors. We all earn stickers for completed chores, even me." I wonder if she earns stickers for the act she just confessed, but I was too embarrassed to ask.

"That sounds a little extreme." I'm getting a little uncomfortable with the conversation. Ruth and I are friends, but now it appears we've crossed over into the realm of confidantes. It's an unwelcome development.

"Well, listen to this, Jenna. When I was pregnant with my fourth child, Ira found out it was another girl. That would mean four girls for us, and he was planning on a son. He gave me an ultimatum. Get an abortion or I'm divorcing you."

"What choice did I have?" Ruth shrugged.

I didn't respond. I already knew the head count at Ruth's house: three girls and... a boy. I thought about my friend Danielle and her heart-breaking unsuccessful in vitro fertilization attempts, a total of seven times. It was so painful. I had offered to be a surrogate mother, but she declined. Suddenly, I didn't feel much like partying. This conversation was a "buzz kill."

"We should go, Ruth. We have to get up early and coordinate all of the shipping for our purchases."

Chapter 33

"Hey, Libby. I haven't heard from you in awhile," I left a message on her cell phone. I'd been really busy at the gallery since the trip to New York.

It had been almost a week since our last phone conversation. This was a big change over the last few months from the hourly cell phone updates of the past few years. Honestly, it's a welcome change. The play-by-play chatter of a disintegrating marriage, even if it is not your own, is draining.

She called back a few hours later. "Well, I thought you might want a break," Libby offered, sounding a little guilty, "I've been talking to Don more. He is going through the same thing with his divorce, so we've been leaning on each other for support."

Not exactly, I thought to myself. The similarities between Don and Libby end with the fact that they are both going through a divorce. Beyond this commonality, Don is an aggressive fighter and Libby is a bleeding victim. Ultimately, every fighter needs someone to wound and every victim wants a savior. This has the potential to end poorly.

After the trip to Mexico, I expected Don to be different somehow. I mean, you hear stories about people almost losing their lives; when they survive, they are inspired to go out to complete acts of public service, ultimately making the world a better place for all. The near-drowning of Don has had a different effect. He is now more inspired to complete acts of personal service, making the world a better place for him. He still does not think it was an angel who rescued him. In fact, that part has completely slipped from his mind.

It's becoming clear to me Libby is always looking for a set of fresh ears to hear her story.

Chapter 34

Later that month, the art arrived from New York. The gallery was packed so full, we could barely move around. Fortunately, I was able to convince my gallery manager to stay with the business. Lisa Wells is always a big help; the gallery is her life. She even kept working for me when I could not pay her for two months during a really slow time. After the trip to New York, sometimes I regret not selling the business to her. She loves it, and because of her loyalty, she probably deserves to own it.

Canvases were everywhere. We had the frame supplier stretch all 430 canvases over wooden bars so they would be ready for customers. This takes up a lot of space.

It was worse than when I moved locations after the baby was born; at least then the inventory was priced and coded. Ruth had been scarce lately, but I figured she was waiting for the paintings.

"Jenna, I'm here." I glance at the clock. She's two hours late and she has two of her kids with her.

"Hi, Ruth. Can you stay awhile? We really need to count and price everything."

"I have about an hour. One of the girls has dance practice," Ruth is forever prioritizing our business behind her activities.

"Here's a marker. Write the date we bought the painting and the price we paid backwards on the wood bars. I'll make the retail prices." Ruth grabs a chair and gets ready to sit down.

"Ruth I've been thinking. We may want to start planning our Art of Giving marketing program with the charities. There is a lot of inventory here and we will need some events to move our new merchandise." I wanted to see her original enthusiasm return for the business. My intuition told me she had already lost interest, but I did not want to believe it. "When would you like to sit down and plan our first event?"

"Let's get this party started..." blares on her ring tone.

"Hi, Doll! Hold on, let me step outside." She covers the phone, "Jenna, keep an eye on the kids?" She winks at me.

Whatever, I say to myself.

I just keep on coding. It will go faster if I do it myself.

"Aaarg...uh, uh." The little boy starts swinging punches at his sister. One lands on her thigh.

"Screech. OOOOOwwww. I'm telling Mom."

Ruth's two kids start pushing each other in middle of the crowded gallery.

A chain reaction starts. A stack of bumped paintings tumbles forward, crashing into the side table holding all of the new lamps. Two of the lamps tumble to the ground, shattering.

The kids are still squabbling and Ruth is outside on the phone.

"Break it up, kids. Stop it!" I yell. That little fight just cost us $100 of new inventory.

They look at me, frozen for a millisecond, and then the youngest one pinches his sister. She promptly starts her waterworks again.

"Ruth, sorry to interrupt." I walk outside and tap her on the shoulder.

She places her hand over the phone, slightly annoyed at being interrupted.

"Why don't you come back tomorrow without the kids?"

"Okay, Jenna, whatever you want," she snips at me.

I walk back inside and start to clean up. There is too much to do to try and figure out what's wrong with her. A few days later, Ruth's carpool nanny, Angie, shows up with instructions from Ruth to help us code everything. Within the week, everything was completed.

"Here, Ruth said I should give this to you." Angie hands me an envelope.

I take the paper from inside. It's an invoice for $725.00. I look at her, flabbergasted.

"Ruth pays me thirty-five dollars an hour to do organizational stuff. This falls in that category. She said the business would give me a check today."

"Alright, Angie, if that's what Ruth says." I write her a check and call Ruth on the cell phone.

"Ruth, I thought you were going to come in to the gallery and help with all of the new paintings."

"Sorry, Jenna, I had Pilates three times this week and I needed to clean out my closets. My mother is coming to visit."

"Gloria called. We need to get into her office and finish up on the contract papers on the business. Also, we should sit down and talk about some logistics. I just had to write Angie a check for $725.00."

"Don't worry, I'll open a line of credit for the business at my bank and I'll bring the papers over for you to sign later. Also, I think I'm going to have Angie cover my shift this Saturday."

"Do I have to pay her $35 an hour?"

"It's only once."

I'd better not tell Lisa, or she will surely walk out. I think I am going to need her more than ever.

Chapter 35

In the three months that followed, there were several shorter weekend jaunts to a variety of places: California, Jamaica, Key West, and Sedona. Steve and I were always invited as friends. What we really were is "front men." Libby wanted to appear to be traveling as our guest.

Steve and I were the white knights charging in to rescue her from her evil cheating husband. We had to take her somewhere every weekend that Blake had the kids. At least this was Don's plan. He was focused on wooing her, whatever the cost or inconvenience.

I don't know if Libby ever considered that we travelled only twice a year all the time we were couple friends. It was cause for suspicion. Libby did not want Blake to learn about her relationship with Don. She was worried about the impact of a relationship with another man on her divorce with Blake and the size of the settlement she was hoping to receive.

The first few trips were fun, like Mexico. Then it started to get weird. Don wanted to be alone with Libby. Libby refused to travel anywhere with Don unless we came along. Their relationship was now comprised of all night phone conversations about their divorces, exotic weekend trips and occasional weekday sex, while the kids were in school.

Every weekend Libby was without the kids, Don purchased a pair of first class tickets just in case Libby would agree to go somewhere alone with him. Most of the time, the tickets went unused, their thousand dollar fares non-refundable. Don was trying everything in his bag of tricks to win over Libby. Libby enjoyed the sport.

Meanwhile Ronnie was livid with me. She felt I had introduced Don and Libby as some kind of matchmaking ploy that was further destroying their marriage. Once again, I could not win in this situation.

"Jenna, you are never going to believe what happened." Libby called me on the cell phone.

"Tell me." The daily dramas in Libby's life were entertaining, if nothing more.

"I was at Don's this afternoon and someone came and started banging on the door." She suppressed a girlish giggle.

"Did you answer it?"

"No way. We hid on the stone floor of the kitchen. Don's condo has so many windows and I could see a woman with her face pressed against the glass looking around. I think it was Ronnie. She was shouting at the top of her lungs. I thought one of the neighbors might call the police." I was a little annoyed.

Rhonda was still considered family, divorced or not. Even though she has not spoken to me since Christmas. Even if I did set them up, it was not intentional. Libby and Don both need to grow up and stop searching for their pirated youth in each other's pants.

"Why would you hide from her like a mistress, Libby? They are separated." *I would have just answered the door like an adult.*

"Well, I don't know, but the kitchen floor was the only spot not visible from the windows. We were lying there on the floor half naked and laughing. She caught us getting a snack after an afternoon romp." Libby was entertained by the sport of it all. "And get this, Amber Atkins is now calling my house and hanging up the phone once I answer. Sometimes, she will whisper *"BITCH"* in a deranged voice." This sent her into laughing spasms.

"Of course Amber is pissed. Someone else is getting the candy from her sugar daddy." I offer an explanation of the obvious. "Libby, have you ever considered that this situation is a mess? Don's wife is now stalking you! His mistress is prank calling you! You have your own divorce, your own kids, at what point is it all too overwhelming? It seems like a lot of unnecessary drama to me."

"Oh, Jenna, did you hear about the Cunningham family at school? He had an affair with his wife's best friend, Gretchen Davis, and she got pregnant; now they are getting married. Beth Cunningham then had an affair with Kim Winter's husband and broke up that marriage. The problem being Kim and Beth are sharing room parents' duties this year for the fourth grade. I wonder how that situation will untangle itself." Libby always has a juicy piece of gossip available to justify her actions. There is always someone else out there whose life is crazier than hers.

Chapter 36

"**B**ang, bang, bang."

"Earl, can you ask your guys to keep it down, my baby is trying to take a nap. There is a hammer ban between one and three every day! Remember?" I shouted an irritated reminder to Earl Hale, the general contractor on our remodel project.

"It's nap time, damn it!" Mia started to stir in the other room; apparently the sound of my voice woke her up.

"Jenna, sorry about that. We're running behind schedule and I want to get caught up this week. I have a line of jobs waiting for me."

"I'm sure you do, Earl, but I'm your wife now, without the benefits. You're not going anywhere until you are done with *my* list." I looked at him and laughed. When we are younger, we want hot studs that can nail us against a wall; now all I want is a guy who can find a stud and hang drywall.

Earl is a nice guy. He's laid-back, fifty-something with salt-and-pepper hair and a Harley Davidson ponytail braid. The stress of construction seems to roll off his back.

"I want you out of here as well. Trust me! But there have to be some limits. Hammering all day long is beyond them." My sanity was already stretched to its limits, as well as my budget. We're three months into this project and there have been many unpleasant discoveries. Like the fact that all of my radiators have holes in them and need to be removed, actually cut from my house with a chain saw. Also, the sewage pipes under the concrete floor in the basement have disintegrated. Apparently back in the day these pipes were made of clay, so basically we are living in a pile of slushy shit. Earl's workers are nice enough, but they don't believe in deodorant. My entire job site smells like the inside of a gym bag. Every night before going to bed I have to shake off the layer of dust that has settled on my sheets. *I never realized a hundred and fifty year old house could need so many upgrades and repairs.*

Faith has taught me that when you remodel a house you remodel your life. It sounds strange but there is a link. For example, when you replace your plumbing, you are working on your emotions; when you rewire you electrical, you are rewiring your viewpoints; and when you paint the exterior you're coloring others perceptions of you.

"Jenna, can you come in the kitchen for a second? I need your opinion on these cabinets," Earl called to me from the other room. While attempting to navigate through my crowded hallway, I tripped over a pile of dusty boxes and scattered building supplies. *This mess is getting out of hand.*

It's time to clean the house, a feat as successful as shoveling sand in a windstorm. Don made plans with Steve to come over and see the remodel and then go out for a drink. He says he has a big announcement to make. I hope we are getting our restaurants soon. Don mentioned it to Steve a few months ago, before the trip to Mexico. I think it was a bribe to make us go along with his plans. Months later, we have yet to see any legal documents concerning the transfer of the assets. I think he's been distracted by his divorce and his harem.

"Do you know when you'll be ready to hang cabinets in the kitchen? I'm tired of living out of the dining room and eating micro waved food off paper plates."

"Soon, Jenna. Maybe next week."

"I'm not convinced, Earl, but I have no choice."

"Oh, and by the way, go ahead and tear out all of the tile and plumbing fixtures in the other three bathrooms. Steve and I have decided we only want the inside of our house torn up once."

"I think you are smart about that, but it will keep us here on the job a month longer."

"I'm aware, Earl. I'm aware."

Chapter 37

The thick envelope landed with a soft thud on the small mosaic table at Adonis's Greek Bistro. Nearby a scantily clad belly dancer dressed in lemon yellow chiffon undulated to the exotic bouzouki music. Her tiny wrist and ankle bells jingled purposefully with each pelvic thrust. I wonder why Don chose this place for drinks. It's fun, if you enjoy a carnival act. But the food is excellent. I must admit the saganaki, or "flaming Greek cheese" made from sheep's milk is otherworldly. It's doused in some Greek liquor [ouzo] then set aflame tableside with an announcement of "Opa!"

"Go ahead! Open it up!" Don was smiling like the Cheshire cat, again. *I've seen this smile before. He must be up to something. It's the smile of the "grand gesture." Is it the contracts? Please, please let it be the contracts to buy the restaurants.*

Steve was reading my mind. "Dad, I was wondering when you were going to get around to drafting the contracts to buy the restaurants." Steve sounded hopeful, even a little pitiful.

"Just open it up, Steve." *I knew right then. It was not the contracts.*

Steve removed a folder with a photograph of a brilliant blue sky offset against a row of crisp white buildings. I at once made the connection with the Greek restaurant.

"We're going to Greece!" Don shouted with enthusiasm.

"Who's going to Greece? You and Libby? You and Ronnie and

the kids? Who?" I was shocked and unnerved. *How could he mean us, we have not even been asked. I guess the puppet master doesn't need to ask the marionette' permission before the performance.*

"All of us, except Ronnie of course."

"Libby's mom is a travel agent. She found us this trip and we're going this summer; you and Steve, the kids, Libby and her kids and me. I hope Gabrielle and Jack will go along too, but right now we are not speaking. At least, they aren't speaking to me."

"Don, if you want to go on a trip with Libby to Greece, just take Libby to Greece. You don't need seven additional chaperones. Do you? Why do you want us along?"

"It will be fun! Beside, Libby can't go with the divorce and all, unless she is travelling with you and Steve." The reasoning of this was absurd. I was certain Blake had figured out about Libby's relationship with Don by now.

We had traveled together a handful of times already this year. Her two boys must have said something about the dark-haired man who acts like Santa Claus delivering gifts all of the time. I'd never know anyone to engage in "travel-dating" before. Whatever happened to a nice dinner, movies, and tickets to a show, an afternoon picnic, and ultimately sex after a month or two of these shared experiences? Instead it's a weekend in Cancun; private sailing charters; spring break with children and a nanny in Jamaica; a weekend in Napa Valley; hot air balloon rides; a spa in Sedona; always first class tickets and first class accommodations. *Now we are all leaving the country for two and a half weeks in August? Eleven people on a group date, spanning the globe to accommodate two people who want to have sex in a luxurious setting.*

"Jenna, I actually need your help with something. The ship is sold out and we were only able to get half of our group on board. You and Libby need to keep calling every day to check for cancellations."

"You want to go on a cruise?" This shouldn't surprise me, but it did. "Perhaps it's a sign this is not meant to be." Don knows about my spiritual beliefs. It's a source of amusement for him. *I believe that it's important to follow the flow of energy and not force things that are blocked. Often a closed door is closed for our own protection, or to prompt us to seek an alternative course.* I could hear Faith in my head.

"I don't believe that. If anyone can make it happen, you can."
Don is always complimenting me on my assertiveness. It's
something he admires about me. I think it's only a remnant left over
from my years as a news reporter. Passive people get passed over for
the top stories, a cardinal sin in the bible of news coverage.

"Here are the details. There's a boat leaving Barcelona, which
travels through Florence, Rome, the Greek Isles of Santorini and
Mykonos, then on to Athens, Ephesus and a few other places. It's a
total of eleven days. Then I thought we could stay in Paris or Italy a
few days on either side of the trip."

Wow! The itinerary took my breath away. I've never been to
many of these places. Steve and I spent our honeymoon in Florence
and Rome and we absolutely loved it. That was almost a decade ago;
it would be nice to see it again and take the kids. The Greek islands!
I am speechless. This is fantasy material. The only problem is, it is
someone else's fantasy, and I feel like a madam.

I look at Steve, who can barely conceal his disappointment. This
dinner was supposed to be his trip to independence; no destination is
as sweet as that. But it's not an option, and the one in front of me is
hard to resist.

"Let me see what I can do. I'm sure Libby can figure something
out." We said good night and walked towards our car.

"Thanks for the invitation." I waved as Don drove off in his sleek
new silver 700 series Mercedes convertible. Steve said he paid close
to one hundred and fifty thousand dollars for the toy, a cash wire sent
directly to the dealership from the company's bank account. It's a
luxurious company car to use for visiting a bunch of taco stands.
Steve was quiet the rest of the evening and on the way home. I could
feel his disappointment over the contents of the envelope. Finally, in
the driveway, he voiced what I'd been worried about for months.

"Jenna, I don't think my dad is ever going to sell me any
restaurants. I think he only tells me what he knows I want to hear, so
I will keep pushing his agenda." He leaned against the car, dejected.

"I have to admit sweetheart, it doesn't look very promising. The
track record is not very good." I leaned next to him, resting my head
on his shoulder and lacing my fingers through his. "We will find a
way to make your dreams come true." He squeezed my hand. Steve's
pain was my pain. That's the way it is sometimes.

Chapter 38

"Jenna, did Don tell you?" Libby excitedly cornered me in the parking lot of Sycamore Creek after morning drop off.

"Last Summer, the Kaplan's and the Smiths traveled to Greece for a grand summer adventure. I've been so jealous ever since. So, when Don and I were talking about where I'd like to visit, naturally I mentioned the Greek Islands. I never dreamed we'd be going there in a few months."

"Whoa! Hold on Libby, I'm not sure this trip is coming at a good time for me. I'm renovating my house and, as the general contractor, I need to be there on the job site every day to supervise. Plus, I have a new business partner, Ruth Simons. You must remember, we just returned from New York. She has not been around much yet for her training."

"Ruth, Ruth, I'm so tired of hearing her name. You know I don't like the woman. She's ugly and bizarre. The only thing she has going for her is her rich husband." Libby has acted jealous ever since Ruth agreed to be my partner.

"Besides, you should have made me your partner anyway. I'm the one with the art degree. Why didn't you ask me?" Out it came. The unspoken animosity of the last few months tumbled to the ground like a pile of volcanic stones sitting between us.

I knew Libby was upset with me about something, but I couldn't put my finger on it. Now I guess I know the truth, but it surprises me.

"Libby, you've told me time and time again that you don't want to work." I tried to conceal my frustration with calmness. "Trust me, owning your own business is a lot of work."

"Jenna, I know and let's just forget it. You and Ruth, it just makes me feel strange. Like you like her more than me. But I don't want to talk about that right now. "

OK, are we in high school again? I haven't been engaged in a feline territory spat in about two decades. The stress of the divorce must be taking its toll.

"It's just business."

Libby cut me off; then stomped her foot like a petulant child, "Business, business. I can't think about that right now. I have to heal myself. This divorce has shattered me. I need to go on this trip!"

"I understand, Libby, I know this has been difficult for you. But you're not the only person in the world to get divorced. Last I checked its one out of every two marriages." *Maybe a slap of reality will jolt her out of her personal pity party. Attending this party everyday for the last two years was becoming a drag. Beside, I'm running out of gifts to bring. Gifts like kind words, constant consolation and time-eating favors.*

"Libby, I don't think I can do it." *For a lot of reasons: the house, the business, my father-in-law, Steve's business, money.* I left the last part unspoken. I now know conversations with Libby are like using a megaphone directly to Don's ear. She hangs up with me and chats aimlessly with Don about our private affairs and everyone else's. Libby's first language has always been gossip. Honestly, that's what attracted me to her years ago. She seemed to be a real "insider." I thought it was funny to know the inside scoop about people I don't really know.

"Oh Jenna, stop making excuses. I'm going and I can't go without you." Libby was acting more and more like a spoiled child these days.

"That's ridiculous, Libby. Blake is not going to *do* anything. He's already living with his mistress, the nurse with the frosted hair in the aqua colored polyester underwear set. Remember her from the picture you found in his trunk? What does he have to say about anything, if you want to go on with your life? You are separated. Right?"

"My attorney says I need to keep things quiet until the divorce is final. Otherwise Blake might be able to get away with paying me less support."

"Or you could find a job and get some independence that way. Didn't you used to be an art teacher?' I was trying to make helpful suggestions.

"Don't be silly, Jenna. If I get a job now, that will hurt me in the divorce as well."

Libby quickly changed the topic to more entertaining fare. "Besides, did you hear about the Sycamore Creek fund-raising progressive dinner? Mary Beth Carsdale did a strip tease on her diving board while singing karaoke before fifty people. Her house was the last one on the tour and was the designated spot for desserts. Apparently, all of the guys got a taste of her tart." She giggled like a schoolgirl. It was contagious.

"Oh my God, is that true? That is so over-the-top. Were you there?" I couldn't repress a laugh.

"Not exactly, but I plan to be there the next time. I wouldn't dare show up without a date." Libby was aghast.

"I can only imagine the look on everyone's face. Libby, you always know the latest dirt." I was still laughing at the outrageous image. I wasn't even invited to the party. The event sold at the school auction for five thousand dollars and thirty families from the school community were invited. It's always the same group. I was sorry to have missed the spectacle.

"Well, Julie Harris said I could stop by; but I chose not to go." Libby always makes certain everyone knows where she stands in the pecking order. Invitations, accepted or not, to events like the progressive dinner are a telling watermark of social status. I've noticed a lot of people at Sycamore Creek are like Libby, using their cars, clothes and connections to set them a step above everyone else. I was starting to learn the details, but I'm still relatively new to the game.

One thing is certain, my minivan is not turning any heads, and my dustbowl house requires an oxygen mask for visitation. I have some things to work on, if I plan to run with this crowd. But for now, Libby's gossipy anecdotes give me the inside track on who's who. She must talk on the phone all day long to collect all of this information. Every time I see her, there is a new piece of juicy gossip. Libby missed her calling as a society columnist for a newspaper.

"Jenna, please." She grabbed my hand and looked at me with those big, blue eyes. "I need this. You and I, we'll have so much fun. Please say yes!"

"OK Libby," I folded like a house of cards. *Greece with my best friend? Who could ask for more, right?* "But we need to get on the ship first." I still had my doubts, but it was too seductive an offer to pass up. Regardless of the strings attached. Later, I'd learn it was so much more than strings; it was a spider's web.

Victorious, Libby jumped in her BMW after a triumphant hug. "Don't worry, I'll make some calls today! Remember, my family owns a travel agency."

"Let me know if you want me to do something." I waved goodbye.

"I'm meeting Don for lunch at his condo." She shouted from the window of her car.

Ira's car whipped into the space next to where I was standing, this was the first time I had seen him alone face-to-face in months.

"Hi Ira, how have you been? When do you want to come down and see what Ruth and I have been working on?" I felt the need to make polite conversation. He intimidated me.

Ira stepped close into my space and said menacingly, "I just want you to know Jenna; I can pull the plug on your little arts and crafts party in an instant. Ruth plays by my rules." He turned and walked into the school.

I knew Ira was a dark cloud in Ruth's marriage, I hadn't realized until now he was a possible storm in my business.

Chapter 39

My bare feet softly pounded the white sand as I ran down the cliff to meet my friends. I knew I was late, but I was not clear why. The sun was high in the cloudless blue sky. It was radiant, warm, and blinding. I stopped for a moment, closed my eyes and captured its brilliance. The powerful light easily penetrated my eyelids and I felt warmed to my soul.

Along the rocky coastline were unusual trees. They looked like olive trees with their soft, wispy, sage green leaves attached to a grayish twisted trunk anchored in the dehydrated earth. As I rounded the corner, a large hot spring was revealed. Threads of steam drifted across the surface as air and water collided. The spring was about the size of a large pond tucked away lovingly within its stone stronghold.

I quickly made my way down to the waters edge using the twisting pathway of granite stepping-stones anchored haphazardly in the sand. The spring was full of nude bathers, many floating quietly in the healing waters of this sacred spring. I removed my white tunic and joined several friends. They looked familiar. Old friends. We embraced. I settled into the hot waters, relaxing after the initial scalding burn had dulled to soothing, saturating warmth. Floating. Peaceful. Healing.

"Beep, Beep, Beep," The alarm clock sliced through my reverie.

Disoriented, it took a moment to realize where I was, still trapped between the world of dreams and the world of Earth. *God, that seemed so real, so vivid.* I tried to collect the pieces of my experience before it drifted beyond my grasp, as most dreams do. A strange, bittersweet sadness crept over me as I longed to reconnect with my friends. Our reunion was so lucid, so brief. Yet, who were they? I didn't recognize them as anyone I know today.

"MOM, MOM! I have to go to the bathroom." My ponderings were interrupted by my daily reality. My youngest child needed her potty-training assistance.

"I'm coming honey! Hold on." The ice-cold wood floor jolted me to attention, wiping away the last delicious haze of sleep. Oh, winter in an old drafty house: it's hard to get out of bed, but duty calls.

"Mom, I can't hold it anymore!" I run to Mia's room and we rush to the toilet shivering. *I'll be glad when these windows are replaced.* The frigid air hisses through the panes at night. It sounds like demons. Most of the time all of my heat-seeking children end up in our bed. Steve and I serve as bookends, keeping the tomes tightly tucked in. We sleep perilously close to the edge of the mattress in unnatural positions, as our children prefer arms to pillows. We have a joke in our family. Dad is the bread. I am the bread. Lucy is the cheese, Cole is the meat and Mia is the pickle. Together we make a giant sandwich. Sometimes, when we hold each other really tight, we call it a wrap.

"Good morning, sweetheart." My husband and I exchange a quick, stinky, pre-toothpaste kiss.

"I had the strangest dream last night. I think it was about Greece."

"Really, was it a nightmare? " Steve is so sarcastic. It makes me smile. He's also less than impressed by Don's shenanigans.

"No. In fact, it was quite pleasant. Amazing. Really. I think I'm really excited to go now!" And I meant it.

"At least one of us is."

I didn't tell Steve that Libby visits his dad at lunch every day to make a wrap of their own in his king sized bed. He's already less than thrilled with the relationship.

"Guys, come on. Get in the car. We're going to be late." I give my fat Corgi dog, Maverick, a boost into the front seat. It's part of the daily ritual of the Route. Maverick rides shotgun. He loves to lick the gusts of wind from an open window, or eat the invisible stream of air from the air conditioning, whichever is available. I don't get the attraction, but its pure heaven for him.

My dog is my constant companion. I adore him. His oversized ears stick up like a clown's. His long body is low to the ground, supported only by four stubby legs. His soulful chocolate eyes are accentuated by a white blaze, surrounded by black and tobacco colored wavy fur. Finally, Maverick has a tail that is always wagging for my attention. D-O-G is really G-O-D in reverse. I don't recall where I heard that saying, but it applies here.

The cell phone rings. It's Libby.

"Good morning Jenna." She sounds chirpy, like a little bird.

"You sound happy today." I was relieved.

"I found us a boat to Greece!"

"Tell me about it." I still had twenty minutes left on my commute.

"Well, it's on Crystal Cruise lines. It's the royal suite, with a grand piano and a spiral staircase…"

"Wow! Wait a minute, Libby. How much is this cabin?"

"It's only one hundred thousand dollars." The amount rolled off her tongue with ease. *We've come along way since our road trip to Myrtle Beach for a stay at a borrowed condo. Total cost, five hundred dollars for a week's stay.*

"That sounds a little high. What did Don say?" I was trying to keep myself neutral.

"He said money is no object." *It sounds like something he would say to someone he is trying to impress.*

"Did you try anywhere else?"

"Yes, but no luck. The only bummer is that this cabin only takes five people and we still need cabins for the rest of us." *One hundred thousand dollars for us to go on a trip that doesn't included everyone? Where is this money coming from?* I'm speechless. *That's more than half of Steve's salary for the entire year. Not mention the fact that he has trouble receiving that on any regular basis. Don manages the company purse strings to his priorities, most of which are personal.*

"Let me try to book a reservation. I'll call you later."

"Make sure I get the travel agent credit. I need the commission to use on the trip." *No wonder she wanted the royal suite, that's more than ten thousand dollars of commission cash in her pocket.*

"Don't worry, Libby, I'll use your Mom's number, if it works out, so you get the credit."

Seconds after I hung up, the phone rings.

"Jenna, it's Don."

"Hi Don, What can I do for you today?" I know he never calls to chat, so I get right to the point.

"I'm not really sure about Libby's mother and her skills as a travel agent. The cabin Libby found sounds expensive. Can you work on this?"

"Sure, I guess." *How can you afford to take this trip, Don? I thought the business was in trouble.* "Oh, and Jenna, don't say anything to Libby!"

"I'll see what I can do." I knew the money was an issue. The big dog lives in a small house, and he has never liked to share his bones.

Chapter 40

"Faith, I'm so glad to see you."

"Hello, Jenna, dear. How are you today?" Her eyes sparkled with kindness.

As I reached over to give her an embrace, I noticed a slight tremor in her body.

"Are you feeling OK, Faith?"

"Don't you worry, honey, I'm fine. I'm just a little tired today. My mother is sick and I've been caring for her." She eased into her chair with a loud exhale.

"You're such a kind person Faith, listening to everyone else's problems all day. Thank you for helping me with mine." I felt a wave of unexpected emotion well up and lodge in my throat. This woman was so nurturing to me. A total stranger, no blood relation, yet she felt like a mother, a spiritual mother.

"Jenna, you're welcome. But that's who I am, plain and simple. I'm happy to be of service to you. You bring me joy."

"You have no idea, Faith. No idea how much I look forward to our meetings." I reached out to grasp her hand in a warm squeeze. After seven years of sharing stories we had a connection.

"So what would you like to look at today?"

"I'm concerned about this trip to Greece. It troubles me on so many levels. The cost, the people going, the fallout, just everything."

Faith closed her eyes for a few moments and took several deep breaths. I placed my hands on tops of her hands lying on the table, palms facing up. Then she did her mantra. "First let's pull the energy down from the heavens into our hearts and release it. Now let's pull the energy up from the earth and into our hearts and release it. We ask in the name of God that the guidance we are to receive today is for the highest good of all concerned. So be it and so it is." I felt a warm shiver race through my body just before I removed my hands.

"First, I think you are definitely going on the vacation. I can see you in that part of the world on a sandy shore line with olive trees scattered along the coast."

"Oh my God! Faith, that's the dream I had last night. I've never been to Greece, but I sensed that was where I was."

"Jenna, you've been to Greece before. Maybe not in this lifetime, but you've been there many, many times." *I hadn't considered it before. Yet, it felt like she was telling the truth. Everything in my dream was so familiar, so real.*

"Faith, we don't even have a cabin yet, or a hotel room. Everything is sold out and I'm supposed to pull it together like some kind of magician." Stress crept into my voice, making it sound thin and shrill.

"That part will work itself out very quickly. You are meant to take this trip, Jenna. If something is part of the divine plan, it will occur regardless of our efforts. Likewise, if something is not part of the divine plan, it will not occur, regardless of our efforts. The key is to relinquish all effort and allow your life to unfold."

I was silent for a moment as I tried to absorb the wisdom of her words.

"Let's pull a few cards, shall we?"

"Yes, I love the cards."

Faith handed me her Tarot deck and I shuffled it like a casino dealer. I've had many card readings in my life, going back long before I met Faith. You might say I'm addicted.

"Now cut it three times with your left hand and focus on your questions." Faith gently instructed.

I completed her instructions and handed the deck back to her. She flipped the cards over one by one and laid them in a spread called the Celtic cross.

"First, here is the World Card, which signifies you are in fact, taking a trip. It's covered by the Ten of Coins, which tells me it will be a very expensive trip on many levels. There is also the card of The Moon, which tells me there is some deception or lying going on. Things are not what they appear to be on the surface. There is the Ace of Cups, which tells me about a new relationship, but it is next to a card which tells me there are hidden motives. Here is something interesting; in the position of the unknown is the card of The Devil, which tells me about dramas, conflicts, and restrictions, which will come unexpectedly. I'm not sure if this relates to the trip or events surrounding the time of the vacation."

"Should I be worried about the Devil card? It looks kind of scary." *I don't get that card often.*

"Remember, Jenna, all of the cards are symbolic. If you look closely, the people pictured on the card are in chains, but the chains are connected to nothing. The people who appear to be enslaved are actually free to walk away at anytime."

"You mean that when I feel trapped, I may not really be trapped at all." *I have been feeling really trapped lately. It fascinates me the way Faith always seems to provide the messages I need to hear even before I know the questions to ask.*

"Exactly. The message of The Devil tells us that we trick ourselves into believing that we have no options, when we always have many options. Free will is infinite. We can choose to walk away from a situation at any time. When we change our perspective, we change our experience."

"Faith, you've given me a lot to think about today. Thank you."

"You're going to be fine, Jenna. You have a truly good heart. I can see your inner light shining, even though you may not recognize it exists in you at times."

After another warm hug, I left, uplifted. A visit with Faith is like drinking a spiritual smoothie: nutritious for your soul.

Two weeks later after leaving messages daily and working with a coordinator for Royal Caribbean Cruise lines, we were on the ship to Greece and Italy. It was just like Faith predicted, a block of rooms opened up at the last minute at a reasonable rate. We were headed half way around the globe on our "group date", with five children under eight, two nannies, a thousand pounds of luggage and four adults, each with an "itinerary" of their own. *Bon Voyage!*

Chapter 41

"Ruth, hi, it's Jenna."

"Hi, Jenna, what are you up to?" I was learning to recognize her phony happiness.

"Do you have any time to meet? We need to talk about some business stuff."

"Why don't you join me at the country club for lunch and a round of golf this afternoon?"

The dark green golf cart with a golden crest pulls up to my car as I unload my clubs. Ruth is wearing a yellow and green argyle print shirt with a matching skirt. It's loud, but within the appropriate range for golf wear. Her clubs are covered by a variety of stuffed animals. I'd seen things like that at the sporting goods store. I always wondered who buys the stuffed animal club covers; now I know. In contrast, I have on a white Nike polo and a black skort. I borrowed my husband's clubs.

"I'm sorry I've been so crazy the last ninety days. Ira's really been on my case to get the house straightened up. He has a whole new series of charts created and I don't seem to be earning enough stars each day."

"I understand. I just want to make sure we're on the same page. The business needs some attention if we are going to grow. Plus we have a lot of inventory to move." I'm trying to be light-hearted. Things are not working out as I expected.

"I promise, next week I will be in with my address lists and we can plan everything. By the way, I heard you are going on a cruise to Greece and Europe."

"Yes, I'm really excited. We leave in two weeks. I've only visited once before, ten years ago, on my honeymoon."

"Who all is going?"

"Well, it's kind of a long story. But here's the list: my family, Steve's father, two nannies, and my friend Libby Peters and her boys."

"That's a boatload. I've always wanted to take a trip like that."

"Call the agent at World Travel, maybe there is still room on the ship." People are always saying things they don't mean.

The afternoon was pleasant. The country club grounds were soothing. I like being outside. I feel better about Ruth now that we've spent some time together. It's probably my imagination that things are different between us.

"Jenna, do you mind if we stop in the pro shop?"

Inside is a variety of golf clothes and equipment. I find an outfit that looks interesting and take it up to the counter to purchase it. Ruth is looking at a set of clubs for her kids.

"I'm sorry, we don't accept American Express, and only members' accounts are valid here." I place my gold card back in my wallet. I don't really need the clothes. They were just an impulse, maybe next time.

"I'll get it for you, Jenna."

"Thanks Ruth, I can stop at the ATM on the way home if you follow me."

"Rick, just put it under the name "Simon." What is it, only $68.00?" She smiles at me.

"Don't worry Jenna, it's nothing. You bought me lunch a few weeks ago, and there is other stuff. It all evens out."

Chapter 42

"Have you guys left your house yet?" Don was already calling us at five a.m., even though our flight was not scheduled until nine-thirty.

"Good morning, Dad. We will be there. We only need two hours before the flight to check in."

"Ok, Ok. Just don't be late. I'm spending a lot of money on this trip and I don't want you and Jenna to miss the plane." Ever since the reservations were made, Don has not missed an opportunity to tell us how much it cost.

"I hear you, Dad. Let me go so I can get everyone together. We'll see you at the airport."

"I knew we should have passed on this trip. I'm already pissed and we haven't even left the driveway," Steve ground out after hanging up the phone. I smiled at him and pecked him on the cheek.

"Mommy, I don't feel well." Mia padded into our room in her pink fleece footed pajamas.

"Come here, sweetheart. Let me feel your head."

"You're not very warm, so no fever. Perhaps you're just a little sleepy still. Lay here in Mommy's bed, pickle, while daddy and I load the suitcases in the car."

"Ok, Mommy. I love you."

"I love you too, pumpkin. You'll feel better soon. I promise."

"Lucy, Cole, time to wake up guys. We need to get ready to leave for the airport. Hurry. Hurry!" I shouted down the hallway towards their rooms.

The kids bounded out of their rooms, excited. Both went to bed last night wearing the clothes they were planning to wear on the trip. For the last month, we've been searching the internet for facts about Greece and reading books with pictures of all of the cool things to see. Regardless of Don and Libby, I planned to make the most of this trip. Lucy and Cole love to travel. It's in their blood. A day long car ride to Florida, no problem; a two-day ride to Arizona, no biggie; an eight-hour flight to Spain, piece of cake; getting there is part of the fun. Getting out the door of our house was an adventure.

"Jenna, our luggage is not fitting in the car." Steve is outside in the driveway screaming and sweating. "What did you pack?"

"Honestly, I didn't know what to pack. There are all these events on the ship: the black tie dinner, the captain's table, casino night. I don't know, I can't even remember everything right now, and the kids need clothes, too."

"Cut this in half, right now. We are going to be late."

"I don't know what to take out. Libby has all kinds of new clothes she is wearing on the trip." I was over there earlier this week while she packed. Her entire travel ensemble was new, sales tags still attached. I don't think it was a going away treat from Blake.

"Jenna, look at me. No one is going to care what you look like, if you're stuck in the airport because we didn't get on the plane. Pack a paper bag and a bikini for all I care. We need to hurry."

I took out several of my evening clothes. I could always wear the same thing twice or share clothes with Libby. I didn't want to take out stuff for the kids; they need extra outfits in case they get dirty, or wet.

"Mommy, my tummy still hurts." Mia still complained as I changed her into a cozy aqua velour warm-up.

"Try to eat some yogurt, honey. Maybe you are just upset over all of the activity this morning." Sometimes Mia gets stomachaches for no reason. After a while they just go away.

"Come here, sweetie. I'll read you a book while mommy and daddy load the car," Cara, the nanny, offered her lap, which Mia happily accepted.

Cara spent the night so we could all leave together at the same time for the airport. Cara has been with our family since she was a college student. Now she teaches first grade. Usually, she baby-sits on Saturday nights. The kids love her, so we asked if she would like to come on the trip with us, as an extra pair of hands. Cara has family in Italy. She plans to visit them for two weeks after the trip. *I wish I had family in Italy.*

Seven twenty-nine, to be exact, we arrived at the airline counter to check in for the nine thirty international flight to Barcelona, Spain, where the boat embarks. Libby and her two boys arrived at the airport fifteen minutes later. I thought Don might wear a hole in his shoes, the way he was pacing back and forth, until they walked into the terminal. Libby also brought a nanny named Maggie. Maggie has been an after school nanny for Libby since Blake left six months ago.

"Tickets and passports, please." A blonde, uniformed representative from the airlines started the process of checking us in for our flight to New York and connecting flight to Spain. Don and I were standing at the counter managing the process for our entourage.

"Excuse me, may I please see a Ms. Libby Peters at the counter, please."

"Me? Okay." Libby smiled and sauntered up to the agent in her new Chanel outfit and her Jackie O glasses.

"Mrs. Peters, it appears your passport has expired."

"What? There must be some mistake. I thought it was good for at least a month after the date of expiration."

"No, Ma'am. This passport is no longer valid and you will not be permitted to leave the United States or to return without proper identification. Also, it expired in April and it is now July."

I glanced at Don, who was looking at Libby, mouth agape in total disbelief. After all, let's face it, the only reason all eleven of us were there was because he wanted to spend this time with her. The airline tickets, her suite on the cruise ship, the hotels, all of it, nonrefundable.

"Well, I guess I won't go then." Libby looked at all of us defiantly.

At that moment I saw what a child my friend really was. A petulant, spoiled child.

"That's not an option." Don sprung into action. Lust is clearly a more powerful emotion than angst.

"Libby, you are going. We will figure it out no matter what." She smiled back at her knight in shining armor.

"What do you suggest?" He asked the ticket agent.

"Today is Saturday, sir, you could try to go to the passport office on Monday morning in New York City and see if you qualify for same day service. Then catch a later flight out of JFK to meet the ship in one of its ports."

"The next stop for the ship is in Rome on Wednesday," said Don, after looking at the itinerary in his briefcase.

"Let me check the flights to Rome on Monday night." I could hear the keys clicking like chattering teeth.

"You're in luck. We have availability in coach. Although your first class tickets for today are non-refundable, I will allow you to transfer them for twenty-five dollars each. How many tickets do you need?"

I could see a bead of sweat trickling down Don's brow. I felt sorry for him. Dating a woman should not be this difficult.

"We need five: myself, Libby Peters, the two Peters boys and Maggie. Oh, and how much would it cost to fly first class?"

"Well sir, it would be a substantial increase, as there is no advance notice. Let me check availability. Here is the price, seven thousand four hundred dollars, each."

"I'll take them." Don reached in his wallet and pulled out what I recognized was the company credit card and handed it to the agent. The total cost, thirty seven thousand dollars.

"Sir, the cost of the coach tickets is only one hundred and twenty five dollars for all five people. Are you certain that you don't want to take advantage of that option? I see here your previous tickets were only $2,500 each."

"No, I only fly first class."

"As you wish, sir."

Libby was laughing and playing with her kids, oblivious to the reality of her oversight. It just cost the company fifty thousand dollars for Libby and Don to go on a date, thirty-seven thousand for the new tickets and twelve thousand for the unusable tickets. I now had the sinking feeling that every part of this absurd excursion was on the company credit card. This amount didn't even include hotels, the cabins on the ship, meals or trinkets.

"Libby has to go home and grab her paperwork. You go on through customs. Hopefully, we will see you on the flight. If not, we'll catch up with the ship later." Don issued some orders as he turned to go get his car to take Libby home for her birth certificate.

"Wait, Dad..."

"I can't talk now. I have to go." Don shouted over his shoulder as he ran through the airport.

"Great, now we are taking a two-week trip to Greece that we can't afford, with a host that we are now unsure will show up." Steve was so mad. I could see the smoke curling from his nostrils. *Now is probably not a good time to mention the company credit card*, I thought to myself.

We rushed down to the gate and boarded the plane right before it was going to take off. The passport debacle had eaten all of our time. Don and Libby and their group were going to have to take the next flight. If we were lucky, we would see them in Rome. Generally, passports take six to eight weeks to process; but sometimes, in cities like New York, they can be processed the same day. As we settled in our seats and prepared for take off, Mia looked at me and started to cry.

"Steve, will you hold her while I strap in the kids," I handed Mia over to his lap, where she proceeded to vomit all over his shirt and pants.

"Damn it!" Steve yelled as the flight attendant rushed over to offer assistance.

Ten hours of flying, no change of vomit soaked clothes, a sick child and half of our group in limbo; this was one hell of a start for the "trip of a lifetime."

Chapter 43

"Allow me, Madam." Our cabin steward effortlessly relieved me of my luggage as he led the way to our cabin. His name was Naseem and he was from India. I've learned that most of the employees on the cruise lines are from countries other than the United States. Places like Jamaica, Portugal, India and Russia, to name a few. Many leave their families behind for months at a time to work in this floating "office". It's more money than they can make at home, but it comes at a price: cramped quarters below deck, long hours with little relief, and severe homesickness. Regardless, Naseem has a warm, delightful smile for us.

"We have arrived." Naseem unlocks the door at the end of the long hallway to reveal a beautiful two bedroom suite with a sitting room and a sweeping balcony that spans the back of the ship.

"Amazing! I had no idea." I was pleasantly surprised at the quality of our accommodations. When we were assigned a location on the ship, at the last minute, I assumed it would be something we could tolerate, since we didn't plan on being in our rooms that much. Instead what I'm seeing is something in which we can luxuriate. I walked out to the balcony and sat in one of the chairs.

The unique location of our suite afforded us a privacy that is not commonly found on a cruise ship. *Thank you, God!* I felt like gratitude was in order; everything up to this point of the trip had been a pile of shit, in my opinion. I was also thankful that Libby and

Don were not on the boat yet. There is no doubt in my mind they would have made us trade rooms. Maybe this is part of the divine plan Faith was talking about? That people get what they deserve? Ok, maybe those were not her exact words, but for now, they work for me.

"Let's go Mommy, let's go see the ship!" Lucy was doing a little jig around my feet.

"Yeah! Yeah! This is so cool," Cole pulled my arm so hard I thought it would dislocate from its socket. All three kids were bouncing up and down in spasms of excitement, and it was contagious. Even Steve seemed a little better. Fresh clothes that don't reek of vomit and a hot shower have a redeeming quality.

"Good work on the room, wife!" Steve offered me a high five. It was clear that we shared the same unspoken thoughts.

"Maybe this trip won't be so bad after all." I was cautiously optimistic.

Our tour of the ship revealed its amusement park qualities: a rock-climbing wall, a simulated wave riding pool, an ice-skating rink, 24-hour cafes, a spa, two pools, a basketball court, miniature golf, and ice sculptures galore. The ship also hosted a kid's adventure club where they could hang out supervised, and meet other kids their age, while the adults enjoyed dinner and drinks. Next, we visited the excursion desk, where we signed up for activities and tours at each of the European ports.

The first stop was Monte Carlo. We docked right in the port. In Florence, we decided to take a bus ride in from the port to see the magnificent city with all of its churches and museums, and to eat its world-renowned gelato. The next day was Rome. This list of ten exotic and ancient ports gave me tingling shivers of anticipation.

"Steve, you have to pinch me! I can't believe we are actually here." I grabbed his arm in an excited squeeze. The adventurer in me was happy to dust off her expedition wear and hit the high seas, ready to explore these new worlds. In all, we managed to plan something adventurous for every port. It's a neat experience to wake up in a new city every morning. This is probably the best part about taking a cruise.

"Hello." Steve's cell phone rang as we were headed back to the cabin to change for dinner. Since we had not left the port in

Barcelona, we still had reception on Steve's phone.

"Hey, it's Dad!" Steve looked concerned. "Dad, where are you?"

"Everything is fantastic! We are here in a suite at the Trump Towers in New York City. Today we visited Central Park and went to a show on Broadway. The concierge at the hotel helped us with instructions and directions to the U.S. passport office for Libby's passport renewal first thing Monday. We're planning to meet the ship in Rome on Wednesday."

I could hear him shouting over the phone in the same enthusiastic tone he uses frequently. He didn't sound angry about Libby's fifty thousand dollar oversight.

"I'm relieved, Dad. I hope it works out." Steve was trying to be polite.

"This is the best thing that has ever happened to me. What a fabulous mistake! Tomorrow is Sunday, so I'm planning to take Libby on a tour of the city, you know, Fifth Avenue, Park Avenue, SoHo. She's never been to New York before. I want to show her the town. We do have the nanny here to watch the boys." Don was so enthusiastic, beyond the usual phony cheerfulness, it was clear Libby was standing beside him.

"That sounds good, Dad. Just call and leave a message about the passport. I hope it works out. I'll check my messages again once we are on land in Florence. Bye." Steve hung up the phone and looked at me. I could see the stress had returned to his face.

"Why does my father always have to be so extravagant with his mistresses?" He sat on one of the benches and leaned over, lacing his fingers through his dark hair. He turned his head to look up at me.

"Jenna, the second round of first class tickets is only the tip of the iceberg. Now he's in a suite at one of New York's finest hotels, and tomorrow he plans to take Libby shopping all day. I hope the company credit card doesn't melt."

"I'm sorry to say Steve, but I'm sure they will do the same thing in Rome. Via Condotti makes Park Avenue look like a Wal-Mart strip center." I loved shopping in Rome when we visited during our honeymoon. It was over-the-top amazing. Everything was supple, luxurious, and unique, in a way that only Italians can create. Think of it, for centuries, this culture has been the home of the merchants of the world, which makes it a perfect fit for the shoppers of the world:

Libby Peters, *diva tout le monde,* and Donald Sinclair, *fou tout le monde.* Respectively, the princess and the fool gorging themselves in the world of wares with their melted platinum plastic.

I thought about all of the money Don spent on Amber Atkins during their affair. Ronnie had shown me a spreadsheet of his "sexpenditures" which she created for her lawyer. They included a house, furniture and appliances, a convertible BMW, designer clothes, exotic trips and afternoon hotel rooms.

These were things Don was trying to keep secret. But how does someone hide a house? It went on and on, page after page; why should this be any different? His girlfriends even have their own credit cards, funded 100% by Don, yet Steve did not even have a company card in his own name. He had to use his own card and wait weeks, even months, to be reimbursed by the company. *Money is tight at the business, Steve. You'll have to wait.* Don always used the same line and Steve was too afraid to ask the tough questions.

"By the way, did he give you a credit card to put down on our room for incidentals?"

"No."

I turned and walked back to the room with the kids. I knew the answer before it rolled off his tongue. One of these days, Doomsday and Don are going to have an epic wrestling match. I don't want to be around to clean up the pieces.

Chapter 44

The morning sun sparkled like scattered gemstones across the dappled water of the Mediterranean. I shielded my eyes from its dazzling brilliance, as we exited the ship for our daily expedition. It was the first port of many in our travels.

Above the shoreline rose a 300-foot ragged palisade that supported the majestic palace of Monaco. It reminded me of an elegant wedding cake, pure confection perfectly presented within the grandeur of its natural setting: a glorious centerpiece. Swirls and curls of ornate ironwork, smooth marble walls merging into endless gleaming floors, and a courtyard of snapping flags caught up in the stiff breezes from the sea demanded our rapt attention. Everything about this place purred elegance, sophistication and savoir faire. I couldn't wait to get inside, to saturate my senses, to imagine…

"Mommy, I'm bored!" wailed Cole.

"Where's the beach?" asked Lucy.

"I'm hungry and I have to go potty," announced Mia.

"Don't you want to see where the princess lives?" I asked the children in an animated voice. In less than a moment, fantasy and reality had a head-on collision. Forget the saturation, now I'm just hoping to be able to glimpse the inside of the palace for a moment. Steve was waiting in line to purchase the tickets.

"Which princess? Is it Arielle or Cinderella?" Lucy asked suspiciously. She'd seen the celluloid castle at Walt Disney World a half a dozen times and this looked nothing like it. *Where were all the colorful singers and the dancers? Was Mickey Mouse coming out any moment to sign her autograph book? Is Daddy coming back soon with our strollers, balloons and cotton candy?* I was beginning to gain an awareness of a different kind: real history is a hard sell to kids saturated with pop culture.

"Come on, guys, let me tell you a story. Once upon a time there were kingdoms and castles and kings and queens and knights and dragons. This is the home to one king and queen in particular and up there on the hill beyond is where the dragon once lived a long, long, time ago." I was trying to make something up to capture their imaginations.

"How do you know it's gone?" Cole asked.

"Well, after we check out the castle, we'll just have to walk up there and see for ourselves." I was planning to visit the tiny stone village of Eze, up the cliff from the palace; dragon hunting would fit into my plans nicely.

"A dragon? I'm not going up there, no way." Lucy gave Mia a meaningful look, which prompted her to burst into tears.

"Will it eat us?" Mia sobbed.

"No, honey, you guys just need to trust Mommy. Come on, I promise you after we take Mia to the potty, we will see so many cool things you won't be able to remember them all. Cole, did you know this is the site of a famous auto race called the Monte Carlo Grand Prix? The cars race through the streets."

"Wow, can I buy one?"

"You will all get little biscuits to remember your trip, but let's save the store for last, OK?" We all held hands and headed to the bathroom before entering the palace.

The morning at the palace turned out to be a pleasant surprise despite the initial speed bump. Cole liked the automobile museum with its glimmering apple red Ferraris and Lamborghinis, and Lucy and Mia found delightful trinkets in the stone-walled shops crowding the village of Eze, instead of dragons.

Afternoon found us at a private beach club on the shoreline of Monte Carlo. Bentleys and Rolls Royces crowded one another in a struggle for the best parking spots in the seaside lot. Bright yellow-and-white striped canvas cabanas dotted the exclusive waterfront like a Boy Scout campout in Happy Land.

It was truly "happy land" for Steve, coincidentally; most European beach clubs are nude, although women usually wear stiletto heeled shoes and swathe themselves in sheer pareos in the café. Nudity and noshing are not in vogue in the Mediterranean, it appears. Neither was my hot pink Land's End tankini, complete with tummy control panel -- in other words, swimsuit girdle -- and enough fabric to craft a cabana. My older kids were too interested in the beach to notice the abundance of breasts, with the exception of Mia, who still remembers nursing.

"Boo-boo, Mommy. Boo-boo!" Mia pointed excitedly at a passing pair of plump, jiggly, grapefruit-shaped breasts adorned with claret-colored nipples. I could tell she was ready for lunch.

Chapter 45

"**I** received an e-mail from my Dad. They were successful at the passport office in New York and are now in Rome at the Hotel Cavallari. They will be getting on the ship the day after tomorrow," Steve told me on our way to dinner.

I felt a combination of relief and disappointment. Relief, because we were in no way financially prepared to shoulder a European trip of this magnitude on our own; yet disappointed because Libby and Donald both have the kind of personalities that demand center stage.

"Oh, that's good," I said brightly. "See, everything always works out as it's supposed to. Like Faith says, there is a divine plan." I tossed out the first thought that came to my mind in response, hoping to mask my disappointment, which was the stronger emotion at this time.

Steve rolled his eyes giving, me a half-smile, half-grimace. My attraction to psychics, astrology and "new thought" has been a point of tolerance in our ten-year-relationship. He listens, but doesn't buy it.

I had an astrologer pick our wedding date, the exact time, date and location for the most auspicious union possible. We ended up barefoot, oceanside in Key West, Florida on June 2nd at 12:06 pm exactly. My Unity minister had specific instructions, which she gladly carried out to perfection. No one attended, just the bride and the groom and the minister, and of course God.

It's kind of a funny story, actually. My mother thought Key West was tacky, although she had never visited. It just sounded distasteful, and Steve's dad thought only a church wedding was appropriate, although he had not attended one in decades. So we decided to get married first for ourselves, secretly, and a week later in my hometown for everyone else. Both events were fantastically fun; but it also foretold of a decade long struggle between what's best for us and what's best for our parents. This struggle is already apparent in our children.

We are required to dress for dinner on the ship. Cole was clad in a tiny navy blazer with a red tie emblazoned with navy stars. It doesn't tie, but instead hides a clever zipper behind the knot for easy wear. Cole likes the look; he fondly calls it his "ribbon." Lucy and Mia are petite princesses in their matching garden inspired pink tulle dresses. The folded layers of transparent fabric encase loose silk flower petals in a variety of festive colors. Yet while the children may look like royalty, they behave like peasants, brawling and screeching throughout the entire four-course meal. The scalding heat of disapproving glares from the other travelers went unnoticed by the children. They were powerless, imprisoned in the chaos by assigned tables next to us for the duration of the twelve-day voyage.

"She got more than me!" Cole was eyeing the elegant shrimp cocktail in a martini glass, in front of Lucy, which happened to have an additional shrimp. I'm so glad he learned to count this year.

"Mom, Cole took my roll," Lucy protested his thievery, an obvious, yet unsuccessful attempt to even the stakes.

"Don't cut it!" Mia burst into tears. "I no hungry."

She defiantly crossed her arms, tears streaming down her face. God forbid, I should touch the sacred food. Where do these tiny tyrants get their criteria? I'll never know. One day the peas are great, the next day poison. One day the steak is tasty, next week it's disgusting. Butter my bread! Pour the syrup! Don't touch my plate! The green beans are touching the ham! Not to mention the fact that they often unexpectedly resort to throwing food and flatware out of sheer frustration, once in a while launching it far enough to encounter a diner at another table. I'm a reasonable parent; but I am also a candidate for a "Supernanny" intervention. We all have our blind spots, I realize.

After the agony of dinner was over for a second night in a row, I turned to Steve. "Do you think we should consider the 24-hour Johnny Rockets café on deck twelve next to the putt-putt course?"

"I thought you'd never ask!"

Chapter 46

Mile after mile of Italian countryside rolled past as our chartered bus chugged along the two-hour drive from the port of Livorno for our six-hour visit to Florence, Italy, or Firenza, as they call it locally. This is the downside of a cruise vacation: too many things to see and too little time to do anything.

The early summer, verde-green, rolling hills were striped with orchards, vineyards and olive gardens, undulating into one another like a gastronomic patchwork quilt. I can't wait to wrap myself in this blanket of culinary bliss. The thought alone makes my mouth water in anticipation. A decade ago, I ate this food on my honeymoon; the taste has remained on my palate, a favored sensory memory. Some encounters are like that: a certain food, a special wine, even a passionate kiss. The experience is permanent, like a tattoo on your soul. We are almost there, after ten years of longing. So get out the ink!

I'm planning to do nothing but eat, all day long. In fact, if the churches don't allow food, I may not be able to play turista and go inside, so great is my appetite for the delectable promise of delicate gnocchi, hand-made pappardelle, savory tomato sauces and creamy, rich gelato, which is displayed in colorful mounds street side behind sparkling glass cabinets. In fact, the entire city of Florence is wearing the perfume of food. I adore the aroma.

"Where would you like to go first?" Steve asked jokingly, as we exited the bus at the corner of one of the many plazas, which make up the layout of this ancient city. My stomach growled in response. He knows how I feel about the food here. Everything I've eaten since my experience ten years ago has somehow suffered by comparison.

We immediately lose ourselves among the cobblestone streets which lace between ornate churches and elegant museums, connected by arching bridges crowded with jewelry and leather merchants and aromatic cafes. The imprint of the powerful Medici family, which ruled the city in the 1400's and early 1500's, still reverberates in the architecture. Everywhere you look in Florence is a feast for the eyes. The city is golden; a million mellowed stones and plaster walls, warmed and colored by thousands of sunsets. Fifteen-foot tall carved wooden doorways line the plazas, inviting visitors to their intriguing entryways, while merchants clatter along the streets under a rainbow of canvasses, beckoning tourists to consider their wares.

This city was the birthplace of the Renaissance five hundred years ago. Art, politics, fashion, culture, religion and revolt all collided here. The spirit of Niccolo Machiavelli's work and the concept of virtu are still evident today. A delicate appreciation of fine art and design, a flexible disposition schooled in many disciplines, in essence virtu, and the concept of the Renaissance man are an ideal still sought after centuries later. It's amazing to me how timeless is the application of truth. Philosophies dating back hundreds, even thousands, of years still apply. Truth and ageless wisdom are one. I really get the sense of that as I'm visiting this city. It makes me feel like an old soul in the body of a thirty-six-year old woman.

"Mommy, what's that?" Lucy was pointing at the statute of Leonardo da Vinci's David. This particular statue was a replica of the original, situated in a fountain spurting at least a dozen streams of water. At almost twenty feet tall, the classic statute was larger- than-life to admirers, and he was sporting a larger-than-life penis. Which is directly where the finger of my seven-year-old daughter was pointed.

"Steve, I hadn't considered the concept of Fine Art Porno, until now. This one is all yours." I walked over to a bench and opened my city guide in the hope of locating my all time favorite restaurant. The piattis, calzones and pistachio gelato I've devoured since my arrival have not managed to fill me up.

On the way back to meet the bus, we stopped at a few of the souvenir stands and small shops. Hand-carved wooden trays embossed with gold and silver inlays, leather handbags in every color and style, lambskin jackets, soft wool pashminas and a smattering of trinkets from shot glasses to snow globes, made it difficult for us to make an immediate decision. I finally settled on an ivory lambskin jacket, which fell just above my knee with a smart, classic design and an oversized suede bucket bag in citron with tawny leather straps and chunky gold hardware. After much debate, Steve could not resist a black leather bomber jacket, so buttery soft; it slid out of our hands several times. Lucy knew immediately what she wanted: a tiny, nine-inch replica of the statute of Leonardo da Vinci's David. *Well, at least her delicate discrimination is beginning to show at a young age.*

Chapter 47

"Ciao! Ciao!" Libby shouted the Italian greeting, running to meet me at the port, as we disembarked from the ship for the daily tour of Rome. Her enthusiasm was contagious and I returned her big hug; dislodging what appeared to be a new pair of Prada sunglasses.

"Oh! I can't wait to tell you our story. We almost didn't get the passport. I had to flash the clerk a big smile, so they would not shut down the office before my turn in line," Libby is forever telling me about the power of a pretty face. I could tell by her tone that any thought of remorse over her expired passport was long gone, like a balloon released at a memorial service.

"I'm really glad it worked out, and I'm glad you're here," I said with sincerity. I meant what I said. I was looking forward to travelling with my best friend. I just didn't recognize her as such anymore. A new persona was gaining strength, drowning out the one I liked so well. But, as Faith says, we all grow and change; some people grow together and some people grow apart. We'll have to wait and see where this is going.

"Are you planning to spend the day with us in Rome?"

"Actually, no, we need to get situated in our cabins, and Don had already arranged for us to have a tour in a private car yesterday. You know, the Coliseum, the Vatican, all that stuff. Oh! And the shopping was to die for!"

At least I'm psychic about some things, I thought to myself.

"You'll love the ship! The kids are having a blast."

"I can't wait to get into the spa for a massage. Is it nice?"

"I haven't had a chance to visit it yet."

"I'm going there first. The last couple of days have been exhausting," Libby said with a dramatic sigh. "Cara can give them a tour."

"We'll see you tonight at dinner, maybe after; we're thinking of trying the Johnny Rockets, instead of the main dining room." Libby crinkled her nose at the suggestion of hamburgers.

"Why don't we send the kids there with the nannies, Cara and Maggie? The four of us can have dinner in one of the other restaurants," Libby offered.

"That's actually a great idea, I had not thought of that. Will you take care of the reservations?"

"I'll have Don do it. I'm too beat from the last couple of days," Libby pushed her glasses up on her head and I noticed a cluster of jeweled bangle bracelets crowding her wrist. "I may just take a Zanax and hit the hot tub." Over the years, I've learned from Libby that one of the perks of having a husband as a physician is easy access to a well-stocked medicine cabinet.

"Just let me know. We should be back on board by six."

Chapter 48

"I can't believe we are finally here! It feels like a lifetime." I look at Steve and the kids and smile behind my sunglasses.

"Welcome! Welcome to Athens." Several young men dressed in suits were calling out to us as we exited the ship, waving us over to their shiny Mercedes and town cars.

"I'd much rather take a limousine than use the bus, please!"

"I agree." Steve answered my plea knowingly. We've taken a lot of bus rides lately.

"Do you have room for five?"

"Yes, sir, but of course." A tall dark-haired young man hopped from his black Mercedes and walked around to open the door for us.

"Is this your first time in Athens?' he asked politely.

"Our first time in Greece." I responded.

"Well then, you need the grand tour. My name is Stephano Spirto, at your service." He swept into a brief bow before reentering the sleek car. I liked him instantly.

"Should we wait for your Dad and Libby and her two kids?"

"You know, Jenna, after last night, I think they can figure it out."

I hadn't wanted to bring it up because I was afraid he would still be angry. The last three ports Don had spent all of his time jewelry shopping with Libby, while we escorted her children along with ours and the two nannies for afternoons of exhausting sightseeing. Libby's boys constantly whined and picked fights with Cole and

Lucy. Five children in an entourage through Europe were more than we bargained for.

Finally, as Libby sat sparkling in her new diamonds at dinner last night, Steve erupted.

"Dad, we didn't come along to be baby sitters. Enough is enough. And Libby, I don't know what to say to you. You're not even divorced from Blake yet, and here you are wearing diamonds like rhinestones on a cowgirl outfit. Dad, hats off to you. You are certainly taking her on a hell of a ride."

Libby gasped with her mouth open and burst into tears.

"Save it, Libby. We've seen your waterworks enough to drown in them." I shut her off cold and she stopped crying as quickly as she started. Like someone turning a spigot off and on. I've seen her cry so many times over the past year, and I've come to realize she uses it as a form of manipulation. Tears make people feel bad. Nobody wants to say something hurtful to someone who is crying, even if it is the truth.

"Libby, what are your intentions here? Are you in love with Don?" I really wanted to know the answer. Her response was total silence.

"You realize that no answer is an answer in and of itself." I refused to let up.

"Don understands that we are taking it slow and getting to know one another. I'm too fragile and bruised to handle another relationship so soon after what Blake did to me."

Don was looking at Libby, a little shocked. He creates fantasies in his mind, and to hear such direct reality… well, all I can say is that fantasy and reality don't always line up. The chasm between is where all of the problems live. Last night, I think we opened Pandora's box.

"Libby, I never in a million years would have thought this about you, but you are nothing better than a gold-digger."

"How dare you say that, Steve!"

"Tell me then Libby, what do you call it? You're accepting lavish gifts on a daily basis from a man you admit you are not in love with."

"I! Augh! I don't know what to say."

"You don't have to say a word. It's very clear to me. Jenna, Dad, if you will excuse me. I have lost my appetite." Steve pushed away from the table and got up to leave. "By the way Dad, you still need to put a credit card on our room. I wasn't planning on taking this trip and it's way beyond my budget."

"I, uh, I thought I did that, Steve. I must have forgotten."

"That seems to be a habit, but I need you to remember. You invited us. Remember? Libby needed us to come on this trip so Blake would not cause problems for her. I wish we had stayed at home. The business needs me." Steve turned and headed for the door.

"Steve, wait for me. I'll go with you," I looked at Don and Libby. Don's mouth was hanging open like a love drunk fool, but Libby flashed me a look I'd never seen from her before in over a thousand play dates, lunches and tennis matches: pure contempt, mixed with a dash of determination. Like most miners who traveled west more than a century ago, she'd been sifting through the dirt most of her life, searching for gold, and the promise of a better life it brought with it. And now, Libby Peters was not about to relinquish her treasure. She'd only just discovered it.

The pictures of last night were still playing in my head as we drove through the streets of Athens on our guided tour.

"First, I will take you to the Acropolis." Stephano had a pleasant accent, yet his English was excellent.

"What can you tell us about the Acropolis?" I asked curiously.

"The Acropolis is an ancient and holy site for the Greeks. Mostly slaves constructed it in the 5th century B.C. Once you climb to the top of the hill, you will see it consists of four main buildings: the Parthenon, the Temple of Athena Nike, the Erechtheion and the Propylaea. There are tour guides available at the top to tell you the history. And, a warning: make sure you hold hands with the children. In many places the stones are crumbling. Last year one of the tourists fell from the temple to his death. Apparently, he was too close to the edge and his footing gave way. "

"Wow, that's a scary thought." Lucy and Cole's eyes were wide as saucers.

"Yes, indeed. During ancient times, virgins were pushed from the edge of the cliff outside the temple of Athena in sacrifice. Prisoners executed. Lovers committed suicide. Many, many have perished here in over five thousand years."

I appreciated his dramatic flair. The children were silent in contemplation of his stories. I looked out the window as we drove by street after street of balconies bulging with geraniums and stone squares fringed with orange trees. The sun shone brightly and the entire city seemed to smile in response. I am transported.

"Oh look, we have arrived." Stephano's voice cut through my reverie.

I exited the car and looked up as far as my neck would allow. A massive stone cliff striped with a zigzag foot trail threading around clusters of olive trees and patches of boulders told me there was no easy way to the top.

"I'll wait for you here." Stephano drew on a cigarette and leaned against his car. I could tell he figured this would take a while. He was thin and athletic, yet elegant in a European way. He was wearing a crisp white shirt, black silk slacks and loafers. Stephano's raven black hair was brushed back from his face and the tamed curls dusted the top of his open collar. His profile was strong, hawk-like, in an attractive way. *Greek men, a gift from the gods!*

The first ruins we encountered were at the Temple of Athena Nike. It was a small structure situated at the gateway to the Acropolis. We climbed the marble seats of the ancient amphitheater, until we reached the top and passed though the large columns marking the entrance to the famed site. Before us the vast, monstrous, Parthenon made me immediately wonder how any human being was able to carry stones of this size up to this site. It's simply unexplainable. It was an effort to carry my own person up to this site.

A tour guide tells us many of the structures in the Acropolis are dedicated to the Greek Goddess Athena, the goddess of war and the daughter of Zeus. The architectural details are breathtaking, regardless of their crumbling state: a massive rectangular building completely surrounded by fluted Corinthian columns, fifty-foot statutes of women dressed in draping, elegant gowns, warriors wielding swords, and noble lions standing guard. Everything was larger than life, everything was crafted from stone; craftsmanship the likes of which we have never seen in this lifetime. It was a visual feast, with more to devour than could ever be accomplished in one visit.

"What did you think of the Acropolis?" Stephano was patiently waiting for us by the car. Again, I was grateful for not being herded into a tour bus.

"It was beyond anything I could ever describe. Amazing, awe-inspiring. I can't find an explanation. I wish I had lived back then and served in the temples, or something. The entire time we were up there, it gave me the tingles all over."

Stephano smiled at me. I could see how proud he was of his country. There is a lot to admire here.

"I've made special arrangements for an authentic Greek meal. I'm certain you will enjoy it thoroughly. This restaurant I'm taking you to, is one of the oldest in Athens and they are known for their many specialties."

"Are you joining us for lunch?" Steve asked Stephano.

"*Ogi*, I mean no, I could not," Stephano demurred.

"We insist. You must to join us. Our treat."

Stephano beamed a boyish smile and nodded his head in surrender. I got the sense that he knew all of the fabulous places to eat and shop, but rarely partook of their delights.

The restaurant was obscure and quietly situated on one of the many hillsides in the city. It had a large tile patio across the entire back of the building surrounded by a stacked stone wall. Providing shade overhead was an arbor made of rustic timber, bursting with a tangle of flowering vines in ruby red and shocking pink. From the arbor hung hundreds of lanterns crafted of battered tin, housing fat white candles waiting for dusk. Our table was covered with a bright yellow cotton cloth in a floral pattern in celery green and tomato red. I felt we had been invited into a secret garden, and beyond its wall the city of Athens lay at our feet.

In the end it was not the view, but the food, which rivaled even my experiences in Florence. Tray after tray of grilled seafood marinated in fresh herbs was brought to our table. Also, warm from the oven pita bread, feta cheese, fresh tomatoes, parsley, oregano, and Greek dishes like, *souvlaki*, a garlic lamb kabob, and *moussaka*, layers of aubergine, minced meats, and tomato topped with a white cream sauce -- somewhat like Mediterranean lasagna. There were sauces: *tsatsiki*, a yogurt garlic spread, and *saganki*, a sheep's cheese served blazing tableside. We ate silently, ravenously, as if we were being served food from the gods. Even the children were licking their fingers in applause for this magnificent meal.

I don't know what it is, but I've come to believe that you have never really touched the heart of a city until you have experienced its authentic food. Food is a life force and a true expression of the soul of a people. The people of Greece have beautiful, delicious, luscious souls.

"You can not leave our beautiful city without visiting the Plaka," Stephano was rubbing his belly like a contented bear.

"What is the Plaka?" I was intrigued.

"It's a shopping bazaar beyond compare!"

"That sounds good to us," chimed Lucy and Cole. Their allowance was burning a hole in their pockets. We haven't had a chance to do much souvenir shopping.

"You enjoyed your lunch?" I ask Stephano in an amused voice.

"Oh yes, Jenna. It was manna from the gods, as they say here in Greece," he smiled at me and I felt we had all crossed the bridge to friendship over our lunch.

"*Efgaristo!* That is the word for thank you in Greece. You know, if you have the time, I would like to take you to visit someone special as a gift of thanks for my excellent meal."

"What do you think, Steve?"

"I'm along for the ride. We are in your capable hands, Stephano." Steve also looked drowsy and contented; all of the tension from last night had vanished. The ship was not sailing for several hours, so we accepted the mysterious invitation.

Our car whisked around the streets of Athens, weaving in and around stone cobbled squares and past elegant villas for a quarter of an hour until we found ourselves on the outskirts of the city, at the wooden doorway of a tiny garden cottage. It was neat and tidy, with a smattering of riotous geraniums in a collection of beautiful cobalt clay pots. I never realized geraniums were so common in Greece; they must adore the dry, warm climate. If plants can be happy, these flowers on the patio of this cottage were exuberant.

"Please, please come in," Stephano waved us into the courtyard and we were greeted by a group of six or seven curious, chubby felines. My hand was greeted by sun-warmed fur, as I reached to stroke a grey and white tabby. She must have been sunbathing. The children squealed with delight. Animals of any kind are an all time favorite with the Sinclair family.

Mystic in a Minivan

Stephano disappeared and returned moments later escorting an old woman on his arm. She wore her silver white hair pulled back from her face in a neat bun. Her dress was a beautiful shade of blue, which reminded me of the shallow aquamarine waters around the islands we were cruising. Her face was lined with the history of a thousand smiles.

"I'd like you to meet my great aunt, Stella. She is a seer. She has agreed to look into your futures." Stella offered us a warm nod.

"Oh!" I was surprised and delighted. It was a perfect gift. How could Stephano have known about my close relationship with an intuitive back home? I don't remember mentioning it. This was a mysterious coincidence.

"Jenna, would you like to follow us? Stella does not speak English, but I will translate for you. I promise to keep your secrets," Stephano offered with a twinkle in his eye.

"Oh, silly, they are not that exciting. Trust me." I taunted him back.

We entered a small parlor with colorful silk sheer draperies in shades of lavender and rose hanging abundantly from the stucco walls. A sunray shone through a small rectangular window topped with an arch, casting a light pattern in the same shape on the terra cotta tile floor. Stella motioned for us to sit on several beaded pillows arranged haphazardly around a low wooden table. Once we were seated, she gently grasped my hand and nodded a friendly greeting. Her palm felt dry, like tissue paper. I returned her nod with my warmest smile. She began to speak rapidly in Greek, and I sat patiently, waiting for the translation.

"First, Jenna, she says, Welcome home, child. You have lived many lifetimes in this land. This is your true homeland. You are one of us deep in your heart."

I was surprised by what she was saying; yet it also made sense on a cellular level, inside my spiritual DNA. I kept thinking about the strange chills I had the entire time we were visiting the Acropolis. All my life I have had a keen interest in mythology, and then there was my sudden urge to burst into tears as we docked in the port of Piraeus. It was as if I was returning home after a long, long journey, like Odysseus. So long ago and so distant that everything had changed in my absence, yet it still felt like home.

"Next she says that you are preparing to embark on your life's work, your soul's song, in the very near future."

"What could that possibly be?"

"You are to be one of the Earth's teachers."

"What am I going to teach anyone to do?" *Navigate the half-yearly sale at Nordstrom's? She must be talking about someone else.*

"No Jenna, she says this is about you. Most of us do not know when life will call us to our true purpose."

"What's my purpose and how will I recognize it?"

"It will keep luring you in different ways until you can resist it no more. To decline the invitation from your Spirit is to die. For we are only alive, when we are living and acting from our higher self."

I looked at Stephano, incredulous. This prediction was far more than I expected. I didn't know what to do with the information. It was terrifying and exciting all at the same time.

"She says you have everything you need inside your heart to guide you. Just be still, and remember: you have spent many lifetimes preparing for this one. It is not a mistake you are here now. You are collecting the fragments of yourself from many lifetimes and many experiences, in preparation for this next leap in your evolution."

I shifted uncomfortably in my seat. The pillows suddenly felt like pebbles on a beach.

"Wait, there is more. She also cautions there are dark times ahead. Do not lose yourself in others' dramas, for you may not be able to find yourself again in this lifetime."

"What does that mean?" They conversed in Greek for a few moments.

"Check in with your heart frequently, Jenna. Your spirit is pure, it knows the right way."

Stella stopped talking and smiled at me compassionately. She gave me a beautiful clear stone from a nearby shelf and said she was honored to meet me. Then she turned to Stephano and said a few more words.

"You are surrounded by angels, Jenna, and though you many feel isolated and cast out in the times to come, you will never be alone. I believe you have met some of these angels before. This stone is to help you remember who you truly are. Think of it as a diamond forged inside the darkness of grinding Earth, molded into its brilliance by tremendous pressure. Only when it is in its true form of perfection is it discovered. Then, and only then, can it show the world its radiant beauty."

I thought about the strange experience on the sailboat in Mexico where Don almost drowned. I believe that was an angel.

"Stephano, efgaristo!"

"Stella, efgaristo!" I impulsively hugged them both.

"This was such an unexpected treat. I'll spend time thinking about what your aunt said." When we came back to the patio Steve had dozed off, and the children were lying on the warm tile floor playing with the cats.

"Steve, would you like to speak with Stella?" I could tell he was in a deep sleep by the way he startled when I touched him.

"No, thanks, Honey. Are we ready to go?"

Stephano drove us directly to the Plaka. True to his promise, it was a colorful crowded marketplace with so many stalls of wares; we could never visit them all.

"Did your tea leaves have good tidings?" Steve loved to tease me.

"I'm not sure."

Chapter 49

Thankfully, we never connected with Libby and Donald the entire day in Athens.

"Jenna, what happened to you guys today?" Libby gave me a big hug. Odd, I have not received a hug from her in a long time. In fact, she has not hugged me since she started dating Don, now that I think about it. I felt strangely empty.

"How was your day, Libby? Did you and the boys go sightseeing?"

"Oh, yeah. We saw the Acropolis and all of the ruins. That walk exhausted me. I think they are a little overrated, just a pile of old stones basically. But I loved the Plaka. We spent most of the day there shopping. The jewelry was to die for, and Don bought me a new bikini. It's virtually all strings with little gold engraved beads on the ends. I usually don't wear bikinis, but I've lost so much weight with the stress of my divorce. You know Jenna, would you like me to give you some of my old clothes? They are all too big for me now. Don has bought me so many new ones. He keeps saying, 'Let me indulge you'. How can I resist?"

Her efforts at extending the peace branch were turning into arrows of insults. I ignored it. But I was relieved we didn't share the day together. Her opinions would have tainted my experience. Everything about our day in Athens was magical. It felt as if it had been pre-planned by the gods. I didn't need a self-appointed goddess as a commentator.

"Well, I'm a little tired. I'm on my way back to the room to rest before dinner."

"Oh, I was hoping we could get a drink or something by the pool. There is something I want to talk to you about."

"If it's about Steve, I'd rather not."

"What about Steve?" I picked up on the cue. When Libby wants to avoid a subject she acts like it never occurred. "Actually, it's my nanny. I read her diary while she was out of the room and I'm really upset about what it says."

"Libby, why are you reading an eighteen-year-old girl's journal?"

"Well, it was just laying there."

"She left it laying out?"

"Not exactly, it was in the pocket of her suitcase, but her suitcase was laying out from underneath the bed."

"I'll tell you what. I'll meet you at the pool bar in twenty minutes."

"Okay."

I quickly raced back to the room to change.

"Where are you going?" Steve asked from the bed in our cabin. "I thought we were going to take a nap together?"

"It's Libby. She read her nanny's diary. I guess it was not too pleasant."

"I can't imagine anyone would have anything pleasant to say about Libby."

"Be nice. She's already over your spat last night, or at least she is choosing to ignore it. Libby is wise that way. She always knows how to pick her battles."

"I don't want to battle with her. I simply don't want to deal with her."

"Well, we don't have a choice now, at least for the duration of the vacation. Once we get home, you will never see her anyway. Maybe she will snap out of it. Maybe it's just a phase." I was wondering when this current haughty, greedy, entitled Libby would be exorcised and my dear friend would return. I hoped it was soon.

"But what about our nap?" He lazily patted the bed, but my curiosity won. *What did the diary say?*

"Can we save if for tonight?" Steve rolled over and ignored me.

Libby was invading his life in more ways than he could handle. "Whatever you've got to do?"

"I'll report back," I called over my shoulder as I shut the door.

Libby had already ordered two tall strawberry daiquiris with pineapple slices and paper umbrellas. She was twirling her straw, agitated.

"Who does she think she is, writing about me, us, in her journal? I invited her on the trip of a lifetime!"

"What exactly did it say?"

Libby reached into her pool bag and pulled out the diary. I gasped in surprise.

"Aren't you worried she will discover it is missing?"

Libby shrugged.

I looked over my shoulder to see if the nannies were anywhere in sight. It didn't feel right, prying into someone's private thoughts.

"Listen to this:"

Dear Diary, I wish I had known them better before I agreed to the TRIP FROM HELL. Mrs. Peters is never around and I have her bratty boys 24/7. All of these people are so spoiled. God, I hope I am never like them.

"Here's another one":

Dear Diary, Mrs. Peters is spending all night out. Lately, she's not even back before breakfast. I thought she was married. Her shit is thrown all over our cabin and she didn't even pack enough clothes for the boys. For two weeks in Europe, she brought each boy one pair of shorts, two pairs of pants, three t-shirts and one pair of shoes, which they are always losing. Their clothes are all dirty and they stink. I'm sick of washing them in the sink. Meanwhile she brought two suitcases full of outfits for herself, and she told me I could only bring a backpack.

"This is total bullshit, Jenna. None of it is true, but she also baby-sits for Blake. What am I going to do if she tells him?"

"Well it's not a crime if you under pack for your kids, I guess. Maybe you should not stay out so late."

"Please, she is making that up."

"What else does she say?"

Dear Diary, Who forgets to renew their passport? I mean, come on. Is this woman a total moron? Now I'm stuck in a hotel room in

New York City for over sixteen hours and they haven't even called to check in. I have no money for the boys, and Mrs. Peters says I'm not allowed to leave the room to take the boys anywhere. They are beating the hell out of each other. This trip is not what I expected. I called my mom for support. She said to hang in there. When they finally showed up, after dark, she had so many shopping bags the doorman had to help her carry them inside our room. All designer names: Prada, Gucci, Cartier. Names I don't even recognize. Thirty minutes later they left again for dinner. We were not invited.

I was surprised Libby was letting me read this journal. I had no idea what was going on in private during this trip. She was too preoccupied with what Blake might find out to consider what I thought about the situation. I, on the other hand, felt sorry for the nanny.

"Mrs. Peters, what do you want the boys to wear for dinner?" Maggie, the nanny approached us at the bar with the boys in tow. My nanny and three kids were with her.

"Is that my journal in your hands?" Maggie was shocked and pissed.

"I, uh, it must have fallen out of your purse. I found it on the floor of our room. You should be careful about things you don't want others to read," Libby said defiantly.

"HOW DARE YOU! My diary was in a zippered pocket in my suitcase under my bed. You had to look pretty hard to find it." Maggie nailed her with a bullshit-shattering sledgehammer.

I was feeling increasingly uncomfortable. I should never have agreed to let Libby read me Maggie's private thoughts. It's just that they were so close to mine these days; it was a relief to have a consensus.

"Maggie, Cara, I am so sorry. I don't know what to say." I stood up, trying to apologize.

Cara looked at me and shook her head. She has worked for my family for years, but I could see she was disappointed in Libby and me.

"Mrs. Peters, I'm leaving. This is the final straw. You, your family, all of you are total nightmares. I'm going home on the next plane." Tears were streaming down Maggie's face as she bolted away from us.

"What's wrong with her?" one of the boys asked.

"Now what am I going to do?"

"Why don't you go after her and apologize? You did betray her trust."

"Oh please, she's lucky to be here. She needs to just get over it." Libby spat back, annoyed.

"Libby, I need to go. I suggest you work this out. We still have a while to go and your options will be limited without a nanny."

Cara walked with my kids and me back to the cabin.

"What were you guys thinking?"

"Libby told me Maggie's diary was full of upsetting information about all of us. She wanted to talk to me about it. I never thought she would bring the book with her."

"You guys really screwed up. Maggie has wanted to go home this entire time. Now you've given her an excuse. If she goes home, that means more work for me. God forbid, I don't want to watch those brats!"

"Don't worry about it. This is Libby's problem. She will have to work it out."

Chapter 50

A gust of salt soaked wind rolling off the waves of the Mediterranean filled our sails, surging us forward. The patches of greenery on the volcanic mountains surrounding us were outlined by a cloudless blue sky. The sun, radiant and welcoming, beamed down on us brightly. So brightly, I could still see traces of its circular outline behind my closed eyelids. Our vessel was over a century old, a sailboat with shiny wooden decks and rails, and a salty-dog captain to navigate our voyage. The captain was a Greek whose idea of English was a nod and a slight grin, which looked more like a grimace. His face was a map of a thousand wordless journeys. It was adorned with a jaunty navy seafaring cap.

The sea around Santorini, Greece is hauntingly beautiful. It now fills a vast volcanic crater where a civilization once existed in the distant reaches of time. Legend says it was the lost city of Atlantis, doomed by a cataclysmic eruption, which sent the land and all who inhabited it to the bottom of the sea in one violent outburst. Modern geologists have determined there was once an island, whole and complete. Now there remains only a crenellated doughnut where modern day Santorini exists. Opposite the city and across the sea filled wound an active volcano still exists, smoking, sputtering and gasping, its rage unspent after thousands of centuries.

I grasped the heavy hemp rope laced between the rails. It was so thick my fingers barely reached my thumb. I closed my eyes and leaned back against the ropes, and felt my heart fill with gratitude. *Thank you, God! Thank you for this experience in my lifetime.*

When I opened my eyes I realized we had entered a cove. *It was the cove from my dream.* Amazing. How can this be true? Yet my own eyes told me it was the same vision from the vivid dream I experience months ago, before we even agreed to take this trip. *I've been here before.* The scattered olive trees, the group of bathers in the hot springs, even the stone path down the hillside; everything looked familiar.

Once anchored, I jumped from the side of the ship, plunging over twelve feet into the shockingly cold water below and swam the 100 yards to the hot springs. No one else wanted to brave the swim. Volcanic gases made the water temperature in this area forty degrees warmer than the sea beyond. I floated silently for a while, absorbing the magical energy of Mother Earth's hot tub.

I was alone in this space, but I felt a mysterious loving presence. It lulled me into a gentle vision behind my closed eyelids. Gabriel, the man from the ocean in Mexico was smiling at me. In that moment I knew I was safe; he was watching over me. In my mind's eye, he led me to a beach flanking the spring where other angelic beings were standing on the shore. They nodded their heads and smiled at me in the same serene way. It was so lucid; I felt their implied assistance and protection. It seemed to me there was a connection between us which transcended time and space.

After a while, I'm ready to swim back to the ship. I paused to take a mental snapshot of this place. I knew that in future I would return to it many times in my imagination. I reached down and grabbed a small, smooth flat stone from the sea floor and held it tightly in the palm of my hand as I swam through the frigid waters back to my family. Perhaps it was a piece of the ancient land that now exists only in the mists of time, a piece of home.

Chapter 51

Don must have paid Maggie a substantial bonus. She was back on duty and button-lipped the next day. We only had a few days left to go, two more ports and a day at sea. Despite a few episodes, I've had a magical time. Faith was right.

"Jenna, is that you? I've been trying to call you all week!" Lisa, my gallery manager, sounded a little frantic.

"Hi, Lisa, what's up? The phone connections on the cruise line are terrible."

"You need to call Ruth. Right away!"

"What's wrong? Has there been an accident?"

"Last week, the Monday after you left, I came in to open the store at ten. Ruth was walking out the door with a box full of papers and loading it in the back of her car. Which was already full of boxes," Lisa continued.

"She said hi, told me not to write any checks, and pulled away."

"Jenna, she took every document out of the gallery. Our inventory lists, our tax records, receipts from suppliers and our bank statements."

"What in the world is she up to?" I felt a stab of anxiety deep in my gut. With each second it was beginning to grow and spread throughout my entire body. "Let me hang up and call her."

Ruth answered on the second ring. "Hello, Jenna, how is your trip?"

"Fine, thank you." I responded curtly. "Ruth, what is going on?"

"Bottom line, Jenna, the business is not what I thought it was. You lied to me, and I want all of my money back in a cashier's check within twenty-four hours. I've added it up Jenna. I want $150,000."

"What are you talking about, Ruth? That's double your investment and you've only been my partner for one hundred and twenty days. I think I've seen you at the business maybe three days. Plus, we bought a lot of inventory." I was trying to keep my voice down.

"I'm on a tour bus in Sorrento, Italy. I won't even be back from Europe until next week. Ruth, everything was fine before I left!" I felt so powerless being a thousand miles from home. "Now Lisa tells me you came in to the gallery on Monday and took all of the records. What happened over the weekend?"

"Ira was looking over the company's bank statements and he thinks there is something fishy going on." *Ira? The husband Ruth wanted to keep out of her "business" suddenly has his nose in mine. I was beginning to see the problem.*

"So, Ira is mad about the money we spent in New York?" Silence greeted me on the other end of the line.

"I've contacted an attorney, Jenna. I want out and I want out fast."

"Ruth, you'll have to wait until I get back. There's nothing I can do before then."

I hung up and look over at Don and Libby. Libby's head rested on his shoulder, eyes closed, as he looked out the window. *Had they heard my conversation with Ruth? Probably, but I could do without any judgments right now.*

The last days of the trip were overshadowed by the impending confrontation with Ruth. *Surely, we could work this out.* I kept going over the deal in my head. *I told her about the construction in the shopping center. She knew she was buying the business from me so I could pay back my equity line. Both of us were in New York together. Buying artwork. Where was the problem? I could not see it.*

Maybe I should see if Lisa was still interested in buying the business. The problem is that we'd bought so much more inventory; the price would need to be much more to cover all of the new expenses. I doubted Lisa could pull that off right now. I know the initial deal was a stretch.

Chapter 52

"Hi, Jenna, did you have fun?'

"It was alright, Lisa. Has Ruth come in here again?"

"Haven't seen her. But you probably should know: she tore up our business checkbook and cancelled all of our business credit cards. Oh, and another thing, she bounced my paycheck and several commission checks to our designers while you were away. What happened to all of our sales this month? I thought we did at least $15,000. That's what the receipt book shows."

"I haven't seen it. But I also don't deal with the banking."

I walked out to my car so I could make a phone call in private to our contact over at the bank. When we became partners, Ruth and I opened a new business account at her private bank with the help of Warren Rhodes, her banker. I didn't mind; she said it would be easier for her. I wanted her to feel comfortable, so I agreed.

"Warren, it's Jenna Sinclair. Could you please explain to me what is going on with my business accounts?"

"You need to sort this out with Ruth."

"Warren, you are a bank representative. This is a business issue, not a sorority dispute. I'm the president of the company, and I don't recall authorizing any changes. Please send over the statements for the last two months, and I need to have new checks and a new business debit card today."

"Ruth has requested that all of your credit cards be cancelled, and she has designated herself as the sole owner of the company. You are no longer authorized on these accounts."

"How can she do that? I'm the president of the company. Doesn't she need my signature?" Silence greeted me on the other end of the line. Clearly, Ruth's stooge over at the private bank was not going to help me today. He was too busy doing her dirty work.

Chapter 53

I picked up the phone and called my friend, Gloria, the attorney who wrote the art gallery contract between Ruth and me. "Gloria, you're never going to believe what happened." I drove straight from the gallery to her office. I forgot to even make an appointment.

"Hi, Jenna. Nice trip?"

"Sorry Gloria, I'm just so worked up. Ruth called me in Europe, told me I lied to her, took all of my business records and shut me out of my bank accounts…"

Gloria interrupted, "Wait a minute! Slow down! What did you just say?"

I exhaled and started again.

"Ruth has changed her mind, Gloria."

"She can't do that. You have a contract. One you two never completely finished, I might add. At least part of it is signed."

"I don't think we'll be wrapping it up now." I said wryly.

"Back up to the part about the business accounts."

"Ruth has shut me out of all of my business accounts, torn up the business checks and cancelled my business credit cards."

"She can't do that. It's against the law."

"Tell that to Warren Rhodes, her private banker. Maybe when you have millions you are above the law?"

"I'm calling the bank right now." Gloria turns on the conference phone in her office and dials the private banker.

"Warren, this is Gloria Coin. Could you please explain to me what is going on with the business accounts for the gallery? My client, Jenna Sinclair, informs me you are denying her access to her corporate accounts. Is this the case?"

"Gloria, I've been expecting your call. Please hold for our legal counsel."

"Hello, Ms. Coin. My name is Melanie Gilbert, legal counsel here at the bank. We would like to request that Ms. Sinclair remove her accounts from our bank today. We will be happy to provide the last two months' bank statements and to wire any funds available to the institution of your choice."

"May I ask how much is in the account?" Gloria repeated the question I mouthed to her.

"Four hundred thirteen dollars and sixty-five cents."

My mouth fell open. We had done over twenty thousand dollars in sales the previous month and another fifteen thousand this month. There should be at least twenty thousand in the account after bills were paid. Where did all of the money go? What was I going to do now?

"Jenna," Gloria covered the phone, "where do you want them to send the money?"

"Back to my old bank, First Fidelity." I was numb.

"Oh, and Melanie, could you fax over all of the bank statements from all other accounts to me at my office immediately? I believe Warren has my number."

I looked at Gloria and started to cry. I put my head down on her mahogany conference table; my wet sobs steaming up its glossy finish.

"Jenna, we will get to the bottom of this. I will help you."

Chapter 54

"Are you Mrs. Jenna Sinclair?" I answered the door to find a sheriff standing on my front porch.

"Yes, I am."

"Could you please sign these papers?"

"What are they for?"

"You're being served in a lawsuit, ma'am."

I ripped open the envelope and in the corner of the court document I saw Ruth and Ira Simon's names. Then I looked further at the details. They were suing for $150,000 plus an additional $200,000 for punitive damages. The lawsuit alleged fraud.

I picked up the phone and immediately called Ruth. "I thought we were meeting next week to decide what to do with the business and the partnership, Ruth? What happened? You are not giving me any time to respond."

"I believe I gave you 24 hours to give me a cashier's check for $150K. You didn't deliver."

"Ruth, you know the business doesn't have that kind of money!"

"Jenna, from now on talk to my lawyer." Then she hung up the phone.

The next day, I hired a hot-shot attorney, Dixon Fox, an acquaintance of Steve's, with a hefty price tag: $250 an hour. Gloria said this latest development was way over her head.

"So I understand you're getting fucked by a member of the

Lucky Sperm Club." Dixon was crude, coarse, and direct. I liked that about him.

"Yes, it's true, my 'trust-fund-financed-ex-friend' wants a refund on the business she bought into only four months ago."

"I've dealt with this type before. If you're not prepared to write them a check today to go away, they will use every legal means necessary to make your life a living hell."

"Thank you, Dixon, for the uplifting words. Truth is, I don't have it. Ruth and I spent the money buying inventory in New York. The money is tied up in the artwork."

"At this point, none of that matters. Roll up your sleeves and put on your gloves, dear. You're in for a hell of a fight."

Dixon was right. I hate how right he was, that first conversation several months ago. Since then, the Simons have used every contact and every legal maneuver possible to drive up my legal fees to the extreme and to harass me into submission. We've sent letters, tried mediation, and even offered settlements: nothing would satisfy their thirst for vengeance against some imagined wrong.

The battle is no longer exclusive to the courtrooms. Ruth has done everything in her power to travel back through all of the social doors she opened for me last year, slam them shut and throw away the key.

It's now escalated to a point where I have no idea how to end the dispute. Ira and Ruth's egos are involved. Even the attorneys are now in a pissing match. This lawsuit has taken on a life of its own.

Chapter 55

"Faith, can you squeeze me in today? I'm on my way home from the attorney. I'd like to talk to you about something."

"Sure, sweetheart. Funny you should call. I had an unexpected visit from a client today. A name I am sure you will recognize. Ruth Simons." Faith's voice was calm and even, but the news felt like a punch in the jaw.

"What did you say?" I managed to choke out.

"Yes, Ruth came to see me. Remember when she hired me to be a psychic at one of her parties? Well, she wanted some guidance on some personal issues."

"Vaguely." I must have referred Faith to her. I'm beginning to think I should hang out a shingle, matches made in hell: Don and Libby, me and Ruth, now Ruth and Faith. I didn't feel like sharing this relationship.

"Well, it was over a year ago I last saw her."

"Did you tell her that you read for me?" *...And that you are my dear friend, my spiritual mother, and my lifeline right now?* I left the latter part unsaid, but my thoughts were so loud she could probably hear them.

"No, and I am conflicted about whether I should share the information with you, Jenna. I do have a confidentiality policy. Yet, you are so dear to me, and I know the struggles that you face from this woman."

"Don't worry about it, Faith, it's none of my business." I was suddenly so jealous; I didn't know where it came from.

"I'm sure it was only a one time visit." Faith read my energy. I felt incrementally better. "Shall I see you in ten minutes?"

"Please come in." Faith offered a warm hug and we walked back to her reading room. It was familiar and comfortable and I felt the previous tension ebb from my body. I notice a slight quiver in her hands as she shuffled the cards. I'd seen her hands tremble a few times during our last few meetings. *She must be tired. Sixty years old and taking care of your aging mother can't be easy.*

"I thought about it while you were on your way over. Here's what I can offer." Faith took a deep breath before continuing. "This woman has more dramas in her life than you can imagine. Her husband is a driving force behind everything you are facing in this lawsuit, and there is an even bigger scenario waiting in the wings right after your situation wraps up."

"Are they going to get a divorce?" I tossed out a guess.

"Yes, and he is using this lawsuit as a way to teach Ruth a lesson about all of the nasty things he can do to her, if she decides to leave him. You see, Jenna, the lawsuit and the trial is not about you. It's about them. Both are determined to take it to the max to teach the other one a lesson. You are just caught up in this situation."

"Faith, are they going to win this case? Is it really going to trial?" She closed her eyes and took several deep breathes before shuffling the deck of cards and laying them before me in a pattern on the table.

"Yes, I'm afraid it will go to trial. They are too stubborn. No, Jenna, the verdict will not go in their favor, but that does not mean that there will not be many personal losses for you anyway."

I didn't need a reading to recognize this truth. Ruth was a master at trashing me in every conversation she's had over the past year. I could see the social damage in the silent stares and whispered comments at the kids' school. *Whatever happened to innocent until proven guilty?* In the court of private school parental opinion, I guess that saying doesn't apply.

"Jenna, there is a karmic lesson here. Sometimes events happen in our lives to force us to grow and evolve into the person we came to this earth to become. These events are never gentle. Think of it as the "dark night of the soul." Here, look at the Tower card.

Everything that is out of balance in your life is going to fall away or be destroyed. But remember that the dawn always follows the night. This all will pass and you'll be in a very different space. A stronger, more empowered space."

"It sounds so scary. I'm so afraid all of the time. Every time the phone rings, every time the mail comes, I'm almost afraid to leave my house, I don't know when the next assault is coming and from where. I don't know how much more I can take." I felt a small shiver travel my spine.

"You are only beginning to know yourself, Jenna. Only beginning to come into your true power. These challenges are part of that process. Embrace them and absorb the lessons. That makes it so much easier. What you fear is only the illusion of what could happen. It's not real. It's not the truth."

"I think I understand what you are talking about." Her energy was so soothing, I felt better. "Oh, I also wanted to mention something about my meeting with my attorney. I'm afraid he's planning to pull out all of the stops in his attack on the Simons."

Faith pulled few more cards and then looked at me.

"Everyone involved will get what they deserve. You've heard the saying 'What goes around comes around'. Well, that's what's going to happen here. They are attracting the embarrassment and judgment to themselves, because they have been so focused on creating it for you. You know about the law of attraction, don't you, Jenna? The energy you send out comes back to you. Both positive and negative."

"I'm beginning to learn that very lesson. Thank you, Faith," I stood to hug her goodbye. " Next week I need to cancel. I have to go to Chicago on business."

"That's good for me too, Jenna. I'm planning to take a few days off to help my Mom. She's moving into an assisted living facility. I'm just feeling extremely worn out these days. I think I need some rest."

"That's a good idea, Faith. You'd better take care of yourself; I don't want you to get sick."

Chapter 56

"Honey, have you felt Mia's head? She feels really hot," I was hugging the kids after walking in the door from my business trip. I was gone a week to finish the details of selling the business. It was bittersweet, but I hoped the proceeds would end the lawsuit with Ruth.

"I didn't notice. She seemed a little fussy, but I just thought she was tired," Steve didn't even look up from the computer in his office.

"Was she sick while I was out of town?"

"I'm sorry, honey, I really didn't notice. She seemed ok. We've had a lot of problems at work this week. Half of the employees' paychecks were bounced by the bank." Steve looked really stressed when our eyes connected.

"What in the world caused that to happen? These are people who work at a fast food restaurant. Aren't they relying on their paycheck to survive? I imagine most of your employees live hand to mouth."

"I know, Jenna," Steve looked irritated.

"Dad decided last month to take over half of the business accounts to manage personally," Steve leaned forward on his elbows, his hands raking through his hair. "As a result, I only have a fraction of the resources to work with that I had before. Yet I still have all of the same expenses; food, employees, utilities. It's causing all kinds of problems. The paychecks are only the beginning."

"Well, are you going to say something to him?" Now I was

irritated. *At some point you'd think this would be a sign to resign.*

"Jen, I haven't seen him in the office for three months. He always seems to be on a vacation. Last week he was in Napa Valley. This week the caller I.D. said Gainey Ranch in Scottsdale, Arizona. There have also been phone calls from St. Bart's, St. Thomas, Laguna Nigel," Then Steve offered up a weak explanation, but I could tell he did not believe it himself. "He says he's thinking about investing in some luxury real estate to diversify our business. He needs to tour the sites first."

"I think he's with Libby." I knew it was true the minute the words left my mouth.

"She told me several months ago they had been taking short trips every other weekend when Blake had the boys for his visitation. Something about her not wanting to be seen with another man in public, around town, until the divorce was final."

"I don't know if I even want to hear anymore," Steve looked more upset than before. *Don and Libby's global playground was draining the bank of our world.*

"That's probably why he wants the money from the business," I was beginning to piece together the puzzle, and it was alarming. "Remember, I told you, I saw him use the company credit card to buy the new plane tickets when Libby forgot to renew her passport for the cruise. That time at the airport alone was thirty–six thousand."

"Jenna, there is something else," Steve looked at me apologetically. "Our paycheck bounced, too."

"What are we going to do, Steve?" I sat down on the nearest chair and put my hands through my hair in frustration. *We have so many payments with the house, groceries for our kids, school tuition; the list is endless. Whatever savings we have would only keep us above water for a few months.*

"You're plugging holes in the business and he's draining it out the back end. Has he ever signed the papers for you to buy the stores for yourself?"

Steve looked at the floor, "He said he'd take care of it next time he's in the office."

I could picture Don and Libby romping on the beach outside a Ritz Carlton somewhere. I know his taste buds are first class all the way. *I'm so pissed.* Despite his promises, I've known for months Don had decided against selling the business to Steve. It was too much of a personal piggy bank for him to resist. Don is vindictive; he'd rather let the business implode than allow someone else to be successful at running it.

Mia started crying again, interrupting our debate. It was a strange high-pitched whine I had not heard from her before.

"Sweetie, are you okay?" My toddler just leaned her dark hair against my chest and sobbed as I stroked her scalding, but dry, head.

I held her face in my hands and looked at her eyes. They were glassy. Then I noticed a smudge of dark blood under her nose. Something was not right. My radar was on full alert now.

"Steve, did Mia hit her nose? Or has she been complaining of a headache or anything?" I'd been gone three days. Lolly was home, and so was Steve, but Steve is not always the greatest with the medicine cabinet, especially now with all of the distractions at work. I looked at my watch. It was three o'clock.

"I'm going to see if the pediatrician can fit us in today." I immediately went to the phone and dialed.

Chapter 57

"**S**o, little Mia, what do we have here?" Dr. Mirrielle Ford has always had such a warm, kind nature with my children. I felt reassured.

"I don't know what's going on, Dr. Ford. I was away on a business trip and when I came home this afternoon Mia was not herself."

"Well, she definitely has a fever, 104 degrees. But what is this under her nostrils? It looks like blood or something?"

"Do you think it could be a sinus infection?"

"I'm not sure. Let's have a look." Dr. Ford was quiet for some time as she looked in Mia's ears, throat and nose with her light. I was starting to feel uncomfortable with the amount of time she was examining my child. *Just give me an antibiotic that will fix it so she can go home, get in bed and be better by the morning.*

"Mrs. Sinclair, can you sit tight for a moment? I'd like to call a specialist and see if he is still in his office," Dr. Ford turned and walked out of the exam room. *A specialist? Okay, now I'm getting really worried.*

Fifteen agonizing minutes later, she returned. "We're in luck. Dr. Ford, an ear, nose and throat specialist, has agreed to see Mia this afternoon. I think there might be a foreign object in Mia's nose. I saw something with the light. Perhaps that is the source of the infection. But I do not have the right tools in my office."

Dr. Ford took out a pad and quickly wrote directions to Dr. Ford's office. I felt a mixture of relief and concern. Mia is always sticking Lego's, peas, paper, whatever, up her nose. It's just a kid thing. Maybe this will resolve itself today after all.

Chapter 58

"Hmm. I think I might see something," Dr. Ford was leaning over my squirming toddler with a nostril-expanding tool and a head mounted flashlight.

"Do you mind if I have the nurse come in and hold your daughter, so we can get the item out? It looks like it might be pretty far back up in the sinuses. In fact, with your permission, I think we should use the papoose."

"Sure, whatever you think. You are the doctor."

Mia was less than thrilled with the straightjacket wrapped around her small body. *Maybe this will teach you not to put things up your nose.* I was worried. I wished this would be over soon. When she's older, we'll probably all laugh about the toy she shoved up her nose.

Dr. Ford sprayed numbing spray up both of her nostrils and I stroked her hair for a few minutes while we waited for the medicine to kick in. Then he took a long thin tool and ventured way up her nose. I could hear it click with the item inside. Mia was crying and squirming.

"Hold on sweetheart, it's a little difficult to reach," he was calm and steady in an atmosphere of hysteria.

Dr. Ford removed the tool and traded it for another instrument. Several minutes passed as the doctor tried to secure the item in Mia's nose with the tool, so he could pull it out. Mia was squirming and crying. *God, please help my child. Help the doctor get whatever it is, the hell out of Mia's nose.*

"I think I've finally got it." *I can only imagine what it is: a screw, a Lego, a part from a small toy, who could guess?* I chuckled a little at the thought.

At the end of his medical pliers, or whatever they are called, was a black and red blob of mucus covering a small silver disc. I look at it mystified. "What is that?"

"This is not good," Dr. Ford said grimly. "In fact, this is the worst possible thing that could be up her nose." At that moment, life changed for my little girl.

Chapter 59

"Jenna, this is Kat at the Soul Center." I had answered my cell phone on the first ring, hoping it was Faith. I really needed to talk to her about Mia, the business, and the lawsuit: just everything. Faith had been sick for a few days. I thought it was the flu. I was so preoccupied with Mia.

"Oh, hello, Kat. I thought you were Faith. Is she feeling better yet?" I tried not to sound too disappointed

"Actually, Faith is in the hospital."

"What? Did the flu turn into pneumonia?"

"Not exactly, Jenna. She wanted me to call you and let you know. She's in the emergency room at St. John's Mercy Medical Center."

"Okay, I'm on my way home from the doctors' office with my little girl. I'll try to get over there as soon as possible." I hung up the phone. *Must everything fall apart all at once?*

The hospital smelled of medicine, half eaten trays of food, and powerful sanitation products. I've never liked hospitals. Long cold tile corridors; soft, sad whispers; the hum of a life support machine: it all seems so bleak and frightening, a place of sickness and death.

"Hello, Faith?" I gently knock on the half open door to the room the nurse said was assigned to Faith. No one responded, so I knocked again.

" Come in." I heard a weak reply. It was Faith.

215

" Hi, lady," I tried to sound cheerful, "What are you doing here?"

"Hi, Jenna." Faith patted the side of the bed, gesturing me sit near her. "Come here, there's something I'd like to share with you." I walked over and clasped her hand in mine. "What is it?"

Faith took a deep breath to steady her. By the grimace on her face, I could tell she was in a lot of pain. I gently squeezed her hand in an effort to send her some strength. *I hope she'd be back to her old self soon; I hated to see her suffer like this.*

"Jenna, dear, I have cancer." She looked me right in the eyes and I knew she had carried this truth for a long time.

"What exactly does that mean, Faith? Are you going to get treatment? A lot of people survive cancer. I know you will be one of them." I was trying to be hopeful, optimistic.

"Jenna, I've known it for a long time. I decided a while back not to treat my cancer. Now, the doctor says it has spread to my bones," I noticed her voice took on a quiet resolve.

"I'm not sure I understand." I couldn't bring myself to ask if she was dying.

"There is a divine design, Jenna. We talk about it all the time. Whatever God has planned for me, I'm willing to accept." *But I'm not willing to accept anything. Especially, when it comes to losing Faith. I need her too much. Now, I feel guilt. Faith is sick, really sick, and I've been loading her up with my frivolous burdens all these years.* I feel so ashamed.

"Faith, I'm so sorry," Tears start to roll down my face. "I've been such a burden to you."

"No, dear. You are a joy. I love you." It was her turn to pat my hand. "It will all work out, child, you will see. Trust the Universe."

At that moment, a nurse walked in. "She really needs to get some rest. Can you come back during visiting hours tomorrow?"

"Sure, no problem." I turned to Faith, "I love you too, Faith. I'll pray for you tonight."

"I'd really like that, Jenna." She sounded drowsy. So I left.

God, what is happening? I didn't even get a chance to ask her about my daughter, Mia. Not to mention everything else. *What am I going to do?*

"Mrs. Sinclair, this is Dr. Ford's office. I'm calling to set up the surgery for your daughter Mia."

"Oh, yes, of course."

"How about the day after tomorrow?"

"Ok, we'll be there."

The silver disc that had been lodged up Mia's nose was a watch battery. Dr. Ford explained to me that the acid in the battery was activated by the mucus in Mia's sinuses, and it had leaked from the battery and damaged the interior of her nose. He said we needed to schedule an exploratory surgery to determine the extent of the damage.

It turns out the dark smudge under her nose was a combination of blood and battery acid. I was sick to my stomach thinking about the pain my baby must have experienced. I still have no idea where she found a loose battery; it must have fallen out of one of the toys.

Dr. Ford wanted Mia to be on antibiotics for a few days prior to the procedure. He was concerned that the raw tissue might be exposed to additional bacteria creating a larger problem. I was all tied up in knots. Faith was too weak for me to even consider asking her about the outcome. *God, please help my child and help Faith.*

I knew Steve would not be able to go to the hospital on Thursday. A group of auditors was coming in to look at the books of the Burrito Bandit, and he wanted to cooperate, since he planned to own it in the near future. Apparently, it was not just the employees who were not getting paid these days. My head has been pounding for days. I don't know which crises to prioritize as the most important disaster.

Chapter 60

"**M**rs. Sinclair?"

"Yes, Dr. Ford." He was still wearing his operating room scrubs.

"We have a wait and see situation with your daughter. I did discover a substantial amount of damage inside her nose. Basically, there is a hole the size of the battery disc where the acid burned away the tissue of the septum."

I gasp. Her nose was so small, how could she have a hole that size? At least it was not visible from the outside of her face.

"Right now, it's not something we can repair. She is so young and the tissue is still growing and expanding. But my concern is that his area of the nose provides the support for the structure and shape of the nose. Without it being present, there is a danger the nose may collapse on the face, creating a cosmetic problem."

I gasp again, this time in horror. *My beautiful little girl, this can't be happening.*

The doctor continued, "I'm also concerned about future problems with the sinuses, damage to the tear ducts, and infections from the scar tissue. It's exposed down to the bone in some areas."

"I'm speechless, doctor," I didn't cry, I didn't move. It felt like Dr. Ford was talking about someone else, totally unrelated to me.

"Let's just let it heal for a while. Continue the antibiotics. Come see me again in two weeks. We will probably not know the outcome here for a while." He offered a reassuring pat on my shoulder and walked off.

I wanted to shout and scream and pound my fists on the ground. There were too many unknowns for me to handle right now. I've never been great with surprises. *Will Mia be all right? Will Faith die? Will Steve get to buy the business? Will I have to go to trial next week? Will Libby and I ever be friends again? Will we get our paycheck?* The list just went on and on, each mystery more daunting than the next.

The second I walked in the door, **"You've Got Mail!"** sounded from my computer. With everything going on, I had not checked it for days.

I saw an email from Libby.

That's strange. We usually speak by phone, although there hadn't been much of that lately. Her life affairs were completely handled by Don these days. He was paying her bills, advising her divorce attorney on strategy, and listening to her endless complaints about Blake. I should be happy, even relieved, but it felt strangely like a desertion.

In addition, I ran into Ronnie at the grocery store, last week. Her angry words are still rattling in my brain. "You think Libby Peters is a true friend to you, Jenna? You are so mistaken. You should hear what she says about you."

"I don't know what you are talking about, Ronnie? Also, I thought you weren't speaking to me anymore." I was poised by my cart in the produce section, between the bananas and the nuts.

Ronnie pushed on, "She said you've always been attracted to Don. In fact, she said, it's really him you wish you were married to instead of Steve. So you could be the true Mrs. Sinclair."

"That's absurd, I am the true Mrs. Sinclair and have been for the last twelve years. Since I married Steve."

"Libby also said you've always been hot for Don and you are jealous of her relationship with him, because he has all of the money and the power. She also said people think Mia is his child, not grandchild, because her complexion is so dark, unlike yours and Steve's."

She stopped her poisonous tirade for a minute to catch her breath. Ronnie was near hyperventilation. "Did you sleep with my husband, Jenna?"

I was shocked. Flabbergasted. Disgusted.

I looked at Ronnie in utter disbelief, and then decided to turn and push my shopping cart away. She was crazy, and I can't reason with someone who is insane.

I opened the email: it was a link to Chicken Soup for Moms. Attached was a note from Libby.

"I heard about Mia. Hope she is okay. Libby."

I didn't even know she had my email address. But it was not what the email said; it's what it didn't say. My child is facing a terrifying health crisis. After years of listening to my friend sob and snivel about her cheating husband, Libby doesn't have the time to pick up the phone and call me to check in? I know she's talking to Don several hours a day. At our peak, her daily phone calls consumed five hours out of each day.

I decided to give her a call.

"Libby? It's Jenna."

"Oh, hi, sweetie. I've been meaning to call you. Blake has been so awful lately. The boys are really upset with their Dad." She didn't even ask me about Mia.

"Libby, will there ever be a time when I call you and I'm not greeted with the daily journal of sins committed against your life?"

"Whoa, Jenna, what's that all about?"

"You know Mia is having this problem with her nose, and you can't even pick up the phone and call, after all of the ways I've been there for you."

There was silence on the other end of the phone.

"Well, I just thought you didn't want to hear all of my problems any more, so I've been talking to Don. Plus he doesn't really like the fact that we are friends. He says it's too invasive in his personal life."

Now it was my turn to be silent. *Were we ever friends? Or was I simply a useful product to be discarded when my services were no longer necessary?*

"Libby. Are you for real? I know the kind of friend I have been for you. Everything was put on hold in my life, so you could feel my love and support 24/7 during your difficult time. Let me ask you a question. What have you ever done for me as a friend? I just want to know the answer."

"I defend you, Jenna."

There was a long, quiet pause.

Here's a twist. I need protection against her. Libby's chronic stream of gossip about my life and her involvement with Don were coming at a high price on many levels. It's a price I'm no longer willing to pay.

"Libby, there are no words left between us. Goodbye." I hung up the phone, my hand trembling with anger.

Chapter 61

With Faith out of commission and so many urgent questions swirling in my head, I decided I still needed some kind of advice, at least until she was feeling better. She was the only psychic I had ever known. I didn't know where to begin to find someone else.

I guess I'll start on the Internet. I typed in the word Psychic and eight thousand possibilities flooded my screen, in groups of ten. *Wow, I didn't realize so many people were intuitive.*

I spent an hour clicking on the possibilities. I came across a website that sounded intriguing. *Need to Get Rid of a Troublesome Person? Stop Your Enemies Cold in Their Tracks?* Read the headlines.

I have a whole list of troublesome people; this looks perfect. What do I need to do? I clicked on the info box and a virtual storefront opened up, offering a variety of spells and hexes. *This is really bizarre. I didn't know spells existed any more and the fact that they can be purchased on line for $19.95 blows me away.* "Desperate people do desperate things" I rationalized. If anyone ever found out I was considering this, I would be toast.

There were over fifty spells to choose from, most were aimed at reuniting with a lover or heating up your sex life. *A master psychic casts all spells and hexes when the moon is right,* read the ad. I'll have to keep those in mind if this works. Then I found the three worth considering: **Extreme Justice:** A powerful hex designed to

222

stop your enemy in their tracks and squish their evil ways, quickly and permanently. Next one to consider: **Banish, Then Vanish Them:** Get those troublesome individuals out of your life forever. And finally: **The Boomerang Spell:** Take all of the evil intentions and negative energy your enemies are sending your way and return it back to them three-fold.

That last one sounded like mega karma. I think I'll try that one out. I don't wish any new problems on someone, but if they need a taste of their own medicine I can be party to that. I just want this lawsuit to be over.

I typed in my credit card number and instantly a receipt popped up with special instructions:

Thank you for your order. Your spell will be cast in the next week when the moon is right. Please fill out the questionnaire below with the name and information about the person to whom you wish to aim the spell casting. Thank you for your business.

I guess the days of back alley voodoo are over. I quickly filled out the form with Ruth and Ira's names and other important information and returned the email. *I wish they could do it tonight.*

A few days later, a noticed an email from the spell casting company:

Dear Mrs. Sinclair,
Please permit this letter to notify you that your Boomerang spell has been cast on Ruth and Ira Simon. From this point forth, all evil intentions and negative energy directed at you by your enemies will return to them 3x3x3.

Please be patient, these spells can take up to a month. However, we do offer a guarantee. If no results are seen in one month's time, we will recast the spell.
Sincerely,
Merlin, Master Warlock

I printed a copy of the letter and saved a draft to my email folder. Just in case I needed to have a double whammy. At least that's taken care of.

A few hours later, the phone rang. It was a mom from school, "Jenna what are you up to? I got a really strange email from you. Something about a spell."

I felt fingers of dread creeping up my spine, "What do you mean?"

"You sent a group email to the auction committee with an attachment letter about a spell that was cast on the Simons. Are you totally nuts?"

Oh shit. Was the boomerang spell accidentally cast on me?

"Oh, that was an accident, it was just a joke email I meant to send to a friend. I must have accidentally forwarded it to all of you," *Oh Lord, how will I ever repair this one?*

Chapter 62

The phone ringing pulled me back from my preoccupation watching Mia watch television. Ever since the incident, I'm always watching, as if by paying closer attention, I could prevent something bad from happening again.

"Jenna, get your ass down to the courthouse, pronto!" Dixon sounded more abrupt than I'd ever heard him.

"What? Dixon, what's the matter? Where are you?" I was completely shaken. For the past month leading up to the trial every phone call, every piece of mail, felt like it might contain my final summons to the guillotine. I don't think the spell worked its magic, other than to make me out to be a total freak. I had hoped we would settle this out of court. After the sale of the business, there was now nothing left to fight about. Now it is all about vindictiveness.

Could this be the call I've been dreading? The stress from the lawsuit is causing all sorts of anxiety based problems all over my body: I have a giant oozing cold sore fighting for real estate on my lip; a smattering of angry red pebbles strewn across my face, too sore to pop; a desire to use coarse grade twelve sandpaper on my raging vaginitis and compulsive eating, which has caused my size twelve jeans to suddenly feel like size twos -- as in too tight -- as my expanding ass fights for growth opportunities outside of the denim confines it was once happy to inhabit. Yes, I am a mess; plain and simple, I am fat and freaked out.

"Dixon, I just spoke with you thirty minutes ago and you said it would probably not go to trial today. Dix, you said there were four other cases in front of me!" I could hear a high-pitched thread of panic squeeze all of the breath out of my words

"Dixon, we didn't even prepare," I groaned. His cavalier attitude was getting to me. Hot lawyer extraordinaire, Dixon Fox, may find this cat fight entertaining, but it's not his fur that is flying, and this squabble has been ruining my life and draining my Prada pocketbook for the last twelve months. I wish I could call Faith for reassurance. She's in the hospital again. I feel so alone.

"I need you here now! We are a GO! I doesn't matter what I said an hour ago, things change." Dixon was all business. He clearly had his game face on. I chose him for his reputation as a junkyard dog. This man is not afraid of a back alley fight, and we've had plenty.

The Simons have tried everything over the past year to discredit the business and me. They used all of their clout to try to buy off other attorneys, so that I would have trouble finding someone to defend me. They called in a favor from a contact at the local police department to insinuate I had committed a crime. It was quickly dropped. But the detective scared the hell out of me. I'm now certain that was their intention. They even tried to involve the Internal Revenue Service, saying I was guilty of tax evasion. All of the accusations were false, everything dissolving to dust upon casual investigation, but I live in a town where if there is smoke, people assume there is fire. The Simons loved to create a lot of smoke, and a person can die from smoke inhalation.

I needed to mentally prepare myself for their latest attack. God, I have to be in a courtroom in less than an hour. The moment I thought would never happen has arrived. I don't even know where the courtroom is; I'll have to call Dixon back for directions. I hung up the phone, lay on my floor face down, and cried.

"God," I sobbed. "Please make this go away! Please…"

"It's enough. I can't take any more." I could feel the carpet fibers coarse across my face. A tuft of cat fur lodged in the carpet mingled with the tears and snot staining my face, causing me to sneeze. Yet, I could not get up. I was face down, humiliated and desperate. I cried and sobbed and begged and prayed for what seemed like an eternity. Face down, waiting: for what or for whom, I'm not sure.

My husband Steve was immersed in his own problems. He also was scheduled to attend a hearing today in a different courtroom with Don about the IRS and franchise problems with the Burrito Bandit. *Why does everything have to happen all at once?*

Steve offered to come to the trial with me for support. I always said emphatically, NO! The Simons would love to drag my husband into this problem; they tried several times and several ways. I was determined not to let that happen. *This was my business, my problem, and my lesson. No point in making it more complicated than it already was.*

Eventually, the sobbing gave way to a quiet sense of resolve. No one was coming, at least not to my bedroom floor, to retrieve me. I could not hear my knight in shining armor climbing the stairs of my newly remodeled Victorian to take me away on his black steed for an afternoon of sex in a sunlit meadow, nor did I hear the trumpets of angels descending from Heaven to elevate me on a golden bridge to a spa in the clouds where I could pass the time until the trouble had passed over me. No, there was only me, covered in snot, tears and pet fur, and I had to be somewhere in less than ten minutes. *Self-pity is a real time eater!* I didn't realize I had been lying there for so long.

Judge Francine Martin's courtroom was standing room only. Over her head was a large state seal depicting an eagle eating a serpent. It was bark bronze and at least ten feet tall. To her right, lining the wall was a collection of a dozen or more men and women dressed in orange jumpsuits, handcuffed, waiting for their turn at justice. The gallery benches held several toothless and tattooed men, and young women covered in piercings, juggling crying babies and squirming toddlers, next to young lawyers in cheap suits with vinyl brief cases so full of documents they were impossible to close. It was a real life circus and I was the next act.

"Hello, Jenna," Dixon offered me a reassuring hug. This unexpected display of affection took me by surprise. He must have sensed my mounting anxiety. "Sorry about the confusion. Come on, let's go into one of the private consultation rooms outside in the hall where we can talk." I heard a cackle of laughter coming from a room right outside of the courtroom. I immediately recognized the vexatious sound as belonging to Ruth. *What does she have to laugh about? Is this all a joke to her?*

The waiting room Dixon led me to was a four-foot by four-foot square cell, with cinder block walls painted an institutional grey. There were no windows, with the exception of a sliver of glass in the one steel door. In the center of the room was a sturdy metal table, circa 1960, with a collection of four wooden chairs for lawyers and their clients to share.

"Have a seat," he held out a chair for me before taking a seat for himself. Dixon was a southern gentleman, in addition to being an asshole. That was part of his charm. He swung the chair around backwards and straddled the seat in a cocky disregard for how things were designed for use. At times like this, he seemed oddly attractive. Although Dixon probably weighs less than me, I know I could never borrow his jeans. His fighting weight at six foot one is probably one hundred and sixty pounds. He's a lean machine, like a high school wrestler primed to hit the mats after a week of carrots and protein shakes. It's a charisma thing. The energy of his bottomless confidence, combined with a "screw-the-world-I-dare-you" attitude, was overflowing into those thirsty parts of myself, and I felt fortified for the first time in weeks.

"Jenna, you have to calm down. Just let me handle everything. I never lose." Dixon obviously thought I was worried about the trial, but in fact, I was absorbed in him. It was as if I was seeing a person for the first time, although I'd known them for ages.

"Of course, Dixon," I shook myself out of my reverie. *Dixon, a hottie? I must be looking for any means of escape.*

"The rest of the day will be devoted to jury selection, then the trial. They have us blocked out for four days."

"Four days?" I groaned and placed my head in my hands face down on the graffiti-laden tabletop. "I thought we might be done by tomorrow."

"I was hoping, but then I saw the stack of legal boxes they wheeled in on a dolly. They are planning for quite a show. I counted at least five."

Are we prepared? I feel so unprepared. Dixon was so impromptu, it unnerved me. At best, he probably brought a file folder and a legal pad to the courtroom. It's clearly too late to choose a different captain to lead the charge, so I'm going to trust my initial instincts.

Jury selection was an interesting study in the pulse of America.

Our options for jurors were as vast as the selections available in a grocery store. One man with shaggy hair and tattoos had just come from a hearing in another courtroom; he couldn't guarantee his four-day availability, because he might be reporting to jail. A young woman brought her infant to the courtroom and proceeded to nurse the baby throughout the questioning. She said she had no childcare, as the baby grunted and squirmed while suckling her pink breast. There was a pediatrician who knew the Simons; a construction worker who had faced two bankruptcies; a retired schoolteacher; a city bus driver; a securities investor wearing a light blue suit and a purple tie who still lived at home with his mother. In all there were over fifty individuals filling the courtroom. Their stories and credentials all congealed into one large blob. *I'm glad Dixon is paying attention. I have a headache.*

In the end we selected twelve, but I can't say it was a collection of my peers, definitely not Ruth's. Private banking, fur coats and country club dues are not even in the vocabulary of most of the reluctant participants in this group. I cringe inwardly. *These people hold my fate in their hands and they are going to hate both of us!*

"All rise, The Honorable Judge Francine Martin presiding," We stood as the judge entered the chambers, ready to start the first day of the trial. Judge Martin was a petite redhead with sparkling brown eyes and a pageboy hair cut. Beneath her black robe, I caught a glimpse of an ivory pantsuit, and on her feet were designer shoes, bridge level, Anne Klein perhaps, maybe Etienne Aigner, in chocolate suede. Respectable, but not over the top, like my leopard print Jimmy Choos. *Judges have to dress for respect, I imagine.* I left those at home and wore a pair of quiet black loafers. Probably no one knew they were Prada but me. It's a mental thing. If I am walking the plank, I plan to do it in style.

Judge Martin spoke directly to the attorneys.

"Mr. Fox, Mr. Harrell, are we ready to proceed with opening arguments?"

"Yes, your Honor."

"Yes, your Honor."

Female judges have it good, I thought to myself, *even a smartass like Dixon Fox treats her with respect.* I looked over at the jury; they looked bored already. *I mean, who wants to be on jury duty anyway.*

Our table runs parallel to the jurors' box. Dixon purposely chose the side facing the jury, so I could make eye contact with them throughout the trial. Or at least they could glare and roll their eyes at me. Ruth sat across the table from me, her back to the jury. All they saw was her wiry black hairdo; shiny with gel, and the kaleidoscope dress she chose to wear to court. I marveled to myself, what *inspired her to choose that outfit for today? Did she purchase it specifically for the trial? Is she dressed to impress?* Her ensemble consists of a wrap dress with a bold triangular pattern; from my angle it looks like lightning bolts in bright purple, mocha, and rose. *I know there is a storm coming, but does she have to be so obvious?* Her jewelry was a pair of glittering chandelier earrings made of pink quartz set in platinum; a long open loop chain in gold hung from her neck; and on her feet were a pair of camel suede stiletto heeled knee high boots with enough fringe to outfit a car wash. *Shazam!* That's all I could think of. A laugh almost escaped my lips, but I pushed it down, deep.

In contrast, I wore a pair of black pants and a black jacket, quiet and unassuming. My mother suggested that I wear a pair of denim overalls or something polyester from the racks at Wal-Mart. She said, "You need to look like you shop at Goodwill, so the jury will feel sorry for you." I considered what she said, but decided against it. Given the content of the case, me wearing a pair of denim coveralls and a lacy tank, like Daisy Duke, would look absolutely absurd. I don't even own clothes like that.

Ira Simons was the only guest in the courtroom. He sat alone on the long bench in the front row, wearing a navy blazer with gold buttons, a lemon yellow shirt and a royal blue and gold rep tie with diagonal stripes. His beady eyes never left my face, in a ghetto stare worthy of the South Texas Padres gang, a group where looks really can kill. *I guess if I had ever questioned how he felt about me, or what his intentions are towards me, it's no longer a mystery.* Steve did not come. I asked him not to. Things with the Burrito Bandit seem to be taking an unexpected turn. He needs to focus on that issue right now. Ironically, we are in the same courthouse today, but we might as well be millions of miles apart. *It's funny really, when you are in the heart of your darkest moments in life, it seems like you always have to face them alone.*

Wesley Corbit is one of the attorneys for the Simons. His boyish good looks and tousled blond hair are a marked contrast to his tightly wound clients. He's been handling the majority of the case. I get the impression that he is new to the practice of the law and that this is a training case for him. He stumbles thorough some of his arguments and motions. It appears he's more comfortable somewhere else, perhaps riding a surfboard or throwing a football. His co-counsel is a man named Edward Harrell. If all people have a corresponding animal for their appearance, Edward Harrell's animal is a lizard. His receding hairline exposes a shiny sloping scalp; wispy white blond eyebrows cap a pair of narrow reptilian eyes. Mr. Harrell is not a member of the Dixon Fox Fan Club. These two men would like to rip each other apart. Edward Harrell has filed every motion available against this case, and Dixon Fox personally. That could be the explanation for the stack of boxes sitting next to our table in the courtroom, on the plaintiffs' side.

"Mr. Harrell, you may proceed with opening arguments."

"Thank you, your Honor." Edward turned to face the jury. His smile looked more like a grimace. I don't think he is used to using these muscles in his face. "Hello, ladies and gentlemen of the jury. Thank you for being here today, and thank for the time away from your jobs and families to deliberate over this case before you." He was walking back and forth in front of the jurors' box, like a caged zoo animal, head down, chin forward. "We believe the evidence will show that Jenna Sinclair knowingly tricked Ruth Simon into becoming her business partner. That Ms. Sinclair knew the business was having financial troubles, but concealed it from Mrs. Simon. We believe that the evidence will show that Mrs. Simon purchased Ms. Sinclair a fur coat for which she has not been repaid." I looked at the jury: the fog of boredom had cleared from their eyes and they were looking at Ed Harrell with complete focus. *Did someone say fur coat? Maybe this might get interesting. Is this a business dispute or a divorce?*

"The evidence will also show that Ms. Simon invited Ms. Sinclair to her country club for a round of golf where she purchased her a golf outfit in the amount of seventy five dollars, but Ms. Sinclair failed to repay her. The evidence will also show that Ms. Simon purchased for Ms. Sinclair an oversized wine glass in the amount of ninety dollars. This expenditure was also never reimbursed. The evidence will show that Ms. Sinclair repeatedly treated the employees of the store to Subway sandwich lunches and paid for them out of the company's money. The evidence will also show that Ms. Sinclair donated several paintings to charity without the permission of Mrs. Simon. The evidence will also show that Ms. Sinclair used money from the company to pay for her retail accounts at Nordstrom, Neiman Marcus and Saks Fifth Avenue." Ed Harrell droned on for a few more minutes, listing all of my alleged sins, retail and otherwise, before taking his seat at our shared table, wearing a smile of smug satisfaction.

"Ladies and gentleman. You are to be commended and revered for your public service here today. Brace yourselves for total and complete absurdity. Everything about this case is ridiculous in the extreme." Dixon gets right to the point and Ed Harrell's jaw dropped to the table. Ruth Simon suppressed a giggle; Dixon's charm was penetrating, extending even to those who hated him.

"Ruth Simon and her husband Ira," Dixon gestured to Ira, who reached up to adjust his banana and blueberry colored tie, while all of the jurors turned to look him over. "He's the dapper fellow, and in fact the only person, seated in the guest area of the courtroom. This pair is what I refer to as members of the lucky sperm club. They come from immense inherited wealth, and this trial is designed to teach my client, Jenna Sinclair, a lesson about how they will stop at nothing to be perceived as right. In fact, I believe the lesson Ms. Sinclair has learned is to be careful with whom you enter into business. What the evidence will clearly show is that Ruth Simon wanted to join the business as a way to leave her troubled marriage." He paused and looked at Ira for dramatic emphasis.

"The evidence will also show that the business has already been sold and that Ruth Simon received a complete return on her investment. This trial is simply the latest spectacle in a series of moves to harass Ms. Sinclair."

"As a previous client and friend, Ruth Simon was well aware of the finances of the business. We will also prove that her "meager investment of seventy five thousand," in her own words, was an amount of little consequence in their household, and that casual tone was conveyed repeatedly to my client.

The evidence will also show that Ms. Simon has a fickle nature, and that she has been involved in several businesses, besides the gallery, such as a massage therapist, a personal shopper, a stockbroker, an exotic dancer and a chocolatier, specializing in the sale of candy confections which enhance a woman's libido. Ms. Simon joined Ms. Sinclair's business as a partner, and within a week the pair travelled to New York on an epic shopping spree where they purchased artwork, fur coats and fine cheeses.

However, after the spending spree, Ms. Simon fails to show up at the business again." Dixon again stops and shrugs at the jury. "Where did she go?" He pauses to add more drama. "What about all of the promises to Jenna Sinclair that she will actively participate in the business? Three months later Ruth demands a full refund of her investment while Jenna Sinclair is out of the county. Not only does she demand the money, but the evidence will show Ruth Simon took over all of the business accounts and began to repay herself out of the proceeds of the business without the permission of Ms. Sinclair." He stops and makes eye contact with each member of the jury. *God, he is magnificent!* "All the while, Ms Sinclair is out of the country and unaware of the actions unfolding in her business. A business she owned for six years independently prior to accepting Ruth Simon as a partner.

"The evidence will show..."

The smug smile had drained from Edward Harrell's face. Dixon was destroying their case with words of truth as effective as bullets from an assault rifle. But I did not want to get my hopes up. There was still a lot of testimony to follow.

Chapter 63

"Ms. Simon, how many sable coats did you purchase in New York?

"None."

"Ms. Simon, how many sable coats did your husband purchase in New York?

"None."

I could tell Dixon was getting frustrated.

"Is it your testimony, Ruth Simon that you didn't purchase any sable coats in New York with Ms. Sinclair?"

"Not sable coats."

"Okay, Ms. Simon what kind of coats did you purchase?"

"They were sheared minks; sable coats would have cost over one hundred thousand dollars each." I looked over to catch several member of the jury rolling their eyes.

Ruth had been on the stand for most of the day, and she looked like a spoiled brat. She kept laughing in a shrill, high-pitched cackle, thrilled that all eyes were on her.

The testimony was all about country clubs and exclusive private banking accounts, and of course our extravagant shopping spree in New York. At one point the judge called the attorneys to the bench.

"Gentlemen, is there no way to settle this absurd dispute? These people do not want to be here listening to this case." Judge Martin was more than a little irritated.

Next was my turn to take the stand. I miraculously managed to stay direct, concise and unemotional. The closing arguments followed.

"This case has all of the elements of a cat fight on the Jerry Springer show and a box of kitty litter," Dixon Fox's opening line of his closing argument drew a wave of snickers from the jury. After three days of debate over fur coats, sloppy contracts and fickle housewives turned businesswomen, this group of twelve men and women looked disgusted and ready to go home.

I made eye contact with a sympathetic-looking, thin black woman in her mid 50's in the front row of the jury box. She smiled at me discreetly. I vaguely recall her saying she worked as a school bus driver during the discovery part of the trial. We must look like spoiled assholes to her, really to everyone in the room. I felt a wave of shame wash over me.

At least it will be over soon. I thought about the mountain of money I now owe in legal fees and immediately the familiar burning sensation of the last few months returned to my abdomen and traveled up my esophagus. I could taste the bile in the back of my throat. My chest felt as it were being cracked open and my heart was awash with acid fear. *Perhaps I need to be medicated.*

It first happened the day I was unexpectedly served with the lawsuit papers by the sheriff. I thought it was a heart attack. Not quite, but it was an attack all right - a psychic one. Now I recognize the symptoms as anxiety and that relieves my fear of dying. It's simply the collision of bile and emotion in my being, eating me from the inside out. Candidly, this is another version of dying, only you still have access to oxygen. Recently, I've been able to shut the fear down to a daily simmer, but it still bubbles constantly deep under the surface.

Chapter 64

Dixon led me to the same little private waiting room with the metal chairs and the table. I could hear the muffled sounds of voices in the hallway. But, this space was like a little incubator, keeping the dangerous world at bay.

"Let's just stay in here and wait until the jury comes back with a verdict." He was pacing back and forth with nervous energy.

I had not slept the last three nights. Fear, anger and frustration had merged together to create a giant adrenaline fireball inside my heart. It ached with an indescribable pain and I could find no relief. It was worse at night.

"Jenna, come on kiddo," Dixon softens his courtroom bravado for a moment. He must have sensed my inner anguish. He walked behind me and started to rub my shoulders.

"God, Dixon that feels really good. I didn't realize how much stress I've been carrying. Please don't stop for few minutes," I closed my eyes as his rhythmic motions started to release some of the tension in my body.

"This is all highly comedic. You should be laughing right now, not crying." His voice sounded like a distant echo, I was so absorbed in the massage.

His hands moved down my back, kneading my muscles. Releasing the knots around my shoulder blades. Next, he moved down my back to my sides and the top of my hips. I was amazed how strong his hands felt. Dixon Fox had such a slight frame, I expected his grip to be weak, but that was not the case.

When his warms lips gently touched the back of my neck, I didn't object. It all merged together in the wonderful sensation of the massage. I needed some nurturing. Everything in my life was hard and cold these days, simply too much reality for a girl to bear alone.

His soft lips trailed down the back of my neck sending little sparks to the top of my head. Then he slowly retraced the path back up my neck to the tip of my earlobe. I was transported. Waves of delicious shivers began to roll through my body.

His strong hands slid around and cupped my breasts. I leaned back against his waist and allowed his fingers to slide inside my lacy bra and gently pinch and knead my nipples into taunt little pebbles. His breath was coming in quick hot bursts down on the top of my head and rolling over my forehead.

I leaned back and felt him hard and punishing against the back of my shoulders as he pushed me further up on the small metal desk. All reason flooded out of me, I was awash in a sexual haze. Dixon grabbed the back of my black lacy thong and ripped the thin fabric away in one swift yank.

"Knock, knock, knock," a strange sound pierced my encounter.

"Jenna, Jenna," Dixon's voice abruptly pulled me out of my lucid fantasy. He shook my shoulders. "Jenna, Earth to Jenna."

Disoriented, I looked at my clothing; it was still intact. I looked at Dixon, who smiled at me sheepishly, but was still dressed in his suit and tie.

"You must be really tired Jenna, that massage put you out."

I blushed deeply from my honey blonde head to the tips of my freshly pedicured cranberry toenails. *That was one hell of a fantasy. It felt so real; it was scary and weird.*

"The jury is back. It's time to go inside."

"Do you mind if I take a quick bathroom break? I need a moment."

Chapter 65

"How's it going?" Steve called me on the cell phone to check in.

At the sound of his voice, I felt guilty about my fantasy. Even though nothing had really happened. I did just have hot dream sex with my attorney in the courthouse waiting room with a window wide open for public viewing. Is that a fantasy felony? And, reality or not, it was the most ferocious sex I'd had in a long, long time.

"Hi Steve, the jury is back with a verdict. I can't really talk right now. How did your hearing go with the lender and the franchisee?"

"Not so great Jenna. They decided to shut down the business."

"What? I thought you were going to buy several of the stores?"

"Dad did finally sign the purchase agreement, as we entered the courtroom, but it was too late. The Burrito Bandit owes too many people money. We were forced into involuntary bankruptcy, so we can work out the money issues."

"Oh Honey. I'm so sorry." I felt my heart drop. This was yet another devastating surprise.

"I know you need to get back into the courtroom. We'll talk tonight. I'm hopeful things will still work out, for both of us."

"I love you, Steve. We'll get through it, whatever comes our way."

Chapter 66

"We the jury find in favor of the defendant, Jenna Sinclair."

There it was, the words I had waited to hear. After months of expensive legal maneuvering, I was vindicated. Ruth threw her pad of paper on the table in a sudden outburst. I could tell it had never occurred to her that she might lose this battle. Most things in Ruth and Ira Simon's lives go the way they want. Ira simply stood up and marched from the courtroom.

Dixon turned to hug me.

"Congratulations, Jenna."

"Thanks Dixon. I owe it all to you. You did a great job." The steamy fantasy of only thirty minutes ago already seemed like a distant dream. In place of lust, now was a deep feeling of gratitude. Dixon, this wiry, spitfire of a human being, had hung in there with me against Goliath.

"You know, I told you I never lose."

"You did say that Dixon, and as always, you were right."

"Oh, and Jenna, my bill is in the mail!"

"I never doubted it Dixon. The best does not come cheap." I smiled and walked to my car. I knew this was not the end of it. I had won in a court of law, but in the court of public opinion, I was still a loser.

Chapter 67

Steve spent the next two weeks trying to patch together his agreement to purchase the majority of the Burrito Bandit locations. He hoped to re-open the restaurants soon, so his employees could get back to work. Some had been with the Burrito Bandit over twenty-five years, long before his Father purchased the business a decade ago.

"Jenna, how are you holding up?" Danielle called me to check in. "Have you read the paper today?"

"No, what does it say?"

"There is a story about the Burrito Bandit on the front page and how they were forced into bankruptcy. Steve's name is quoted."

"Oh," I sighed with disappointment. "Don refused to testify at the hearing and Steve wanted to preserve his ability to purchase the stores. So he got up and spoke on behalf of the company. Now he's going to look like the fall guy in the media."

Why does shame always have to be so public? School just started last month and everyone in town reads the papers. I didn't think it was possible, but it appears my social decline has mushroomed into a landslide, actually a mudslide to be exact.

"Have you heard from Libby lately?"

"Sometimes, I see her at school, but we haven't hung out together for a few months. Once she got really hot and heavy with Don, our friendship took up residence at the North Pole. It really ended on that trip to Greece, or shortly after."

"Well I have a story to tell you. You better be sitting down."

"My friend Mara works in retail at Nordstrom. Long story short, we were chatting and she told me about a girl who comes in shopping with her sugar daddy boyfriend several times a week. This has been going on for months. He's one of the top spending customers at the store right now. In retail, it's everyone's business to track the big rollers. Apparently he spends thousands upon thousands of dollars each day, all designer brands. St. John, Prada, True Religion Jeans. You name it."

"Yeah, okay."

"Well the very next day, this same girl comes back and returns every single item for cash. To date, she has cashed in on fifty thousand dollars at this one store alone."

"The girl is Libby." We both said it at the same time.

"How did your friend know?"

"She recognized Libby from one of our girl's lunches at the café last year."

"She said all of the clerks are pissed at Libby, because her returns are screwing up their commissions."

"It's even worse Jenna, Mara has a friend in retail at Neiman Marcus and Libby is pulling the same routine over there. I think the cash figure on the returns at that store is even more, close to one hundred thousand dollars. I know because they track all of the sales and returns as a way to enhance customer service. Everyone is talking about her. The blonde bimbo who is cashing in on her unsuspecting boyfriend."

"You know that was all money from the company."

"I figured. But, I thought you should know."

"Thanks, Danielle."

"Call me if you need anything. By the way, how is Mia?"

"She seems a little better. No fever. We're scheduled to go to the doctor in a few weeks." I had to go drive the route. "Thanks for the update. I'll talk to you later."

"See you later. Hang in there."

Chapter 68

"Hi Dixon, I didn't expect to hear from you?" It had been almost three weeks since the trial.

"You are quite the celebrity Jenna."

"Oh really Dixon, why is that?"

"I have a friend, who is a reporter at the Suburban reader, who wants to run your story."

"She thinks it's interesting. She read about the case from the article in the Courthouse Review. You remember the one, it was titled Star-crossed art gallery at the center of debate over fur coats, country club outings and wineglasses.

"I had already forgotten about that little blurb. Who cares Dixon?"

"She has enough info to run the story whether you cooperate or not."

"My story is over Dixon. Case closed. I just want to forget it and move on."

"That's what you think Jenna. They are talking about an appeal of the verdict." *Darn it. I knew the Simons would be sore losers.*

"You need to talk to this woman. It's important."

A week later, I opened the Suburban Reader and the headlines Desperate Housewives glared back at me. My hands were shaking as I read the article, which portrayed Ruth and I as frivolous, moronic, domestic divas, clashing over our sheared mink jackets and our

Chinese oil paintings in a county courtroom.

In ten short absurd paragraphs, my fate was sealed. The events of the last month had succeeded in totally destroying my reputation; a reputation I had spent years cultivating. Someone basically did a full out lawn job in my botanical garden. Not an errant blade of goodwill grass was left.

Ruth's mudslinging campaign against me regarding the lawsuit and the newspaper articles about our businesses, true or not, had worked their magic, I was rendered socially invisible. Now, every day, as I walked to the classroom to pick up Lucy, no one acknowledged me with a wave or a nod. The phone was as silent as a frozen pond in an isolated winter glade. No one wanted a play date with Lucy and no one wanted any volunteer hours from me either.

I was even being shut out of the Girl Scouts as a parent coordinator. A group of parents simply moved in and suddenly my services were no longer necessary. I think that's they way one fires a volunteer. There were no waves from manicured fingers in the carpool line or smiles of acknowledgement from familiar faces. I was also beginning to suspect Libby had launched her own subtle smear campaign to counteract anything I might have said about her relationship with Don. There was no longer any doubt, my social plummet was humiliating and complete. At least Lucy was getting a good education. In time, I hoped everything would blow over.

"Mrs. Sinclair, may I have a word with you?" Ms. Abbott, The head of the Sycamore Creek Early Childhood Development center beckoned me from the doorway of her office.

"Sure, Ms. Abbott. What can I do for you? Sorry I haven't signed up for any committees this year. I've not had a chance."

"It has come to my attention, Mrs. Sinclair that you have not paid your tuition for this school year. It has also come to my attention that there have been some unsavory articles published about you and your family in the local papers." She cleared her throat before continuing. "Mrs. Sinclair, this is not the type of notoriety we seek to achieve here at Sycamore Creek. I've spoken to the board and we've decided to ask your family to leave our program effective today."

"What? Leave the program? Today?" I was flabbergasted. "My child has not done anything to hurt anyone. She loves it here. Ms. Abbott I was also cleared of every accusation. This is not fair." I started to lash out, then, I decided, I did not have the energy to do so. I knew Ruth was not leaving the school.

"Mrs. Sinclair, please do not make this anymore difficult or embarrassing than it has to be," her eyes looked down to the ground.

"Fine, Ms. Abbott, you win. I'll clean out Cole and Lucy's desks today," I turned and walked down the hall to my little girl's classroom, defeated.

Chapter 69

"Hello Faith, I brought you some fuzzy socks and a lavender pillow."

I stopped at the hospital for another visit. She still seemed weak, but the doctors said she could go home for now. I pulled back the sheets and slid her feet into the new soft pink socks.

"Thanks Jenna, those feel really good. My feet have been cold in here. You are always so thoughtful." She offered me an appreciative smile.

Then I gave her the heart shaped pillow. "Just know how much everyone loves you, Faith." She placed it on her chest and deeply inhaled the lavender scent, which is supposed to promote relaxation.

"Lavender is my favorite, how did you know?"

"I'm glad you like it," I gently patted her arm.

"Jenna, I'm sorry I have not been able to support you through the trial and everything else. I've felt to weak."

"I understand Faith. You've supported me for years. Your voice and words were with me even though you could not personally be there. Besides, I won. Now I just need for things to turn around with Steve."

"It will all work out in the end. Trust me on this Jenna. I see a lot of brightness around you."

"I hope you are right, Faith."

"Take care of yourself. Get some rest. You'll be back to yourself in no time." I prayed she'd be one of those people miraculously cured of cancer overnight. As I left the hospital, I wasn't sure when I would be able to see Faith again. She was moving an hour south of the city to stay with her mother.

Chapter 70

"Ring, ring." I could hear the phone ringing throughout the house. Demanding attention.

"Steve, why don't we just take it off the hook?"

"Whatever, you'd like Jenna," Steve was sitting in the brown leather chair in his office staring out the window. It was a seat he had occupied daily for the last couple of months.

Depression does strange things to people. He's up all hours of the night, I hear him pacing the house. Not to mention the fact that he's eating everything in sight. Right before my eyes my darling husband has turned into a fat, unbathed, zombie, lost in a fog of self-pity.

The phone is ringing again. It never stops. The complete implosion of our businesses earlier this year, has sent our financial life into a frenetic tailspin. Now, instead of friends calling, a host of rude and threatening debt collectors from a variety of companies are stalking us mercilessly.

I wish we had never paid for company expenses on our personal credit cards. Steve always thought it would be a matter of days before the business would transfer to him, he never considered that it might not happen. Everything was a pile of ashes at our feet. Not only do we have unpaid business expenses on our personal credit cards, but we no longer have health insurance. That was one of the things Don had stopped paying, opting instead to splurge on luxury travel with Libby, my ex-best friend. *However, as an aside, once the articles hit the paper about the Burrito Bandit, Libby dropped Don like a hot tamale. He was way too loaded for her plans of social ascension.*

All of Mia's medical appointments and her surgeries were rejected by insurance for non-payment from the company. Now in addition to the credit cards bills, we are facing a mountain of unpaid medical debt, close to fifteen thousand dollars.

Today, a certified letter came in the mail from the IRS. Steve is being personally assessed for all of the unpaid taxes from the Burrito Bandit, even though he was not in control of the company finances. Don refused to sign his name to the employee paychecks. Without a signature, no employees could be paid, so Steve stepped up to the plate. Now, according to this letter, he's on the hook for almost a million dollars of liability.

The IRS letters were strewn around Steve's feet in a crumpled mess. *This is the worst case scenario times one million.*

"Steve, we really need to talk," I walked into his office, risking a swing from his bear claw. He has definitely turned into a grouchy bear. I can't say I blame him.

"Yeah, what do you want?"

"Have you come up with any ideas for a new business, perhaps considered putting together a resume? I'm worried we are not going to be able to go on much longer like this."

"You think? What do you want me to do about it? I lost the business. It tanked. End of story." He sounded so bitter, so resentful.

"Steve, how can it be the end of the story? We have three small children. Thank God, my mother has stepped in and offered to pay our mortgages and some basics like food and utilities while we get back on our feet. Otherwise we'd be on the street right now."

"Oh yes, your mother, she's so great," His face contorted into a nasty sneer.

"I'm sorry Steve that Don screwed you over. In the end every single thing he promised turned out to be a lie. I don't know many fathers like that. Most men want to take care of their children and grandchildren. They want to protect them from harm."

I knew I should stop, but I couldn't, "Your father threw you on the sword to save his own skin. It has always been that way. Don is first."

Steve just sat there silent, brooding.

"Steve, you also carry some of the blame here. Why did you not leave the business and make other plans?"

Steve remained silent. This made me angry.

"We have to try and figure something out on our own, before it is too late. No one is going to come and rescue us."

Chapter 71

"Knock, knock," I walked to the front door. "Steve, are you expecting someone?" I shouted through the house. He didn't answer.

"Hello, may I help you?"

"Hello ma'am, I'm here to pick up a silver minivan, license plate FHT 769."

"I don't understand, it's not broken and we didn't call for a tow."

"I'm here on behalf of the finance company. I'm reclaiming the asset due to non-payment."

"What?"

"Yes, ma'am. Would you like a moment to remove your personal belongings?"

"Yes, of course." I stammered. "I'll be out back, give me moment."

"Steve what in the hell is going on?" I shouted into his office. He was there in his chair again staring out the window.

"What do you think is going on Jenna, we don't have any fucking money?" he screamed back at me.

"Okay, so could you have at least told me you decided to stop paying the car payments? Now they are here to repossess it!"

Steve just sat there and shrugged.

"Hello, are you in there? What happened to you?" My voice was near hysteria, "You're not dead. Where is the bottom? How far are you willing to let our family slide before trying to save us?' I stormed from the room, hot tears streaming down my face.

I grabbed a laundry basket and headed out to the car still sobbing. A stack of my CD's, Mia's car seat, several tubes of lipstick, Maverick's dog bed in the passenger seat, a backpack of workout clothes and the kid's sports bags. I collected it all. The whole time it felt as if the unknown man in the mechanic's jumpsuit was actually hauling me away, not simply my well-loved silver minivan.

Lolly was waiting for me at the door, a sympathetic expression on her face. She took the laundry basket from me, set it on the kitchen table and gave me a big hug.

"Doesn't life just suck sometimes," she offered consolation in her country twang.

In spite of my misery, I laughed.

"You know something Lolly, you've been such a great friend to me. Thank you." It dawned on me she was one of the few friends I had left in the entire world.

"Hey, I kinda like you too." We smiled at each other; her kindness soothing my broken spirit.

"You know something Jenna, I think I'm going to come here for a while free of charge." She must have read my mind. Lately I was dreading the fact that I could no longer afford her services, but didn't know how to say so after eight years together.

"I love the kids, you're ok too." We laughed again. "I know when things get better you'll make it up to me."

Chapter 72

"Maverick are you ready to go outside?" I called out the dog's name from the front door. For some reason, he had not come upstairs to sleep next to me in the bed last night. Lately Steve had moved into the guestroom. My little dog was a source of great comfort in my otherwise big empty bed.

"Maverick, where are you?" I called again, he didn't come, but I heard a whimper from the back hallway.

"Mav, are you back here?" I walked around the corner and he wagged his tail at me in a greeting, but still did not get up from his bed.

"Come on let's go outside. We need to hurry so we can get everyone to school on time." The kids had ended up a few blocks away at the neighborhood public school. It was anonymous, and that was fine with me. My mom Jackie had once again come to the rescue. She'd rented me a car for a few weeks until we could figure something out.

I walked over and stroked his dark fur. He yelped as I brushed over his leg.

"Baby, what's wrong with you?"

I looked at his leg and noticed it was cocked at a strange angle. He must have injured it.

"Steve, did something happen to Maverick?"

"Last night he fell off the temporary deck steps. I had to carry him back inside." Nothing seemed to faze Steve these days. He was frozen.

"Steve, I think you left him downstairs all night with a wounded leg. I hope it's not broken."

"Mrs. Sinclair," the vet was warm and friendly, but the news was devastating.

"We took an x-ray and your dog has a severe fracture of his left paw. Every bone in this foot area is broken. It's not something that will heal on its own." He pointed to injured area on the lighted x-ray display box.

"What do you recommend?" *And how much will that cost?* I was worried.

"There is a specialist in town. I will send the x-rays over to him today. They will get back to you with a prognosis and an estimate. My guess is he will probably need surgery."

"Thank you doctor. When can I see my dog?" I was missing Maverick terribly already. He's been a source of deep comfort these past few months.

"Why don't you call in this afternoon? We knocked him out for the x-ray and I am sure the techs will need time to put him in a temporary bandage to stabilize the break."

"Sure, Okay. I'll call around four after I've brought the kids home from school."

I walked out to my rental car and started crying. *What's next? God, please tell me what's next?*

"Mr. Sinclair? This is Amy from Dr. Gordon's office. Veterinarian Specialty Services. We are calling about your dog Maverick?'

"Oh, yes. What did Dr. Gordon think about the break?"

"He's like you to come in for an appointment and consultation later today. Say one o'clock?"

Later that day, I drove to his office stroking Maverick's head as he was gingerly seated in the front seat. I could tell by his eyes, he was in pain.

"Hello Mrs. Sinclair. I'm Dr.Gordon."

"Hi, Dr. Gordon, how soon can you fix my dog?" I spurted out. "He means everything to me," the anxiety was taking it's toll.

"Well that's what I wanted to talk to you about," I picked

something up in his tone and it sent shivers down my spine.

"What is it?'

"Upon closer inspection of the x-ray, I'm afraid there may be an additional problem with your dog Mrs. Sinclair," He snapped the film into the light box. "Do you see this area here inside the body? It looks like a suspicious mass. I'm afraid your dog may have cancer Mrs. Sinclair."

A broken leg and cancer? I dropped my head to my hands and started pulling at my hair. *No, God please no! Do anything to me, but not this. Not now.*

"Mrs. Sinclair, there are treatments for cancer. It doesn't have to be an immediate death sentence," Dr. Gordon compassionately touched my shoulder.

"How much doctor? How much will it cost? To fix the leg and cure the cancer?" I wasn't sure if either result was possible.

"The surgery for the leg is about eighteen hundred dollars. Cancer treatments start around twenty-five hundred." My heart shattered.

In another lifetime, I would have whipped out my credit card and bared no expense to save my dog. Now it was impossibility, all of my credit cards were maxed out with residual business expenses and lawyers fees.

"How much time do I have?"

"To operate on the leg, we need to get in there within five days for a successful outcome. As for the cancer, if you chose not to treat it, he has as long as he has, until there is a decline in his quality of life. With every animal it's different. It could be a couple of months, it could be years." Dr. Gordon's voice was kind, but it did not lessen the blow.

"Do you mind if I take a few days to think about it?"

"Sure."

"Right now he can't walk at all with the broken leg, I'm carrying him everywhere." At fifty-six pounds, that would not be an option for long.

"I don't doubt it. But, it will take several months to heal." Dr Gordon confirmed my growing fears.

I wiped my eyes, shook his hand and carried my baby to the car. Once inside the faucets turned on again. Tears poured from my eyes mingling with a torrent of snot from my nose. I turned away from the truth. I knew what needed to be done; yet I could not even bear the thought of considering the option. It shattered me. I was a thousand tiny shards on the pavement after a fatal accident.

Maverick and I drove back to the house. I carried him up to my bed and we laid there together for hours while I cried into his fur. He seemed to understand in the quiet way animals do. *I'm sorry, I'm so, so sorry. I want to help you. I need to help you, but I don't know how I can. Oh sweet little man, I adore you so much. You've been such a gift to me.* I cried and sobbed and stroked his soft fur while holding him tightly to my body.

Maybe I can sell something? Maybe I can borrow the money? I racked my brain for solutions. *Maybe Don will help? Isn't my dog more important that an outfit from Nordstrom's for Libby. The same girl who no longer returns your phone calls?*

I sat up on the edge of the bed, a small ray of hope brightening my mood. I walked to the phone and dialed the number. He answered on the second ring.

"Don, It's Jenna."

"Oh, hi Jenna, I thought you were Steve. Listen, I'm out of town right now and in a meeting. I'll be back next week. Can I catch you then," Don hung up on me. Even since my split with Libby we have not talked much. Steve always stays connected; it's his dad. But I'm now an outsider, a traitor.

I dialed his number again; this time he did not even answer. In my desperation to save my dog, I did not care about a deal with the devil. Next, I called my mom, Jackie. Ever-practical Jackie.

"Mom, there's been an accident with Maverick, he broke his leg."

"Oh no dear, you've had such a rough time these past few months. I'm so sorry to hear that." Her sympathy was genuine and it brightened my spirits a bit. In contrast to all of her tough love over the years, I know her heart is with me when it really counts. This was one of those times.

"They can fix it, but the surgery is close to two thousand dollars."

"Jenna, I'm already cashing in some of my stocks and my retirement savings to keep you and the kids off the street right now. I'm so sorry. I can't help out with the dog. Really sweetheart, I'm sorry, but it's more than I can do."

"I know mom," I started to cry again. Then I told her the other horrible discovery. "They also think he has cancer."

"Oh sweetheart, you poor thing. Life has not been kind to you lately. I know how much you adore your little dog. He's been a dear friend to you. Animals are like that," She continued to sooth me with sweet and comforting words. "Jenna, you know what you need to do, don't you?"

"Yeah mom, I do."

I kept Maverick close to me for the next two days, right up to the deadline for the surgery. Hoping for a miracle. We slept together, I carried him outside to go the bathroom, and I carried him to the car to ride the carpool with me. It wasn't the same; I could see he was uncomfortable. On the fifth day, I made an appointment to see Dr. Gordon.

"Dr. Gordon, I've decided not to get the surgery for Maverick." A wave of immense grief rolled over me.

"Mrs. Sinclair, I think you have made the right decision. I did not want to mention it as an option the other day, you were already so distraught."

"So how does this work?" I was trying to be brave.

"He will receive a sedative to calm him followed by an injection that will stop his heart. Nothing is painful, it is fast and very peaceful."

"Do I need to make an appointment,' the tears were silently rolling down my face.

"No, you are only prolonging the inevitable, without the surgery today, it will be too late to fix the leg. You can't carry him around forever. Also, I'm sure the fracture is causing him a great deal of discomfort." Dr. Gordon was matter of fact. He turned and left the room to collect his supplies.

I had a sudden urge to grab my dog and run for safety before it was too late. He looked fine, other than his leg. He was the same old friend who had driven the route with me for years, my furry little sidekick. But in my heart, I could tell he was not the same. He was being stoic for my benefit.

"Don't worry baby. I'll be here with you." I stroked his fur and scratched his favorite spots. He closed his eyes in appreciation.

"I will always love you Maverick," I hugged him tightly my tears dampening his sweet smelling fur. "You've been my best friend. No matter what."

Dr. Gordon stepped in the room, asked me to sign the forms and then administered the injections. He waited a moment to make sure they took effect and left the room. There was no drama, not a sound, no whimper, not bark, just silence followed by peace. I could tell he was gone. I felt his spirit leave his body.

I sat for a few minutes and cried and clutched his fur. *It's too much God! It's too much!"*

I left the vet clinic and got into my rental car, the passenger seat now strangely empty. The drive home was a fog. Thank God, Lolly had stepped in and driven carpool for me this past week. I was out of my head.

I walked to my room and crumpled to the floor.

No, no, no... I kept saying the word no over and over again, sobbing and lying on the floor in a ball of anguish-riddled flesh. I laid there for hours, as day gave way to night. Eventually, I crawled into my bed, a new bottomless well of fresh tears pouring from my burning eyes. *What happened to me? Where is my life?*

My business: gone. My friends: gone. Steve's business: gone. My child's nose: gone. My minivan: gone. My dog: gone. My friend Faith: gone. My money: gone. My dignity: gone. My reputation: gone. My spirit: gone. My heart: dark. There is nothing left of me, Jenna Sinclair.

I am dead.

Chapter 73

I hit the snooze button for the fourth time thinking to myself, how many times will an alarm clock continue to alert you, until it gives up. Today, my soft sheets and my coverlet of sleep-induced denial feel too difficult to remove.

I probably should have turned it off. But what's the point? I need to drive the route regardless of whatever assault the day has in store. I'm beginning to get the sense of a war zone with its constant unexpected, life-changing attacks. Recently, the best part of my day has been the end of it. Uneventful is a welcome blessing.

Now, the phone starts ringing. Between the alarm and the phone, I feel compelled to start the day. First, I check the caller id. If it's an unknown caller, that means it is a bill collector, so I don't pick those up. I've already explained a thousand times, as soon as Steve is back on track, we will take care of everything. For some reason, honesty is not enough. They call relentlessly between the hours of eight in the morning and nine in the evening, as if harassment would alchemize money from thin air.

The caller id said it was the Soul Center.

"Hello."

"Jenna, it's Kat. I have some news for you."

I knew it was about Faith. They never call. I held my breath. *Is she dead?*

"Faith is moving into the residential hospice program at St. Mary's today."

"What exactly does that mean? Do people ever come home from of residential hospice?" I knew the answer to the question as soon as I asked it.

"I'm sorry Jenna. Faith asked me to call you. She's been in terrible pain. She's too tired to speak, and with her broken arm, unable to dial the phone. She wants to be in an environment where there is more pain medication. The last week has been unbearable."

"I just saw her two weeks ago when I gave her a ride into the center. I thought she had turned the corner for the better. She looked so vibrant and happy."

Then I thought about others I knew, who had passed on from this life. Often they had looked a little better right before they died. It must be patterns of Grace, where they are able remind their loved ones what they were like before their illnesses ravaged them. This explanation made sense. Bone cancer was not supposed to be curable. Faith was in the final stages last fall.

"Is she allowed visitors? Does her family care?" I didn't want to intrude on anyone's farewell to his or her mother or grandmother. Although, I had often felt Faith was a "spiritual mother" to me. We had known each other intimately and she was a dear confident for the last seven years.

"Jenna, of course you are welcome. She loves you."

I start to cry now, large quite tears. The kind of tears that fall with the final recognition of a battle lost, but hard fought.

"Thank you for calling me Kat. It means a lot."

I decide to give Faith a day or two to settle in, yet I am afraid to wait too long. I don't know if she has several days or several weeks. Meanwhile, I want to bring her something to comfort her, but what? I search my heart for ideas. What can someone who is about to leave this earth possible need or want? The obvious is peace and comfort and, of course, love. But how do you show that? When she first went into the emergency room last fall, I brought her fuzzy socks for comfort and a lavender filled heart shaped pillow to give her something to hold on to when she felt alone or scared. I feel now she is beyond that. I'll have to think on it for the day. Perhaps an idea will come to me before I can visit. What can you give to someone who has given so much to you? Right now my mind is drawing a total blank. God knows I can't afford to buy anything.

The next morning when I woke up I was still thinking about something for Faith. After carpool there was still nothing: a card, flowers, food... it all seemed so trite. She is too special for me to settle on the obvious. I just needed to give it a little more time. God will guide me to what Faith needs. In fact, why don't I just say a quick prayer and ask right now?

"Lord, what is the best thing I can give to my dear friend Faith to give her comfort during this time?"

I waited silently awhile but still no answer.

Later that day, my friend Danielle and I were talking about Faith (although they had never met). Despite everything, Danielle hung in there, and never flinched at all the dramas in my life. Danielle knows a lot about death. She lost her sister, uncle and cousin in a terrible accident at an amusement park. Danielle told me she heard that the last sense a person loses is their ability to hear. In fact, the dying can hear long after they have lost the ability to speak.

I thought about what she said for the rest of the afternoon. Then it came to me.

"That's it! I've figured out what to do for Faith."

I said aloud to myself as I was driving the route to pick up the kids. I always used to hear that I had a great voice when I worked in television as a newscaster: authoritative, yet soothing and reassuring.

"I will use my voice to create something to comfort Faith. I'll record a CD for Faith on my computer of some inspirational thoughts and prayers." The idea was starting to take shape in my mind.

I thought at least she can listen to it while no one is available to visit her. But what prayers should I choose? I'm not even sure if I own a Bible and I haven't been to church in ages. I don't even know what church I would go to right now, if I wanted to. All religions hold some appeal, but I don't belong to any one. I like to think of myself as more spiritual than religious, but I do believe in God.

But that aside, for whatever the reason, prayers seem like the right thing. I could feel it; the tingle of confirmation was there. I sometimes feel this tingle when I know I'm making the right decision about something for my kids or my husband. Over the years, I have tried to trust it. Faith once told me, "That tingle is your intuition talking to you, reassuring you that you are on the right track. Follow it and you will be guided in the right direction."

Then I remembered the box of books I had found when I was pulling things out of the attic to get ready for my big garage sale next month. These books went back a long way, in fact I was surprised to see I still had them.

Fifteen years ago, back in graduate school at UCLA, my friend, David Grace, a student in the film school used affirmations. He would type them up and then cut and tape the words into a long strip of paper, which looked like a shoelace.

This "affirmation shoelace" was then wrapped around his recently completed screenplays or projects like a ribbon around a gift. David Grace said it helped keep positive energy around all of his projects. I was curious, actually fascinated. We were both trying to break into tough businesses and I could use all of the positive energy available. He asked if I had ever heard of affirmations? I said no, but I wanted to learn.

Then he gave me a book called the <u>Dynamic Laws of Prosperity</u> by Catherine Ponder. He simply said, "Read the book. I use affirmations for everything. They work."

So, I read it. For the next couple of years of grad school and beyond I used the affirmations to help me navigate my television career. Sometimes, they really seemed to work.

The discovered box had not been opened since I graduated from UCLA. I knew there were some books inside. Perhaps there were some affirmations and prayers on healing or peace in those books?

"It's funny," I thought to myself, Faith often said to me, "Everything in life you need, you already have."

I walked upstairs to the third floor and easily located the box. It was taped shut and covered with dust. On top, in black marker, was scrawled JENNA'S WISDOM, in handwriting other than my own. David Grace helped me pack. He was always so sarcastic, funny as hell. I had used the affirmations, like a magic spell, to attract news directors to my audition reel. Eventually it worked. I dusted off the top of the box with my hand and a cloud of dust flew into my mouth causing me to cough.

"You guys have been waiting patiently for a long time." I said to the books inside as if they were real. In a way they were. Books have been my friends for many years, especially when people have failed. Ever since I can remember, I've had a love affair with books. I love the way they feel in my hands, especially hardbacks with their weight and substance. I love the way the written words of fiction come to life in my imagination, transporting me a million miles away from the issues of today. And, the common sense information and "how-to" instructions of non-fiction books have taught me countless truths. Yes, when all else fails, books deliver. That's probably why I never gave the box away. After all, a girl needs her "wisdom." You never know when you will need a reference, and this situation is a perfect example. I was suddenly proud of myself for my foresight, a tiny victory in a sea of recent crippling defeats.

I carry the heavy box downstairs. Remove the dirty tape and discover there were at least twenty titles inside. Funny, I didn't remember having so many books. In fact, I only remember using a handful of books to find the right affirmations more than a decade ago: three books, maybe four tops. All of my books were written by the same author, a Unity Church minister named Catherine Ponder. She was the "Affirmation Queen" back in the early 1960's. She's been around a while; I didn't discover her until the early 1990's. As an author, I remember her being pretty straightforward with her words, not too heavy on any particular religion, just plain straight-talk on Spirit for everyday people. I liked it then, I like it now for the same reason.

Her book, The Dynamic Laws of Prosperity was on top.

"I could use some prosperity now!" I said aloud.

I opened the book to one of the dog-eared pages and found this declaration highlighted with instructions to make a list of what you would like to see happen in your life:

I give thanks for the immediate, complete and divine fulfillment of these desires. This or something better comes forth now with perfect timing, according to God's rich good for me now.

I remember using that one a lot. It seems I had a lot to ask for at the time. In television, "No Thank You," is the most common response to applications from first time reporters fresh out of college.

I had a file folder full of rejection letters; eventually I knew someone had to say "yes." And they did finally say, "YES," at a television station in Florida after more than fifty "NO's". I wonder if the affirmations worked. I think they helped.

Inside one of the books on top was an envelope sticking out. I opened it and looked in amazement. It read:

Jenna,
I thought you might use these someday. Enjoy! They are too expensive to ship back to England.
In Spirit and Love,   David Grace

David helped me pack my things to move home after graduation. He must have put these books in the box then, thinking I would open it up as soon as I arrived at my destination. Instead my mother stored the box until I married. It was one of the boxes that arrived via her van when she downsized her house last year.

I had heard a few years ago that David Grace was killed in motorcycle accident in Los Angeles. We had lost touch once I married. Steve never felt comfortable with the fact that a lot of my good friends were guys. It was another part of myself I had discarded to take on the role of wife. But, I've always remembered David's positive outlook. Now, it was as if he was reaching out to me from heaven, in an answer to my prayer about Faith.

It made me feel better knowing that she would not be alone, especially with good people like David to meet her. Another quiet tear slid down my face. There had been so many "deaths" lately: Maverick, my business, Steve's business, many of my friendships, and now the imminent death of my dear friend, Faith. Death seems to surround me, to isolate me, to consume me. *What or who else was I going to lose?* I quickly dismiss the terrifying thought from my mind.

Lucky for me Lolly is working the next two days. Steve has been preoccupied with his owns problems and unable to help with the kids. Her presence frees me to dive into the box right away and discover its treasures. The first book I find is actually a collection of four paperback books housed in a cardboard sleeve by an author named Emmett Fox. His books were titled, <u>The Power of Constructive Thinking</u>, <u>The Sermon on the Mount</u>, <u>The Ten</u>

Commandments and Find and Use Your Inner Power. The next book
I pull from the box is titled Spiritual Growth: Being Your Higher
Self written by Sanaya Roman. Then came the Science of Mind by
Ernest Holmes, The Superbeings by John Randolph Price, and
Autobiography of a Yogi written by Paramhansa Yogananda. I had
never heard of any of them. Now a pile of unearthed and unexpected
treasure leans against my leg, as I sit on cross-legged on the floor of
my sun porch.

My sun porch, which is my home office, is a converted sleeping
porch, the kind that existed before air-conditioning was invented.
Originally, this space was one of the areas I fell in love with when
we bought the house. However, the sleeping porch was badly in need
of repair and sloped away from the house. It was one repair on a list
of many in my house, Dora.

I offered it up as a sacrifice when our remodeling dollars didn't
stretch as far as we had hoped. It's better for this kids to have an
updated bathroom, than for me to have a home office. Miraculously,
the appraiser didn't agree with my viewpoint. She wouldn't agree to
give the house the value we needed for the construction loan without
the restoration of the two-story porches flanking the back of the
house. I am eternally grateful for her intervention.

It's a lovely room surrounded on three sides by eleven five-foot
tall windows. Three windows are situated on both the north and
again on the south side of the room and the remaining five face the
east. It's an aquarium in the sky. Instead of fish and water, there are
birds and leaves. Branches from a dozen century oaks fight for space
in the vista outside my window creating a tree house experience.
Sometimes in the early morning, when the rest of the world is asleep,
I relax in my favorite down chair, a "chair-for-two" and a matching
ottoman. I open the windows allowing for a gentle dewy breeze to
meander through my space, entangled with nature's breath is a
sprinkling of birdsong announcing the dawn. Every morning ushers
in a new avian melody.

But, by far the best time of the year on the sun porch is when a
winter storm comes to call with it's fierce winds chasing flurries
around the moody January sky, only to have them dance beyond its
grip in mirth-filled chaos. The earth below is coated white, cloaking
the boundaries between neighbors. All the while, I am cozy and

nestled inside, enjoying the soundless snowflake skirmish unfolding outside.

I leaf through a few pages of each of the newly discovered books. The words are immediately soothing and I feel a sense of warmth and hope for a moment. Then I look up and notice the clock. I close the box. The rest of the books inside will have to wait for another day. I'm certain I will be able to find something suitable to record for Faith's tape. I've scheduled an appointment for tomorrow morning with Bob at the Apple Store in the Mall. They offer free one-to-one training on your Mac laptop with the purchase of an inexpensive membership. I plan to come prepared, an hour goes by fast and I want to visit Faith tomorrow afternoon.

Chapter 74

"Hi Bob."

"Hey Jenna, How's it shakin," he greets me with a friendly smile as I enter the store with my laptop. I plop down and unpack at the small counter designed for tutoring called a "genius bar." It's where you drink in the technology.

Bob is a "computer wizard" by day and a civil war re-enactor the rest of the time. His affinity is with the confederates, but I try not to press for much more info. I know he is passionate about his pastime and travels the country visiting various battlefields recreating their tragic history on the once blood soaked soil. Perhaps, he's having a hard time getting over that past life? God forbid, I tell him my house was built by a Civil War Captain; he might follow me home and never leave.

"Bob, I have an unusual project that I am working on. I want to make a CD for my friend in the hospital."

"Will it have music? Or voices?"

"Actually, I'd like both."

"OK, then we will have to do this in Garage Band." He clicks on the picture of a guitar at the bottom of my screen.

"Bob, this is like taking Dorothy out of Kansas. I didn't even know this program was on my computer."

"Don't worry it's so easy." He clicks on a new song and then asks if I want to use a synthesized computer generated voice or my own voice for the voice track.

"I'm going to do it myself." He clicks on the word instrument. "I guess in the world of Mac my voice is an instrument." I think to myself.

I see some bars moving on the screen indicating that it is time to start speaking. The store is loud, but I want to learn what to do. I'll obviously have to create the CD in the quiet of my sun porch. I decide to read part of the book instead of saying the prayers in a public place. It feels strange to be praying aloud in a store at the mall. *Isn't prayer private? Or is it?*

Next he showed me how to layer in background music.

"When your finished Jenna, click on "share." This will send your completed project or song to your itunes playlist. From this list, you can burn as many discs as you please."

"Oh and Jenna, you may want to purchase a microphone. It will sound better."

"How much are those?"

"A hundred dollars."

"Wow, I don't know about that." It seemed frivolous in light of everything going on.

That was more than I wanted to spend. Honestly, more than I could spend. Then I remembered I had a store credit left over from my previous purchase.

"Bob will you look up my .mac account and see if I have a credit on file. It would be from last year sometime."

"Yep, you sure do. Two hundred and twelve dollars to be exact."

"Great, I'll take a snowball mic!" Things were flowing today, so I decided to go with it. I still wanted to get the CD finished.

"Bob, that was amazingly easy. Thanks. I'll schedule another appointment next week."

Back at home, I open the box and remove my new microphone. True to it's name it is white and shaped like a snowball. Across the front in metallic silver is the word Blue, indicating it is manufactured by Blue Microphones. A single chrome post atop a petite tripod supports the cute six-inch diameter ball, the instructions tell me the unique shape is designed to create professional quality sound without a studio.

"Technology is cool!" I feel part of an old self of mine break free from its dusty quiet repose and come down off the storage shelf that I had locked away long ago.

I think I can still do this, I say to myself as I start to read the first prayer for Faith's CD. I first picked a prayer that I remembered from childhood. The prayer is called The Lord's Prayer. It is from the book of Psalms and it's listed as one of the most powerful prayers of all time in one of my newly discovered books by Emmet Fox.

Isn't that what my friend needs right now, Power Prayers.

"Our Father…" I look down at my script.

Our Father, who art in Heaven, hallowed be thy name. Thy kingdom come, thy will be done on Earth as it is in Heaven. Give us this day our daily bread and forgive us our trespasses as we forgive those who trespass against us. Lead us not into temptation, but deliver us from evil. For thine is the kingdom, the power and the glory for ever and ever."

The replay button tells me I have done something wrong. There is not a sound recorded.

"Ok, let's try again."

"Our Father who…" I look down at my script.

I hit the replay button, again nothing. What am I missing! Technology sucks!"

I pull out my notes from Bob. I refuse to give up. Twenty minutes and few expletives later, I have figured it out. Prayer one is in the can, complete with background music. I feel as if I have climbed a mountain.

Now, I'm ready to begin recording prayer number two. At the rate I am going today, I think this is all that is going to be on my first CD. Two prayers. It will have to be enough.

"If she dies before I can finish my project, that defeats the entire purpose, doesn't it Jenna?" I've been talking to myself all day. Frustration has a funny way of venting itself.

Prayer two, I quickly laid down the voice track. I only had to start over once this time because the phone rang in the middle, breaking the mood. I also used the same gentle background music as on prayer one. I grab the finished CD and rush out to the car. Lolly is picking up the kids and with any luck I'll beat rush hour traffic.

The hospice building is located a half a mile back from the main road nestled between a small grove of dogwoods on one side and an open field of wild flowers on the other side. A colorful landscaping of perennial flowers and ornamental trees hugs the brick and stone structure. I know the building is less than ten years old. My grandfather spent two weeks here before he passed when it first opened. It's funny how we keep returning to the same places in our lives, yet for different reasons.

Outside every window was a bird feeder or a birdbath. I assume these are soothing focal points for each of the residents. "What a nice thought." I know Faith loved to watch the birds. She told me once when I called to see if she needed anything. I hope she has something to enjoy outside her window.

I'm so excited to see her, yet nervous at the same time. Does hospice change the way you look? It has only been two weeks since I last saw her, but I don't know what to expect. I've tried not to call her more than once a week over the past months. With all the chaos in my life, anymore frequent would be unfair. I fear I would burden her with my problems, even telepathically. I know she has not felt well. Energy is a precious commodity to the sick.

Hospice does not look like a hospital. The interior is pleasantly furnished in a home-like setting. The sitting room in arranged in an inviting layout with comfortable couches and a collection of chairs. Elegant oil paintings depicting landscapes and attractive botanical prints are framed and hung around each room. The next area reveals a large cherry wood dining room table with chairs enough to seat twelve. Beyond this space is a general waiting area with a large screen flat panel television and several comfortable couches. Down every hallway, there are three, I see small clusters of couches and chairs designed to give families and friends a place to rest outside of the patients' rooms. The nurse's station and information desk is situated where all three wings of patient rooms connect in the heart of the building.

"Excuse me. Could you please direct me to Faith Monroe's room."

A nurse smiles at me, her white teeth brilliant against her chocolate skin. "Room 11, down the first hallway on the right." She points in that direction. I return her contagious smile. It dissolves some of my apprehension. Her nametag says, "Wanda".

"Thanks, Wanda."

The door to suite eleven is slightly ajar the room inside is dark; at least in the way a room can be dark on a sunny day with the blinds tightly closed. Little slivers of light slice through the slats in the mini blinds creating subtle bands of gold on the beige walls. The only sound in the room is the "puff and release" of Faith's respirator. She appears to be sleeping in her bed. It has been turned to face the window.

"Faith," I say her name quietly.

No response. She must be asleep. I decide not to wake her. I walk over to the recliner in the corner of her room and sit down. I can wait. Perhaps she has a magazine or something? I see some books on the table in the corner. I pick one up noticing the author is Emmet Fox. It makes me smile. What a strange coincidence. He was the author of one of the books I used to find the prayers for Faith's CD. The gift books from my friend David Grace. I open the book and sit down. You could tell it was a well-loved book; pages are dog eared, sentences underlined and the corners are blunted and curled from years of use. I've always thought books like this must have something important to say otherwise why do their owners refer to them so much. After all, this is the inspiration she chose to bring to her deathbed. Seeing the book is confirmation that I'm on the right track with the CD. I feel my body tingling.

The very first page causes me to pause. Emmett Fox writes:

All power lies in creative thought. Thought is the key to life: for as a man thinketh in his heart, so he is. Your destiny is really in your own hands, because it is impossible to think one thing and produce another your mental conduct, your hour-by-hour thinking, produces specific conditions. Fear is the ultimate cause of all sickness, all failure and disappointment.

This is what I call a Eureka moment. My hour-by-hour thinking has been in the pits for as long as I can remember. In fact, the only time I haven't been plagued by fear of the phone, fear of the mail and fear of the doorbell, has been the last few days that I've spent working on the CD. This past year of trauma has handicapped my life in ways I've only begun to consider. Every time the phone rings, I fear it's an inquiry about an unpaid bill I can't pay. Every time the mail comes, I'm afraid it will be another notice from my attorney or Steve's attorney about lawsuits beyond our control. And every time the doorbell rings, I fear it's someone coming to serve us with papers for another lawsuit, or worse to evict us from our home for an unpaid mortgage statement. Even though we've been able to keep up so far.

That's not even skimming the top of the tower of personal terrors: I'm terrified for my children's health and well-being, afraid that my marriage is deteriorating before my eyes, and afraid I no longer have any value in this world. It's no wonder I can barely get out of my bed in the morning without an overwhelming sense of duty to drive me from the sheets. Am I attracting these conditions into my life? The words I've just read somehow imply that I am responsible, that I have the power, yet I feel completely powerless. How can that be true?

"Ouch! Ow, Ow Ow... Auh, Auh....No." Faith moans in anguish, thrashing in her bed obviously in tremendous pain. She seems to be fading in and out of awareness. I rush to her bedside and grab her hand.

"Faith, can I help you? Please, what do you need?" She does not respond but continues to cry out. I feel powerless.

"Do you need more pain medicine?"

She squeezes my hand. I take that as a yes and walk into the hall to find a nurse. It so happens that Wanda, the nice woman from the desk is walking by. I recognize her.

"Wanda, my friend needs some pain medication quickly!"

"I'll take care of Ms. Faith. Don't you worry about it."

I return to her side. "Faith do you need water?"

She nods, not opening her eyes, as I held the straw up to her cracked lips, surrounded with the white paste of dehydration. Eventually, she takes a sip. I walk into the bathroom, wet down a washcloth with cool water and return to gently wipe off her mouth. I stroke her forehead.

"Faith, the nurse is on the way." She never opens her eyes, but I can tell the action is soothing to her; the tension in her face seems to ease.

"Ms. Faith, how are you this afternoon. I'm here with your

medicine." Wanda announces cheerfully as she walks in the room still smiling. I guess there is even joy in hospice, although, I would have never expected to find it here. I leave the room for a moment so Wanda can do an assessment of my friend. As she left the room, I asked her the question I was so afraid to consider?

"How long Wanda? How long does she have to live?"

"Well, that all depends. Usually, when they stop eating and drinking it can be anywhere for one to three weeks."

"Has Faith eaten anything?"

"Not in the last two days. The pain medication makes the patients extremely sleepy."

"Thank you, Wanda. By the way my name is Jenna Sinclair. Is it okay if I play a little CD I made for Faith in her room?"

"Sure, there should be a player in there."

Faith appears to be drifting back to sleep. I grab her hand trying to catch her before she floats away from the reach of my voice.

"Faith, it's me Jenna. I want you to know that I am here. I made you a CD of prayers. I'm going to play them softly for you. I hope you like them." I know I need to say goodbye just in case there is no tomorrow for this lifetime. I'm holding her hand still. I softly say the words my heart prompts me to say, "Faith, you are so dear to me. I just want you to know how much I care about you. You have been there for me in so many ways. I can't imagine how I could have survived this past couple of years, especially this last one, without your kind words and encouragement." I'm holding her hand still but there is no response.

"I guess I always thought you would get better Faith. This just doesn't seem right. I can't imagine this world without you in it. I know this sounds strange Faith, but will you visit me? Will you come to me in a dream of something and let me know you are okay? Please, I just don't want to lose you forever." I squeeze her hand firmly and she opens her eyes for a moment connecting with me.

"I love you Faith. Thank you for being such a blessing in my life." Faith squeezes my hand weakly as she turns her head away drifting off to sleep. In sleep, her pain is shut out; but so am I. I guess it's time to go.

I wipe the large quiet tears from my eyes. The player is on the table by the books. It has a repeat feature so the two prayers will replay continuously. It starts on the second prayer I recorded, The Good Shepherd, also from the book of Psalms.

"The Lords is my Shepard; I shall not want..."

I could hear my voice gently, slowly filling the empty spaces in her room. It doesn't sound like me. It sounds smoother, richer. Our voices sound different in our heads, than through our external hearing. I almost don't recognize myself.

The prayer continues:

He maketh me to lie down in green pastures: he leadeth me beside still waters. He restoreth my soul: he leadeth me in paths of righteousness for his namesake. Yea though I walk through the valley of the shadow of death, I will fear no evil: for though art with me; thy rod and thy staff they comfort me. Thou preparest a table before me in the presence of mine enemies: thou annointest my head with oil; my cup runneth over. Surley goodness and mercy shall follow me all of the days of my life: and I will dwell in the house of the Lord forever.

I leave patient suite eleven wondering if I will ever see Faith again. I also wonder if anyone will play the CD I made for her. It doesn't matter as long as she gets to hear it once.

Driving home, my thoughts keep returning to the first pages of the book I'd read in Faith's room before she woke up. I knew the author's words were true. It's funny we always recognize Truth when we hear it. I thought about David Grace and his affirmations. Once, long ago, I had really believed in those affirmations. Now I probably would not even recognize that young woman I once was. Let's face it; I didn't even recognize the voice on the CD as my own. I am so disjointed and disconnected, I'm like a pile of bones from a disassembled science room skeleton. I need to put myself back together again.

"If anyone is going to fix this Jenna, it's going to be you." I was talking to myself again. That's a start! Someone or something needs to set me straight it might as well be the voice in my head.

Chapter 75

I bought the house because I loved the sun porch. The appraiser said it must be completed to get the money needed for the construction loan on the entire house. Events had conspired together to create this beautiful space for me, yet I have failed to claim it as my own. The kids' toys are scattered across my room. Books, bills, discarded art projects and a variety of papers are stacked in the corners; clutter is everywhere.

I walk in and look at the room with fresh eyes. My new mission has given me the focus of a laser.

"How can anyone do anything in this mess? This is my place I want every one else out, TODAY!" I make the pronouncement, even though all of the kids are at school and I am alone. It feels more official this way.

I grab several laundry baskets, one for each child, and start sorting the toys, videos, and other items. Everyone else is moving out and I am moving in. I'm merciless in my selections. If it doesn't belong to my personal self, it is banished from my room. This process takes the entire day.

I moved the household bills down to the desk space in the kitchen, then pulled out every finished paperback book, catalogues from mail order companies, and the dozens of virtually unread magazines from ten subscriptions and placed them in a box to donate. I filled two giant trash bags full of stuff that should have been pitched long ago. I unplug the phone and move it to another room. I vacuumed and washed the slipcovers on my favorite chair and my couch liberating the fabric from food stains accumulated over the past months. I moved the furniture around in a way that enhanced the fabulous views. And I cleared everything off my desk but my computer and my printer. I wielded the pledge and the Lysol like a true domestic goddess. My space is now sparkling and surprisingly vacant.

"I love it!" I say aloud to myself as I collapse on my favorite chair the freshly laundered slipcovers releasing an aroma of Bounce, the fabric softener, instead of the scent of wet towels and spilt soft drinks. It feels really good to do something for myself.

Next to my chair, I've unpacked all of the books from the discovered box and placed them on my pale green wrought iron bookcase. On the top shelf is my new CD player alarm clock, kidnapped from my bedroom, so I can listen to music when I read. On the other side of my chair, I've placed a small painted table with a collection of my crystals from Arkansas on top. I love the way the light from all of the windows illuminates their transparent structure. I used to keep them wrapped up in newspaper in a box, but they seem happier here in the new space. Next to the crystals, is the feather from Faith's reading room. It was a gift from her when she went into the hospital. I also found a fountain upstairs while organizing for the garage sale, it must have been a gift from someone that was misplaced before it could be opened and assembled. I don't remember who gave it to me, but I really appreciate the sound of the flowing water in my new space. Everything feels balanced and orderly, calm and quiet. I now have a refuge from all of the chaos swirling around in the rest of my affairs. As a final act of defiance, I install two sets of white blinds from Loews, covering the glass on the French doors leading to my sun porch. This creates a cocoon effect, now I am truly cloistered from the outside world, up in the trees, closer to heaven.

Aside from the blinds, I didn't need to purchase a thing. Like the books, everything I needed to make my space perfect, I already had in my possession. Today, for the first time in a long time I have accomplished something only for myself. Baby steps, that's all it is, but I feel an awareness of a long lost companion flickering faintly in my being. Happiness has relit its tiny flame. I hope tomorrow doesn't stamp it out.

Later on, after the kids have gone to bed, I decide to make Faith another CD before I stop by to visit tomorrow. I'm planning on visiting her at least three times a week until there is no reason to visit. Perhaps she will be awake this time. Now that I have figured out the technical kinks the CD is made in less than an hour.

"Hello. Faith." I knock gently on her door. She appears to be asleep, but this time she is not alone.

"Oh, hello. Am I interrupting anything?" I was ready to leave and come back. Faith's family comes first.

"No not at all, Mom loves visitors."

"I'm Jenna Sinclair, a friend of your mom's."

"Hi, I'm Trudy Williams. Faith's youngest daughter."

I could see where dried tears had created streaks down the powdered blush on her face. Trudy looked to be in her early thirties, she had a blonde pageboy cut and was casually dressed in shorts and a t-shirt.

"Jenna Sinclair?" Trudy said my name again as if trying to pinpoint her knowledge of me.

"We've actually never met." I volunteered.

"I know that, but are you the one who left the CD for my mom?"

"Yes, I'm sorry about that. I hope you're not offended. I know religion is not everyone's thing."

"Oh, that's not the case at all. I was wondering how to thank you. Mom seems to really love the CD. She's asked the nurse to replay it for her several times. The prayers are a comfort to her."

I exhale in relief, "I wasn't really sure what to do for your mom, but I had to do something. Your mother means a lot to me." I smile at Trudy as my eyes well up with tears. *What right do I have to cry? She's losing a mother; I'm only losing a friend.* I feel selfish.

"By the way, I made Faith a new CD with a lot more prayers on it. The first one was a little rough. There was a learning curve." I laugh to myself. Truthfully, it was a huge learning curve. I almost gave up.

"I'll go ahead and leave you alone with your mom. It was nice to meet you Trudy." Perhaps next time Faith will be awake when I visit.

At least she liked the CD. That was enough.

"Hi Wanda, How are you doing today?" I recognize the nurse from my last visit on my way out. She smiles at me. I love the size of her smile.

"It's Jenna, my friend Faith is in room 11."

"Oh yeah, Hi Jenna. Have a good day."

"Thanks Wanda. You have a great smile. It brings a lot of sunshine to this place."

I could see my compliment turned up her smile a watt or two, as if that were possible.

With the visit cut short and kids in school, I had the entire morning and part of the afternoon available to read in my new space. An unexpected treat! When I got home, I took the phone off the hook and went straight upstairs. Where do I even start? I see the book from Emmet Fox, the same author from Faith's room. It was a "gift" book from my friend David Grace. The title is <u>Power Through Constructive Thinking</u>.

I curl up in the chair and dig in. The content seemed obvious, but it was clear departure from my current thinking. On my way to pick up the kids I ponder the author's words. I must be on the right track with the CD for Faith. Fox says prayer is the answer to any problem. He calls prayers a "treatment." If anything is not going right in your life the best prescription is to pray about it. Fox also says that when things go wrong, we need to declare constantly that we are not afraid or intimidated by any external conditions. Whether they are your health failing, your money disappearing or your friends deserting you. These are all outer expressions of your inner world. The more you are afraid of these events, the more you need to declare, "God is my refuge, and I am not going to be afraid." You need to keep saying it until your knees are no longer knocking.

"God is my refuge, I am not afraid. God is my refuge I am not afraid. God is my refuge, I am not afraid…" It was a lie of course. I am terrified of everything these days.

Yet, I keep saying the affirmations out loud all the way to the kid's school and through the carpool line. I'm sure drivers in the cars next to me think I'm a freak carrying on a conversation with myself. But, I'm beyond caring.

One day led to another in my new "sacred space." I can't wait to get the kids to school, so I can retreat to the sun porch and drink in the wisdom from my new "friends," the books. I can feel the words of the authors, many long dead, penetrating me on a cellular level. It's as if I am being reprogrammed like a computer recovered from a virus. My perspective has been upside down. Sleeping beauty is waking up and she doesn't even need a prince to do it.

At the end of the week I decide to go and visit Faith, I bring her a new CD, this time I have recorded healing affirmations from Paramhansa Yogananda, a popular and enlightened yogi from India who passed away in the 1950's. I'm learning that Truth teachings are timeless.

"Hi Wanda."

She looks up from her chart and smiles at me as I walk past the nurse's desk on my way towards Faith's room.

"Oh Jenna, wait a minute. I'd like to ask you something."

"Sure Wanda, what's on your mind?" I like this woman. She makes me feel warm and happy.

"I hear that you are the voice behind the prayer CD's in Faith's room."

"Yes, that's me." I say modestly, embarrassed to be acknowledged.

"Girl, you're really good. It has made a difference in Faith. She's very peaceful. There is a calm presence in her room, as if someone is standing vigil. In fact, several people have ask me where they an get a copy of the prayer CD."

"Oh! Really? Well I guess I can make you a couple of copies on my computer."

"How much do you want to charge?"

"That's crazy, Wanda. I'm not going to charge anyone money for a prayer. I'll bring them next time I come and visit."

"Jenna, you are an angel."

"Wanda, there is no way that is true, but thanks anyway."

I walk into room eleven. This time the CD with my voice is playing gently in the background. Faith is asleep. I don't want to wake her. She looks thinner, gaunt. I know she has not eaten in over a week. Time is coming to an end for my dear friend. I sit quietly with her for thirty minutes, sharing the space. Maybe next time she will be alert.

I gently squeeze her hand as I leave, "Goodbye dear friend, I'll see you soon." I wondered if that was the truth.

Chapter 76

Steve and I spend the weekend relaxing with the kids at the community pool. The weekends are great because the phone rarely rings and we just hang out as a family. Friday nights are always pizza and a movie at home. Saturdays are busy with kid's sports activities. The rest of the time in the summer is sun and fun. Steve and I are trying really hard not to let the children in on how far our life has tumbled in the past year. We look for free fun and cheap eats whenever we can. They don't notice, one of the perks of having Daddy home all of the time is that they get to play with him. There is always a silver lining. Before the collapse of the business, they never saw Steve, and when they did he was stressed, grouchy and exhausted.

I notice I feel happier, more present than I have in a long time. Perhaps the "God is my refuge" affirmations are starting to work. I've been saying them everyday for almost a week. A little more light is starting to filter into my black hole. Even Steve is in an uncharacteristically good mood. Perhaps my prayer sessions are having a trickle over effect.

Monday morning I stopped by to visit Faith and drop off the copies of the prayer CD's for Wanda. I made ten; I hope that's enough. I left my phone number and an email address in case she wanted more. There is no change with Faith. My CD is playing in the background. Even if she never wakes up while I am visiting, I know that I am with her through the prayers.

It's back to my new course of study in my "sacred space." I feel as if I have entered a self-crafted graduate program; there is a lot to learn, a lot to absorb. I call it self-u, abbreviated for self-university. I just go wherever I am guided. Several of the books I'm reading talk about meditation. I've never mediated before. I think I might fall asleep. *How can I sit still for that long? Maybe I need some soothing music?* Several of the books have instructions for different meditations written in the back of each chapter. *How do you read the instructions to yourself and meditate at the same time?*

Before I pick up the kids on the route, I decide to stop at the Soul Center, Kat will tell me what to use to start my meditation practice. She pulls out several selections of CD's and places them on the counter. Some have music, some use special sound waves for relaxation, and some feature a person's voice. One in particular catches my attention, it's by an author, Dr. Wayne Dyer, and it's titled <u>Getting in the Gap</u>. On the CD, Dr. Dyer guides the listener through the first ten words of the Lord's Prayer focusing on the spaces in between the words. The spaces he fills with a series of "ah" sounds or "Om" chants. I like that prayer and I know Faith likes it too. So, *In the Gap,* it is. I learn from his book, "Om" is another form of prayer.

"Jenna, what are you doing up in your sun porch all day?'

"I guess you noticed. I'm sorry Steve, have I been ignoring you?"

"No, I just want to make sure you're OK. I know a lot has happened to us lately and I just want to check in."

"Honestly Steve, I just need to recalibrate myself. I feel really out of whack. This time alone seems to be the only thing that is helping me cope right now."

"Believe me, I need to get my head on straight too. I still can't believe everything that has happened. I really miss my business. I'm sorry that we've come to this point. I saw all of the signs but I ignored them."

When he says this it breaks my heart. At every crossroad he made the wrong choice. It has hurt our marriage.

"I'm sorry Steve. I wish things had worked out differently for you. It doesn't seem fair. Do you mind if I take some space just for myself? It'll only be a couple of weeks. I feel like I really need it."

"Is everything OK with us? I'm sorry about the money problems. I know my dad will help with more of the bills until we are back on track."

"Yeah, I hear you. This is about me," ...*and us.*

"Do you want me to sleep in the guest room? I know I've been snoring," Steve says apologetically.

"You don't have to, but you're pretty loud. I think it's the stress.*"*

"You've looked pretty exhausted," Steve was sympathetic.

"Now that you mention it, I am. If it won't upset you, I'd like the space. I'm beyond what I can handle right now."

"OK, whatever you need Jenna. We're both hanging on by our fingernails right now. But in the end, I think everything will work out. You have to believe that."

"I do Steve. I do believe it will all work out. Now more then ever," I used one of my new affirmations.

"What are you grateful for?" The words stare back at me from the page I'm reading. They feel like an accusation.

"Grateful?" There's not much I'm full of appreciation for these days.

"Thank you for destroying my business, thank you for dissolving my social life, thank you for a mountain of legal bills with no money to pay." My list could be endless if I wanted to explore it. Now I'm starting to get pissed. It's easier to chant and forget about my problems. Perhaps, I have better things to do than sit on the sun porch today.

"I would not say there are grounds for much celebration. Thank you God, is not the first sentence out of my mouth every morning. In fact, I've felt more like saying damn you." I'm talking to myself again. Well, at least we are developing a friendship, me and myself, especially now that there's no one else to talk to.

I read on. The book says, "Gratitude is the gateway to God's grace."

This part is interesting. Basically, what you focus on expands. So if you focus on all the things you are thankful for: your health, your family, your marriage, the food you eat, the air you breath; these points of intention will expand and fill your life with positive energy. As this positive energy expands, the negatives in your life dissolve and fade away. I think about this idea for a while, allowing it to absorb.

"Well, I am thankful for my children, and I do have a loving husband, even though I don't agree with his career judgment. I love my house, warts and all. I'm thankful for my mom Jackie who has been an angel. And of course, I'm thankful for the sun porch and the time to read these books. I'm grateful for Faith and my dear friend, Danielle."

It appears my gratitude list is longer than I thought. I get an idea. I'm going to write all the things I'm thankful for in a gratitude letter to God. I'll just read it every morning with my other affirmations. In the letter, I decide to include things that I would like to see happen in my life. Many of my books instruct me to be thankful for some future event I'm dreaming about and to act as if it has already occurred. Why not, I'm already in uncharted territory right now.

Dear God,
I love my Life. I am extremely and infinitely grateful for the many blessings in my life now.

Thank you for my beautiful children. May they have lives filled with happiness and joy. I am so grateful to be their mother and to share their incredible journey. Thank you for my loving, sweet and funny husband Steve. He is a dear companion with whom to share life's many twists and turns. Thank you for my darling pets. They give me a million reasons to smile each day and I celebrate their playful antics. Thank you for my family, my parents and Steve's parents. Thank you for giving me life, thank you for your support on whatever level (This is about all I can manage right now, God).

I am thrilled and grateful for my dream home. It is a beautiful home, where I am filled with comfort and warmth. It is a perfect and evolving reflection of myself and I celebrate the opportunity to live in this stately home and to have the resources to restore it to its magnificent origins. It is the home I wish to raise my children in and to give them a lifetime of beautiful happy memories of the family time and traditions we are creating in this perfect space.

Thank you for my many loving friendships. I am so humbled by the joy, love and affection that have been shared with me over the years from my dear friends. Some are near, some are far, some are no longer part of my life, but to all I send my deepest love. Life without friendship is like the sky without the sun. Whether we will walk the same path again in this lifetime or not, I am profoundly and humbly grateful for the time we've shared.

Thank you for who I am. Thank you for my healthy fit body. Thank you for my intelligent and creative mind. Thank you for my happiness and sense of peace.

Thank you God for my constant and continued abundance. I am financially secure, debt free and building a financial nest egg to support my family for generations to come.

Thank you for my being a citizen of the United State where I have freedom and opportunity and wealth and safety. Thank you God for the many successes I have already had in my life and the countless more I look forward to in the future.

Thank you God for the many blessing in my life, both anticipated and unexpected.

AMEN

Chapter 77

"Hi, Doctor Ford. I'm sorry I haven't been in with Mia for a while. We lost our health insurance."

"It's okay Mrs. Sinclair. Life has its shares of ups and downs. So how is my little charmer here?"

"She seems to be doing fine. I've been looking for some of the symptoms we discussed last summer when the injury occurred and so far nothing has happened."

"I'm happy to hear it. I was concerned about sinus infections, scar tissue on her tear ducts and even a collapse of her nose structure. But from the front view here, I believe she looks pretty good. You know though, that the hole will never completely close up on it's own. It was too large and the area was pretty raw."

"I understand Dr. Ford. As long as all that is there now is a hole, I can live with that."

Dr. Ford gave Mia a big smile, who returned it warily. She remembered the pain of the last exam.

"Ok little one, let's take a look." Dr. Ford got out his light and started the exam. He was taking awhile and I was beginning to feel uneasy.

"Is everything alright?" I couldn't stand it anymore.

"Mrs. Sinclair, I don't know what to say." Dr. Ford was scratching his head befuddled.

"What do you mean? Is something wrong?' *Things are starting to feel better, Please God, no bad news!*

"Not exactly, I'm looking in your daughter's nose and there is no evidence of trauma. Her tissues are perfectly healthy and the hole has vanished. It defies explanation."

"Not for me Doctor," I was smiling ear to ear.

The angels had given me a gift. I knew it was the power of prayer. I had been praying for Mia everyday. Wow! Prayer really works! From that moment on, I decided to call my daily ritual *Power Prayers*. Then I considered something, had God set up the scenario with Mia so I would have proof of his divine power? I think the answer is, yes. The sweet blessing of answered prayer had brushed its wings over my child, I knew nothing else mattered now.

Chapter 78

After reciting my gratitude letter for a few days and the news from Mia's doctor, I feel another ray of light joining the others in the darkness of my heart. It's a little brighter in there. May be my perspective has been off. I don't really like to think of myself as a victim. But I realize I've been in that role for a while now. I look at the clock; there is still time for a quick visit to Faith before I pick up the kids.

"Hi Jenna Sinclair. Your ears must be burning girl."

"Oh, hi Wanda, you got the CD's."

"Jenna you are a hit here at St. Mary's. People want to know who the person is with the velvet voice. Is there a way for people to get more CD's?"

"You're flattering me, Wanda. Stop it. I'm glad people like the CD. It's okay to give out my email and please drop me a note if you need something. It's really no problem. How is Faith?"

Wanda offers me a compassionate smile. I know that there is not much time left.

"Faith. Faith can you hear me?" I want her to wake up and connect with me, but I can see she is beyond that. I sit next to her and gently take her hand.

"Faith, I've been reading a lot lately. You would be so proud of me. I'm starting to figure some stuff out without running to you for every bump in the road. I wish you were here and you could explain to me more about everything I am learning. You were always so wise and kind, Faith. What am I ever going to do without you?" I stop to catch my breath as a sob breaks forth from my body.

"I've dialed your number a few times these past weeks, before I remembered you were here. Thank you Faith. Oh God, Faith, thank you so much. Have I ever told you that? I can't remember now." I'm feeling really guilty. Was I part of the draining energy that made her sick? The thought makes me cry harder.

"In so many ways you've saved my life. Saved me from myself. You always saw more in me than I could ever recognize. I hear your voice inside my head, your amazing advice. It feels like it's coming directly from the angels themselves. You are my dear angel, Faith, my guardian angel on earth. I am going to miss you forever."

Tears are freely rolling down my face as I sob. I know this is goodbye. I don't know if I can bear another farewell. Gentle or violent, goodbye has been an overused word in my vocabulary this year. It hurts like hell.

Later that day, I got the call I had been expecting from Kat at the Center. "Jenna, I thought you would want to know, Faith passed away this afternoon." I hung up the phone and cried solitary sobs for what seemed like hours.

"You seem a little sad today, Jenna," Steve commented.

"Oh, a friend of mine died today." I choked back a sob.

"Who was it?"

"Faith, from the Soul Center. I don't think you ever met her."

"I don't recall the name. Jenna, is your period starting soon? Lately, you cry over everything."

I turned and walked out of the room. It was not worth the energy of an explanation.

Over the last few months, I'd left books and CD's on Steve's desk as a subtle way to encourage him to shift into a happier state of mind. I noticed they remained untouched. For longer than I can remember, Steve and I have been orbiting different planets.

Chapter 79

My life has started to take on a routine of sorts. For the past few months, I've set my alarm for 5:45 am, so I have uninterrupted time to meditate, read my gratitude letter, say some affirmations and write a few observations in my journal, before I have to run the route. It is a daily ritual and I'm finding comfort in the consistency of my practice.

I've heard from Wanda a few times via email. Apparently, I am praying with several of the patients in hospice through the CD's. It's funny to think my voice is comforting someone I've never met. It makes me feel good inside, useful in some small way. A few family members sent me email messages.

"Thank you for giving dad comfort during his final days. Your voice and calm prayers were a balm to our chafed hearts. Warmly, Sue Duncan."

"You are an angel, dear girl. Thank you for speaking your kind words of prayer to my wife. It seems to have eased her suffering. I know it helped mine. I hope you don't mind, I've taken the CD home to listen to. It keeps the house from being too quiet without my wife of 50 years. Sincerely, Earl Thompson."

"God says his messengers speak to us through many channels.

You were a channel for us during the death of our darling son. It gave me strength to let go and know that Billy will be safe in heaven. Thank you from the bottom of our hearts, Sara Ragsdale."

Chapter 80

"Bob, can you help me out with something?" I sat down at the genius counter in the Apple store for another training session.

"Is there a way to email copies of my prayer CD's to people who request one?"

"Sure Jenna, you can publish your work as a pod cast on itunes and offer it as a free download."

"Really. Say it again in English Bob."

"Basically, you already have twenty song and prayers made. Let me see if there is a category for prayers on itunes, I will help you publish them right now. When you make a new one add it to your list."

"You mean the itunes that's available to the whole world?"

"Jenna, that is how the internet works silly."

"It sounds simple enough."

Bob opens up the area for prayers and I notice there is not much competition. At the most there were fifty free downloads available and most were replays of catholic masses.

"Who am I to be offering prayers on the Internet? This is beyond bizarre." I'm talking to myself again. *"Come on, I'm competing for airtime with the Bishop of Canterbury. Prayer one, read by anonymous housewife, prayer two, read by archbishop. The absurdity makes me laugh. What kind of spiritual authority do I*

have?" My inner debate continues. Bob is totally unaware.

"There is one issue Jenna, you need to create your own music, or you need to get permission to publish the songs that are underneath your voice track. Permission is expensive and difficult to get."

"Okay Bob, now Jenna, who can't carry a tune, is supposed to become a musician." I could feel my idea dying on the concrete floor of the retail store.

"Actually, it is easier than you think. Garage Band, the program you have been using to create you CD's, offers all kinds of instruments and music tracks. Let me show you."

An hour later, I left the store with a head full of tips about song making and a new Garage Band disc called World Jams. My store credit was used up, but now I have instruments like the Tibetan Peace Drum and the Chinese Zither at my fingertips. I was ready to create my new musical masterpiece.

That afternoon while I was making dinner for the kids, the Oprah Winfrey show came on the television in the kitchen. There was a group of authors appearing as guests on her show talking about their new book <u>The Secret,</u> by Rhonda Byrnes. It sounded similar to the books I've been reading lately. I made a mental note to pick up a copy the next time I was at a bookstore. Lately, I have been browsing the shelves at the bookstore looking for anything that catches my eye. That's part of my curriculum at self-u. It's like I have a hunger for new knowledge that only books can feed. I know I'm on the right track, because each new book seems to answer any questions raised by the previous book. So I'm boiling noodles and sautéing my signature sauce when one of the guests on the show, makes a statement that floors me.

"Unforgiveness is like drinking poison yourself and expecting the other person to die."

I repeat what the man, an author of <u>The Secret</u> named James Arthur Ray said aloud:

"UNFORGIVENESS IS LIKE DRINKING POSION YOURSELF AND EXPECTING THE OTHER PERSON TO DIE."

Wow! Doesn't that just sum it all up in one powerful statement? Over the sizzling of my tomatoes, the blowing range fan and my boiling noodles, I recognized the Truth of his words.

"I have been drinking poison for a long time now, no wonder I

feel sick; no wonder I died."

By now me and myself are good friends, we talk to each other all of the time. Is this the definition of schizophrenia?

"Now that I know better, I'm not doing it anymore. Even if I have to forgive Ruth and Ira and Donald and Libby, and every other person who has hurt me over the past few years."

After books were read and kisses given to the kids, I spent some time in my sacred space. *Where do I even begin?* Rage and anger have tightened their black fingers around me in the vise grip of a lifetime. I was prepared to carry these grudges to the grave. A hall pass for these "life-ruiners" was not part of the plan.

I remember that one of my books had a chapter on forgiveness, but which one was it? The first one I opened fell exactly to the page I was seeking. I noticed a lot of these coincidences were happening lately. The book says to use prayer, of course, and to ask that God help you to forgive the person who harmed you. But there is more, you need to forgive yourself and also ask for forgiveness. Am I ready for this? The next idea is a relief. All of this is not direct contact with the perpetrator; it is handled through prayer or a written letter, private between you and God. Apparently the souls of everyone involved pick up the messages and they work everything out.

I say a prayer:

"God, help me to forgive Ruth and Ira for all of the pain and suffering they have caused me. Help me to release her from my life. And God, if I can't seem to let go of them and this situation completely, find the part of me that wants to forgive, no matter how small it is, and make that part stronger, so I can be free and clear of the poison. Thank you God for your time. Oh and by the way God, feel free to send your Archangel Michael, who I understand is in charge of Truth and have him let everyone know what really happened. Jenna."

I say it again and again for everyone else I can think of. This forgiveness business is exhausting. I'm ready for bed. Plus, in three weeks is my garage sale, the one that I have been working on for the last three months. I hope I make some money. God knows we need it.

My new book, <u>The Secret</u> gives me an interesting idea. The author Rhonda Brynes says to treat the Universe as a magic genie in a lamp and to ask for whatever you'd like to see happen in your life. The only limitation is your own imagination. Anything is possible if you act as if it has already occurred and, here's the key, you have to *BELIEVE!*

"Wow, no wonder this is a bestseller."

I know what I want. I want to win the "Powerball." The multi-state lottery that is now up to sixty-seven million. Winners receive half of the jackpot. I could do a lot with thirty-two million dollars. I'm already in a great mood thinking about it, all of the ways I would spend my riches.

In the book are some suggestions on how to make your "wishes" feel more real. I spend the entire day looking through old travel magazines tearing out pictures of the places I'll be visiting as a new millionaire: Bora-Bora, Africa, Greece, Colorado. Of course, I'll be paying off my house for cash, after I add a fabulous swimming pool, extensive gardens and a four-car garage filled with new automobiles: I've been driving a borrowed car from my mother ever since my van was repossessed.

Then I take out my checkbook and proceed to write checks to everyone I owe money: my lawyer, my mortgage loan, my electrician; I went through the entire list. I write symbolic checks for a thousand dollars, ten thousand dollars, and a million dollars; the amounts don't matter, I am an up and coming lottery winner! I place all of the checks in an envelope just waiting to be sent next week when I win. I'm really starting to get into this.

Then I think about a charity I'd like to start to help all of the causes I believe in. I'll call it the Grace Foundation, in honor of David and Faith. I set up accounts to pay for the kid's college. I'd help a few friends who are also having money struggles. All of my ideas are laid out in detail on the pages in one of my journals. This exercise is great fun. Yes, if <u>The Secret</u> is right, all of my problems are solved by the end of the month. I pick up a Powerball ticket that afternoon while driving the route. Drawings are held on Wednesdays and Saturdays. Don't worry that one hundred and forty six million people are also playing this week. The "law of attraction" says the odds are on my side.

For the next couple of weeks, planning for my Powerball victory gives me great joy. I read the section, "winner's stories" on the Powerball web site, so I could plan my press release. I've really come to believe that any one of these Wednesday or Saturday night's in the near future is the day my life changes forever. I am rescued! I feel like just sitting on the porch and waiting for the announcement.

The jackpot is growing larger every time no one wins one of the bi-weekly drawings, I can barely get my mind around the idea of $150 million dollars, but I mentally manage to invest more money and beef up the amount I will give to charity. I've been adding notes in my "millionaire journal" to this effect. Steve doesn't even know what I am up to; I keep it a secret. Isn't that why the book is named, The Secret? But he has noticed, I've been happier lately. Not as freaked out by the phone calls and the official–looking mail. After all, I know payday is right around the corner.

I purchase my ticket for Wednesday night's drawing. This is five dollars less in my empty gas tank, but it is an investment I can't afford not to make. This is definitely the one. I imagine the Powerball ticket in my hands is made of pure gold, instead of the fraud control paper it's actually printed on. I hurry home to go over my notes in my "millionaire's journal" and to look through my scrapbook of vacations I'm planning on taking. I can barely wait until 9:59 pm when the little white balls whirling in the air on FOX news will announce the victory I've been rehearsing in my head for weeks.

It's 10:01pm. There's a winner in the Powerball! I rush to get my ticket.

It's not me.

In fact, I don't even have one matching number. I am a complete loser. I feel my self deflate like a hot air balloon hit by a cannonball. I walk straight up to bed, crawl in the sheets and bawl like a colicky baby, until the mercy of sleep takes over. If the Powerball lottery is not going to save me from the hell of my life, what else is there?

The next day I'm really dragging. This disappointment has wiped me out.

"I heard you crying last night Jenna, are you OK?"

"Yeah Steve, I'm having a bad day." I could not even form the words to tell him I was disappointed that I'm not the one person out of one hundred and forty six million people who won the lottery last night. He wouldn't get it. I don't get it. So, I blamed it on my period, even though I never have PMS.

I went back through some of my books after the kids went to school and I came upon this explanation. "To have a certain experience you need to first create that experience for someone else."

I think about this for a while. "To win the lottery you need to be the lottery for someone else." I say the words out loud. Is that what the statement means? How am I going to be the lottery for someone else? I can't even afford to buy groceries these days.

I say my affirmations and read my gratitude letter half-heartedly before starting to set up for my garage sale this weekend. Lately, in addition to God, I have also been petitioning the archangels like, Michael, Raphael and Gabriel for assistance. I've also prayed to the ascended masters, the saints, and a whole slew of heavenly helpers. I feel like I need the extra dose of divine intervention.

Outside it has been dark and rainy for the last four days. I'm concerned about the sale tomorrow, but I've already placed the ad in the community newspaper and I am counting on the money. I organize everything in the garage. Raindrops are pelting the side of the house, they are falling diagonal, from the force of the wind; it does not look promising. If the weather breaks in the morning, I will drag everything outside first thing. I need to make at least five hundred dollars. That will pay for the basics.

The alarm sounds at five a.m. It's garage sale day. Miraculously, for the first time in five days, it's not raining. I rush outside and with the help of Lolly and we drag out all of the tables of my unwanted stuff. "Please God let people come out to shop, despite the history of the weather." I send a silent plea.

Someone was listening. Business is brisk right from the start at seven a.m. I sell kids clothes, kitchenwares, baby supplies, toys, and furniture. I'm not sorry to see all of the clutter leaving my house. The way I used to spend money, before the world collapsed, seems so foreign to me now. *What possessed me to buy all of this stuff?* A lot of it looks new. I know my kids barely played with most of the toys. They did not even recognize many of the items as I pulled them from the attic. There were so many toys; they filled my dining room. It made me feel a little nauseated to realize that I could outfit an entire preschool with my rabid materialism. I wish I had all the money I spent then, right now!

Mid-morning the bad weather returned. Lolly and I started to pull the tables of unsold items back into my crowded garage. *We'll try again another day.*

A small, beat up, blue Toyota Camry pulls in my driveway. Both the front and the back bumper were totally covered with bumper stickers declaring religious and political views about children and the world. There were so many stickers, half of the words on one sticker; were covered by the slogan of another. It was like a religious outburst - coming and going. Out of the car emerges a man not more than five-foot-four-inches tall. He was round and jolly, dressed head to toe in black polyester. He walked over to the collection of my kid's bikes, unaffected by the pouring rain splattering his spectacles.

"How much for these here bicycles?" He had an accent, Irish perhaps.

"There's a price tag on each one, but I'll give you a deal if you want more than one."

He starts to walk around, looking at all of my items.

"This would be so nice for a family I know, they have nothing you see. I'll take this for them." He's pointing to several different items now, remarking about different people and their needs.

"Do you have any small books, I'm sending a box to Africa?"

"Sure, what do you have in mind?"

"Mrs. Rodgers over on Elm Street," he points in the direction of the unknown woman's house on the familiar street, "is having a large Garage Sale at the end of the month. All of the items are donated and the profits all go to fund our parish project in Haiti. It's a orphanage."

"Are you a priest?"

"Why yes, I am. Call me Father Marty."

"I'll tell you what Father Marty, you can have my entire garage sale. Every single unsold item." The offer flew from my mouth one angel's wings. I was even surprised to hear my voice saying the words.

"Oh! Bless you child!" He exclaimed. Exuberant.

"I'll just have someone from the parish come and pick up the items. Is today too soon?"

"Today is perfect, Father."

He asks me to help him load the bikes into his small car. I notice his dashboard is covered with a brown car carpet monogrammed with the words, Fr. Martin. At least, I know he is really a priest and not some imposter taking away all of my potential profit. The bike's tires and handlebars are hanging out of the windows of his rolling billboard. He could not wait to take the bikes to his parishioners. Amazingly, once I counted the money from the early part of the sale, I realized we made four hundred and ninety-eight dollars. Thank God!

A few days later an envelope came in the mail. Inside was a letter hand-written in ten different colors of marker. It was covered with stickers of hearts and teddy bears.

Dear Ms. Jenna Sinclair,

You are an angel on Earth. Thank you for your generous donations to our fundraising garage sale. Thanks to you, this will be the biggest one ever. We have never before been blessed with so many nice items. Thank you again. We have won the lottery! The money we will raise at the sale will save many children's lives. You are an answer to a prayer.

Love to you and many, many blessings,
Lisa Rodgers

Enclosed with the letter is a pamphlet with pictures of babies sitting in muddy, desolate conditions. It talks about the orphanage in Haiti. My life is a dream compared to their nightmare. Also in the envelope is a tax letter for deductions itemizing the thousand-dollar value of the donations with a thank you note from Father Marty. I looked at the envelope again and realized the address in the upper left side said Church of the Archangel St. Michael. There really is no such thing as a coincidence. Lately, all of my surprises have been fun. Perhaps surprises aren't so bad after all.

Chapter 81

The next couple of months were blessedly uneventful. I'm still waking up early to do my daily ritual: I read the gratitude letter, say some affirmations, meditate and record my prayers. Some of the listeners from itunes have sent me nice emails about my power prayers; similar to the ones I received from the hospice. I ask Wanda to direct all of the listeners to my free download. It makes it easier for her. Hopefully, Steve will get a job soon. I pray for that above everything else.

Meanwhile, Steve's consulting opportunities are picking up and money is not as tight. Things are feeling almost normal, just a scaled down version of my previous life. A few of my old friends have even started to come around, and they call more often. I've even made a few new ones. I think people get scared when the see blood in the water; they run for solid ground. So I'm not really mad about being deserted. In fact, I'm not really mad at anyone anymore.

"Hello."

I rush to grab the phone as I'm carrying in groceries.

"May I please speak with Jenna Sinclair?"

"This is she." I hope I'm not walking into a "bill collector ambush."

"Hi Jenna. This is Edward Windsor. I'm the New Talent Coordinator for Enlightenment Entertainment. How are you today?"

"Oh fine. But I'm kind of busy right now and I don't want to enter any contests. So thanks for calling." I'm hanging up the phone when I hear.

"JENNA, PLEASE DON'T HANG UP!"

"Excuse me?"

"I'm not with the Prize Patrol. I'm calling about your prayers on itunes. You know the ones called Power Prayers."

I immediately sit down.

"Yeah, what about them."

"Well I'm a big fan! I'd like to invite you to our offices in New York to discuss a business opportunity?"

"Is this for real? I mean, I know the prayers have been a number one download for the last couple of months. But they're free and I'm only competing with Catholic mass. You know, there's not a lot of competition in the prayer department."

Edward laughs.

"Why don't you fly to New York and listen to what I have to offer. It could change your life."

"Excuse me, what is your name again?"

"Edward Windsor. But you can call me Ed, if you'd like. Does next Monday work? You'll only need to spend one night and our firm will take care of all of the arrangements."

"Um, I'm sure it will be OK."

"Great, Jenna I look forward to meeting you. See you in a few days. Our travel representative will call shortly to arrange all of the details."

When I step off the plane in New York, a uniformed driver holding a name card "Jenna Sinclair" greets me. I'm escorted to a waiting limousine. This is more than I expected. As the car glides through the streets of Manhattan, I think about the last time I was here. Ruth and I had a great time at the art show; it makes me smile to think about the fur coats and the cheese bistro. Too bad it turned out so ugly. I know she is divorced now, that's probably a good thing, considering everything she told me. I hope she is doing well; being a single parent can't be easy.

This line of thinking makes me realize how far I have traveled over the past couple of years; most of my anxiety and angst has been crowded out by a general sense of well being, although not much has changed in my external life. I'm still juggling payment plans with more than a dozen companies, the kids had to leave private school and I miss my dog, Maverick and my dear friend, Faith. Yet, I feel okay inside. Actually I'd even go so far as to say, I feel happy.

Being in New York feels like a treat. It gives me an opportunity to dust off my "sophisticated-career-self. " Instead of flip-flops and sweat pants (my mom uniform), I'm dressed in a smart black Tahari suit with a pair of Prada pumps. Recently my hair was highlighted a honey blonde, my nails are sporting an American manicure, the more natural version of a French manicure, and I've lost a fair amount of weight. I'm a city girl! This is a fun space to inhabit.

The lobby of the building where the offices of Enlightenment Entertainment is located in a minimalist, clean New York style with all glass, black marble, and a collection of chrome chairs. Their clean lines and thin black leather seats tell me they are here more for looking, than for sitting. An attractive young Asian woman, dressed in a crisp white suit, greets me from behind reception counter crafted of glass and granite.

"Jenna Sinclair to see Edward Windsor."

"Enlightenment Entertainment is located on the twenty second floor, they are expecting you."

I'm a little nervous now. This isn't bush league. *What do these people want with me?* My stomach is fluttering and I have to go to the bathroom. It's a nerves thing. During the trial I had to pee every break, the stress was a trigger. I stop in the ladies room before entering the office. Lipstick and make-up have not dissolved from my face revealing the true unglazed housewife I am inside.

"Jenna Sinclair, could this be you? We are so excited to meet you."

"Edward Windsor? Hi, nice to meet you." It was clear from the expression in his striking blue eyes that he was pleasantly surprised. I could have been a heifer from the heartland; pudgy, bleach blonde with bad teeth. A pleasing voice is no guarantee of a pleasing appearance. My years in TV as a newscaster had taught me how to put on a "spit shine," that's what they call it in the military when you want your gear to look its very best.

"Please follow me." He led me to a conference room with a wall of windows looking out over the Central Park. I summed him up from behind. Tall, athletic, mid-forties: he looked like tennis pro with his carefree tousled tawny hair and big easy smile. He was not wearing a suit, instead a pair of unstructured silk black dress pants and a linen shirt with driving moccasins; Gucci, I think. His voice held a bit of an accent, later I learned he was from South Africa.

"You're probably wondering why you are here? First I'd like to spend some time with you explaining things, then after lunch if it's okay with you we'll meet with some other individuals who will be instrumental in your future." It was easy to be charmed by his voice, lilting and pleasant.

"Spirituality is the hottest genre out there in the world right now. A majority of the bestsellers in bookstores across the globe, and on-line, through outlets such as Amazon.com, are written on the subject matter surrounding holistic living, being in balance, communion with spirit. Your Power Prayers, as you call them Jenna, have touched a chord in the psyche of this dynamic field."

"Okay, well I didn't plan that when I started at the Apple Store. The first CD was a gift for my friend in hospice. She'd die if she knew I was here now." I thought about what I just said. God, I sound like an idiot.

We chatted for a while about my background in TV news, my family, my schedule and any goals I had for myself. I talked about my spiritual practice and how much comfort it brings me. I said a little about the past year, my history in the art business and my irrational partner. I figured he'd read about me on Goggle anyway. The direct approach always works best. Edward Windsor was interested. I couldn't believe it. I never told anyone about my morning ritual; the prayers, affirmations, meditation, and chants! I don't even attend church.

In fact, aside from my husband, no one knew I was even submitting prayers to a podcast on itunes. Steve even thought it was amusing and a little weird. I didn't tell him how important the podcast had become to me, or how much the heartfelt emails of thanks warmed my embattled, lonely heart. My blossoming spirituality was my secret, now my two worlds were about to collide.

"Here's my proposal. Now that I've met you, I'd like to create an entire workshop around your personality. It would consist of your power prayers, advice on building a spiritual practice and guidance on living a balanced life."

"Wait a minute. You don't know me. I am a disaster. There's no way I can be a spokesperson about balance, it's would be a total hypocrisy."

"Why do you say that Jenna. Everyone has trials in their lives. It's not the events that define you; only your response to the events. You responded to the events in your life through Grace. You simply surrendered, allowed them to occur and focused on the Divine. Do you not see that?"

"Well, if you put it that way. I had no choice but to surrender. I was ambushed and hog tied, Edward."

"But you didn't die darling, although it may have appeared that most of the things in your life were destroyed. Through the experience, you seem to have been born into who you really are. Even if you don't recognize or acknowledge who that person is right now. I see a lovely, incredibly bright, compassionate woman, who cares about others more than herself. You are a spiritual being. You are the perfect person for what I am proposing. What do you think?"

"What about my children? They are so small and still in school? I could not leave them. They need me. My husband, too." Despite everything, I still love Steve; he was caught up in the landslide too.

"Most workshops are scheduled on weekends, either one or two day events, generally once or twice a month. They are usually hosted at luxurious resorts. Why could you not bring them along? The rest of the work could be done from your home with an occasional trip to our studio space here in New York to record a series of CD's. I have a musician lined up who would love to work with you."

"Edward, you mean you're not a fan of my Garage Band soundtrack?" I laughed. I never could get the hang of many variations with the instruments and used the same couple of tracks I created over and over again.

Edward then handed me an envelope.

"I've written an offer for you on the paper inside. Let's break for lunch; you can check into your hotel have lunch in your room. I have you booked at the "W" across the street. Take some time to think. I'll see you back here at 2:30 p.m. We'll have dinner tonight to celebrate." I didn't say the hotel was my personal favorite.

Back in the room, I opened the letter. The staggering amount offered in the contract forces me to sit down and catch my breath. I don't know whether to laugh or cry. There is an amount for the CD series of Power Prayers and an additional fee for me per workshop, plus royalties, plus all accommodations and travel and a large signing bonus. I feel as if I have won the lottery, only better! Because this is not a random jackpot, it's an acknowledgement of me and my personal value.

"Steve, you are never going to believe this. Are you sitting down?" I told him all about my meeting, the offer, the travel. It all seemed unreal; even as we spoke about it on the phone.

"If anyone deserves it, it's you Jenna. You are the most loyal person I know. You've stuck it out with me through the darkest of times. I think a lot of other people would have left."

"You're crazy, Steve. I love you and our family. I created my fair share of problems too. Now I think we're really turning the corner and putting the past behind us."

"Maybe I should start using some of those Power Prayers!" It made me happy to hear him say this. I've encouraged Steve in that direction, but you have to come to this space on your own terms; in your own time.

"All I can say, Steve, is that prayer is the solution to every problem. Now I have proof," I was preaching and Steve laughed at my enthusiasm.

"I love you. Have fun the rest of the trip. I'll see you tomorrow night. Maybe we can take the kids and go out to celebrate."

"That's a great idea. I'd love to do that. Love you too sweetheart. Bye,"

I felt a door unlock in my heart towards my husband that had been closed for awhile.

The afternoon meetings were a whirl. Apparently an entire team has been assembled to help create these workshops and to help groom me into the spokesperson. A stylist, my own personal assistant, a musician, a travel coordinator and Edward Windsor and his business partner Hope Conway. Hope was an attractive woman in her late fifties with white hair and intelligent eyes. I learn she's the brain behind many of the inspirational seminars held by some of the new authors I've been reading over the past couple of months.

Over dinner, we celebrated with a champagne toast. I'll need to come back to New York a few more times to work out all of the details. The target date for the first workshop is next summer, eight months from now, in Colorado. Followed by events in Hawaii, California and North Carolina. We also talk about a possibility of an event in the Caribbean. As part of my contract, for all of the long distance locations, I'll be given extra days to stay and relax with my family and sightsee. Between now and then, everyone needs the time to create and release the CD and to launch the marketing campaign. I also plan to take some time to explore this new thought genre and see what all of the buzz is about. Everything I've done so far has been alone in my house.

Back in my hotel room, I called Steve and the kids to say good night. The silky cotton sheets in my "heavenly bed" at the Westin hotel are irresistible and quickly usher me to sleep. Where I experience the most amazing dream; so clear it felt real.

I look down at my feet and see that they are bare. I'm walking along a path covered with diamonds. Flanking both side of the glittering trail are wave after wave of golden wheat, as far as the eye can see in both directions. The route is not long; it's short like a driveway, indicating I have already reached my destination. Sitting atop a hill is a giant crystal castle. The front door is open, inviting me inside. In the main hall is a crystal banquet table set for me; I'm led to the head seat. Surrounding the table are my friends and enemies and some unknown faces, including Faith, Ruth, Ira, Libby, Donald, Danielle, even the new people I've met, Edward and Grace. It's a perfectly peaceful and delightful meal. I excuse myself from the table and enter a room full of radiant light. In the center of the room is a man seated in a lotus position wrapped in a cloak the color of a Valencia orange. One of his shoulders is bare. The minute we make eye contact he starts laughing. His laughter is joyful and robust. He is filled with mirth as if he has just heard the funniest joke of his life. At first, I am taken aback. Is he laughing at me? Am I the joke? Then a realization dawns on me from within. Like when you get the punch line of a joke. That he and I are the same. We are one. I suddenly am laughing as hard as the jolly monk. I understand the joke! What could be more hysterical than a monk living as a Midwestern housewife loaded up with a life full of kids, carpool, and chaos. Not a peaceful, quiet, cloistered monastery in sight. Then I woke up.

"The Universe has a sense of humor." I comment aloud on the

lucid dream as I got out of bed to get dressed.

The next day, we had more meetings at the offices of Enlightenment Entertainment. I suggest we call the series "Monastery Within," drawing from my dream last night. I didn't tell anyone the source of my inspiration. Everyone was easy-going and pleasant. They seem to respect and honor my ideas. At three o'clock it was time for my afternoon flight home. I feel like I've lived a whole lifetime in the last twenty-four hours.

The kids smother me with hugs and kisses as I get in the car.

"Mommy hold me!"

"Hug me!"

"Can I sit on your lap?"

"I've missed you guys too. Wait until I tell you about some of the fun places we will get to visit soon." They are bursting with excitement.

I decide the first thing I am buying with my advance is a shiny new silver minivan. In fact, I may go get it next week, as a way to celebrate.

For the first time in a long time, I felt a tiny breath of hope come alive inside my heart. The losses over the past years have left me feeling numb, dead inside. Sure, my coffin was metaphorical, but I was buried deep nonetheless; deep in my own sorrow, deep in my own self-pity, deep in the drama of my departed self. Coincidentally, none of that seems to matter anymore.

Sure, I'm still an addict. Now, my vices are obvious. I'm addicted to Spirit, affirmations, and prayer.

The End

Reader's Guide

If you liked the book, Mystic in a Minivan… Lets take the journey a step further…

You're now invited to unlock the deepest Truth about you. Will you accept this key?

Once you accept, it could transform your life in a profound way. It won't cost you a thing, most spiritual gifts are given freely. But, accepting this journey will encourage you to look deep within yourself and uncover the roadmap of your Spirit. We all have one, an internal compass. It's part of our spiritual DNA. So take a moment and consider where you are RIGHT NOW, because that's all that matters… just today.

Are you going in the right direction? Is it time to make a u-turn? Perhaps you've even been stalled out at a rest stop and don't have enough energy to get back on the road? Wherever you are, I'll meet you there…

Please visit my website for a free downloadable workbook. Messages from the Mystic.
www.kristenwhite33.com

Be Empowered! Plug into the Universe!
In Love and Light,

Kristen White

About the Author

Kristen White is an intuitive life coach, medium, energy therapist, spirituality mentor, entrepreneur, talk show host and mother of three young children. She holds a business degree, BSBA, from the University of Arizona and attended the University of Southern California and Arizona State University for her graduate work in journalism and communications. Kristen spent more than a decade working as a television news reporter. Now she is the founder of a holistic wellness center located in the Midwest called, The Energy School.

Kristen White is a popular motivational speaker with her series Messages from the Mystic and Spirituality Bootcamp. Please visit her website at www.kristenwhite33.com for more information. She also hosts a weekly radio show, Reporting Live from the Universe with Kristen White on Contact Talk Radio www.contacttalkradio.com and on the Law of Attraction Radio Network, www.LOAradioNetwork.com

As an intuitive life coach, she consults with clients privately. She also teaches a variety of workshops and seminars on-line. Visit www.theenergyschool.net for a complete schedule or to book a private session.

QUICK ORDER FORM

Fax orders: 770-217-6884. Send this form.

Telephone orders: Call 800-611-2768 toll free. Have your credit card ready.

Email orders: orders@mysticinaminivan.com

Postal Orders: Mystic Media, LLC 9849 Manchester Road, Suite #22 Saint Louis, Missouri 63119-1200 USA. Telephone 314-724-8859

Please send the following books, CDs or reports. I understand that I may return any of them for a full refund–for any reason, no questions asked.

_____

_____

_____

Please send more FREE information on:
❏ Books and CDs   ❏ Coaching Sessions   ❏ Newsletter
❏ Speaking/Workshops

Name: _____

Address: _____

City: _____ State: _____ Zip: _____

Telephone: _____

Email address: _____

Sales tax: Please add sales tax to all products shipped to Missouri addresses.

Shipping by air

U.S.: $4.00 for first book or CD and $2.00 for each additional product.

International: $9.00 for first book or CD; $5.00 for each additional product (estimate).